NO PEACE FOR THE WICKED

Love, loss and danger in 1950s Soho...

Quiet, unassuming Lizzie Robbins lives in Soho near her friends Maggie, Bert and little Rosie, who run a café in Old Compton Street, but her well-ordered life changes dramatically when Peace comes to stay. A beautiful half-Chinese girl, Peace has run away from boarding school, and doesn't intend to return. When Peace goes missing a second time, Lizzie asks T.C., Rosie's policeman dad, to accompany her to the seedy docks around Limehouse where she thinks Peace may be hiding. Home to the Chinese community, it's a very dangerous place indeed...

NO PEACE FOR THE WICKED

NO PEACE FOR THE WICKED

by

Pip Granger

Magna Large Print Books
Long Preston, North Yorkshire,
BD23 4ND, England.

British Library Cataloguing in Publication Data.

Granger, Pip
    No peace for the wicked.

    A catalogue record of this book is
    available from the British Library

    ISBN   0-7505-2462-6

First published in Great Britain in 2005 by Bantam Press
a division of Transworld Publishers

Copyright © Pip Granger 2005

Cover illustration © Andy Walker by arrangement with
P.W.A. International Ltd.

The right of Pip Granger to be identified as the author of this work has
been asserted in accordance with sections 77 and 78 of the Copyright,
Designs and Patents Act, 1988

Published in Large Print 2006 by arrangement with
Transworld Publishers Ltd.

Magna Large Print is an imprint of Library Magna Books Ltd.

Printed and bound in Great Britain by
T.J. (International) Ltd., Cornwall, PL28 8RW

This one's for Ray
and in memory of my dear friend
Terry Pizzey

Prologue

If only my mother could have seen me: on my knees deep in the heart of sinful Soho, with a mouthful of pins, taking up the hem of a stunning creation in sequin-encrusted scarlet. The gorgeous gaudiness of the dress on its own would have had her praying so hard her poor knees would have been quite worn out. Such sinful waste! And scarlet, the colour of harlots and fallen women! But the fact that it was being worn by Freddy the Frock would have finished her off completely, despite the innocent explanation: being on the short side, Freddy often stood in for absent customers when a hem needed seeing to. Mother would have died of mortification anyway, if she hadn't already done that when I married Sid – or so my aunts always said. Luckily, if the old darling could see me at all, it was from the safe haven of 'the other side', where shame couldn't kill her for a second time.

Anything could bring on an attack of mortal shame in my childhood home: dropping an 'h', talking with one's mouth full, wearing red, showing a knee, lipstick, laughing on a Sunday, whistling at any time, playing with the children at my school or worse, in the street. I remember the hours I spent with my nose pressed to the window, watching the other girls, skirts tucked into their bloomers as they leapfrogged over their giggling friends or did handstands against the sooty brick walls along our road or skipped, using someone's mum's washing line purloined for the purpose. I longed and longed to join them, despite my mother's and aunts' holy horror, or perhaps because of it. But I never did – at least, not until some time after I had met Sid, and by then, I was too old for it; well, almost. I did once run amok in Regent's Park with a skipping rope and leapfrog over the chunky black bollards that kept vehicles out, but I didn't tuck my skirt into my underwear. I was definitely too old for that.

It certainly was a stretch, the journey from my early years in Islington to the theatrical costumier's in St Anne's Court where I worked. However, all that's another story. This one involves some of the best friends I have ever had, and a lovely girl called Peace. And it all began in the first few weeks of 1956, not long after I moved into the small flat above Bandy's, a drinking club that nestled in an alley just round the corner from Old Compton Street.

1

Everybody called it 'Freddy the Frock's', but in fact the theatrical costumier's where I worked was owned and run by Freddy and his partner Antony. My job had become the best part of my life since I had been there. I loved the shop and its gorgeous fabrics, I loved the colourful customers and I adored my two bosses. I thought I had strayed into Wonderland the very first time I walked into the place and it still felt like Wonderland to me a year or two later.

The immediate thing that confronted me as I walked nervously through the door on my first day was a hundred empty eye sockets belonging to a display of masks on the wall opposite the door. Some were glamorous jewelled eye masks, incredibly elaborate in shape and decoration and held on sticks. Others depicted fearsome characters like phantoms, monsters and devils, and were fixed to the head with elastic that was meant to be hidden by an appropriate hat. In the back room were stands that held whole heads, like asses or cows with crumpled horns; but we didn't keep many of those, as they took up too much room. They were hauled out of storage as and when they were needed, along with the theatrical armour, Puss in Boots's boots, Tinkerbell's wings and Captain Hook's hook and jacket, complete with ticking crocodile.

The counter ran the whole width of the shop so we could roll out bolts of fabric and measure them against the brass yard rule attached to its edge. The counter of mellow beech wood had seen years of service, long before Freddy and Antony's time. Some time in the eighteenth century, number 7 St Anne's Court had become a haberdasher's, and was one still when Freddy and Antony had taken over the premises just after the war.

Located right in the middle of Soho, the shop was close at hand for the many theatres and clubs of the West End. We also had a modest sideline in bespoke evening wear for ladies. In 1956, glamorous evening wear was a must for any self-respecting, well-turned-out lady with a social life. The theatre, smart restaurants, clubs and, of course, the debutante circuit all required the right formal clothes. Freddy and Antony were just the chaps to design and make them, and all the local show business girls and cabaret artists, as well as the ladies of leisure from the posh squares round and about, knew it.

On the wall behind the counter were shelves piled up with bolts of fabric that filled every inch available. Silk, satin, sequin-, jewel- or ribbon-encrusted voile and plain old cotton organdie glowed in every colour imaginable. Then there were the trims. A whole wall was devoted to trims – rhinestones, diamanté, sequins, silk flowers, tassels and pearls sewn on backing strips and sold by the yard.

Beneath the counter were drawers and drawers of buttons, hooks, eyes, press studs, zips, bias binding, sequins, jewels and pearl drops sorted

14

by colour and type. A full-length mirror disguised the door to the workroom behind. Tucked away in one corner was the stockroom with the lavatory and basin.

The place was an earthly heaven for a person as starved of colour as I had been all my life, and I took to being the shop's assistant and general dogsbody like a duck takes to its pond. I felt as if I had come home – which was strange when you consider how drab my home had really been. But as time had gone on, and to my utter astonishment, it had become apparent to my bosses that I had an unsuspected talent.

'I've never known anyone with an eye for colour like our Lizzie's. She just has to give a body the once-over and she's taken in skin tone, eyes, hair, the lot,' Freddy boasted to a plump Widow Twankey as he stuffed a set of huge false bosoms down the front of the frock. 'Next thing you know, she's back with just the colours to suit. She never fails. What's more, she's got a colour memory second to none, ducky, second to none!'

Freddy completely ignored the fact that I was standing right next to him and was blushing furiously. I wasn't used to being shown off like some kind of prize. I'd been taught to stick close to the woodwork and leave the limelight for others.

Freddy reminded me of a brilliant little dragonfly as he darted back and forth, tweaking a sleeve here and a dart there, head tilted and eyes narrowed as he assessed the figure before him. Freddy was small for a man, being around five and a half feet tall, with a slender, wiry figure and small hands and feet to match. He had the face of an angelic schoolboy, complete with thick dark hair that flopped fetchingly over his forehead in a fringe. His narrow face was blessed with large, beautiful, brown eyes that could sparkle with merriment, melt with sympathy, flutter with pleading or glitter with irritation as the situation demanded. He also had several inches of thick, dark lashes, envied by every woman who ever crossed his path.

Had he been an actor, he would have been the young man who skipped on to the stage wearing tennis trousers and a Fair Isle sweater, waved a racquet and asked if there was 'Anyone for tennis?' The resemblance disappeared when he spoke. His appearance may have suggested the playing fields of Eton, but his voice was pure East Acton alley.

'It means she can hold colour in her mind's eye, and doesn't have to take a swatch with her,' Freddy explained to Widow Twankey – whose mind was firmly fixed on the three o'clock at Aintree, judging by the well-thumbed racing paper in his hand and the dog-end that smouldered unregarded in the corner of his mouth.

'I've seen her do it.' Freddy carried on blithely, utterly unaware of his unresponsive audience and his squirming assistant. 'We were in some fashion department, Selfridges I think, poaching ideas, when she swooped down on this scarf which was the exact same shade of blue as a frock we'd made a fortnight before! Now blues don't always go with each other, and there's loads of different shades, so it's not easy to match, or complement either, not from memory it isn't. Madam over

16

there does it easy as you please.' Freddy shrugged philosophically, indicating that there was no explaining the phenomenon. Funny thing was, I'd never thought anything of it. I thought everyone could do it, but apparently not.

'So now we always send her out to pick up any bits and bobs we might need to finish a garment.' He gave an almighty yank to Widow Twankey's left sleeve and there was an ominous ripping sound from the tacking stitches that held it on. 'Oh bugger! Can you sew that back on again, Lizzie, while I get the skirt right?' Freddy asked.

Antony had the idea a few hours later while Freddy was perched on a chair, clad from Adam's apple to bony ankle in scarlet sequins, doing duty as a dressmaker's dummy once again. The Widow Twankey had left and we'd moved on to a dress for a cabaret singer.

As I looked at Freddy twinkling in the workroom lights, I thought how strange it was that I spent part of my days dressing men in women's clothing, as if it was the most normal thing in the world. And of course it was in a theatrical costumier's in the middle of Soho – but in my childhood home in Islington, and the cheerless Chapel Hall just up the road, it would have been an outrage. I had never seen a pantomime as a child, as they smacked of fun and thus were branded as Devil's work. The likes of a Widow Twankey or a Mother Goose never crossed my path until I worked at Freddy the Frock's. It was funny how times changed, I mused, as Antony's cultured voice broke into my thoughts.

'I've been thinking, Freddy dear,' he said, turning him slightly so that he could get another bit of hem pinned up. Antony was the exact opposite to Freddy to look at, and in his manner. He was tall and very fair, and while Freddy was as chatty as a flock of sparrows, Antony was quiet and thoughtful for the most part, although he could have flashes of 'artistic temperament' where his work was concerned. Because he was the quiet one, everyone thought that Antony's was the business brain behind the shop, but it wasn't. Freddy was the shrewd one who made all the business decisions: Antony made the artistic ones.

'We've been so busy over the winter season, what with the pantomimes, Christmas shows and so forth,' Antony continued quietly, 'that we've hardly had time to breathe. I think we should seriously consider training Elizabeth up to take on some of the fancier work.'

Freddy nodded. 'Cinderella's still not happy with her bodice and I've worked and reworked that bloody thing until my poor fingers are numb and bleeding. She's always been a cow, that one.' He huffed and turned another few inches. 'You're right, it would help a lot if Lizzie could turn her hand to more than just the schlep work.'

As it happened, the schlep work had suited me fine up until then. I looked forward to Monday mornings the way a starving beggar looks forward to a square meal. Work meant that I could forget the awful, gnawing hole where my heart and my home life should have been, ever since my daughter, Jenny, had died a year and a half before. While I was dashing around after the demands of

18

customers and my bosses, whole stretches of time passed when I didn't think of anything except the task at hand. What's more, I had discovered that, for me, aimlessness was the way that madness lay. I had teetered very close to that particular brink and had been pulled back in the nick of time by my employers and a shop full of wonder. So naturally, I was very interested in any plan that would increase my skills and keep me even busier.

'We're too busy at the minute to do anything much about it, ducky, but we could ask Sugar to show you a thing or two,' Freddy suggested as we talked about it some more later that day. 'What do you reckon, Lizzie? Would you mind learning fancy work from Sugar, if he'll do it? He's the best person with a needle we know: he can embroider, do fancy detailing and he's good at design too. The man has the lot at his fingertips.'

'I think I'd like it,' I said cautiously. 'I'm fond of Sugar. He's a nice man.'

And so it was agreed. I'd ask Sugar for lessons the very next time I saw him.

2

Sugar Plum Flaherty, my friend and neighbour, lived and worked with Bandy Bunyan, the owner of the drinking club below my flat. He was her right-hand man, chief barman, cook, bottle washer and closest confidant. Rumour sometimes had it that they were lovers, but rumour was equally insistent that Sugar was not a ladies' man, but a man's man when it came to romance. The truth was, nobody actually knew, because nobody had ever seen Sugar with a known lover, male or female. Speculation often ran riot though, especially round at Freddy the Frock's.

'The problem is that he's never given anyone even an interesting glance, let alone a full-blown lecherous leer in my presence, or in yours, Freddy dear. So whatever *we* think is pure guesswork. What about you, Elizabeth?' Antony asked. 'Have ever you noticed Sugar eyeing anyone?'

I shook my head. Sugar always seemed to be equally interested in everyone in a general sort of way. Naturally, he was more fond of some people than others. He adored Bandy, for instance, would do almost anything for her, but he was also the only one brave enough to stand up to her when she was being difficult, which was fairly often. Freddy and Antony were special favourites as well, but then they all shared an interest in fabrics, sewing and women's clothes; Freddy and Antony designed and made them and Sugar designed, made and sometimes wore them.

Sugar went in phases, like the moon. On the street, he dressed his tall frame in a relatively conventional way, if you can call a jaunty beret, bright scarf and three-piece suit conventional. But at other times, in private, he liked to dress in women's clothes. He even had phases with those too. Sometimes he went for glamour: high heels, sequinned gown, long gloves, wig, false eyelashes, nail polish, full make-up, jewellery, everything. At other times, he could be someone's favourite aunt, comfortable, homey. It all depended on his mood. He liked to be dressed up when in company, but naturally, he had to choose that company very carefully. He restricted it to like-minded chaps, home, very private parties at the club and a few close friends.

When I first encountered Sugar in a frock, I had to admit I was surprised. Shocked, even. I'd led such a sheltered life. Our church had boasted one or two mustachioed spinsters and a chap who'd been arrested for something unspecified in a public lavatory near the station, but no men in frocks as far as I knew. So Sugar in full regalia came as something of a facer the first time. Then, I'm ashamed to say, I found it rather funny. But when I got to know Sugar, really know him, I was grateful to be one of the few friends he trusted enough to know about his private passion.

He said it was the way that clothes felt that did it for him. The soft feel of fine fabrics and yarns against his skin, the whiff of Shalimar behind his ears and at his throat, the soft lines and freedom of movement, or, sometimes, the opposite; the restriction of tight skirts and high heels did something for him that nothing else could do. As did wearing cavalry twill, flannel and stout cotton, when he was in the mood for being 'a butch bastard', as he put it.

For Sugar, it was all about freedom in a funny kind of way, even though it was so hidden and secret. It was about the freedom to be whole, or so I understood it when we talked. It had sounded wonderful to me, who had never felt that way in my entire life to date, and I suspected that dressing up as a man wouldn't do it for me. Sometimes, I did wonder what *would* do it. The nearest I'd come to it was motherhood, and that had been taken away.

I didn't see Sugar for days after Antony suggested I ask him for embroidery lessons, but that wasn't all that unusual, despite living in such close proximity. Not only did we keep very different hours, but Sugar was known to simply vanish from time to time. No one ever knew where he went, and if Bandy knew, she wouldn't say. Sometimes he'd be gone for days at a time and then he'd return with no explanation beyond a quiet, secretive smile.

As it turned out, I eventually found him skulking round at the cafe in Old Compton Street when I popped in for some tea on my way home from work. I hadn't had time to shop, so sardines on toast and a cup of weak, sweet tea at home were the order of the day. The cafe was another important place in my small world. It was just around the corner from where I lived, so it was handy, but that wasn't why I went there. I went for the warmth of the welcome I invariably received from Maggie, her husband Bert and their adopted daughter, Rosie.

It was Rosie who had first brought me to the cafe. She'd been Jenny's very best friend at school. When Jenny had become too ill to go to school, Rosie had come to play with her at home. What a ray of sunshine that child had been in those dark times. Rosie had made Jenny's last days so much less lonely with her chatter, school gossip, mischievous laughter and her touching presents. I remember a cardboard theatre in particular, complete with characters, costumes and scenery. That theatre had kept Jenny absorbed in a world of make-believe for many, many hours.

Maggie and Bert were legendary among the locals for their kindness and generosity, so their establishment was one of the hubs of local life, especially when the pubs were shut. Everyone who lived and worked in the area turned up at the cafe at least once a day. It was an important meeting place as well as a good cafe. Some people practically lived there, like Madame Zelda, Clairvoyant to the Stars, who when she wasn't at the cafe, lived and worked next door; and Luigi Campanini who was from the delicatessen two doors up. They seemed to be there almost as often as Maggie and Bert.

Maggie was born to be a mother of a fine, large brood. She even looked like a fertility goddess, being big-bosomed and generous around the hips. But the brood wasn't to be, so Rosie, Bert and her many favourite customers became her chicks. She mothered us all. Maggie embraced life and people with equal enthusiasm, and it showed in her almost permanent smile, ready laugh and her plump body encased in a wraparound pinny. A mother hen with glittering rings, she had at least one for every finger, leaving only her thumbs free.

Bert was not quite such a presence, largely because he spent most of his time in his kitchen. He, too, was a cheerful soul with more than a passing resemblance to Humphrey Bogart, and according to Madame Zelda, he had set more than one girl's heart aflutter in his time, including hers. 'But he's the faithful type. Loves his old woman to death and his Rosie and that's enough for him. He wouldn't do nothing to upset them and everything he could to protect them,' she'd told me once, and I'm sure she was right. Bert Featherby was that rare being, a thoroughly contented man.

Which is more than could be said about my husband, Sid. I first got to know Maggie and Bert when Sid took it into his head to desert Jenny and me for another woman. Times had been very lean then. Jenny was ill, Sid had gone and I was unable to leave home to work because Jenny needed me to care for her. It was then that Maggie, Bert and many of my neighbours stepped in to make sure we were fed and kept a roof over our heads. I have never known such kindness as I received in those awful months around the time that Jenny died.

'Wotcha, Lizzie, what can I do you for, love?' asked Maggie, round face gleaming with the effort of washing a sink full of crockery in scalding hot water. Maggie prided herself on her spotless china and cutlery and it took lots of hot water and elbow grease to get them that way. I'd just managed to scrape in before Maggie and Bert battened down the hatches for the night. Sugar was ensconced at the corner table.

I gave my order and carefully counted out the money. It was Thursday and I got my wages on Friday evenings, so it was a case of chasing the last farthing around a virtually empty purse.

Maggie smiled at me. 'Go and join Sugar and

I'll bring your food over to you when it's ready. Here's your tea.'

I took it gratefully and joined a rather glum Sugar. 'How's life treating you?' I asked, more for form's sake than anything. I could see how it was treating him. Sugar looked depressed, a state of mind I could recognize all too easily.

Depression didn't really suit Sugar, who was normally a gentle, good-natured giant. He was tall – over six feet – and well made, with wide shoulders and long legs. You couldn't call him thin, but he certainly wasn't fat either. There was no sign of a paunch. I suppose he was in his mid-thirties, but it was hard to say because his slightly rounded face and wide eyes gave him the innocent, cherubic look of a younger man. He kept his thick brown hair a little on the long side and swept back from his broad forehead, but a lock of it tended to flop in a cowlick and he was continuously pushing it back with a massive, spade-like hand. It was hard to imagine such a hand wielding anything as small as a needle, but it did, and beautifully too. The man was an artist, everyone said so.

'Hello, Lizzie,' he said. 'Not bad, sweetie, but not good either. Middling, I s'pose you'd call it middling. Bandy has got herself a new man and that usually bodes difficulty, at the very least.'

I knew what he meant. Bandy, the owner of the drinking club which was the haunt of Soho's literati, the artists' set and the simply thirsty or curious, would launch herself at romance with the remorseless single-mindedness of a battleship on manoeuvres; but, just like a battleship in

25

enemy waters, she was quite likely to explode at the end of it. Bandy was nothing if not volatile.

'She's at the permanently horizontal stage at the moment, which makes work tricky,' Sugar continued. 'She's too busy in the boudoir to see to things like the ordering in the usual way.' He brightened slightly. 'I don't suppose you fancy doing a spot of waitressing while her ladyship is otherwise engaged, do you? It'd free me to do the stocktaking and whatnot if you would; just for a couple of nights a week until she rises again. I'd pay the usual rate of course.'

'I'd love to, Sugar,' I said, a vision of my empty purse firmly in my mind. Apart from the extra money, I loved any excuse to get out of my empty flat. 'When do you want me to start?'

The big man shrugged. 'Is tonight too soon? I really do have to get to grips with the drinks order. We're almost out of gin, and that will never do.'

'I'll be down when I've had a bath and changed, then,' I told him. 'But I'll have to leave before last orders. I've got work tomorrow.'

'That's all right. Just serve the after-work crowd early on and I'll see to the hardened boozers later. A couple of hours should see me right for the ordering. Then, after that, could you do Fridays and Saturdays to help with the crowds? There's too many those nights for one pair of hands, let alone my poor old feet.'

I looked up as Maggie delivered my food and pulled up a chair to join us. She'd taken the precaution of bringing a pot of tea, a jug of milk and a spare cup for herself.

'How long do you reckon Bandy'll be out of commission, then?' Maggie asked, winking playfully at me.

'There's no telling,' Sugar said mournfully. 'Depends on the geezer's stamina, I expect.' Maggie laughed and I smiled. Sugar shook his head at us. 'It's all right for you to laugh, but it could be weeks before we get any sense out of her. You know Bandy. She didn't come by her name for nothing.'

I looked at Sugar, then at Maggie, my eyebrows raised in enquiry. How *had* Bandy come by her name? As little Rosie had once pointed out, Bandy's legs were as straight as anybody's.

'According to my Bert, Bandy's ... er ... staying power is legendary, so it's "Abandon hope all ye who enter here," and "Bandy" for short.' Maggie blushed slightly. 'Or so Bert says.'

Sugar nodded. 'That's it. That, and the fact that her name really is Hope, Hope Bunyan. She's the younger sister to Faith and older sister to Charity, or so she told me not all that long ago.'

I was amazed. Faith, Hope and Charity, whatever next? I just couldn't imagine Bandy as one of the Virtues, and I said so.

'Me neither, sweetie,' Sugar agreed. 'Let's face it, she abandoned virtue a long time ago.'

Maggie chortled. 'Who's been sleeping in the knife drawer, then?'

'I know, Maggie, I know, but it gets on my wick. Whenever Bandy lands a new bloke, I get dumped on until she comes to her senses, then I have to mop her up. I love old Band like a sister, you know I do, but I do wish she'd pick a better

27

class of bloke, someone who'd treat her right and make her happy. But no,' Sugar sighed long and hard, 'she picks the dregs, sweeties, the absolute dregs!'

Maggie and I nodded sympathetically. Bandy did have lousy taste in men, we could testify to that, but I thought it politic to keep my mouth shut on the subject. I remembered my own husband, Sidney, with a shudder. I was no shining example of how to get it right, that was for sure. Then I looked at my friend Maggie and thought that she, on the other hand, was. She and Bert had one of the happiest marriages around.

'Who is the new fella anyway?' Maggie asked. 'Do we know him?' The question had been hovering on the tip of my tongue, too, but I'd been too polite to ask, an unfortunate throwback to my childhood.

'You might do. Name of Malcolm Lamb, fancies himself as a poet, lives in Peter Street.'

'I know,' Maggie answered after a moment's thought. 'Tweedy sort, dark hair, needs a good shave most of the time. Wears sandals all year round and reeks of French baccy.' I applied my mind and thought I knew who she meant.

'That's the one,' said Sugar. 'But French baccy isn't the half of it. He could do with a damned good bath on a regular basis *and* a trip to the Chinese laundry with his togs while he's at it.' Sugar sniffed. 'I call him Malodorous for short.'

Maggie almost choked on her rich tea biscuit. Sugar thumped her back a few times, shifting the crumbs enough for her to sip her tea.

'That's not short,' I objected. 'That's long.'

'That's as may be, but it's accurate,' Maggie assured me, taking a deep breath. 'The bloke does honk a bit.'

'A bit! By the end of the month the man can make your eyes water at five hundred paces. Bandy says it's manly, but I say it's simple slackness, sweeties, in the washing department.'

Sugar's voice was a little sharp; time to change the subject, although I secretly couldn't wait to meet this paragon of grime. I brought up the subject of embroidery lessons and, to my delight, Sugar agreed at once.

'Oh yes, flower, I'd love to. It'll get me back to the soothing silks myself. Nothing like a bit of handiwork to calm a body's shattered nerves. There was never a tremor in my hands all through the Blitz; cool as a cucumber as long as I had my needles, my embroidery ring and my silks.'

This was not strictly true – the odd shoddy stitch in his 'war work' attested to that – but we let it go. Distance had lent enchantment to quite a lot of our memories of the war and Sugar was far from alone in putting something of a gloss on it. If all the blokes who said they'd been heroic at Arnhem had actually been there, there'd have been no room for the Dutch, the Germans or the Americans to stand, let alone fight.

A clatter of young feet on the stairs that led up to the flat above brought my thoughts back to the cafe. Rosie burst into the room, closely followed by her friend Kathy Moon. My eyes welled up again and my heart lurched, because just for a second, Kathy could have been my Jenny, laughing and bounding into the room like a young

29

horse, all legs and youthful enthusiasm. But she wasn't my Jenny of course – Jenny was gone and she wasn't coming back.

Somebody must have noticed a bleak expression on my face because I felt a warm hand find mine and give it a gentle squeeze, then the moment withdrew and I came back from the brink of utter desolation to hear Rosie's cheery voice. 'Hello, Auntie Lizzie, how're you?'

'I'm all right, sweetheart, and you? How's school?'

Rosie laughed and rolled her eyes and said in mock exasperation at the predictability of grown-ups, 'People *always* ask that. School's school, what else is there to say? If you mean, how am I doing at school, then I'm doing OK, thank you.

'Kathy and me are going round to see Mademoiselle Hortense, to help finish off that piece of scenery for Saturday's show. What time should I be back, Auntie Maggie?'

Maggie glanced at the large, round clock hanging above the doorway to the kitchen. 'No later than half seven. You've got school tomorrow. And make sure your homework is really finished before you scamper off,' she said suspiciously.

Homework began with the build-up to the eleven-plus examination and had rapidly led to conflict between Rosie and Maggie. Maggie and I had had several planning sessions, trying to find ways to get Rosie to knuckle down to the hated chore. Bribery seemed to work the best: no homework, no pocket money, harsh but effective. I wondered briefly what strategy I would have used on Jenny. It wouldn't have been pocket money,

30

that much was certain; there'd never been enough cash for that kind of thing. I sighed. I probably would have fallen back on nagging and getting cross, good old standbys when all else failed.

'Bye-bye, Auntie Lizzie,' Rosie's voice whispered close to my ear as she flung her bony arms around my neck and plonked a smacker on my cheek. She did the rounds and kissed Sugar and Maggie in their turn, sang out 'Bye, Uncle Bert,' in the general direction of the kitchen, then followed Kathy out on to the street.

'Bye love,' came a voice from the rear of the premises and Bert appeared in the kitchen doorway, wiping his hands on his long, white apron and smiling broadly. How that man loved that child! Fatherhood suited Bert Featherby as well as motherhood suited his Maggie.

I felt a pang of envy for this happy little family, and then snapped out of it. Envy is, in my opinion, one of the more repulsive of human emotions, dishonest and punishing if it's allowed to get out of hand. I really didn't want that. Envy makes people unkind. Few people are able to say, 'I'm being horrible to you because I envy you like mad.' No, they're just blindly spiteful and then blame the object of their envy for deserving such treatment. I certainly didn't want to turn into one of those poor souls, and gave myself a stern talking to. Self-pity is so hard to control when a person actually has reason to feel sorry for themselves. I had to keep reminding myself that others had known personal tragedy without being soured by it. Some had even managed to become better people, but I wasn't sure I was up to that. The best I hoped for was not to allow the terrible loneliness to turn me into a bitter person.

I squared my shoulders, mentally counted to ten, and brought the subject back to my embroidery lessons. Sugar and I agreed that Sunday teatime was best for us both.

'I'll tell you what,' I said, 'I'll swap you one evening in the bar a week for one lesson, then if you pay me for the other session, that'll seem fairer to me. I can't afford to pay you for my lessons, you see.'

Sugar stuck out a hand. 'Done!' he said. 'And you have been! You could have had the lessons for nothing,' he chortled. I looked around the cafe at the familiar faces and thought that although the hand I'd been dealt had been a hard one, it had led me to all these dear friends in a roundabout way and for that I was truly grateful. Good friends could make even the hardest things in life more bearable.

3

I could hear the murmur of voices as I walked downstairs from my little flat to the club just before eight. Tobacco smoke made the air fuggy and faintly blue on the last leg of the descent. 'Bandy's Place' had a reputation for its atmosphere, its clientele and, first and foremost, the double act formed by Bandy and Sugar. They had a chemistry that drew people like ants to honey –

or 'flies to cack', as Bandy rather tastelessly put it.

The lady herself was sitting on her usual stool at the end of the bar, where she could lean casually against the wall if she was a little the worse for wear after a long night talking and drinking.

Bandy's looks were as striking as her wit. She had a strong, bony face, pale but full of character. It was the kind of face 'that sank a thousand ships', according to Bert – who was, luckily, a good friend of Bandy. She used to scare me to death, before I got to know her better and realized that beneath her hard, often cruel outer shell was a rather decent person.

'Ah, Elizabeth, good of you to help us out at such short notice. It will stop that damned Sugar from grumbling about being worked like a Singapore coolie.' Bandy took a sip of her drink, a long drag on her cigarette and blew a perfect smoke ring into the air.

'Hello Bandy,' I said. 'How are you?'

'Never better, Lizzie dear, never better. When Malcolm turns up, we're off to some ghastly poetry reading above the Coach and Horses. As I was saying to Sugar, at least there's a well-stocked boozer to numb the pain.'

I smiled. 'Why go if you hate it so?' It seemed a reasonable enough question.

'To keep the little man happy,' she answered promptly. 'You know how it is. I have to let the poor chap up for air from time to time and that's what he likes to do, read his poems out loud to a load of dreary people. I go occasionally, to show the flag.'

I was astonished. I couldn't imagine Bandy in

the middle of a group of bohemians; they always looked so drab in their black clothes, so humourless too and more than a tad depressed. Whereas Bandy wasn't any of those things. She was a passionate person who prided herself on taking life 'by the balls' and not simply allowing life to happen to her.

Her worldly enthusiasm for the good things in life was partly what made people flock to her bar. She sat on her bar stool, with a Passing Cloud smouldering in a long, slender cigarette-holder in one hand and a large gin in the other, and dispensed pithy stories, observations about life and insults to anyone within reach of her hoarse but plummy voice. The customers lapped it up.

The other half of the successful team was Sugar. He was the one who mopped up the bleeding egos that Bandy's sharp tongue had managed to wound. He remarked on new hair-dos or clever makeup, noticed men's triumphs and glossed over their disasters. As fast as Bandy knocked them down, Sugar picked them up, dusted them off and sent them back into the world thinking they were the bee's knees. It was a winning combination and Bandy's Place was rarely empty unless it was closed.

The club itself had two separate identities. The daytime one began rather shabby and faded as Bobby Bristowe, the only male cleaner I had ever met, whipped around the threadbare, red-patterned carpet with a vacuum cleaner. Bandy and Sugar swore by their 'little treasure' who was, in fact, far from little. Bobby had been an all-in wrestler in his day, and still looked the part, having one of those necks that seemed just as wide as his bald head. Every morning, bright and early, Bobby flicked a large duster around the red and gilt chairs and stools scattered about the room. He emptied the ashtrays, wiped down tables and dusted the huge, gilt mirrors with a feather duster on the end of a long, slender pole. Finally, he polished the bar carefully. It was his pride and joy, and he liked the mellow wood to gleam in the lamplight. Once Bobby had finished, the place had the air of an ageing sleeping beauty who was way past her best, but who still waited with quiet dignity for her admirers to return and bring her back to sparkling life.

And of course, they did. At night the club took on a vibrancy as the lamps beneath their ruby glass shades were reflected back into the room by the mirrors. Then, the place glowed invitingly. All you noticed was the glitter of bottles and glasses, the blue swirls of smoke, the hum of talk and much laughter. Bandy was always threatening to close the place for a week and have it repainted, but she never did. The truth was, people liked it that way. It radiated warmth, companionship and good cheer even on the coldest and foggiest of winter nights.

My heart lightened as soon as I walked through the doors. I certainly lived a more colourful life now. When I was young, we'd all crept about trying hard not to be noticed for anything other than the perfection of our front step, the crispness of our curtains and our devotion to a wrathful God on the sabbath – and on every other day. Men who loved men, women who loved women, anyone

35

who loved anyone outside of holy matrimony – or sometimes even within it – and men who wore dresses, or women who wore trousers, were hardly to be imagined; and if they were, they were damned to everlasting Hell, no doubt about that.

I was brought up to believe that a state of grace required dull cheerlessness at the very least, but abject misery was better. That way, a body went to meet their angry and vengeful Maker with some semblance of the enthusiasm that would have been missing if life had been a jolly affair. It had, therefore, come as a bit of surprise to me when Sid and I moved to Soho after the war to find brightly clad men and women engaged in the enjoyment of all sorts of unusual activities with one another, and more or less getting away with it. At least, they got away with it without bringing down the wrath of God; no bolts of lightning, no pillars of salt, nothing like that. True, it did end in court sometimes, with knuckles rapped and fines to pay, but in Soho nobody seemed to mind that much. They didn't worry about what the neighbours thought, largely because they were pretty sure their neighbours were at it too.

Besides Bandy in her corner and Sugar behind the bar, the only other people in were regulars. Bobby and his wife, Pansy, had a table by the door. Madame Zelda sat with them, nursing a port and lemon. Anyone less like a pansy than Pansy Bristowe was hard to imagine. When she'd first introduced herself to me, she'd stuck out a beefy, red hand and said, 'I know, I know, more of a small brick khazi than a Pansy.' She'd laughed. 'I put it down to wishful thinking meself. Me mum was praying I'd look more like me dad than her, but it wasn't to be. There was no mistaking whose little blossom I was.'

'Well, you're my little blossom now,' Bobby had interjected gallantly, and I swear that Pansy blushed.

'All right Lizzie?' they smiled as I walked past their table. I nodded, smiled back at them, and left them to continue their quiet conversation.

Freddy and Antony sat in a corner, discussing business over a bottle of their favourite 'Poo'. When I'd asked Freddy why they called it 'Poo' he'd explained, 'Champagne, shampoo, get it?' I continued to look blank. 'Oh, please yourself. It's what we call it anyway.'

Sharky Finn, a local lawyer and Madame Zelda's landlord, sat with T.C., an ex-policeman who was Rosie's father. T.C. was a nice man, fairly recently widowed, his wife Pat having finally succumbed to a long illness. It was during that illness that T.C. had fathered Rosie, but Pat was not her mother. That was Cassandra – Cassie to her friends. T.C. and Cassie had met in the war and had a passionate, on-off love affair for many years.

I have often wondered if T.C.'s wife knew about it, but if she did, she'd kept quiet on the subject – in public, anyway. She had certainly always been very sweet to Rosie when she saw her and, if not exactly matey with Cassie, then certainly cordial. Rosie looked a lot like her father. She had his curly hair, slightly stocky frame and blue, blue eyes.

At the table next to them was another regular, Dominic, who worked for the BBC, and his brother Brendan, who was fresh from Dublin

37

and looking for a good 'crack', as he called it. What he meant was, plenty of talk while the booze flowed and possibly a good-natured brawl at the end of it. A visit from Brendan always made for fireworks, and poor Dominic was often left to put out the flames.

I straightened my shoulders. It was likely to be a lively night. Brendan could talk the hind leg off a giraffe – and that is some leg. The Irish that came to the club were able to drum up a party atmosphere in the most unlikely and unpromising of company. They could even tempt a smile out of Bandy when she was in one of her moods, and that took a real gift.

Sugar's face softened with relief as I joined him at the bar. He was wearing a smart, three-piece suit in navy blue, with the thinnest of stripes; a white silk shirt that could almost have been a blouse, but wasn't quite; and a flowing, multi-coloured silk tie that was almost a scarf, but wasn't quite either. I noticed that his nails were the colour of seashells, the palest of pinks, and polished to a shine, while his lashes were suspiciously black. I looked down. Sure enough, he was wearing his sultan's slippers – maroon leather, tooled in gold, with the toes hugely elongated and turned back upon themselves, like puppies' tails.

'Not that many in so far, Lizzie. As long as you keep the Guinness flowing, Brendan will be happy. If he kicks up, just give us a shout and I'll rush to your aid.' Sugar paused, then brightened as a new idea struck him. 'Or ask him about his latest work, that gets him back from the brink, usually. Even Brendan finds it hard to fight and quote his plays at one and the same time.'

Sugar sketched a little wave as he disappeared into the stockroom, but was back in a second, brow creased with concern. 'And if he threatens the mirrors, kill him first and ask questions later. At least hurl him to the ground before he can throw anything or *thrust* yourself into the firing line. Anything, but don't let him smash the mirrors whatever you do.' And on that worrying note, he was gone.

'T.C., dahling!' I heard a woman screech as she made her entrance into the bar. 'Cassie's on her way. She'll be here in just a moment.' Her heavily painted face took on a troubled look. 'Although perhaps I should warn you that she's bringing a friend. Sharky, dahling, get me a little drinky, there's a good boy. Sylvie will love you for it later.' She dropped into a chair alongside the man I assumed was her latest lover.

Sharky nodded and raised a finger at me. He made a little circle in the air, to indicate another round for himself and T.C. at the same time. I smiled, nodded in my turn and shoved a glass under the vodka optic, once, twice. Sylvia didn't trouble with singles. I poured a brandy for Sharky – he rarely drank anything else – while T.C. usually drank beer or the very occasional malt whisky.

T.C. still carried a bit of a torch for Cassie, anyone could see that. She was the mother of his only child, after all. I noticed the poor man wincing as Sylvia prattled on about Cassie's new friend.

'The man's loaded, stinking rich, name of Harry,' she gushed, oblivious to T.C.'s bowed head as he stared into the dregs of his beer. I hurried to finish the order so that I could interrupt Sylvia's tactless flow, but you can't hurry a pint of brown ale through the pump. I arrived at the table to hear the end of the story. 'Met him gambling,' she continued. 'Saw the size of his wallet and took him home for the experience of a lifetime. Hasn't let him out since. It's been three days since they last surfaced.'

Bandy barked with laughter. 'Sounds like a gal after my own heart,' she roared, and slapped Malcolm's backside as if he were a horse. 'Drink up. It's time we shook a leg.' She slipped from her bar stool. He'd arrived in time for a quick one before the poetry reading.

'Right you are, Bandy my dear.' Malcolm threw back his shaggy head and poured his drink down his throat in one go. 'Let's be having you.' He put an enormous arm around her shoulder and they left, laughing about something as they went. Despite Sugar's dislike of Malcolm, he seemed to make Bandy happy.

I was back behind the bar, filling another order of Guinness for the Behan brothers, when Cassie arrived with a slim, bespectacled, well-tailored man in tow. She made her way to the table where Sylvia, Sharky and T.C. were sitting, and introduced everyone.

Sharky and T.C. had stood at Cassie's approach, so it didn't take long for T.C. to shake Harry's hand and murmur an excuse I didn't hear. He began to walk away and I heard Cassie cry, 'Don't be silly T.C. Do stay, we don't want to break up your evening.'

The look of pain that shot across his face made

me want to help him.

'It's all right, Cassie,' I sang out. 'T.C. said he'd help me reach down the Teacher's and fix it to the optic.'

'Thanks, Lizzie,' he whispered as he approached. 'You saved me from a dreary evening. I couldn't think of a single polite excuse for not joining them. Now, where's this Scotch that's out of reach?' he asked loudly. He had his back to the table and didn't see Harry move closer to Cassie and put his arm possessively around her waist as if sensing he had a rival. I delivered Cassie's gin and it to the table, along with Harry's whisky sour.

For a while all seemed to be going swimmingly. Brendan, Dominic and pals were in an unusually quiet, reflective mood, and had shown no signs of evil designs on Sugar's precious mirrors. Cassie's party had grown by another couple, a toothy, rather florid man and a brassy blonde I'd never seen before. Although noisy, they were too busy drinking and flirting among themselves to trouble anyone outside of their golden circle. All the while T.C. seemed content to help me serve a slow, but steady trickle of customers. We knew things would pick up once the theatres and the pubs had chucked out, and we were enjoying the relative peace and quiet while we had it.

'She's beautiful, isn't she?' I asked, nodding towards Cassie's back, which appeared to be shaking with laughter. She had looked so lovely as she walked across the room. Her cornflower blue, heavy silk two-piece hugged her tiny waist and matched her large eyes. She wore it with a crisp, white blouse, the collar starched and turned up to

41

frame her elfin chin. Her blond hair was swept up in a French pleat. The silk of her suit had swished expensively as she walked and sat elegantly, as only the best tailoring does.

The long pencil skirt reached to her shins and tapered from the waist and hips in an elegant line. The sweet little jacket flared slightly as her hips swelled and it had a neat belt in the same silk as a finishing touch. Cassie wore black stiletto-heel shoes and clutched a bag made from the same leather. Over her suit, she had worn a mink coat I had never seen before, and that I had safely stowed in the cloakroom. She'd obviously allowed Harry out of bed long enough to go shopping, I'd thought rather nastily as I stroked it and put it on its hanger.

T.C. smiled sadly. 'Yes, she's very beautiful. I'll always care for her, naturally, but there's been a lot of water under the bridge since she and I... No, no, it's the drinking that worries me. She always winds up in tricky company and bad situations when she hits the bottle.'

I didn't say anything. Another rush of customers had come in and T.C. and I worked our way through them in a companionable silence. Then, towards midnight, a fight broke out. Thank God the Behans had moved on to pastures new before it started, as they wouldn't have been able to resist joining in.

It began as I cleared the glasses from Cassie's table. Only Cassie, Harry, Toothy and the blond woman were left at the table, Sharky and Sylvia having left with Freddy and Antony an hour or so before. Bobby, Pansy and Madame Zelda had also left much earlier in the evening, to get something to eat. Toothy was well-oiled and was slurring badly as he spoke to me. I leaned forward to hear him better and his hand snaked up my skirt. I shrieked and jumped back, startled.

A voice from behind me said, 'I don't think so, chummy!' It was T.C., who'd vaulted the bar and landed close to the offending party. His hand shot out and he grabbed Toothy's arm. 'Out!' he roared into the astonished silence that followed.

'Fuck off!' slurred Toothy. 'S'only a bit of fun.'

'I say,' said Harry. 'Have a care. You almost had the drinks over then, old chap.'

'OUT!' T.C.'s finger was rigid and his expression unflinching as he showed Cassie's friend the exit. Toothy picked up a heavy-bottomed whisky glass from the table and swung it threateningly at T.C., as if he was about to bowl a cricket ball, but it slipped from his grasp and crashed to the floor. Blondie screamed and lurched to her feet, her dress ruined by flying glass, whisky and Toothy, who had tripped over his own feet and fallen against her. Blondie shoved him hard, sent him reeling into T.C. who stepped smartly aside so that he stumbled into a couple of Bobby's wrestling pals, unwinding after a show. Before I knew it, there was a full-scale fight going on between Toothy, Harry and the wrestlers. Needless to say, the wrestlers won and Toothy, Harry and Blondie were cast into the night.

Cassie hung back just long enough to collect her mink. Her blue eyes flashed with fury as she confronted T.C. 'My hero!' she spat. 'Now who is going to pay for the supper? Not to mention the damned rent! Not you, Sir Galahad, that's for certain.' She swept out, calling, 'Harry, Nigel, Mary, wait, wait for little old me. We can still salvage the evening. Perhaps you'd all like a drink back at my place...'

'Did I miss something, sweeties?' came a voice from behind us. Sugar was standing in the doorway to the stockroom.

'Just a bloke taking liberties with Lizzie,' T.C. told him. 'It was soon sorted out by our friends here.' He nodded towards the two wrestlers, who nodded back.

'A quiet night then,' Sugar observed. 'I'll get you a drink for your trouble. Gentlemen, T.C. what'll you have?'

'Do you know,' T.C. grinned, 'I think I fancy a nice cup of tea.'

'You're on,' Sugar chuckled. 'Lizzie, do the honours will you, and join us if you like? I want to put a proposition to T.C. Get our two friends whatever they fancy.'

When I brought the tea to the bar, the men were deep in conversation. 'Yep, I'm short on all the spirits, by at least a bottle, sometimes two. And Bandy and I have both noticed the takings are down. Not by much, say a tenner every now and then, but it mounts up.' Sugar smiled his thanks to me and patted the seat beside him. 'I want you to look into it, T.C.'

T.C. held his hand up. 'Bandy could be being particularly vague at the moment,' he pointed out. 'Or it could be someone else altogether. Who else has access to the club when it's quiet? There's Bobby for starters.'

Sugar shook his head. 'Nope, we've had Bobby for years and the man's straight. I know that swine Malodorous is stealing from her – I just need to prove it, that's all. Until then, I'll keep my suspicions between you, me and Lizzie here. I want you to keep your eyes peeled too, Lizzie. These thefts are getting serious.'

I finished my tea, bade the two men goodnight and walked up the stairs to my empty fiat. I had enjoyed working with T.C., and was relieved he'd rushed to my aid when that awful Toothy had taken a liberty. It had been nice to know there was someone watching my back. Drunks could be a tricky lot; OK one minute, seriously hostile the next.

I got ready for bed in double-quick time. I was exhausted after my full day at work and my evening shift at Bandy's and was glad about that, because it promised a decent sleep for once. I hadn't really slept well since Jenny got ill. Usually the awful emptiness of my nest kept me awake. I had never lived alone in my entire life before and I still wasn't used to it. I sometimes wondered if a person ever got used to it.

4

Peace arrived a few days later on the coldest day of the year.

She was beautiful in a delicate and small-boned way. Although technically Anglo-Chinese, Peace looked more Chinese than Anglo, with her glossy black hair, pretty brown eyes and tiny build. She was a boarder at a girls' school somewhere in Essex. Before that, she'd lived in Hong Kong, where she had been born sixteen years before. She'd flitted in and out of our lives like an exotic little bird for a good couple of years, arriving each school holiday and disappearing again when term began, leaving absolutely no trace behind her.

'I have run away, Mrs Robbins,' she said to me, standing miserably in front of the counter of the shop. 'And I am never going back. Never!' It's hard to be convincingly defiant when your teeth are chattering like typewriter keys in a typing pool, but Peace did her best, poor little scrap.

'Ooh, ducky, sit by the two-bar, do,' clucked Freddy as he guided her towards the electric fire that warmed the area behind the counter.

'Lizzie, get the kettle on. We'll all have a cuppa and try to thaw the poor thing out.'

Freddy's tone of distressed concern brought Antony out of the workshop to see what was going on. 'I've got just the thing,' he said, having assessed the situation in a moment. He dived into the stockroom and returned with a length of the black and white furry fabric that we'd used to make Dick Whittington's cat. He wrapped it around Peace's shoulders and found a remnant of pantomime horse for her legs. He tucked her in as tenderly as you would a baby. 'There, you'll soon be as warm as toast, young lady.'

I handed out cups of tea, Freddy found more chairs and we were soon seated in a circle around the fire as we stared at Peace. She, in turn, stared

46

back at us as she sipped her drink.

After much silent prompting from Freddy, in the form of nods towards Peace and furiously waggled eyebrows, I finally broached the subject.

'So, when you say you've run away, Peace, we presume you mean run away from school?'

She nodded in answer to my question, but said nothing.

Bandy had become Peace's guardian while she was being educated at St Matilda's, and that's roughly all any of us knew about her, except that she always referred to Bandy as Aunt. Just who had given Bandy the responsibility for the girl, and why she had taken it, were matters of speculation.

'When you say you're never going back, does never really mean never?' I asked. 'And does your aunt know?'

Peace's face set in stubborn lines and her eyes narrowed. 'Never,' she hissed, 'I will never go back and she can't make me.' She raised her chin slightly. 'And no, Aunt does not know because I have not seen her. I went to the flat, but there was no answer. So I came here.'

'And quite right too. You could've frozen to death hanging about on the streets today,' Freddy reassured her. 'Have you eaten?'

Peace shook her head and took another sip of her tea.

'Righto. Well, we'll soon see about that. You come upstairs with your Uncle Freddy and I'll whip you up some scrambled eggs on toast. You come as well, Lizzie. You and Peace can have a nice little chat while I'm cooking.' Freddy turned to Antony. 'You can hold the fort for ten minutes,

47

can't you, Ant?'

Antony agreed that he could. The three of us went out into St Anne's Court and Freddy slipped his key into the anonymous green door beside the shop. He ushered us into the kitchen and turned on the gas oven full blast, leaving its door open so that the heat would soon fill the small space. Then he set to, beating eggs and pouring milk into the bowl, while he chattered on about nothing in particular, putting Peace at her ease. 'Sit,' he ordered, motioning us to the table by the window, 'while I cook.'

I took my cue. 'So, can you fill us in with a little more detail?' I asked as gently as I could. I could see that the girl was badly rattled, by the way her eyes darted about. 'Like why you've run away and are never going back? That's a good place to start.'

'I hate it there, Mrs Robbins, I really hate it there,' Peace whispered in a voice so quiet, I could barely hear her.

I could understand this. Chilly old Essex was a far cry from Hong Kong, I imagined, and life in a cheerless English boarding-school was probably anything but cosy. 'I can see how you could hate it, but what happened to make you run away now? There must be a reason.'

Her eyes began to dart about again, as if she expected someone to jump out of the walls at her, but she said nothing.

Freddy handed me a cup of coffee, put a plate of scrambled eggs on toast in front of Peace and sat down beside her. 'Well ducky, looks like you're in hot water all right. Still, chin up, I'm sure Bandy can sort the school out if anyone can,' he

48

said in a cheerful voice as he patted her hand tenderly. 'Don't you worry, Peace, things have a way of working out in the end, you'll see. Meanwhile, you scoff your breakfast and Lizzie'll take you home to see if she can track down that aunt of yours. How about that?'

He smiled at me. 'Take as long as you need, Lizzie, just make sure she's safely tucked up before you come back to work, that's the main thing.' He walked to the door, then turned. 'Just pull the doors to when you leave, and remember to turn off the oven.' He sketched a little wave, 'Toodlepip old things,' and he was gone.

Once Peace had mopped up every crumb of her meal, I put down my coffee cup and asked her again what had happened. To my astonishment, she burst into tears. Peace, who had solemnly taken in her stride all the strange events and people life had thrown at her, never showing anything other than polite interest, was weeping buckets.

'Oh dear! What on earth is it, you poor girl? I didn't mean to upset you.' I got up and put my arm about her skinny little shoulders. I was reminded, suddenly and painfully, of Jenny, the last child I'd held in my arms.

'Do you want to talk about it, sweetheart?' I asked as I rocked her gently and looked down at the dark head now burrowed into my midriff. At last, with great shuddering gulps, Peace was able to stop crying and lift her head to look up at me. 'They call me the Chink or the Yellow Peril or the slanted-eyed swot. They laugh at me. And they call me "Bunions" too.'

'I have no friends, not any more, not since Sally left. Sally N'kozi was my friend and she was big and strong and no one bullied her or called her jungle bunny to her face, never! Some of the bigger girls bully anyone who is friendly with me and call them names as well. It is very hard, Mrs Robbins. It is very hard indeed to bear it.'

The tears welled up again and I found myself joining in. She sounded terribly lonely, and felt so small and frail in my arms. 'Have you told Bandy all this?' I asked.

'I did not want to tell Aunt about it. I was told before I came to England that I must not be troublesome to Aunt. I thought it would get better and it did. Sally saw to it that no one was nasty to me.'

Peace took a deep breath. 'But Sally has gone. She did not return after the Christmas holiday. I miss my friend very much.' If Sally N'kozi was all that stood between Peace and total isolation and insults at school, I thought, then this had to be the understatement of the century.

How could children be so cruel? But they are, I could vouch for that from my own schooldays. It didn't do to be different, I knew that only too well. Being different was an invitation to the bullies to pick on you, and however hard you tried to fit in, they wouldn't let you. Bullies always need a target and if there isn't one handy, then it's their job to set about making one. A stranger from a strange land was a gift to any bully because, by definition, they had few if any allies handy to help out.

'Did you ever tell the headmistress, the matron

or any of the mistresses about your troubles with the other girls?' I asked, knowing the answer. You didn't tell the authorities anything if you wanted to survive. That was as true of girls at English public schools as it was of any children at any school – and indeed, of the citizens of Soho, or what the racier Sunday papers referred to as 'the denizens of the underworld'.

Peace shook her head. She was a bright girl, and knew about survival in strange set-ups. 'Watch and learn' was her motto, I'd noticed that. She would know that sneaks did not prosper. Sneaks got beaten up at worst, and even more backs turned upon them at best.

'So, if Sally left before you got back to school, what happened yesterday to make you run away?'

Peace hung her head. 'I hit someone,' she whispered. 'I hit someone and threw her on to the compost heap that the gardener keeps behind the bicycle sheds.'

I raised my eyebrows. I could see that running away could appear to be the best option in the circumstances, but I was blowed if I could see how such a tiny little thing had managed to throw anything bigger than potato peelings on the compost. 'What did the headmistress have to say about that?' I asked. 'Or did you run away before she could say anything at all?'

Peace nodded silently, and squeezed her eyes shut tight in an attempt to keep the big tears from oozing from beneath her eyelids.

I felt helpless. 'I think we'd better tell Bandy what's happened, dear. She may be able to help,' I said, although for the life of me I couldn't see how.

5

Peace and I could hear Bandy yelling into the telephone in the bar as we entered the building. 'What do you mean, missing? How the hell can she be missing? Shouldn't she be in maths or something ghastly like that?' There was a pause as she listened to a reply. 'Don't take that tone with me, madam. You're paid to care for and educate the gal, not to bloody well mislay her.'

There was another, more lengthy pause, then a throaty chuckle. 'The compost heap you say? I expect the little madam deserved it. It's not like Peace to rear up over a trifle. Peace by name and peaceable by nature, that's the gal I know.'

Another silence, then a bellow of pure outrage. 'If she has turned into a thug, then you, madam, are responsible for this miraculous transformation, because we put you in charge of her moral and social development as well as her education. That's what fucking boarding-schools are for, dammit!'

Then, 'I'll use any language I choose because I am not one of your damned gals, thank God. You're the one who lost her. It is your moral duty to bloody well find her. Keep me informed. Good day to you.'

There was a crash as the receiver hit the telephone, and I felt Peace shrink against the wall in alarm. I gave her the key to my flat and whispered

52

to her to go up while I told Bandy she was safe and well. Peace looked grateful and scuttled up the stairs. I took a deep breath and pushed open the door to the bar.

'Hello Bandy,' I said as casually as I could manage. I wished like mad that Sugar was there, but he wasn't. The only other person in the bar was Bobby Bristowe, who was flitting about with a feather duster as far away from Bandy as he could get and still be in the room. He may have been an all-in wrestler once upon a time, but he also knew when to keep his head well down.

'Piss off, Lizzie, there's a good gal. I've got a crisis on my hands,' said Bandy as she lit up a Passing Cloud.

'And I've got her upstairs in my flat,' I answered, standing my ground. 'She's very upset. She's had a rough time at that school and now her only friend's gone and she's on her own.'

Bandy looked surprised. Her Brillo-pad hair was sticking out at all angles as if she'd been plugged into the mains. Her gold silk dressing gown was pulled tightly around her and tied with a wide, black, fringed sash. There wasn't an ounce of spare flesh on Bandy, 'apart from her hooter, that is', as Freddy had once rather unkindly pointed out. It was true that Bandy's was a nose to be reckoned with. When she was cross, it looked like the prow of a Viking ship bearing down on a cowering enemy. I'd tried to tell Freddy that it gave her face character; 'Yes,' he'd agreed, 'and plenty of it. It scares the hell out of me, ducky, that's all I can say.'

'Well, thank God she's safe,' said Bandy,

recovering her composure. 'And what's all this about chinning the hockey captain and slinging her on the dung heap?'

It was my turn to look surprised. I knew nothing of any 'chinning'.

'She threw someone called Penelope Smedley on the compost, or so I am informed by Peace's form mistress. Apparently, Miss Smedley made some remark to which Peace took exception and Peace lifted her bodily and dumped her on the steaming mound. The crime is not at issue; there were witnesses. The burning issue is why? The Smedley girl denies provocation, and swears Peace simply went berserk.'

I took a deep breath. 'I think the girl said something about Peace being a slant-eyed, yellow swot and Peace took exception.'

Bandy thought about it for a moment. 'I see. Then it seems that the hockey captain got her just deserts. You can't insult a Bunyan, whatever its colour and studying habits, and expect to get away with it.' There was a pause as Bandy gave the matter some more thought before she pronounced judgement. 'The gal did well in defending her corner. Take me to her.'

Peace's unexpected arrival was the main topic of conversation when I had the first of my sewing lessons with Sugar that Sunday. We were sitting at the kitchen table at Sugar and Bandy's flat upstairs from mine. 'You could have knocked me down with a bat of your eyelashes, sweetie,' he said. 'She's supposed to be safely tucked up at school.'

He paused and fingered a piece of fabric he had

54

in his hand. 'If you do titchy running stitches, you can thread a seed pearl on every few stitches to make a fetching little detail, or you can ruffle it up a bit – that can be a good touch, specially if you get it nice and even and do several rows of it; it's like tiny pleats. Then you add the trimmings after.' He ran the fabric through his fingers, to show me the effect. 'If you press it, it looks better, neater.' He moved his work this way and that so that I could appreciate the play of light on the gathered fabric. His stitches were minute and even, and the ivory-coloured scrap of silk shone in the weak sunshine by the window.

'You can do it on cuffs too. Add some pearl trim top and bottom and it'd look smashing on a wedding gown. You could use sequins for stage work, or maybe a nice bit of your genuine paste diamonds, if the punter can run to them.' He paused for breath at last. 'Now, what was I talking about?'

A husky voice from the kitchen doorway answered for me. 'Peace.' Bandy coughed. 'Any coffee in that pot?'

'No, but if you park yourself, I'll make another.' Sugar stood up as Bandy sat down beside me at the kitchen table. It was cluttered with several pairs of scissors, pieces of bright material, spools of thread and a plump pincushion made of a patchwork of velvets in jewel-like colours, trimmed with thin gold braid and with a tiny tarnished-gold tassel at each corner.

There was a small chest on the table. It could have been Chinese; it certainly looked it to my untrained eye. It was mainly black, with birds, butterflies and flowers picked out in slivers of carnelian, beryl, jasper and other semi-precious stones. Abalone and mother-of-pearl shone here and there, softly reflecting daylight back at us. The lovely chest had many narrow drawers, each one filled with skeins of embroidery silks. There was a drawer full of blues, from the palest sky to the darkest midnight shade of indigo; another held the yellows, right through to burnt orange; a third held pinks from sugar ice to puce, and so it went on, through the rainbow hues and beyond. It was a treasure trove and, judging by the way Sugar's hand often strayed towards it to give it a little stroke, he loved it. So did I. It was a wonderful object, full of delicate detail, and it filled me with sheer delight whenever I saw it.

'What's this, the Sunday sewing circle?' Bandy fished about in her dressing-gown pocket and, finding a pink packet of Passing Clouds and her gold lighter, lit up. Then she fitted her cigarette into a holder, took a deep drag, coughed again and raised her slender, arched eyebrows in enquiry.

'You could call it that, if you can form a circle with just two people,' I answered. 'Sugar's teaching me some fancy stitchery. How are you, Bandy?'

'In fine fettle, thanks Liz, despite the Peace problem. The girl's refusing to go back to school. Sugar suggested we let her get her breath back, allow her time for mature reflection, that kind of thing, then boot her back to school and the dorm, where she belongs, but I have an awful feeling it's not going to be as simple as that. Meanwhile, we're stuffed to the rafters up here, barely room to move. Ah, here comes Malcolm.'

I could have sworn I heard Sugar groan as the door burst open and a large, hairy figure padded across the floor to catch Bandy in a massive hug.

'Put me down, you idiot,' wheezed Bandy, but she sounded pleased all the same.

'Ah, fair Hope, the morning light glimmers palely beside the glory of your exquisite radiance,' Malcolm's voice boomed. I swear that beneath it I heard Sugar mutter 'Prat!' – which summed up my sentiments exactly. I may have opted for something more polite, like 'Phoney', but it amounted to the same thing.

'I think you'll find it's afternoon, around three,' Sugar announced as he delivered a pot of coffee to the table. 'Coffee for everyone?'

To my disappointment, the sewing equipment was cleared away, and we were settled at the table with cups of coffee and a plate of biscuits called 'cats' tongues' made by the French pastry chef Pierre, who worked at the pâtisserie around the corner from the cafe.

At last, we got back to the original subject of our talk. When Peace had stayed for the school holidays in the past, she was so quiet – 'deep', according to Sugar, who had grown fond of the girl – that you would hardly notice she was there.

In my presence too, Peace was unfailingly polite, helpful and utterly enigmatic the way adolescent girls so often are, 'but with knobs on', as Maggie would say. Privately, we all thought Bandy had been giving her lessons in being secretive and unreadable, because she herself could have won prizes in that.

But in some ways, I think Soho may not have been quite so alien to that poor girl as school had been. At least when Peace was in Soho she was in the heart of a busy city, and quite a few Chinese businesses had opened up in and around Gerrard Street recently, especially since so many of their people had been bombed out of Limehouse during the Blitz. Peace could even get Chinese food if she fancied it, because a small wave of Hong Kong citizens were emigrating to Britain, on account of political unrest in China.

Sugar said that Britain being another small island made it feel the tiniest bit familiar to the incomers, who certainly seemed to fit in seamlessly. Mind you, the Chinese kept themselves to themselves and never seemed to have any problems with the authorities. Sugar said it was because they were quiet, hardworking people who liked to take care of themselves and each other and not to trouble their hosts too much, if at all.

I could not help feeling that it must have all been a shock to poor Peace, just the same. One minute she was Chinese and going about her business in Hong Kong, and the next, she was trussed up in a gymslip, lisle stockings, blazer, scarf and silly hat and expected to be an English miss. She had been thrust into a public school in chilly old England, without warning, and in the school holidays she lived above a bar stuffed full of the oddest types, not least of which were her Aunt Bandy and Sugar. No wonder she was quiet; it's a tribute to her strength of character that she wasn't struck completely dumb. I said as much to the assembled company.

'You're right there, Lizzie,' said Sugar. 'She's adaptable, that one. And clever! You should see her reports. What that girl can't do with numbers ain't worth doing, according to the maths mistress. She's good at music too, plays the piano a treat. They often go together, according to the school, music and being good at sums.'

Sugar was puffed with pride. I noticed that he had turned slightly away from Malcolm, who'd sat down between him and Bandy, but being excluded from the conversation didn't seem to bother Malcolm in the slightest. He was too busy leaning over Bandy to murmur sweet nothings into her ear.

I don't know what he was saying but Bandy looked faraway and dreamy, and suddenly they were gone, only their empty cups and the crumbs of cats' tongues to show that they'd been there. That, and a lingering odour made up of Passing Clouds, French perfume, fresh coffee and something less pleasant.

'Eau de armpit,' explained Sugar knowledgeably. 'It's that Malcolm. He had his bath on New Year's Day as usual, and there's aeons to go before the next one,' he added, with just a touch of malice, as he got the embroidery things out again.

'Surely the baths aren't that rare,' I objected. 'You're exaggerating!'

Sugar giggled. 'Well, perhaps a tiny tad. But the man doesn't like soap and water any more than he likes a razor, a fine badger brush and Mr George F. Trumper's scented shaving soap. He is unclean, I tell you – but when I complained to Bandy she said he was "masculine", something she feels I know little about. But even our Bobby doesn't smell like that – and what's more he never did and he was a *wrestler* before he cleaned for us. You don't come much more butch than that! His Pansy would never let him leave a venue without a proper hose down and fresh togs. I expect you've noticed that Bobby's nails are immaculate, even when he's giving that bar the benefit of a thorough buff with a soft cloth and the Johnson's Lavender. You don't have to be a slob to be a proper man. It's not compulsory, you know.'

I had to agree, although I was aware the majority of the population didn't. Around half of us still couldn't get used to having running hot water, let alone enough for regular baths. We'd been used to eking it out when it was scarce, and couldn't get past the idea that it was precious stuff, along with soap, washing powder and shampoo. Others thought that liberal use of soap – *any* soap, be it carbolic, Lux, Wright's Coal Tar or Imperial Leather – was very suspect indeed if used by a man, because as everybody knew, real men stank. Apparently, Caitlin Thomas had had to tempt her Dylan into the bath with his sweet tooth: she had arranged dolly mixtures tastefully around the edge, or so she informed the entire bar one night when they'd been in. And as Bandy had pointed out, Dylan had lacked little in the masculinity department, if the testament of several experienced ladies was anything to go by.

'But that didn't clinch the argument,' Sugar informed me. 'I could show Bandy some seriously butch types who'd pass the Sugar Plum Flaherty hooter test any day, Maltese Joe and that nice

Luigi from the deli to name but two. All the Campanini boys are clean, got the bathing habit from those lovely Roman ancestors, I expect. Nobody casts nasturtiums on Maltese Joe's manhood, I notice, and I happen to know for a fact he uses a cologne that smells of violets that he gets sent from some place in France.'

'So who won the argument in the end?' I asked as I unwound some emerald green thread from its spool, before packing it away in the deeper bottom drawer of the little chest.

'Neither of us. It still rumbles on. Bandy's besotted with that smelly sod and insists I'm jealous, which of course I'm not. Who can be jealous of a giant, hairy armpit, I ask you?'

I decided it was better not to say. I didn't want to hurt poor Sugar's feelings, but the truth was, he probably *was* a little jealous. A change of subject seemed tactful. 'You were telling me something about Peace?'

'Oh yes. Hang on a tick.' Sugar got up, pushed the club door shut and rejoined me at the table. 'It seems Peace has been asking awkward questions about her parentage, and Bandy's been trying to dodge them.'

'Why?'

'Apparently Bandy's been sworn to secrecy, by both parties concerned – mum and dad, or at least by the people that represent them,' Sugar answered shortly. I could sense what he thought of such promises.

Then his attitude softened slightly. 'Actually, Bandy's in a bit of a spot with one of the parties concerned, on the Chinese side. It wouldn't do to stir up any resentments there. There's a sort of code...'

His voice trailed off and he swallowed. 'It's just that Chinese culture takes a dim view of bastards in general and half-European ones in particular. If certain parties found out who Peace's father was...' He trailed off again, then brightened. It seemed to be his turn to change the subject. 'So, Elizabeth, how have you enjoyed your first lesson?'

'Immensely, thanks. I hope I've been an apt pupil.' I was hoping for some reassurance on that point. I didn't feel very apt when I looked at Sugar's fine stitches and mine.

'It'll come easier with a bit of practice; almost everything does,' he assured me. 'You love the fabrics and the bits and bobs, that's the main thing, and you've got an eye. You can't teach that; you've either got it, in which case it can be refined, or you haven't, in which case there's sod all you can do about it.

'To some people, one frock's pretty much like another, 'specially if it's in the same colour. They can't see the possibilities in a piece of jersey wool, silk chiffon or lawn cotton. Some of them can't even tell the differences between them, believe it or not. But you *do* see.' Sugar smiled. 'What's more, you're a whiz with colour, nobody to touch you in that department, apparently. Freddy was telling me only the other day that he and Antony are determined to get you trained up, so that you can turn your hand to anything in the frock-making line. They say you're gifted and it'd be a criminal waste to let you go completely untrained. So it's practice, practice, practice for you my girl, until you feel like Cinderella condemned to knock up the ballgowns, but never to attend the ball.'

'But what's the point in having this "eye" you all talk about if you don't get to wear your own creations now and then?' I protested. It sounded too much like the aunts to me; I knew then that I wanted, eventually, to have the courage to wear one of the confections I helped to produce.

'My sentiments entirely, petal. There's nothing quite like the feel of fine silk sheathing the old body in my view and chiffon is just plain heaven! It's like wearing clouds.' Sugar had a faraway look in his eye. I knew what he meant; I'd often draped myself in it when I was alone in the shop. It's impossible not to feel delicate and feminine in yards of floating chiffon. 'So different from cavalry twill,' Sugar added.

Yes, it must have been very strange for Peace to meet her aunt and her friends, I reflected, looking at that dear man going dreamy over chiffon. I wondered if they had bohemians, boozy women, or even transvestites and suchlike in Chinese culture. They must have their own brand of misfits, it stood to reason. But that didn't mean that Peace had met any, any more than I had before I moved to Soho.

6

The cafe was full of familiar faces when I went there for tomatoes on toast on my way to work the following Friday morning. I loved tomatoes on toast, and liked to have breakfast among friends now and then. There had always been people around when I got up in the mornings, all my life, until Jenny died in the summer of 1954. And then, suddenly, I was alone.

I still hadn't got used to how quiet it was as I cleaned my teeth and chose my clothes for the day. A year and a half on, any changes around me or in my circumstances still really upset me. I couldn't seem to help it; I simply hated the way time had a habit of marching over all my carefully cherished habits and routines. I had the irrational feeling that if things just stayed exactly the same, right down to my wearing the marcasite poodle brooch that Jenny had saved and saved to buy me for my birthday, then nothing awful could happen.

I wore that brooch every single day, which was ridiculous, because I was wearing it the day my darling had died – and that was the most terrible day of my entire life. Up until then, I hadn't realized there was anything worse in this whole world than hearing that my baby was dying. Then she had actually died, and I knew that there was. There were two deaths that day: Jenny's, and my belief in a fair and just God.

I'd learned that on the bad days, when the silence threatened to overwhelm me, breakfast at the cafe would soon put me right. Maggie's usually smiling face, Bert's wonderful breakfasts and the comings and goings of the morning regulars gave me a feeling of belonging that I had never had before, even as a child. I was thankful that they opened early every day, except Sunday, when they didn't open at all.

'Morning love. Usual, is it?' Maggie asked me, as she handed over a cup of tea to Ronnie from the market.

'Yes please, Maggie.' I glanced over at the corner table. Rosie, Luigi Campanini, T.C. and Madame Zelda, the fortune teller with consulting rooms in the house between the cafe and Campanini's delicatessen, were munching on pieces of toast, sipping tea and chatting idly. I could never quite work out if Madame Zelda was a fraud or not; my religious relatives would say that she was far worse, that she was an instrument of the Devil. I found that hard to believe of Madame Zelda, who was too good-hearted and sensible to be anybody's evil instrument. What's more, every now and then she'd surprise everyone, including herself, by making a prediction that came true.

Rosie, who was getting ready to go upstairs for a final wash and scrub up before school, had been the first to spot me weaving through the busy tables.

'Morning, Auntie Lizzie,' she grinned. 'Sorry I've got to go, but I've got to find my kit for netball. Yuck!' She screwed her nose up. 'I hate netball,' she explained, unnecessarily.

'Off you go then, Rosie. You don't want to be late. I'll take your nice warm seat. Hello Madame Zelda, T.C., Luigi,' I said and sat down.

'Morning love,' said Madame Zelda, between sips of her creosote-coloured tea. It could strip paint, her tea. 'We was just talking about them teddy boys. There was a load of 'em up here Saturday night. Came from all over and met in Leicester Square. We was just saying, we don't know what all the fuss is about, they was as good as gold. Didn't snap a matchstick, let alone smash up a pub or anything. They got a bit sparky in The French, Luigi says, but Frankie, Luigi and Danny the Dip just had to stand in doorways for a minute or two and they quietened down like lambs.

'I've had a few of their girls in in my time, too. The things they want to find out from their palms or the tarot cards are the same things girls always want to know. Will they find true happiness, and what's his name? Or for those that already have a lad, does he really love me? They may look tough with their leather jackets and their hair like bleached birds' nests, but they're just like girls everywhere.'

T.C. nodded, blue eyes creased in laugh lines as he smiled at Zelda. 'Most of them were no problem when I was in the Force. It's just the odd one or two who want to cause real trouble. With the rest, it's high spirits mostly.'

Luigi laughed. 'They all want to be James Dean. Can't say I blame 'em neither; it sure does pull the girls, that look. Thought I'd get Ernesto to give me a James Dean next time I'm in having my barnet cut.'

66

Madame Zelda wheezed around her fag, exhaling a cloud of smoke as she did so. 'Yes, but the poor boy wound up dead, didn't he, and not all that long ago? Wasn't he racing about in fast cars? Bloody motorbikes can't be any safer, can they? Nothing between your nut and the road if you take a header. Nasty things, I've always thought.'

Maggie plonked a plate in front of me and admonished her friend. 'I don't think it was his haircut that caused that poor boy's accident, Zelda. Anyway, you told me once all about getting a lift on a motorbike in the war from some Yank, and you said you loved it! The open road, the wind in your hair, all that. Motorbikes wasn't nasty then, I notice. It's because you was young then. The young like speed, danger, it's only natural. The trouble is, it scares the daylights out of the rest of us, specially if you've got impressionable kids growing up. Isn't that so, T.C.?'

T.C. nodded gravely. 'There certainly seem to be more temptations and pitfalls around nowadays. I don't know about you lot, but I've looked like a younger version of my dad more or less as soon as I could stand.'

'Well, I can assure you I didn't!' Maggie told him archly. 'My dad had an enormous moustache. But I suppose I looked like my mum in miniature, even to the wraparound pinny.'

'I'm not sure if I ever looked like my papa,' Luigi said, with a slightly worried frown. Papa Campanini was a short, round man, while Luigi was slender and rangy. 'I don't look like my mother either,' he added. She was also short and round and had several gold teeth in her flashing smile.

'P'raps you was left on the doorstep, Luigi, with the bread sticks,' Madame Zelda suggested, rather unkindly I thought, but everyone laughed, including Luigi. Personally, I could see a lot of his dad in Luigi: the masses of thick hair and the sad, brown eyes, and he definitely had his mother's saucy smile. I looked back at myself as a child. Like Maggie, I was a carbon copy of my mother. Both of us wore the same neat, plain, serge skirt, white blouse and home-knitted cardigan in shades of brown or grey. Everyone in my childhood had worn black, or shades of brown or grey. They were serviceable colours that didn't show the dirt and didn't draw attention to the wearer – both desirable attributes, according to Mother. In winter, a pale, pasty face – hers or mine, or that of any one of the aunts – would peep out of a grey felt hat topping off a grey flannel coat.

A voice penetrated my memories. 'A penny for them,' Maggie said. 'You was miles away then, Liz; bloomin' miles away.'

'I agree with you and T.C.,' I said. 'I was brought up to be just like my mother. It never occurred to me it was possible to have a style of your own. I think all this stuff in the newspapers about "teenagers" being feckless and out of control is simple jealousy from a generation who never got a chance to do the same because of war and rationing. It's sour grapes, a lot of it.'

I was absurdly pleased to see T.C. nodding and smiling as I spoke.

'How's it working out for you at Bandy's?' he asked me, changing the subject entirely.

'What're you doing there?' Maggie enquired.

68

I smiled. 'Don't tell me, Maggie Featherby, that something has happened around here and you don't know about it!'

Maggie stood on her dignity. 'The odd thing does occur that escapes my notice, but not for long. Cough it up, gel, what are you doing at Bandy's?'

I explained about my temporary job on Friday and Saturday nights, and the embroidery lessons I was getting in return. Maggie immediately pressed for details of everyone who passed through the hallowed doors; who they were with and what they said. All the loneliness I had been feeling evaporated as the cafe weaved its magic and wrapped me in its warmth. 'I can't tell you all that,' I smiled. 'I've got to get to work. And anyway,' I asked innocently, 'isn't a barmaid sworn to secrecy, like a priest?'

Maggie turned to Zelda and shrugged. 'It's too late, Zeld. Sugar's nobbled her already. She'll never spill the beans now. And Sugar won't talk because he says Bandy's is the only place in the world where some people can relax and be themselves. It's a crying shame.'

'It is that, Maggie. It is that,' Zelda agreed, with a slight twinkle in my direction. I realized that Madame Zelda had a great many secrets – her customers' – that she was unable to share. According to her, being a fortune teller was like being a priest in that regard.

'I promise I'll pass on the odd titbit – a harmless titbit that is,' I told them, 'but it'll have to wait for another time. I'll be late for the shop, and there's a rush order for the chorus at the Windmill.'

69

As I rose to go, Luigi glanced at the clock, high above the counter. 'Is that the time? I'd better be going, too. Things to do, people to see, money to collect, all that. See you lot later.' He grinned and ambled towards the door.

I made to follow him and Madame Zelda got up too. 'I'll walk out with you, Liz. I've got my first client coming soon. I'll be seeing you, Maggie, T.C.' She buttoned her coat for the short nip next door.

We parted on the doorstep and I turned my face in the direction of St Anne's Court. As I walked to work, I marvelled at how a little human company – as long as it was the right company – could dispel the bleakest of moods.

7

There was a flap on when I got to the shop. Antony was standing in the middle of the workroom at the back looking furious. 'What do you mean she won't wear green? The designer *said* green.' His voice was quiet, but steely, as he waved a thick sheaf of design notes from the Windmill job at Freddy. Antony's blue eyes flashed dangerously as a pink stain spread rapidly across his pale features. His languid manner had been replaced with the fieriness that he reserved for creative matters.

'We have to dress four complete acts and the whole chorus for the next season's shows and time's running out as it is, so changes at this stage are definitely not on.' His voice remained quiet, but it was being forced between the gritted teeth of a very angry man. 'It's in these notes right here, in black and white. "GREEN," he says.'

'I know, I know,' Freddy gabbled sympathetically. 'But she simply won't wear it. Says it's unlucky. She won't even try it on, won't let it touch her body. Says the minute it does, bad luck will follow. You can't reason with a person like that.' Freddy broke off as he spotted me in the doorway. 'Tell him, ducky, tell him how blind these superstitious types are to reason,' he pleaded, sidling towards me then nipping behind my back, so he was out of Antony's direct line of fire.

I tried to be soothing. 'It's true. I had an aunt who wouldn't leave the house until she'd kissed the budgie. Said the one time she forgot, the house was robbed.' I noticed that Antony had stopped waving his papers about.

'Really?' asked Freddy. 'How did the budgie feel about that? Did he like to be kissed by a non-budgie?'

'It's hard to say with a budgie, especially as he never actually said much more than "Pretty boy" and "More tea, minister?" But he did bite her lip, she'd got the scars to prove it. Sometimes he made her bleed.'

'So why did she keep shoving her smoochers through the bars?' asked Freddy, fascinated and exasperated at the same time.

'She'd decided it was a good luck charm against robbery,' I reminded him.

'But it makes no sense,' Antony snapped, his

71

mind still on the thorny question of the green dress.

'You see!' said Freddy triumphantly.

'I see what, exactly?' Antony's voice tightened dangerously. I piped up swiftly, to deflect the threatened artistic outburst. Antony was a gentleman at all times, except when the flow of his 'creative juices', as Freddy called them, was being stemmed by things beyond his control.

'What Freddy means is that superstitious people often don't make any sense,' I explained. 'After all, there's green everywhere. She can't escape it all.'

Antony was slightly mollified. 'I suppose so, but if the featured artiste just refuses to wear her costume, where does that leave us?'

I thought for a moment. 'It's the same design as the ones the chorus girls are wearing, isn't it? If you take it in a little, you can swap it with the one that's still left to do, the yellow one. There was blue, green, pink, yellow and then the red, wasn't there? You've done them all except the yellow, so they can swap. No serious problem.'

My employers thought about it for a moment then Antony smiled slowly. 'You're a genius, Elizabeth dear, that's the solution. I'll start on the yellow straight away,' he said, then picked up his large cutting shears and snapped them playfully at Freddy, like a crocodile looking for breakfast.

Freddy dodged aside and held up a tentative hand. 'Except she's a redhead; she'll look dead uggers in that shade of yellow.'

Antony set his jaw, put his hand on his narrow hip and tapped an elegant foot in mock high dudgeon. 'And?'

'True, true,' murmured Freddy hastily. 'If she wants to be a fusspot then she can wear the bloody yellow and like it.'

'Precisely!' Antony snapped the shears a final time for emphasis and picked up a bolt of yellow silk jersey. He flipped it expertly on to his workbench so that the fabric spread itself out like a carpet of buttercups. Even in the pale winter light, the silk gleamed richly. Antony began to pin paper pattern pieces to the cloth and Freddy sighed in relief. Antony could be a holy terror when anyone got between him and his creations. He'd been known to down needle and thimble, point blank refusing to sew a stitch, if a customer had upset him too much. More than once, Freddy and I had toiled deep into the night to finish an order while Antony sulked.

'So which aunt was it with the budgie?' Freddy loved to hear about my eccentric aunts. 'She certainly did the trick just now, taking his mind off her ladyship's green frock.'

'It was Auntie Glad, only she wasn't glad at all, because she was married to Uncle Cyril, who was something of a misery. But then he had his reasons. He'd been gassed in the trenches. That, and the fact that it was Auntie Glad's proud boast that he had never "troubled" her "in *that* way", and that she would be returned to God "unopened". That probably upset him a bit as well.'

Poor Freddy choked on his tea, and I had to act quickly so he didn't splutter it all over a bolt of purple silk. I was busy thumping his back when Cassie came through the door, closely followed by the same bespectacled man I had seen her

73

with at Bandy's. As Freddy said later, with a sniff, 'If the cove had been any closer, she'd have been wearing him.' The man did seem reluctant to let Cassie out of arm's reach, and a short arm at that. I greeted them while Freddy gathered some breath to do the same.

'I want something pretty made. May I look at some taffeta?' Cassie asked. I nodded and pulled down a bolt of dark blue. Given her colouring, blue was always a good place to start with Cassie.

'No thanks, Liz. I have a yen for something different, I could do with a change. May I have a look at the rose pink?' I replaced the blue and pulled down the pink. It was a lovely shade, the colour of an old damask rose Uncle Cyril had grown in his back garden. London clay was good for roses, and the sulphur in the air kept black spot and other nasties at bay, or so Uncle Cyril had said. It was a pity he'd never managed to 'open' Auntie Gladys; he was good with children. I had spent many happy hours pottering about with him in his garden and shed. He'd always been very nice to me.

'What do you think, Liz?' Cassie asked, holding the fabric up to her face.

'It suits you,' I answered. In fact, it suited her very well. It brought a touch of colour to her pale cheeks.

Freddy had recovered himself, and joined in: 'Tell you what, stand over by the long mirror and we'll get a length swathed around you, you'll be able to see for yourself then how smashing you'll look. Lizzie, grab a length of that drop pearl trim,' he instructed, having assessed the thickness of the man's wallet to the nearest pound simply

74

by looking at his clothes. The Turnbull & Asser shirt, silk cravat and hand-made-in-Bond-Street brogues gave the game away. One glance and Freddy had decided the chap could run to top-of-the-range trimmings.

I did as asked, and we traipsed over to the long mirror on the back of the workroom door. We could hear Antony singing a snatch of 'Oh! What a Beautiful Morning' as he cut out the final costume for the Windmill's order. Freddy and I exchanged relieved glances. Harmony reigned once more.

We spent a happy hour in the shop, as we plucked bolts of fabric from the shelves, then indulged in an orgy of tucking, pleating and swanning about in ostrich feathers, pearl drop and rhinestone trim, while Cassie's friend watched adoringly from behind thick-lensed glasses.

Cassie finally settled on Uncle Cyril's damask rose pink, which she wanted made into a strapless sheath with a drop pearl trim around the bodice. Freddy, a salesman down to his socks, went in for the kill, skilfully addressing not Cassie, but the man with the wallet. 'Of course, if you wish to see the lady in it any time soon, a nice lined shawl will be required, to save the poor darling' – Freddy hesitated slightly, so that Cassie's admirer could get his imagination going – 'from freezing to death.'

It took a matter of moments to scribble the order into the book for the matching shawl, lined with the softest pink ostrich feathers for extra warmth. That done, the man handed over a hefty deposit, in guineas, and Cassie was signed up for her first fitting.

'You'll need to have the dress boned, to keep it up. Fitting's really important when you're expecting teeny weeny bits of whale to defy gravity and keep you modest on the dance floor. When suits you best?' Freddy asked as he flourished a large, leather-bound diary. The appointment was soon made and Cassie and her friend were gone.

'I wonder if she'll stick with him long enough to get the dress? Or whether she'll ditch him and reclaim the deposit?' Freddy tapped his teeth with his pen. 'Hmm, I think we'll hold off until she comes in for the fitting, just in case. Antony can always cut it out on the day, if it happens. It's not a complicated number. What do you reckon, Lizzie? Is it a goer or will she be back in a day or two, little hand out for the readies?'

'I'm not sure,' I said. It was true that Cassie had sometimes cancelled orders and, on behalf of her male friends, had taken the deposit, even though she hadn't paid it herself. And she got away with it for the most part. We'd only had irate men in chasing their money a couple of times.

'I am,' came Antony's voice from the back room. 'She'll stick him out for a while, because that Harry is, according to current gossip at The French, worth about a million and counting; Grandmama hasn't snuffed it yet.'

'How on earth do you know that?' Freddy asked.

'I was in there the other day when he came in looking for Cass. Quentin and one or two of the others were in there, too. They said everyone had given him the once-over and made enquiries, but he was mainly interested in girls.'

'Oh well, then,' agreed Freddy, 'go ahead and

cut it out. She's in for a fitting on Thursday. She's opted for the expensive trim, too, *and* the ostrich feathers, bless her heart. I do love that girl. When she's got it, she does so love to spread it about.'

'Even when it isn't hers,' I said under my breath. Nobody had ever offered to buy *me* rose pink taffeta with drop pearl trim and ostrich feathers, pink ones.

'*Especially* when it isn't hers, dear,' Antony sang out as he went back to his cutting table, carrying the bolt of cloth for Cassie's frock. 'Especially when it isn't hers. That's the whole point.'

'Luckily, the bank manager doesn't give a damn as long as it winds up being his, via our account,' Freddy added.

There was no arguing with that, so I went to make us a cup of tea and thought about all the beautiful colours I'd spent the morning with. I loved it. When I returned with the tray of steaming cups and a plate of assorted biscuits, a slight, damp figure was being blown through the door by a vicious gust of wind and rain. When the figure came to a halt in front of me and a pair of almond-shaped eyes blinked through a nest of very black and very wet rats' tails, I realized that Peace was in the shop. Her normally glossy hair was sodden, as was the rest of her.

'Peace!' I exclaimed. 'What are you doing here?' It was not the way Mother had taught me to greet visitors, but Peace had not been in the shop since the day she had arrived.

'Do you know where Aunt Bandy is, Mrs Robbins? I've rung the bell many times but neither she nor Mr Sugar are answering it.' I suspected

77

that her aunt might have still been in bed with her poet Malcolm, and it was anybody's guess where Sugar had got to. He'd taken to making himself scarce outside of opening hours at the club.

'Don't you have a key, dear?' I asked; not a very bright question in the circumstances, but the best I could come up with.

Peace shook her wet head and dropped her eyes to the floor for a moment. Her face was solemn, but then it usually was.

'Well, you'd better let yourself into my place, dry yourself off and at lunchtime we'll go and have a look for them,' I suggested, taking my key out of my bag. Peace whispered her gratitude. There was definitely something wrong with her, and I was more likely to get to the bottom of it if we were tucked up in a quiet corner like my flat, than I was in the shop, with Freddy and Antony to listen in on us.

8

Peace was very quiet, very polite, but her mind was far, far away – way across the China Sea I shouldn't wonder. When I got in for lunch an hour or so later, I saw that she'd dried herself off and climbed into my winter dressing gown that I kept on the back of my bedroom door. I loved my winter dressing gown; Freddy and Antony had made it for me for my first Christmas at the shop. It was fire-engine red velvet with black trim around the mandarin collar and narrow cuffs. It made you feel warm just to look at it, and the cuffs guaranteed the sleeves never dangled in the washing-up or cups of tea. Peace was curled up on the settee in front of the gas fire, reading. She stood up as I walked through the door and looked demurely at the floor as she greeted me.

'Hello, Mrs Robbins.'

'Hello, Peace,' I answered, thinking as I did so how nice it was to have someone to greet me when I came home. It had been a long, long time since I'd had that particular comfort. 'I'll get the kettle on. I'm parched.'

I made beans on toast for two for our lunch, and we settled down at my tiny kitchen table to eat it, with the gas oven on to keep us warm.

'So,' I began, 'why were you hanging about in the street this morning getting soaked to the skin? Why didn't you at least have a coat and hat? You could have caught your death out there.'

Peace hung her head and stared at the yellow Formica table top. I was so proud of that table; one wipe with a cloth and it was clean, and such a cheery colour too. 'I am sorry to have worried you, Mrs Robbins,' she said.

'Oh for goodness' sake, call me Lizzie, everybody else does.'

'But you are my elder, it is not respectful to call you "Lizzie", Mrs Robbins,' Peace argued seriously; still not answering me, I noticed.

I thought about it for a moment, then found a compromise. 'I am older than you, but I am also older than Rosie, and she gets round the problem by calling me "Auntie Lizzie". You could do the same if you like,' I suggested. 'And you can also tell me why you were running around in the pouring rain, in inadequate clothing, getting soaked to the skin, when you could have been nice and warm at home.' I added a smile to show that she wasn't in trouble.

'Aunt and I had an argument last night and I ran out this morning, before she woke up and could start shouting again.' She paused briefly, then added, 'Aunt Liz', with a small smile.

'I see,' I said, although I didn't quite. 'What did you argue about, if you don't mind me asking? Was it very serious? Were things said that can't be unsaid?'

'Aunt wants me to return to St Matilda's and I said I would not.' Peace hung her head again, so that I couldn't read her expression. She either had to be very brave or very desperate to argue with her formidable aunt.

I thought about it for a while. 'Would you like me try to talk to your aunt, to see if she's calmed down a little?' I asked, more casually than I felt. Truth to tell, Bandy scared me to death when she was cross. I treated her with caution even when she wasn't.

Peace nodded. 'Yes, please.'

Bandy flung open the door a few minutes later and scared me so much that I took a step backwards. Her hair was in a wild tangle around her strong, hawk-nosed face, and her eyes glittered dangerously. As always, she was in her dressing gown. A rumpled Malcolm stood behind her, scantily clad in his underwear, and scratching. I stood on the small landing outside her flat, trembling slightly – with cold, of course.

'What do you want?' she asked, rather rudely I thought. Really, she was a very frightening sight when she started her day around lunchtime, even on normal days, and this one was obviously far from normal. Something had got on Bandy's wick and she was cross, very cross indeed.

'Well, spit it out, gal, I haven't got all bloody day!' she barked. Something about the 'gal' annoyed me. I was a grown woman, same as her, and only a few years younger.

'There's no need to be rude, Bandy,' I said, sharply.

I could see Bandy was taken aback by my nerve – as was I, a little. Her mouth snapped shut the way the till at the shop snapped shut on a fiver. Her thin, arched eyebrows disappeared into her unruly hair and her eyes took on a speculative look.

'I see, showing a bit of spunk, eh? Well, it's about time. You've been creeping about like a church mouse, apologetic for taking up room, for far too long in my book. But I've had a telephone call from Peace's school, wanting to know if she's ever going back there. Meanwhile, it seems the child's gone AWOL yet again. She was missing at roll call this morning.'

'That's what I came to tell you. She's down-stairs. She turned up at the shop again, looking like a drowned rat.' I paused and looked over Bandy's shoulder at Malcolm, who was still standing behind her, and still scratching. His vest was a few days off clean. 'She tried to come back here, but got no answer, so she came to the shop to find me. I sent her back with my keys and she dried off downstairs.'

Bandy raked her hair and mumbled something like, 'Thank God for that!' before raising her voice again. 'She wouldn't be bloody frozen if she'd remained tucked up in her bed, now would she?'

I could see she was working up to another outburst, so I changed the subject. 'Where's Sugar?' I asked, innocently.

'How the fuck should I know?' Bandy exploded. 'The bloody man's never here nowadays. Your guess is as good as mine.' She was about to say something more but got as far as, 'He's probably off with that fucking...', thought better of it and clamped her mouth shut.

'Oh bugger!' sighed Freddy, when I related the encounter to him and Antony back at the shop that afternoon.

'Seconded!' said Antony. 'We've been longing to find out about Sugar's *amour* for simply yonks now.'

The rest of the afternoon was relatively uneventful, unless you count Cassie panting in just before closing to grab 'her' deposit back.

'So much for her hanging on to the millionaire.' Freddy sniffed. 'Now what the hell will we do with her frock? Did you cut it out, Antony?'

'No need to get your nerves jangled,' Antony sang out happily from the back of the shop. 'I decided to err on the side of caution and stay my scissor hand until I saw the whites of Cassie's eyes at the fitting. Always a wise move when it comes to that one.'

Freddy clapped in delight. 'Oh well done, Ant! I convinced myself her millionaire would turn out to be a keeper, but there you are. As you say, you can never tell with Cassie.'

As I made my way home, I could not help reflecting on how a person's mood can be turned upside down in the course of a day, sometimes several times. I'd started so desolate that morning, but I had wound up laughing with my bosses and looking forward to the next instalment of life in the flat above mine, where there was rarely a dull moment.

In fact, I could hear a full-scale row going on in Bandy's flat as I arrived home. Peace was sitting on the landing outside my front door. She smiled shyly, not sure she would be welcome for a second time in one day. I smiled back at her, to assure her that she was. In fact, she was very welcome indeed.

'Hello again, dear,' I said. I didn't need to be bright to work out why she was waiting for me: she was a refugee from the war in progress in the flat above. We both jumped as a plate or something hit the door with a resounding crash. I pulled a face and whispered, 'Some people do carry on so, don't they? Let's have a nice cup of tea, shall we?' I settled Peace down at my kitchen table while I took off my outdoor things and put them away, then I put the kettle on. I fished my slippers out from under the dresser and put a pinny over my work clothes.

I thought of the lonely chop on its plate in the larder and wondered what to do. I could hardly tuck into it in front of the girl and leave her out, but on the other hand, one chop is one chop and there's no way to make it look like two. Having decided disguise was impossible, I settled on a recipe that'd stretch it to two if necessary and be fine for one if not. I made a pot of tea and left Peace to pour her own while I laid the little chop in a small casserole dish and surrounded it with onions, peeled and chopped potato, carrot, turnip and some diced swede. I added a dried bay leaf, salt, pepper and some water and popped it in the oven. Dinner could cook itself while I took care of my guest, who hadn't said a word as she watched and listened to me chatter about nothing while I prepared the meal.

Now I could afford to relax. 'Let's go into the other room,' I suggested. 'It's more comfortable in there and it'll be warmer once the fire's on.' I lit the gas fire, which hissed then popped as the flame caught. At full blast, my tiny living room would be toasty in minutes.

We sat down. I noticed tears glinting in Peace's eyes as the muffled shouts and banging continued. She sniffed, and I handed her a handkerchief. She blew her nose.

I waited, but nothing was added to that small blow. I was a bit at a loss; to probe or not to probe, that was the question. I knew that Peace was a very private girl. It was not her way to chatter, gossip or to talk much at all. Come to think of it, neither did her aunt. Even when in a temper, Bandy didn't give away personal information. Sugar had sworn to me that Peace turning up and calling her 'aunt' was the first he had heard that Bandy had sisters at all, let alone that the Bunyan family had been based in China for most of Bandy's childhood. Naturally, the girls had come back to the old country for schooling, hence Bandy's cut-glass accent and lofty manner.

'She never talks about it, though,' Sugar had said. 'There's no childhood stories about Great-Aunt Augusta singeing the cat or anything interesting like that. Can't have been much fun for poor old Bandy.'

'You never talk about your own childhood, Sugar,' I pointed out, 'so that's the pot calling the kettle black right there.'

'Mine wasn't much fun either,' he said shortly.

Soho had taught me that it didn't do to pry into people's backgrounds. The castaways that washed up in that small district of London generally told you what they wanted you to know and nothing more. It was safer that way and easier to stay lost, if that's what they wanted. And they often did.

Despite being a reluctant informant, Peace began to talk a little about her fears for her present and her future. What it boiled down to was that she simply didn't know what either held, although she was determined never to go back to St Matilda's – that much was certain.

'They are cruel, Aunt Liz, very cruel and I will not endure it. But Aunt says that I cannot stay here for ever with nothing to do. She says that she is not the stuff of which mothers are made, even stand-in mothers, and that is true.'

'What does Sugar say?' I asked her, fairly certain his attitude would be gentler.

Peace smiled a small smile. 'He is very kind to

85

me. He has let me have his room and he sleeps on the sofa. He says that as Aunt is my guardian, it is her job to make sure that I am safe, happy and well cared for. Aunt is very angry with him for not taking her side, I think. She is also angry because Mr Sugar does not like Mr Malcolm.' Peace's smile faded. 'I do not like Mr Malcolm, either; he looks at me in a funny way. Mr Sugar has also noticed this. I think that is what started the argument they are having now.'

I had my mouth open to ask more questions when the noise above ceased abruptly. The door slammed and large feet thundered down the stairs, followed by those of another, lighter person, who stopped at my landing and hammered on my door. Peace and I gave each other a startled look, like rabbits in a spotlight, then I went to answer the knock. Bandy was standing on my doormat.

'Come in,' I said and in she came.

'Time you stopped pestering Elizabeth, Peace. Come on home.'

'But you tell me it is not my home, Aunt, and that I am a temporary guest. I have no home.' Peace's words held such terrible sadness that, for a moment, Bandy seemed lost for words.

'Yes, yes,' she rallied. 'Well, we'll talk about it later. Say thank you to Elizabeth for her kindness and we'll go.'

'Have you and Mr Sugar stopped fighting?' Peace asked pointedly.

'You, young lady, are bordering on the verge, the very *verge* of cheek,' Bandy told her niece severely. 'But yes, we have stopped our ... er ... discussion. I'd prefer to call it a frank discussion.'

'Talking doesn't break china, Aunt, but fighting does.' I looked hard at Peace. The tearful child I had been talking to had been replaced by a miniature Bandy, but without the nose and the wild hair. It was quite extraordinary.

I could hear the two of them bickering all the way up the stairs, right up until their front door slammed. I turned back into my flat, closed the front door quietly and leaned against it and listened: there was no other heartbeat in the vicinity, no one breathing, no sounds of movement. I was alone again – just me and my solitary chop.

9

On one Saturday in three, I got the morning off. This was my Saturday and I was luxuriating in a leisurely start at the cafe. We never worked Saturday afternoons, just ten until one, but that three hours really cut into the day. I was sitting at the corner table with some of the regulars, enjoying my second cup of tea and the full fry-up – egg, bacon, sausage and fried slice. I'd been paid and it was a ritual treat. What's more, the whole day stretched in front of me, mine to do what pleased me. All I had to do was decide what that was. Running through the possibilities in my mind was at least half of the fun. I could be dutiful and catch up on cleaning my flat and top it off by doing some much-needed mending. Or I could squander my time by idling at the cafe, gossiping, with a trip to a cinema in Leicester Square in the afternoon for a treat. Or I could simply feed the ducks on the Serpentine. My thoughts were interrupted by the conversation at the table.

'So what do you reckon then – will they ever put a bloke on the moon?' Luigi asked no one in particular.

'I reckon, eventually,' said Bert. 'Do you suppose there's life out there somewhere?'

'I don't see why not,' Madame Zelda mused. 'There's life after death, after all. I've got my spirit guide, Chief Running Water, to prove it, so why not people out there?' She waved her arm vaguely in the air, indicating way beyond the cafe's smoke- and steam-stained ceiling, to the heavens invisible.

Bert winked at Maggie. 'I thought you got the idea for his name after a cheese sandwich and pickled onion supper, Zelda. It kept you awake half the night and dreaming nightmares for the other half. You said it was the gurgling of the pipes as the khazis flushed in the other flats that got you to thinking about running water.' He laughed and Madame Zelda tutted.

'You're a bad man, Bert Featherby. You know that ain't true. I did have dreams after a cheese supper, that bit's true, but the rest isn't and you know it.' I knew Madame Zelda had to say this, as there were several of her clients in the cafe. It didn't do to cast doubts into their minds. Madame Zelda's purse depended on their faith remaining unsullied.

Bert laughed. 'Only teasing, Zeld, only teasing. If there are spirits on the other side, why shouldn't there be spirits everywhere? And where there's spirits there has to be your actual live ones, before they become spirits. It stands to reason, that does. Don't it, T.C.?'

'I have no idea what you're talking about, Bert,' said a voice behind me, 'but I'll take your word for it. Any chance of a bacon sandwich and a cup of tea?'

I turned round. T.C. smiled and made to sit beside me. 'I hope you don't mind?' he asked, hand holding the back of the chair, ready to pull it out and sit down. T.C had the kind of smile that crinkled the corners of his blue eyes, thick, coarse, fair hair that would have curled if he'd grown it long enough and a strong, wiry build. I suppose he was the better part of six feet tall. He had a pleasing face; warm and friendly, but with deep grooves beside his mouth that testified to years of unremitting strain.

I had a mouthful of sausage, so simply nodded, then shook my head, confused. I choked slightly, righted myself with an inelegant swig of tea and managed to splutter out, 'Of course not,' before convulsing in a fit of coughing. I was mortified. When I finally came to a stop, T.C. had sat down and I was red in the face, with my heart hammering in my throat, like a trapped bird battering its wings against a window. Or that's how it felt to me.

'Morning all,' T.C. grinned, sounding just like Jack Warner as Dixon of Dock Green.

'Morning T.C.,' Luigi answered pleasantly. He was a nice boy, that one. All Mamma Campanini's children were well-mannered; she made a point of it, she said.

'I'll get your sandwich,' said Bert, getting to his feet.

'And I'll get your tea.' Maggie followed Bert to the counter.

'Morning, T.C.' Madame Zelda also got to her feet. 'It's not that you smell or nothing, but I've got a client in five minutes. Got to limber up the old Third Eye and all that.' She chortled and left.

Luigi took a final swallow of his coffee and grinned, 'Sorry folks, I gotta go, too.'

Suddenly it was just T.C. and me at the table. He eyed me warily. 'You're not going to make your excuses and leave too, are you?'

I shook my head. 'Not on your life. I'm only halfway through my fry-up.'

'Good. I was beginning to feel the general exodus had something to do with me. Policemen have that effect on people, even ex-policemen.' His lovely smile was rather sad, I thought.

'Well, *I'm* always pleased to see you,' a voice announced. It was Rosie. She flung her arms around T.C.'s neck and planted a kiss on his beaming face. I was struck again in that moment by just how much Rosie looked like her father. The curls, the merry blue eyes, long eyelashes and the compact shape were all his. She could do worse. What went to make up a pleasant enough looking man, made for a very pretty girl. It was the eyes and hair that did it. That and the fact she'd inherited her mother's pointed chin and little, elvish face. The eyes looked huge in that face.

Laughing so that the corner of his eyes stayed creased, T.C. held his daughter at arm's length. 'Morning Rosie, my love. Stand back and let's get a good look at you.' He looked her up and down, then gathered her in for another cuddle, saying, 'My, you're a sight for sore eyes this morning. Fresh as a daisy, that's you; fresh as a daisy.'

Rosie squirmed and was released. 'Morning, Dad. You can put me down now, because I've got to meet Kathy round at Mademoiselle's for our lesson, then we're meeting the others at the milk bar for a shake. What're you doing today?'

T.C. paused before answering, obviously at a bit of a loss. I knew he was finding it hard to fill his time with no work to go to, but he didn't want to tell Rosie that, because it didn't do to burden children with adult troubles. Once again, I took pity on him.

'I'm going to the Serpentine later, to feed the ducks, seeing it's such a fine day. You could join me if you fancy it.' I blushed, suddenly embarrassed by my suggestion. I hoped it didn't look as if I was being too forward.

'What an excellent idea. I'd love to come with you.' T.C. sounded enthusiastic and just a touch relieved. I could understand why: being suddenly single again, for whatever reason, left weekends wide open and not always with opportunity. Sometimes, as I knew only too well, that gap seemed like a gaping great hole.

I noticed a flash of uncertainty cross Rosie's face as she looked from her father to me and back again, then she smiled widely. 'Have fun with the ducks then. See you later, alligator.' Rosie waited a moment and then rolled her eyes. 'Dad, you're useless! You're supposed to say "In a while, crocodile." I've told you and told you.'

'I know, but I'm just too old and too square to catch on. You'll have to make do with plain old "Cheerio", I'm afraid. I'll try to do better next time.' T.C. fumbled in his pocket and found a shilling. 'Here, put this towards your milkshakes.'

Rosie looked at the shilling and then shot a glance towards the counter and her Auntie Maggie, who turned her mouth down and shook her head very slightly. Rosie nodded just as slightly and flashed an enormous grin at her father. 'Thanks, Dad, but I've got my pocket money and Auntie Maggie says I must learn to live within my means.' She leaned forward and whispered, 'And she's watching. I'll get into trouble if I take it.' She plopped a kiss on T.C.'s forehead, smiled at me and was off.

T.C. watched her go with a proud but bemused look. 'How on earth did Cassie and I manage to make such a little smasher?' He paused. 'But of course, we didn't. Maggie and Bert did. Well, we may have made her, but they turned her out.'

'Let's just say it was a joint effort and leave it at that, shall we,' Maggie suggested as she arrived at our table with a tray of tea things and a bag of bread crusts for the ducks. 'So what's this I hear about World War Three breaking out round at Bandy's then?'

I thought back and remembered Peace's miserable face. 'Bandy was in a bad mood because Peace's school had telephoned her asking when they could expect the girl back. Sugar was also missing when he was needed, and she was cross about that, so I suppose she was a fight looking for an opponent when he finally walked in late last night. And from what I could hear, Bandy was already engaged in a fairly heated exchange with poor Peace. Sugar took Peace's side and then war broke out in earnest.'

'Have they made it up yet?' Maggie asked tenderly. She was fond of them both.

'I don't know, Maggie. All was quiet when I left this morning. But I'm seeing Sugar tomorrow for our sewing circle, so I'll gather the details then. He's asked if we can hold it at my place, so things are obviously still not comfortable at home.' I paused. 'Of course, he really doesn't like Bandy's new chap, either. He tends to make himself scarce when Malcolm's there, which is most of the time.'

'Hmm. Can't say I blame him. It's a mystery what she sees in that Malcolm. The attraction's not obvious to outsiders. It's probably something to do with' – she looked around to make sure there were no young ears about, but spelt the word anyway and mouthed – 'b-e-d. It usually is when it's that hot and heavy. It'll burn itself out soon enough,' she said comfortably.

T.C. and I had a smashing time in the park. It was bitterly cold and the poor ducks skidded across ice to get to their crusts, but they were grateful, we could tell. After the ducks, we walked for a while, not talking much as the cold air took our breath away. We walked through to Kensington Gardens and found a place for tea in the High Street. Once we were sitting in the warm, it became easier to hold a conversation.

We explored the weather, our friends and related topics, and we were on to our second cup of tea and the remaining halves of our Chelsea buns when T.C. suddenly asked, 'How do you manage – you know, moving from family life to living by yourself?'

It was an enormous question. 'Well, at first, I didn't manage all that well,' I began cautiously; the wounds were still tender. 'But I had a new job with Freddy and Antony and with it, new friends, and they've been wonderful to me, absolutely wonderful.' I stopped again, realizing that I had just placed a very large clodhopper right on one of T.C.'s tenderest spots. He had no job and hadn't had one since he'd parted company with the police force.

I hurried on, wincing inwardly at my tactlessness. 'Sundays were the worst of course, but Maggie and Bert have been very kind, along with Mamma Campanini. They didn't let me sit alone on Sundays for a long, long time and wouldn't let me now, if I didn't insist that I am mostly all right on my own. If I wasn't at one flat for Sunday lunch, then I was at the other. And of course, I have my sewing with Sugar, which I enjoy, and the evenings at the club. So, I suppose what I'm saying is, I manage with the help of my friends and by keeping busy.'

I asked the obvious question, working on the theory that he probably wanted me to. 'How are you managing? You know, since Pat passed on?'

He sighed and looked down. 'I miss her,' he said simply. 'I miss her every day. But, God forgive me...'

He couldn't go on, so I finished the sentence for him. 'You feel released. And you're grateful that she is too.'

There was a long silence from the other side of the table and then he whispered, 'How did you know?' He laughed a bitter little laugh. 'I'm an idiot. You know because you felt it too.'

'Yes,' was all I could say for a while. 'I felt terrible about feeling that way. I felt so guilty, I thought I'd never learn to live with it, but it was Madame Zelda who put me straight.' I took a deep breath. 'I'll pass on her pearls of wisdom if you like; they helped me.'

I waited until I saw him nod. 'I broke down one day and told her all about it. About how, just before the end, I'd stood over my child with a pillow, willing myself to smother her to put her out of her misery. She was so ill and every moment had become a struggle for her. But I couldn't do it, and I don't know what made me feel worse: wanting to do it, or not being able to. Then, when Jenny went – I mean the instant she stopped breathing, I felt a rush of relief. That was my first feeling – relief...'

My voice cracked and a lump the size of Liechtenstein formed in my throat. I couldn't speak any more for a while. A warm hand found mine and squeezed very gently. We sat like that for quite a time before I could pull myself together.

'But Madame Zelda was lovely. All matter of fact, the way she is. She told me it was the most natural feeling in the world, to want a loved one's suffering to come to an end. What's more, she said it was also natural to be relieved for myself, that I was to be free of the sick-room. I can hear her now. "It's only one of your feelings, petal, just one among many. It's the life force. It's selfish by nature and there ain't nothing you can do about it because it's elemental to all living things. Nothing to do with your will or your brains, any more than breathing is."

'What she meant was, I had to go on living and the relief was part of that. The worst thing was the waiting for the inevitable. You must know that: you did it for years. There's always part of you, once you accept that they're going to leave you, that wants them to just jolly well hurry up about it, so you can get on with the inevitable pain of grieving.

'Of course, another part wants to hang on to them until the last possible second. There's no real logic to it. You swing from one to the other all the time. But I think that's what Zelda meant about being allowed to be relieved and the life force and all of that. It's natural to feel that way.'

T.C. didn't say anything; he simply stared at a potted palm in the cafe window. His warm hand squeezed mine again and he coughed once. At last he squared his shoulders, turned to me and smiled sadly.

'Thanks for that,' he said. 'What do you fancy doing now?'

We wandered back across the park and wound up having lunch at a Lyons Corner House. After much wrangling, he allowed me to pay for my own omelette at least. Nothing I could say or do would persuade him that I could stand him his liver and bacon, though.

'I may be hard up, but I'm not that hard up. Anyway, I think I may have a commission.' He grinned enigmatically.

'What sort of commission?' I was interested, I hadn't realized you could commission ex-coppers.

'Sugar wants me to look into some missing stock, and he thinks the till's been a bit light on occasions, too,' T.C. told me quietly. 'He wants me to keep an eye on Malcolm. I know he's mentioned his suspicions to you, so I'm not talking out of turn.'

I remembered their private talk on that Friday when I began to help out at the bar. Sugar was convinced that the poet was 'liberating' the odd bottle of booze from the stock cupboard and occasional sums of money from the till. He'd tried to tell Bandy about it and had had a large soup tureen thrown at his head for his trouble. Relations were certainly strained in the flat above mine.

'He says he'll pay me the going rate, whatever that is. I said it didn't matter, but he said that it did, that professionals ought to get proper fees and that he'd look into it. Do you reckon he just feels sorry for me?' T.C.'s brow creased in concern. 'I mean, I know life's taken a downturn and all that, but I'm not up for being a charity case – not yet.'

I hastened to reassure him. 'Oh no, it's not that. He needs proof. He says the dinner service can't afford to lose the other tureen.'

'And there's something else,' T.C. continued. 'Apparently Sugar recommended me to a rather grand young lady, who he met just a couple of nights ago, through a friend. She wants me to find out if her old man's playing away.' He paused. 'I'm not sure I want to get into that game, meddling in people's private lives. Seems mucky to me.'

He smiled sadly at me. 'And I'm hardly in the

97

position to throw mud about, am I? After all, I did father an illegitimate child while married to another woman. It seems a bit too much like the pot calling the kettle a kitchen utensil to me.'

'I can see your point,' I answered quietly, not wanting the whole of Joe Lyons to know every little detail of T.C.'s private business. I'd noticed the couple on the table nearby leaning in our direction, to hear us better. 'But on the other hand, investigating *is* your area of expertise, you *are* broke and you *do* need to find something to do with your time. Time hangs really heavily when you're lonely, as you very well know.'

T.C.'s eyes crinkled again, making my heart give a peculiar little lurch, and he held his hands up in surrender. 'You're right, I know you're right.' He laughed.

I smiled back. 'And anyway, just because you may look into it for the lady, it doesn't mean you're setting yourself up as some kind of judge and jury. You'd simply be reporting the facts to her, that's all.'

'You've talked me into it. I promise I'll meet this lady and find out what exactly she wants me to do.'

We raided the market on the way home, laying in provisions for tea and for Sunday. It seemed natural to invite T.C. to tea at my place and he accepted gratefully. 'It's been a nice day,' he said. 'Thanks. I'll buy the cakes at Pierre's. How about that?'

Luckily, my tiny flat was tidy and it didn't let me down. The living room warmed up in a jiffy and I laid the small table in front of the fire. I had a pretty linen tablecloth, embroidered by Sugar with a twining pattern of nasturtiums, and my grand-mother's good plates. I'd found a Susie Cooper teapot in a tiny shop hidden down an alleyway still lit with gas lamps and the cups came from a shop at Seven Dials. I took them out of the sideboard and placed them beside the tea plates on the table, then went to the kitchen to fill the pot, returned and placed it on a brass trivet in front of the fire.

I was proud of my treasures and the way they looked in the flickering light of the gas fire and the small lamp on the bookcase. It was cosy, with just a touch of elegance, I thought. We had potted shrimps on toast, then toasted crumpets on a fork in front of the blue, yellow and orange flames given off by the small gas fire and ate them with some of my Aunt Dora's raspberry jam. To finish off, we each ate a cream horn from Pierre's.

We didn't talk much, just listened to some music on the wireless and to the rain battering against the window. The sunny day had given way to a dreary, wet and windy evening. The strains of the *Moonlight Sonata* faded into silence and T.C. sighed gently and stood up. To my utter astonish-ment he began to collect up our plates and cups. What on earth was he doing?

'I'll just give these a rinse,' he said.

'It's all right, I'll do them.' I headed towards the kitchen at a clip.

'How about if you wash and I wipe, then?' T.C. suggested, and so it was settled.

My kitchen's tiny – minute. Passing one another was out of the question, so I was rooted to the sink, which was near the small yellow table that overlooked the street, while T.C. stood in the narrow space between me and the door. I could smell the comforting scent of his Harris tweed jacket, he stood so close. A Hebridean woman once told me that the distinctive Harris tweed smell came from lanolin in the sheep's wool and the memory of the peat fires that heated the crofters' weaving sheds.

Whatever it was, it made me want to snuggle into it for warmth and safety, and I blushed deeply at the thought of it. I stared hard at the soapy water, willing my flaming cheeks to return to normal. T.C. dried each item carefully and stacked them in the hatch between the kitchen and the living room. He'd noticed that my china lived in the sideboard, but then he *was* a policeman; he was trained to notice things. I finished the washing, and gave the sink and draining board a brisk wipe around with a cloth. Satisfied, I turned away from the sink. T.C. finished the last saucer, looked up from the task and smiled.

'Here,' he said. 'Here, you've got a blob of cream on your chin.'

He moved towards me and tipped my face up to the light to wipe at my chin with a corner of the tea cloth. For a moment, we stared into each other's eyes. His seemed dark blue-grey, like the sea on days when the weather can't make up its mind between sunshine and showers. We stood close and still for what seemed an age. Then he tipped my face a little further and moved a shade closer. I could smell Aunt Dora's raspberry jam on his breath. I could hear ragged breathing – his or mine, I wasn't sure – and I could feel my heart hammering.

I went rigid, as if set in stone. My skin became clammy and my breathing shallow with blind panic. I remembered Sid, sneering at me as he left for the last time. 'You're such an ugly cow. But it hardly matters, does it? I mean, who looks at the mantelpiece when he's poking the fire? But you've got no fire neither. Shagging you is like trying to shag a plank.'

T.C. saw the panic in my eyes and let me go immediately. His voice was husky. 'I'm so sorry. I … er … didn't mean to take advantage. I think it's time I went.' He hurried into the living room and gathered up his coat, hat, scarf. Before I knew it, he'd thanked me for a lovely day and gone. And I was left with the lingering memory of distant peat fires and raspberry jam.

10

I slept very badly that night, partly because I kept kicking myself for my frigid response to T.C. I wished like mad that I had done things differently. Sadly, wishes at three o'clock in the morning change nothing, and the next day I was still plagued by the memory of his hurt, bewildered embarrassment and hasty departure.

The other reason for my wakefulness was yet another furious argument raging in the flat above. The occasional crash of china hitting the walls testified that Bandy was involved and the sound of two masculine voices and another female one led me to believe that the entire household had joined in. There was one point when I felt like putting on my dressing gown, marching up the stairs and having a go myself, but I thought better of it.

It was a relief to see the first chilly fingers of dawn creeping over the chimney pots. As it was Sunday, I was still in bed, with a cup of tea and the latest Ellery Queen. I had found that reading was a great antidote to anxiety and loneliness, especially when it was too early in the morning to seek out human company or to make a noise doing the housework.

I heard a slight scratching at my front door. At first I thought it was a mouse in the wainscoting and tried hard to ignore it, but soon the scratching turned into a tentative knocking. I got up with a sigh, put on my velvet dressing gown and opened the front door to find Peace looking a little desperate on my doormat.

'Come in, Peace. You needn't explain, I heard the fighting last night. Have you had breakfast?'

A small shake of her head sent me to the kitchen. I lit the oven for warmth and put the kettle on. 'Sit at the table and I'll rustle us up something to eat.' I looked in my cupboard. 'Tea and toast do you, will it?'

Another small nod accompanied by a whispered, 'If it is no trouble, Auntie Liz.'

It wasn't long before I was sitting opposite her and tucking into my breakfast with enthusiasm. It was nice to have another person across the table from me first thing in the morning. It had been a long, long while. I smiled encouragingly at my guest. 'So, what was it all about this time?'

I thought Peace wasn't going to answer at first, but she finally raised her eyes from the table and looked at me sadly. 'Everything. It is about everything. Aunt is angry with me because I will not agree to go back to school. Aunt is angry with Mr Sugar because he does not like Mr Malcolm and because he keeps disappearing when she needs him to help her. And Aunt is angry with Mr Malcolm because we are overcrowded and his flat is not clean enough for her to want to stay there instead. Aunt is angry about everything and with everybody.'

I could imagine that squeezing four people into a flat no bigger than my own would be troublesome for someone whose life was as busy and as complicated as Bandy's life was. I munched my toast in silence for a while, then a thought struck me. 'What will you do about your education if you don't go back to school? I understand that you're a bright girl. It would be a pity not to make full use of a good education.'

'I suggested that I attend a day school, but Aunt says that still leaves the problem of my living quarters.' Peace looked so forlorn that my heart ached for her. It was hard to reconcile the little scrap before me with the tigress that had taken on her formidable aunt a few nights previously and had held her ground to an honourable draw. Bandy had not carried out her threat to bundle Peace on to the first train back to school, or any other train for that matter.

I made another pot of tea and we drank it quietly, each deep in our own thoughts. The beginning of an idea was stirring, and I wanted to think through all the possibilities before I put it to Peace. It could well solve several problems at once. I made up my mind.

'Do you think it would help if you came to stay in my spare room? It's not that big, mind, but you could make it comfortable.'

Peace's face began to glow with tentative hope. 'I would be very good. I would be no trouble. I would help very much with the cooking and cleaning,' she assured me earnestly. 'Do you think Aunt would allow it?'

'I have no idea,' I told her honestly. 'We'll just have to ask her and find out.'

In the end, I left Peace to wash up our breakfast things and climbed the stairs alone, a little worried about the reception I might receive.

Bandy and Malcolm were up and eating croissants at the kitchen table. A coffee pot stood between them, along with a muddle of used plates, cups, saucers, cutlery and a brimming ashtray. It was easy to see that Sugar wasn't around much. He would never have tolerated such squalor. Sugar was the housekeeper when he and Bandy lived alone, but he'd obviously gone on strike once Malcolm had moved in. I understood Bandy's ineptitude in the housewifery department: she'd been brought up with servants in Hong Kong and an army of skivvies had cleaned at her boarding-school.

Most men, in my meagre experience, expected household chores to be done by women: mothers, sisters, wives or a 'daily' who came in and 'did' for bachelors. Malcolm's domestic habits came as no surprise at all to me. It was Sugar and, indeed, Bobby Bristowe who were the shockers, because they seemed to *enjoy* cleaning, and what's more they were good at it.

'Take a pew,' suggested Bandy through a haze of cigarette smoke. 'Care for a coffee? It's fairly fresh.'

I took a deep breath. 'No thanks, I can't stop for long. I've got Peace downstairs and I've had an idea that might help ease the overcrowding for you...'

I went on to outline my plan. Bandy listened intently as Malcolm yawned and scratched a bit. I could see why Sugar loathed him so; there was something repulsive about the man. He was just beginning to run to seed for one thing. His skin wasn't a good colour and he was getting a tiny bit flabby around the middle. And there was something about the fleshy, red lips that spoke, somehow, of unwholesome appetites. I shook myself, and waited for Bandy's reply.

'It's very kind of you, Elizabeth, and it would certainly help in the short term, but I am hoping to persuade her to return to school eventually. Still, it would certainly help to overcome our immediate problem. Perhaps if Sugar gets his room back, he'll spend more time at home.' There was a long pause while she took a deep draw on her cigarette, then seemed to come to a decision. 'Thank you, Elizabeth, I think it would help enormously. Now about the rent...'

We argued a little about the idea of rent for such a tiny room, but in the end we settled on a contribution towards gas, electricity and food. Bandy stuck her hand out and shook mine. 'It's a deal,' she said firmly, and we were both happy. I had company again, Bandy had more room and Sugar would get his own room back. Of course, to make his life complete, he'd have to get rid of Malcolm, but it was a small step in the right direction.

Peace was relieved and happy when I told her the news, and set about moving her things down the stairs immediately. Round about lunchtime, Sugar appeared. We celebrated the new arrangement with cauliflower cheese because that was all that I had in my larder. Then we spent a happy afternoon sewing and gossiping while Peace arranged and rearranged her room until she was satisfied.

I smiled to myself. A stranger could look through my living-room window at that moment and see a typical little family scene, mother, father, daughter. A closer inspection would reveal that father was wearing a tweed skirt, an understated pair of pearl earrings and a little subtle make-up and that, although the daughter looked Chinese, the couple did not.

'A penny for them,' Sugar said as he saw my smile.

'I was thinking that we felt like a family, albeit a rather strange one,' I told him.

'There are all kinds of families, sweetie. The main thing is to be loving and loyal, and the rest – well, that's just the window dressing.' Sugar laughed and I joined him. The sound of my laughter came as a bit of a surprise to us both. It had been such a long time since either of us had heard it.

11

It was Wednesday; three days since Peace had moved in with me.

Winter Wednesdays were popular round our way because it was steak and kidney pudding day at the cafe. Freddy, Antony and I always closed the shop promptly on Wednesday lunchtimes and hotfooted round to Old Compton Street to get in before the rush. Madame Zelda usually saved a table for us and any other regular who cared to join us. T.C. was sitting with her on this particular Wednesday.

I stopped dead in the doorway in confusion, causing Freddy to crash into me. I didn't know quite what to do. The last time I'd seen T.C. had been when he had tried to kiss me and I'd managed to ruin the whole thing by choking him off. My heart hammered so hard, I thought I'd be sick, but Freddy, unaware of my mortification, simply gave me a shove and muttered, 'Get a move on, ducky, I'm freezing my goolies off here.' He barged in and strode purposefully towards our table.

'Wotcha, Zelda, T.C. Nice day for it.'

'Wotcha all.' Madame Zelda grinned. 'Nice day for what?'

'I dunno what. It's just a nice day – but a bit parky,' Freddy answered.

'I see, or rather, I don't, but then I don't really need to. Your puds are on order. Should be here in 'two shakes of a lamb's wotsit,' she reassured us.

'Hello, Freddy, Antony, Lizzie.' T.C.'s eyes crinkled pleasantly as he smiled but I noticed that he didn't quite catch my eye when I returned the greeting, and my heart sank.

A blast of air told us that the door had opened again, and Peace hurried in from the cold. There was a general shuffling about of chairs and tables and finally we wound up with a table for eight, leaving two chairs for any latecomers.

Maggie approached the table smiling and took the new order, but she needn't have troubled because Peace opted for steak and kidney pudding. 'One more please, Bert,' she roared across her counter and through to the steamy kitchen at the back.

'Right you are, Maggie, my love,' Bert roared back. 'Mrs Wong's on her way with the first five plates.'

Maggie returned to our table and beamed at Peace, the latest recruit to 'the Wednesday pudding club' as she called us. 'Hello, dear. What's this I hear – that you've moved in with our Lizzie? Settling in, are you?'

'Yes, thank you, Mrs Featherby,' Peace answered shyly. 'I am very happy to be staying with Auntie Liz.'

'Ah, here comes Mrs Wong with the first of your dinners. Yours won't be long, dear.' Maggie stood aside to allow Mrs Wong near enough to the table to serve the steaming plates from her tray.

Silly of me, I know, but it had never occurred to me that Mrs Wong and Peace might have met before, but a look of recognition flashed between them as Mrs Wong approached the table. She smiled and bowed slightly to Peace, who bowed her head respectfully in return. Mrs Wong said something in rapid Chinese while she doled out the contents of her tray, and Peace replied, in equally rapid Chinese.

I felt absurdly proud of her, for being able to speak a foreign language. But then, it wasn't a foreign language to her; she'd been brought up with it. I was always impressed by local children being able to speak French or Italian, even when they *were* French or Italian. I suppose it was because I could only speak one language myself and found it wonderful that children could be so clever.

Not that Peace was a child exactly, I reminded myself sternly. She was on the brink of woman-hood, not eleven as my Jenny would have been. It was important not to mix the two up in my mind, however tempting it was to pretend that Peace was my own daughter, especially as nobody else seemed to want her. Peace was simply on loan to me, perhaps only for a short while. That was all.

Mrs Wong withdrew to the kitchen and Peace appeared much more relaxed than she had been when she had sat down. Politely, she translated their brief conversation for the rest of us. 'Mrs Wong welcomed me to Soho once again and said she hoped I would have a happy time.' She smiled sweetly. 'She said that I had fallen among good people and that I was a very lucky person. It was very good to speak Cantonese once again, no one spoke it at school. It is good that Mrs Wong and I speak the same language, because I know hardly any Mandarin at all.'

'Well I think you're a very clever girl to be able to speak two languages, let alone three,' Freddy said between his first and second mouthfuls of pudding. 'God, this is good, Maggie, you've out-done yourself. Hasn't she, Ant?'

'She certainly has, Freddy dear, she certainly has. Delicious, Maggie, absolutely delicious,' Antony assured her with a blissful smile. Maggie returned to her counter, blushing at the praise. Approval from Freddy and Antony was praise indeed, because they adored good food and spent many happy hours pottering about in their kitchen.

'Look what the cat dragged in,' Madame Zelda muttered as she swallowed a mouthful of cabbage and took a swig of tea to wash it down. The assembled company looked towards the door to see Sugar, dressed immaculately in what he called his 'civvies', or street clothes, standing on the threshold laughing with Luigi. Sugar bade him farewell with a wave of his hand and finally entered the steamy cafe.

'The usual please, Maggie,' he sang out gaily. 'I'll join my friends if you would kindly deliver it to their table.' He smiled broadly at us, put the brown paper parcel he was carrying and his tailored camel hair coat on one spare seat and sat down on the other, carefully hitching each striped trouser leg as he did so. 'Hello, sweeties,' he said to the table in general. 'Freddy, Antony, that little commission you delivered will do very nicely, very nicely indeed. I've added the finishing touches, so if it's all right with you, I'll hand it over now.' My bosses grinned in unison and gave their consent. The rest of us at the table looked on in bewilderment.

'Oh very enigmatic,' said Madame Zelda. 'What are you on about?'

'Not that it's any of your business, but as you're here, you nosy old bat, you'll find out soon enough,' Sugar answered with mock severity. He turned to me. 'This is for you,' he said, handing over the parcel. 'Bandy and I thought we couldn't have you lowering the tone of the bar with that black top and skirt you keep trotting out, so we commissioned the boys here to knock you up a decent frock to work in.'

I was flabbergasted. I could hardly wait to tear the paper off, but T.C. smiled a caution at me. 'Watch it, you'll dip it in that gravy if you're not careful.' His voice and eyes were warm and I felt the knot in my stomach that had been there throughout my lunch, loosen slightly.

'You're right, of course, T.C.,' Antony said sternly. 'Contain yourself, Elizabeth.' He sounded just like my mother when she was cross. 'When we're back in the shop, where there are no gravy hazards, you can try it on in safety. I hope it fits. We didn't dare spoil the surprise with a fitting; that would have been no fun at all.'

'But how are *we* going to get a look at it if she waits till she's back at work?' Madame Zelda complained.

'I second that,' said Maggie from so close behind me that I jumped and almost dropped the precious parcel. I put it down safely and tried to be patient. But it wasn't easy; I wasn't used to

111

getting presents.

Sugar stood firm. 'You'll just have to drop in to Bandy's Place on Friday or Saturday night when she's wearing it for work. So, how's it going with you two sharing a flat?' he asked Peace solicitously. 'Working out so far, is it? I certainly hope so. No offence, but I like having my own room back.'

Peace was too shy to answer for us both, but she managed to reassure him on her own behalf. 'I am very happy, Mr Sugar. It is good that you are happy too.'

'Well happier, certainly. I'll only be truly happy when we're shot of that oily poet – or should I say greasy?'

'Ooh, meow!' Freddy sniggered slightly.

I hastily changed the subject. Sugar could be tetchy about Malcolm, very tetchy indeed. 'I've been thinking, Sugar,' I said, as if I had never entertained the idea before it struck me at that meeting of the pudding club, when in fact, I'd talked it all over with Peace during the last few days. 'Don't you think it'd be an idea if Peace enrolled in a local day school? She's hanging around with nothing much to do. That's never good for anybody and her brain needs stretching, otherwise it'll get sloppy from under-use.' I smiled across the table at the girl, my co-conspirator. 'And what about a Saturday job? It'd help her to buy her own stockings, and things like that. She is sixteen, after all. It's time she learned some responsibility for her own money and some of her own needs.'

Sugar grinned amiably at me, then at Peace. 'Let me guess: you two want me to broach the subject with Bandy.' He shook his head in wonderment. 'If you were any more transparent, we could call you windows and have done with it. I'll have a go, that's all I can promise.'

He turned to T.C. 'That woman I told you about says to meet her at some place in Sloane Square tomorrow morning. I've written it all down. Looks like you've got a job, mate. Two in fact.' He shut up abruptly as the questions began to form on Madame Zelda's face.

'Just doing a favour or two for friends, Zelda,' T.C. assured her, 'Looking into one or two private matters.' He tapped his nose with his forefinger.

Did I hear the words "Saturday job"?' Maggie asked, coming to the rescue. 'Because if I did, me and Bert have been talking about getting a Saturday girl in, to help Mrs Wong when it gets so busy with all the trippers in from the sticks for a day up West. It'd give us a longer break too, by adding an hour or so to our Saturday evenings.' She looked at Peace. 'So if you fancy it, the job's yours. But only if your Aunt Bandy says it's all right.'

Peace's face was radiant as she thanked Maggie for her kind offer. She had allies at last: me, Sugar and now Maggie and Bert. Every little helped in her campaign to stay in Soho.

I fingered my parcel. I could hardly wait to get back to the shop and get a look at it. I checked my watch. 'It's time I got back to work. I'll open up if you want to linger,' I told my bosses.

'Not on your nellie,' said Freddy. 'I want to see the frock on.'

'Me too,' Antony chipped in. 'It may need some altering before it's fit to wear.'

'I'll wait until Friday' – Sugar waved an airy

113

hand – 'when I expect you to make a grand entrance to the club, Lizzie my sweet. Anyway, I want to finish my Kate and Sidney pud. Peace can stay with me if she likes.' He looked towards her, eyebrows raised.

'I want to see Auntie Liz in her dress,' she said, slipping out of her seat to join the group forming by the door and getting into coats, scarves, gloves and hats.

T.C. laughed. 'I'll keep you company, Sugar.' He looked straight at me. 'And I'll see you in all your finery over the weekend, I expect. I'm looking forward to it.'

12

Rosie was flushed with excitement when she came to tea on my Thursday afternoon off. She'd made a habit of having tea with me every now and then. It had started when we had both missed Jenny so much, we thought we'd never be able to bear it, and we had continued the practice ever since. It was an arrangement I certainly enjoyed and I'm pretty sure that Rosie did too. Unlike most young girls, Rosie didn't seem to find adults boring; quite the opposite in fact.

It probably had something to do with her not having any other children in the family, no brothers or sisters or cousins to play with when out of school. However, in compensation she was bright enough to understand a lot of the doings of the world about her, the people in it and the conversations that they had, so she was rarely bored. And, of course, the cafe meant she was surrounded by an endless parade of people, some fascinating, some not. Not many children have that much stimulation. I thought it added an unusual richness to the pattern of her daily life.

'So what's it like living with Peace?' Rosie asked almost as soon as she saw me when I answered her knock. She was peeping round me, hoping to see my house guest, no doubt. 'Auntie Maggie says she's coming to work at the cafe on Saturdays,' she announced as she rushed through my front door, shedding her cherry red, woollen winter coat with the black trim and buttons as she did so. I retrieved the coat from the floor, where it had slipped from the chair, and hung it carefully on a hanger on the hook behind the door. 'Thank you, Auntie Lizzie,' she said. 'I would have picked it up, honest.' She sounded slightly ashamed of her carelessness with her mother's recent Christmas present.

'It's not settled about the Saturday job yet. Sugar's got to ask Bandy about it first, and she may not agree,' I warned.

'Where is she?' Rosie asked as she landed with a thump in an armchair. 'I was sure she'd be here.' Her face was red as her coat in all the excitement and the cold air of the streets. 'I asked Auntie Maggie if she'd be here and she said she thought that she would, unless she'd started at a new school already and had homework to do, like me. I thought Peace might be excused homework if she had a proper job, but Auntie Maggie says definitely not. Doesn't seem fair to me!'

Rosie kicked the table leg lightly, to emphasize her point. The dreaded homework was obviously still an issue in the Featherby household. 'I know that Auntie Bandy can be a tough lady, but surely she'd let her off some of it! If she lets her take the job, that is. Do you think she will?'

'I think Bandy may still be cross that Peace ran away from school and refuses to go back,' I said, putting it mildly for the sake of young ears.

'Cross! Uncle Bert says that Bandy's still eyeing Peace's guts, to see if she can turn 'em into a decent set of garters.' She seemed hugely amused. 'So where is she?'

Rosie'd lost me for a moment. Then the penny dropped and I smiled. 'She's nipped round the corner for me, to get some milk. How about we start the tea so it's ready for when she gets back?' We settled on scrambled egg on toast followed by the jam tarts I'd baked earlier. 'We'll scramble the eggs when Peace gets back, but we can toast the bread in front of the fire and get it buttered ready,' I suggested.

We settled down in front of the fire to gossip while Rosie made toast on the end of my long toasting fork and we waited for Peace. 'You seem pretty excited to have Peace in the cafe. Why's that?'

'Well, you've got to admit, she's interesting. The only other Chinese person I know is Mrs Wong, and she's very quiet. She doesn't chat at all, and you never hear hardly anything about Mr Wong and all the little Wongs. Of course, Mr Wong died years ago, but that's all I know about him.'

'Are there little Wongs?' I asked, fascinated. Rosie was right. None of us knew much about Mrs Wong, except perhaps Maggie and Bert. And if they knew anything, they certainly never discussed it in any depth, if at all. All I knew about Mrs Wong was that she was a hard worker, that she was a widow, that she could throw a knife with deadly accuracy – according to the Featherbys and several others who had witnessed it – and that keeping 'face' was very important to her.

'She has three,' Rosie replied, 'but they're not little any more. Lucky's twenty-two, Jackie's twenty-one and Bubbles, her baby, is seventeen.'

'What unusual names. How do you know about them?'

'I asked her when I was little. You can get away with all kinds of things when you're young,' Rosie explained, sounding like Old Mother Time. ''Specially with people who really like children. And Mrs Wong really likes children. She dotes on hers. You can tell if you know what to look for. The names are nicknames. I don't know what their Chinese names are; Mrs Wong did try to tell me once, but I couldn't take them in. I was too young and I don't understand Chinese at all.'

'Have you met them?' I was intrigued.

Rosie shook her head sadly. 'No. They never come to the cafe. I'm not sure why. It's something to do with it not being kosher for a Chinese lady to be working in an English cafe, or something like that.'

Rosie examined her thumb for a moment and took an exploratory nibble of her nail, then frowned and dropped her hand sharply. 'I'm

117

giving up nail-biting. It was my New Year resolution; that and not squandering all my pocket money on comics and sweets.'

'Why isn't it right for a Chinese lady to work for English people?' I asked. I knew very little about the Chinese, except that I'd noticed some of the run-down shops in Gerrard Street, just on the other side of Shaftesbury Avenue from Soho, had been taken over by Chinese businesses in recent years. Another Chinese laundry had opened up, along with two tiny cafes, a larger restaurant and a grocery store selling all sorts of exotic foods I had never seen before. I'd tried to shop there once, and the lady behind the counter, although bowing politely, seemed not to understand a word I said. I couldn't read a single label on the cans or recognize any of the shrivelled, dried foodstuffs in jars, so I finally gave it up. It had been fascinating, though, that dark little shop with the bowing lady in black behind the counter and the small group of women waiting silently and watchfully for me to leave.

There were also several blank store fronts in Gerrard Street, with discreet notices in Chinese on the doors, but no welcome for strangers. I had no idea what went on behind the curtained, whitewashed or boarded windows, and neither did anyone I'd asked. It suddenly occurred to me that I could ask T.C. when I saw him next. If anyone would know about the mysterious blacked-out shops, he would. He had got into all kinds of places as a bobby on the beat, I was certain. It went with the job.

'Are you listening to me?' Rosie's young voice

demanded and I started guiltily.

'Sorry Rosie, I was thinking about all those blank shop fronts in Gerrard Street. I thought T.C. might know what goes on there. What were you saying?'

Rosie rolled her eyes at me and began again in a voice loaded with patience. 'I *said*,' she began, 'that Luigi told me that Lucky told him that they call us "ghosts" because they like to pretend we're not really here, and anyway, we're such a funny colour, so pasty and white that we all look the same to them.'

I smiled. 'Well, that makes a change. It's what we've been known to say about them.'

'I know. Do you think Peace will be stand-offish like the others?' Rosie asked. 'I hope not, because I'd like to get to know her better. We've got stuff in common, after all.' Rosie hesitated and blushed slightly. 'There's our parents for starters. I mean, it was ages before I knew who mine were and Peace still doesn't know who hers are; nobody does. It's hard, not knowing. At least I see mine from time to time. Poor Peace wouldn't know hers if she fell over them, would she?'

Rosie had a point. I knew for a fact that the question of her parentage was an extremely vexed one for Peace, because Sugar had told me she'd asked more than once if Bandy was her mother. 'I mean,' he'd said, 'if you start hoping Bandy's your mother you've got to be desperate. Bandy has all the maternal instincts of a municipal paving slab, and is about as cuddly.'

It was an unkind observation, but a true one. Bandy liked children well enough: she held

119

legendary children's parties at the club, but they were festive occasions, not real life. And anyway, Bandy was doing what came naturally being a hostess, but a hostess was a far cry from being someone's mother. You couldn't send your kids home when you'd had enough, or because they bored you, the way you could your guests. I couldn't imagine Bandy smoothing a fevered brow, clearing up vomit, making breakfast before school, washing a nappy, rubbing zinc and castor oil cream into a chapped bottom or giving up a night on the tiles to take care of the children.

'And then there's this boarding-school business.' Rosie's voice brought me back from my musings.

'Peace's been to boarding school, and Auntie Maggie and Uncle Bert are beginning to think that I should go too. It's all my mother's fault; well, her relatives anyway. I don't think my mum cares one way or the other, to be honest. They always send their kids away to school in that family,' she added darkly, as if they were being sent to a deep, dark dungeon to be tortured. 'They don't think Soho is a fit place to bring me up really. That's what I heard Auntie Maggie tell Madame Zelda. My Great-Aunt Dodie, my mother's aunt, talked them into it. She's dead set on it, and now so are Auntie Maggie and Uncle Bert.'

Actually, this wasn't really true. I knew that Maggie and Bert were merely putting a brave face on it. They hated the plan, but they also knew that it would offer Rosie more choice in later life. 'There's no doubt about it,' Maggie had said. 'Those schools open doors that slam in your kisser if you go to an ordinary school. I mean, if she stays put, she'll wind up running the cafe, probably, or something like it.

'Not that there's anything wrong with that, I'm happy in my work. But if she goes away to a school, she could do anything, *be* anyone. She could inherit that bloody great business of theirs, or marry a diplomat even, and know what to do at them banquets they have to go to, with all them forks and knives...'

Her voice had trailed away as her blue eyes grew moist with unshed tears. Poor Maggie didn't want her beloved Rosie to marry some snotty diplomat and move away, but being the good woman that she was, she realized that she had to equip her little girl to make some of the difficult choices that lay in her future.

Cassie, Rosie's mother, was high-born by local standards, and had come from money before she'd discovered booze and hard times. So far, Rosie was the only heir to the family business and fortune. Cassie had drunk her shares, and Rosie's Uncle Charles was what Maggie called 'a confirmed bachelor' and unlikely to have children. That left illegitimate Rosie the only viable heir to Loveday-Smythe Engineering. As Maggie said, she had to be equipped to deal with it and whatever came her way.

I tried to explain her Auntie Maggie's point of view, but I didn't need to. Rosie understood why she had to go. Maggie and Bert had been preparing her for it for quite a while. 'I thought, seeing as how Peace had been to one of those schools, I'd ask her for some hints on how to get on.'

'Remember, though, dear,' I pointed out, 'it's

121

not the same school as you're likely to wind up at. And Peace obviously didn't do that well with fitting in, poor lamb, otherwise she wouldn't have run away.'

'I know. It was because she was Chinese. It made her different from the rest.' Rosie's voice grew small. 'But I'll be different, too. So I thought I'd ask, then maybe I can be ready for them.'

There was nothing I could say. Poor Rosie knew she'd be likely to have a rough ride at school, what with her background and accent. If I told her it wasn't so, I'd be lying. I knew as well as anybody how cruel children can be, especially to an outsider. I'd been one as a kid. Children can be natural bullies, even so-called genteel ones.

Rosie sighed and dropped the last piece of toast on the bread plate. I buttered it, cut it in half and added it to the pile. Her mind was on more important things. 'How about another jam tart while we wait, Auntie? They're delicious.'

'Let's wait until Peace gets back with the milk or there'll be nothing left for her. Anyway, you're supposed to eat your scrambled egg before the tarts, you naughty girl. I was so busy nattering I didn't see what you were up to.' It was so good to have her around. She reminded me of Jenny. Not in her looks; Rosie had fair curls, peaches and cream skin like her mother's, and her father's merry blue eyes, with just a touch of sadness lurking in their depths. My Jenny's hair had been straight and much darker; she'd been darker altogether, in skin tone and her hazel eyes had pretty speckles of darker brown and honey gold if you looked closely.

My own eyes filled with tears for a moment, but I swallowed the lump in my throat at the sound of Peace's key in the door. The girls were awkward together at first, but the ritual of tea in front of the fire helped to ease their shyness and an hour spent working together on my appearance made them fast friends.

Rosie started it. 'Let me see your new frock, Auntie,' she pleaded as we finished the washing up after tea.

'Oh yes, do show it to her, Aunt Liz.' Peace's eyes shone as she turned to Rosie. 'She looks very nice in it, but she needs to do something with her hair and, of course, some make-up would help.'

'Let's give her a new hairdo and a face job,' Rosie suggested, as if I wasn't there. I noted the determined look that flashed between the girls and sighed with resignation. I was about to be turned into a guinea pig. I could feel it 'in my water', as Madame Zelda would have said.

Sure enough, Peace and Rosie had me sitting in front of my dressing table with a small bowl of warm water, some setting lotion and a bag full of curlers and hair grips almost before I could agree to the plan.

'She needs some curl in that hair,' Rosie had said firmly. 'She's always on about my lovely curls, so it's time she had some as well.' She grinned at me. 'It might stop her from ruffling mine quite so often if she's got some of her own to play with,' she added cheekily.

'Yes, you are right. I have seen the girls at school do it,' Peace assured me earnestly. 'So I am pretty certain I know what to do.'

'So am I,' Rosie added. 'I'm always doing Kathy Moon's for her when we're in Mademoiselle Hortense's shows. Her hair's almost as straight as yours,' she informed Peace gravely, 'only not as dark and glossy.'

I have to say that between them they did a pretty good job. When they had finished, my fine mousy hair was softly curled around my face with pretty little kiss curls. They'd given my hair a bit of height and volume by using large rollers on the top, which was far better than the scraped-back French pleat I normally wore to keep it out of my way.

I didn't own a great deal of make-up, so they had to make do with powdering my shiny nose and putting a little lipstick on my mouth. Peace stood back and looked at me critically. 'You still look too pale,' she told me. 'What do you think, Rosie?'

'You're right. She is a bit pasty,' the younger girl agreed.

I was a little nettled. 'Do you two mind? I'm sitting right here, you know, and I have ears and feelings just like the next person. Pasty, indeed!'

'Sorry, Auntie Lizzie,' Rosie giggled, not sounding at all sorry.

Peace stood deep in thought for a second, then her solemn face broke into a radiant smile. 'I have it. I saw Cynthia Mortimer-Rendalsham do it when she went out after lights out. She had a boyfriend in the town,' Peace explained, 'and she would creep out to meet him. She would put a little lipstick on her cheeks, to make them pinker. Just a little, then you rub it in. Like this.'

She dabbed a blob of lipstick on each of my cheeks and then rubbed her fingertips across them gently, in a circular motion. It was very soothing and when she'd finished, I did look brighter and healthier. It was a tip I would remember, I decided, as I looked closely at the result.

'Now for the posh frock,' Rosie sang out excitedly. 'Put on your posh frock, so that I can see it.' She rushed to my cupboard, where she found the dress immediately. It stood out as a splash of colour in my otherwise decidedly dull wardrobe.

'OK,' I agreed, 'but out, the pair of you. I'll only be a minute.' I shoved the giggling girls into the hallway.

'All right, Auntie, but be careful of your hair and don't get lipstick on your frock,' Rosie instructed as I closed the bedroom door on her excited and smiling face.

As instructed, I lowered the dusky pink silk gently over my new hairdo, being careful not to smudge my lips on the fabric while I was at it. Freddy and Antony had done me proud. Even I could see that I looked good in it, the first time I had tried it on. With my hair and face done, I looked even better, almost beautiful.

The dress itself had a narrow, fitted bodice that hugged my shape as if they'd painted it on. The boned bodice emphasized my bust and narrowed my waist so that the flared skirt, with its stiff net underskirt stood out proudly. It was held up mainly by whalebone, but thin, spaghetti shoulder straps also helped. Freddy had even taken the trouble to provide me with a strapless brassiere, knowing that I would never have owned such a thing. Luckily, I had a small waist and my hips were in proportion, something for which I

125

thanked providence on a regular basis, so he didn't need to provide a corset or roll-on as well.

As a finishing touch, Sugar had embroidered a large spray of briar roses in a slightly darker pink across the bodice, so that the green stalks and leaves were grouped on the left-hand side of the waist and the blooms themselves were scattered up and across until they petered out on my right breast. It really was a stunning creation.

I took a deep breath and stepped out of the bedroom to meet the critical gaze of my two young dressers.

Rosie's face split into a huge, delighted grin that made my heart stop for a moment. She looked so much like her father, only without the crinkly bits. Peace smiled widely too.

'You look smashing, Auntie Lizzie, absolutely smashing.' Rosie danced and clapped around me like an excited imp. 'I've never seen you look so gorgeous. I love the embroidery. Did Uncle Sugar do that?' I nodded, delighted with her uninhibited approval.

'You look very lovely, Aunt Liz, very lovely,' Peace assured me with her solemn smile. 'But I believe you also need to buy mascara and some blue eye shadow to complete your face. That is all. The rest is very lovely.'

I found I was looking forward to some unashamed showing off when I next went to work in Bandy's bar. I had a beautiful dress that made me look pretty and I had no mother breathing down my neck telling me that I looked like a Jezebel in my make-up and brand new finery. Freddy, Antony, Sugar and Bandy had been so kind to provide me with my first-ever posh frock, that I didn't even know where to begin to thank them.

Rosie brought me back. 'Put it away,' she told me severely, 'before you get it dirty.'

13

It was Friday, and I was due to make my grand entrance in my new dress. Rosie popped round and joined Peace in attending to my face and hair before I set off. Once I had their seal of approval I kissed them both and walked with them down the stairs. Peace had offered to see Rosie safely home as, being winter, it got dark early, and she herself was off to the Wongs', having been invited to pay a visit for the evening.

It hadn't taken Mrs Wong long to issue the invitation once she realized how desperate Peace was to speak her own language and to taste some good, Chinese home cooking. She probably remembered homesickness all too well. Peace had also been looking forward to renewing her tentative friendship with Bubbles Wong, which had begun during one of her previous visits to Soho during school holidays. I was pleased to think that Peace had a friend around her own age who knew what it was like to be a Chinese girl in England.

Having seen Peace and Rosie safely out of the alley I walked back into the building and shrugged off my coat. There was no point in ruining my entrance with my shabby, grey flannel.

As promised, Freddy and Antony were waiting at the bar. To my surprise and embarrassment, T.C. was there too, chatting to Sugar in the corner. Bobby and Pansy Bristowe sat with Madame Zelda at a table at the back. Freddy spied me first, although I'd crept in, my nerve having suddenly abandoned me at the last moment.

'There she is!' he screeched, clapping his hands together in excitement. 'Ducky, you look fantabulosa, just fantabulosa. I told you you'd look better for some slap and a bit of riah shushing. Didn't I tell her, Ant, when she tried it on the other day, didn't I say about the hair and the face?'

'You did indeed, Freddy dear, you certainly did,' Antony agreed. 'And you were right. You do look very nice, Elizabeth, very nice indeed. That pink looks so good on you, and Sugar's embroidery...' Antony kissed his fingertips in appreciation. 'I said it the first time I saw it and I'll say it again, that man is wasted in a bar, simply wasted. He should be working for us.'

Sugar laughed as he came up to give me the once-over. 'Yes Antony, you're probably right, but I know for a fact that you pay peanuts and I ain't no monkey.'

Sugar grew serious as he walked round me and studied the whole ensemble, then his dear face lit up with the widest of smiles and he positively twinkled at me. 'It's official, Lizzie, you're a bona fide stunner – Sugar has spoken!' He flung his arms wide in a grandiose gesture and gathered me into a bear hug that lifted me off my feet.

'Watch the schmutters!' Freddy squealed in

alarm. 'Put her down: you'll snap the straps if you're not careful.'

Sugar put me down gently and flapped his hand at T.C. and the others. 'What do you think? We thought she needed a cocktail dress for the job, what do you think?'

'Very nice, very nice indeed,' said Bobby Bristowe, gruffly.

'Smashing, Lizzie dear, you look smashing,' Pansy offered more enthusiastically. 'Doesn't she look smashing, Zeld?'

Madame Zelda smiled appreciatively. 'Yep. She does scrub up quite well, don't she?' she asked no one in particular.

I glowed beneath all the unaccustomed praise, but self-consciously waited for T.C.'s verdict. He stood at some distance from me and smiled widely, his head on one side as he considered what he was seeing. 'You look beautiful, Lizzie,' he said finally, making my heart leap into my mouth. 'Really beautiful.'

The spell was broken by the arrival of Bandy, who was obviously in a filthy temper. She peered at me through a haze of Passing Cloud smoke and growled, 'Is that the frock? It looks a bloody sight better than the togs you usually turn up in, I must say. I told Sugar you lower the bloody tone and that we ought to do something about you. Get you to fit in more with the ambience if you're going to be working here regularly. Glad to see that we've managed it.' She turned to Freddy and Antony: 'Another fine job, boys, you've surpassed your-selves.'

Bandy took up her usual place on her stool at

the corner of the bar. It was the first time in ages that she had made an appearance at work. I couldn't believe she'd come specially to see me in my dress and I wondered why she had disentangled herself from Malcolm. It wasn't long before we found out.

'So to what do we owe the pleasure?' Sugar asked as he handed Bandy her first gin of the evening. Bandy lit up another Passing Cloud and carefully fitted it into her long cigarette-holder before she answered.

'I had a look at the books earlier, and the takings are down. Seems this place goes to the dogs without me.' She took a deep drag on her cigarette, and followed it up with a hefty swig of gin. 'So I thought I'd better put in appearance, encourage the customers and keep an eye on things at the same time.' Bandy looked towards the door as Cassie, accompanied by one of her regular men friends, Neville, and also Sylvia and Toothy, piled in noisily. Sharky Finn, Sylvia's usual escort, was nowhere to be seen.

'See what that lot want, Elizabeth,' Bandy instructed. 'They look as if they're off out somewhere and we want to make sure they get their full quota on board before they go. There's little profit in allowing the customers to leave the place stone cold sober.' I hurried to do her bidding.

While I was away taking their orders, Bandy and Sugar began to quarrel quietly. They were still at it, hissing through gritted teeth, as I stood behind the bar to pour the drinks and put them on my tray. They were obviously so deeply involved, they simply didn't notice me. T.C. winked

130

and smiled at me while we both eavesdropped.

'Don't give us that, Band,' Sugar told her sweetly. 'You've known about the shortfall for a while now. I've told you before that I think Malodorous is more than a tad light-fingered, but you won't have it. It's not just money either; bottles are going missing from the storeroom.'

'Anyone could have their fingers in the till.' Bandy looked and sounded rattled. 'It doesn't have to be Malcolm. It could be Peace getting her own back, or Bobby or Elizabeth in need of a little extra.'

I took in a sharp breath. How dare she?

'Don't be stupid, Bandy, please.' Sugar sounded exasperated. 'Peace was still at school when I first noticed the takings were down. Lizzie wasn't even working here then, and anyway, she's as straight as an arrow. Just ask Freddy and Antony if you need proof. And Bobby? Are you mad? We've had him for years. Why would he start now, and do you honestly think Pansy'd let him?' I think it was the first time I'd ever seen Sugar angry, really angry, with Bandy or, indeed, anyone. 'Anyway, I've asked T.C. to look into it.' He glared at Bandy, then turned to T.C. in appeal. 'Tell her, T.C.'

T.C. nodded. 'It's true. Sugar has asked me to look into it and I've taken certain steps already, but we won't discuss them here. Walls have ears and so do boozers.' He was trying hard to keep his attention on Bandy, but I noticed that his eyes kept straying to Cassie's table, as the noise grew from that quarter. I can't say that I blamed him. She was looking lovely in a sea-green silk two-piece.

'I don't remember authorizing any kind of in-vestigation.' Bandy looked alarmed and her voice had even more of an edge to it. 'Why don't you mind your own business for once?'

'Because it *is* my business. I own a quarter share of this place, in case you've forgotten. What's more, you're casting suspicion on people I care about, so the sooner the little matter is cleared up, the better for all concerned.'

Bandy grew louder when she saw that she was cornered. 'You've never liked Malcolm. You're a jealous sod, Sugar Plum Flaherty, because nobody'll take an old pervert like you on, well not in public anyway. What person in their right mind would want to be seen with a man in a fucking wig and false tits?'

'I can see the extra classes at charm school paid off handsomely, Band,' Sugar answered sharply. 'Don't take it out on us just because your bloody boyfriend's pissed off for the evening. Although he's probably living it up on your booze and your money as usual.'

Sugar paused for a moment, face pale with rage. Then he remembered his audience and lowered his voice. 'Correction – *our* booze and *our* money – and I, for one, don't feel I'm getting any satis-faction for my contribution. I get the smelly bastard cluttering up my life, and if I'm right – and I *know* I am, it's just up to T.C. to prove it – he's also stealing from me, and *that* I will not have!'

Bandy had her mouth open to reply when Toothy roared across the room. 'Do hurry up with those drinks. It's like being trapped in a bloody desert over here.'

I jumped as I realized I had been standing listening to my employers' argument with my mouth wide open and my hands full of tray. T.C. grinned sympathetically and relieved me of the tray. 'I'll take them over. You might as well start on the refills straight away. If I know that lot, they'll want topping up very soon.'

Bandy stood up, glared at Sugar one final time, and swept out of the bar. The minute she left, we all heaved a sigh of relief; Sugar, me and the customers.

'Thank Christ for that,' said Cassie as the door closed behind Bandy's black silk back. 'I thought I was going to have to leave, the woman was such a misery. What the hell's got into her, Sugar? Love life in the doldrums, is it? She shouldn't take it so seriously. Love 'em and leave 'em I say, before they can do it to you.'

Sugar opened his mouth to answer, but Cassie ploughed on. 'I've a couple of men spare, if she feels the need. I don't think they're that fussy. Well, they're certainly not when they have a few drinkies on board. Speaking of drinkies, how about sloshing another gin and it in a glass, Lizzie, and bringing it over here? Make it a double, there's a dear. Oh, and put it on Neville's tab.'

I was about to do as Cassie asked when T.C. drifted up to me. 'Make it a small one, will you, Lizzie? It looks to me as if she's been at it all afternoon,' he whispered. He was so close to me that I could feel the heat from his body against my bare shoulders. I suddenly remembered the feel of his fingertips on my face when he'd been about to kiss me and shivered slightly.

Once I'd served Cassie's table with their drinks the place went very quiet for a while. The theatre crowd had drifted away, Bobby, Pansy and Madame Zelda had disappeared around the time Bandy had started getting tetchy and that just left Cassie and her friends, T.C., Sugar and me.

'So, did you see that woman, whatever her name was? The one with the wandering old man?' Sugar asked T.C. absentmindedly. His mind was obviously still on his row with Bandy. It had been particularly unkind of her to bring up Sugar's dressing habits, because that evening he was elegant in an evening suit, complete with fancy white shirt, cummerbund and bow tie, to complement my cocktail dress. He said that he didn't want to let me down by being a scruff. Not that he was ever scruffy, whatever outfit he was wearing. He was such a sweet man and I didn't like to see him hurt by Bandy's unkind words.

T.C. nodded. 'Yes, it's all set. As I can't be in two places at once, Bobby's going to do some of the watching and Pansy too, if need be. The client understands that I have to hire in help on a job like this, and Bobby's keen to help.'

'Glad it worked out, T.C. It could be a nice little earner,' said Sugar vaguely. He cheered up as the Behan brothers turned up with a large group and demanded drinks all round. They kept him busy serving and gossiping and the tension soon eased from his face.

The rest of the evening was busy and I was run off my feet. Several people told me how lovely I looked in my new dress and I glowed with pride and happiness as I darted between the tables. It

134

was some time before I realized that T.C. had left. I asked Sugar where he'd got to and he nodded towards Cassie's table. She had gone too.

'Cassie dragged him off about half an hour ago. Neville's hooter's way out of joint, 'specially as she's stiffed him with the bill,' he told me as he passed on the way to deliver another order to the Behans' party.

'Carrying a bit of a torch, are you, Lizzie?' Sylvia's voice made me start and I felt my face redden.

I shook my head vehemently. I didn't want Cassie's friend gossiping out of turn. T.C. and I had got over our embarrassment, and as I had to see a fair amount of him, I wanted to stay on those easy terms.

'Just as well, dearie, because you'd be batting on a very dodgy wicket with that one. All Cassie's got to do is bat her eyelashes and reach for his flies and T.C.'s a goner, an absolute goner. Always has been.'

Sylvia smiled, but her eyes remained watchful. 'Cassie can't help herself either. She may have a dozen men on her hook, but it's always T.C. she goes back to. He must be good in bed or something. He certainly has no money to speak of, and with our Cassie, it's usually money that talks.'

I didn't know what to say. I simply stared at Sylvia for what felt like ages but was probably only moments. She smiled again, still without a trace of humour, and said, 'Another round of drinks for me and the boys, and make it snappy.' She paused for a heartbeat. 'There's a good girl.'

'What got into Miss Nasty Knickers over there?

135

What did she say to you to upset you?' Sugar swiftly cleared his tray of empty glasses and began to put fresh ones on it as I poured them.

'The silly woman seems to think I carry a torch for T.C.,' I said with as much dignity as I could muster, with my knees wobbling beneath my beautiful dress. 'Any fool can see that it's Cassie he wants, even if I did have ideas, which I don't.'

It seemed to me at that moment that no matter what anyone did, even dress me in the most beautiful frock in the entire world, they'd still never be able to turn this particular sow's ear into a silk purse – however hard they tried. I felt something warm run down my cheek, trickle round to my chin and make a tiny 'ping' as it dripped on to the rim of the empty glass I was holding. I felt Sugar's warm hand take the glass from me and put it on the bar, then he gently dabbed at my tears with the sparkling white linen tea towel we kept for polishing the glasses.

'Don't drip on your frock, sweetie, it'll leave wet marks on your silk.' He leaned closer and whispered in my ear. 'And that prat T.C. will come to his senses, you'll see. He's more than halfway there already. This is just a hiccup, a tiny little hiccup.'

He pulled back again and grinned his lovely, huge grin and said louder, 'Now you go home to Peace and I'll take care of that little bitch Sylvie. It's time she and the boys buggered off and left me and the Behans and their pals to a nice night of pure Irish whiskey and even purer Irish blarney.' He patted my shoulder and gave me a little shove towards the door. 'See you tomorrow, sweetie. Pleasant dreams.'

I walked slowly up the stairs and put my key quietly into the lock, so as not to wake Peace, then crept in and made ready for bed. Once I'd hung up my dress, I wrapped myself in my velvet dressing gown and tiptoed to Peace's door. She'd left it slightly ajar and I could hear her breathing softly. I was soothed enough to go to bed and straight to sleep myself.

14

Life settled into a rhythm over the next few weeks. Peace and I became used to living together and sorted out the routine that suited us best. Sugar, knowing Bandy better than anyone, picked the day after their very public row in the bar to approach her about letting Peace continue her education at a day school. He also suggested the Saturday job at the cafe.

'She'll be feeling guilty about letting her mouth get away from her and casting her nasty suspicions everywhere except where they belong,' Sugar assured Peace and me when he saw us the next day. 'She'll want to make amends, mark my words. I'll catch her the minute she emerges from bed. She's always at her most fragile then. What with the guilt and the hangover, it'll be easy. What's more, if I get between her and her first coffee and fag of the day, she'll agree to almost anything just to get at them.'

He was right, too. Sugar had Bandy's agreement to both plans within minutes of her ungluing her reluctant eyes, or so he told me at our next sewing circle. Neither did it take long to find Peace a place in a day school at Marylebone. Bandy grumbled a bit, but it had no heat in it. Peace had won the battle of the schools, and Sugar and I privately believed that she'd never go back to St Matilda's, except to pick up her things.

Getting Bandy's agreement to Peace's Saturday job was easy too. Bandy approved of Peace earning some of her own money and taking some responsibility for providing for herself. 'According to her ladyship, "It's the Bunyan way," apparently, "to encourage hard slog in its young,"' Sugar reported. 'Only it doesn't seem to have taken with Band. Well, not lately, anyway,' he added bitterly.

So it was settled. Peace started at her new school, and although she was quiet and shy, she managed to make one or two friends almost immediately. She joined the school music and chess clubs, both after-school activities, and that helped a lot.

Her two favourite friends, Beatrice and Angela, came to tea with us occasionally, and Peace went to tea with them. The girl blossomed. Her solemn little face began to light up with laughter as she giggled and gossiped with her chums and her manner became much more relaxed generally.

Peace's friendship with Bubbles Wong also grew steadily, although Bubbles rarely came to tea. When she did, she was very shy and quiet if I stayed in the room, so I tended to serve them up a little something then disappear for an hour or two to let them get on with it. I'd go to visit Madame

Zelda, or Maggie and Bert, or perhaps one of the Campanini girls – Gina was my favourite.

Bubbles would usually thank me very politely before she left, but she always left immediately I returned. The kitchen would be spotless after one of her visits, her mother having taught her well. I know that Peace really appreciated the opportunity to speak her mother tongue and that that was a huge bonus in her new life. She also enjoyed Mrs Wong's cooking enormously, and would relay what she'd had to me. Not that it meant much, as I'd never eaten Chinese food. Peace was horrified when I told her I had never tasted crispy duck or noodles.

The following Saturday she came home from work with cooking equipment borrowed from Mrs Wong. She called the strange, dish-shaped pan a 'wok' and had a set of bamboo steamers as well. Her bag bulged with strange ingredients that I didn't recognize. She'd saved some of her earnings especially to buy them.

'Mrs Wong has taught me how to make some of my favourite dishes and I shall make some for you tomorrow,' Peace told me. 'It is terrible that you have never tasted Chinese food. I have asked Mr Sugar and Aunt, but Aunt cannot come because she has to go somewhere with Mr Malcolm.' Peace paused and gave me a sly look. 'So I asked Mr T.C. when he came into the cafe today, because I know that you like him.'

Like an idiot, I blushed. 'Of course I like him,' I protested, 'he's a very nice man. Everybody likes T.C.'

'Yes, that is true, but you like him very much, I

think.' Peace grinned a wicked grin. '*Very* much.'

'What makes you say that?' I asked defensively.

Peace pretended to think, forefinger to her lips and eyes pointed to heaven, as if for inspiration. 'Well, let me see...' She ticked off each of her reasons on her fingers. 'You go a funny red colour when you see him. You get flustered, too. You always listen carefully when his name comes up in conversations, even if they are not your own. You are always looking towards the door when you are in the cafe, but you stop looking when he comes in.'

I hadn't realized I was quite so transparent. It seemed that everyone *and* his brother or sister knew that I carried a torch for T.C., except the man himself, that is. He'd been friendly enough, but there had not been another attempt to kiss me, or even to be alone with me. And now I had to face the fact that he was seeing Cassie again.

I tried to be nonchalant, but my pride was injured. 'Did T.C. accept your invitation?' I asked at last. I simply had to know.

'Yes he did,' Peace beamed. 'But Mr Sugar has cancelled. He has to go somewhere suddenly. He didn't say where, but I think he goes to meet his lover.'

'Peace!' I said, a little shocked. 'What do you know of such things?'

Peace gave me a withering look. 'I am not a baby, Aunt Liz, and Mr Sugar did look very happy for a man who was giving up a free dinner.' Peace paused. 'He asked me to give you his apologies, but there will be no sewing tomorrow, either.' She grinned. 'So you can devote your attention to Mr T.C. exclusively.'

It turned out to be a very pleasant afternoon. As promised, Peace kept herself in the kitchen and left T.C. and me to chat as we ate. The meal began with tiny bowls of clear soup. Just a very few slices of some kind of cabbage and spring onion, so thin that they were virtually transparent, floated in the tasty liquid. There were also dumplings that we chased around our bowls with chopsticks for ages, until we were helpless with laughter and Peace had to come in and teach us how capture them. I settled for spearing mine. It was very effective as long as I could stop them from slithering about, which I did by using a finger to anchor them.

'That's cheating, that is,' T.C. told me, as his dumpling leapt from under his chopstick, shot across the rim of his bowl and landed with a plop on the carpet in front of the gas fire.

'And that's sloppy,' I said, popping my dumpling into my mouth, then gasping as I bit into it and steam escaped in a little cloud.

'No, no, no, Aunt Liz, you hold the dumpling between your chopsticks thus,' Peace explained patiently. 'Then you bite into it a little, to let the steam escape, then more small bites until it cools and then you eat the rest at once.' She demonstrated, but the moment she was gone, we each resorted to our favoured method and used our fingers, licking them clean before our tutor could tell us off.

Those dumplings were delicious. They were stuffed with a spicy mixture I found hard to identify, but T.C. thought was pork. The soup itself had a subtle flavour of good chicken stock, herbs and a very few vegetables. Next came crispy duck, supplied by Mrs Wong already cooked. She, in turn, had got it from her cousin who cooked for the Chinese restaurant that catered for the local Chinese workers. Or so Peace told us. 'It would have taken a very long time to cook it here and so that is what we did. But I made the sauce and the vegetables,' Peace told us proudly. 'And next you will have my special noodles.'

T.C. and I ate our meal with appreciation. Peace's cooking was so good, and the blend of flavours and textures was so subtle, it was hard to describe because it was all so new to us. Peace beamed with happiness and pride as she cleared each emptied bowl and listened to our praise and grateful thanks.

I was a convert to Chinese food and told her so. 'I'll be expecting more now that I've tasted it, Peace. It's absolutely delicious. No wonder you haunt Mrs Wong's table. I would too – if only she'd have me.'

'I second that, Peace,' said T.C. 'You'll make prospective husbands very happy indeed when they find out you can cook like this. You'll be beating the young hopefuls off with clubs. Beauty and cooking skills are a winning combination.'

T.C. and I chatted idly about the people we knew as we ate and drank fragrant jasmine tea. Eventually, we got around to the continued thieving from the club till and stockroom.

'He's a crafty beggar. Nobody's managed to catch him at it, so now I've left some specially marked bottles and the same with some bank notes. We're going to leave a float of marked notes in the till when it's not being used during business hours. Then, if and when they begin to disappear, we'll try to think of some way of checking our main suspect's sideboard for the bottles and wallet for the lolly,' T.C. explained.

'That's the tricky bit. Sugar thinks he can get a look in Malcolm's wallet when he's otherwise engaged with Bandy, but the sideboard's more of a challenge. Getting into his flat may not be that easy. Mind you, it helps that Maltese Joe is his landlord. Sugar says he thinks he'll hand over a master key if he's approached right.'

I was intrigued. 'How have you marked the notes and bottles without being too obvious? Surely if he sees a whole load of notes with pen marks on them or bottles with crosses on, he'll twig.'

T.C. nodded. 'That's why I used that invisible ink that they sell to kids who want to play French Resistance, British Spies or Sexton Blake or whatever it is kids play nowadays. They sell it in Hamley's; it shows up if you apply a little acid. Lemon juice will do, and there's always plenty of that in the bar. I got some invisible ink for Rosie last Christmas, that's how I know about it. She loved it. All you've got to do is rub a little slice of lemon on the top left-hand corner of a suspect note and if the letters "SPF" show up – they're Sugar's initials of course – then it's one of the planted notes. I've also written down their serial numbers, just to double-check if we find any of our notes in circulation. If one of them does show up, make a record of who gave it to you, will you?

Then pass it on to me. I'll look into it.'

I agreed that I would. 'How do you like being a private eye?' I teased. T.C. didn't seem to fit the part somehow. 'How's the posh lady's erring husband?'

'Actually, I don't mind it at all. As you so rightly said, looking into things was my stock-in-trade, after all. So far, the erring husband is sticking pretty close to home. Maybe he's got wind of his wife's interest, or the fling he was having is over, if he was having one that is. Funny thing is, I could swear I've seen him before, but I can't for the life of me think where.'

T.C. stared at the last piece of crispy duck clenched between his chopsticks. I'd resorted to a knife and fork myself, much to Peace's disgust. 'Still, I expect it'll come to me.' He grinned, looking just like his daughter for a moment.

We ate in companionable silence for a while, then he asked, 'And you, how are things going with you?'

'Very well, thanks. Peace has settled in nicely. She's made a few friends, including Mrs Wong and her family. She goes there a lot. It must ease her homesickness quite a bit to hear and speak Cantonese and eat childhood foods. I know I find bread and butter pudding a real comfort. My Auntie Elsie used to make it for me specially when I was a kid. What's your favourite childhood food?'

'Jam roly-poly and custard,' T.C. answered promptly. For some reason, I wasn't surprised. He was just that kind of man. Once we'd finished our meal, we helped Peace to clear up. Then T.C. escorted her round to the Wongs' and I was left at a loose end. The flat felt very lonely when they left, and I was forced to do some ironing to take my mind off it. It had been a nice afternoon and it seemed to me that T.C. and I had finally got over all trace of embarrassment in each other's company, which was a relief. Naturally, I had been itching to ask how his relationship with Cassie was working out, but I didn't like to appear too interested, in case it led to more uneasiness between us.

It seemed that Toothy had now taken up with Sylvia. Sylvia said she'd ditched Sharky Finn when she caught him with another woman, but rumour had it that he'd simply drifted out of her grasp as he was wont to do. Nobody could nail Sharky Finn down, not even the wife, children and mother-in-law he was rumoured to have stashed away in Golders Green – or was it Finchley? I was never sure, because nobody had ever actually clapped eyes on them.

Harry, the man with the glasses, had only been to the club the once. Neville was much more in evidence around Cassie most evenings, according to Sugar, and T.C. didn't like Neville one little bit. The feeling appeared to be mutual. Neville lacked enthusiasm for T.C., sensing that he was, in fact, his only serious rival for Cassie's attention. It was a muddle all right. Although I yearned to know quite how T.C. fitted into it, I hadn't had the nerve to ask him.

Everyone had their theories, however. Peace, who saw a lot of Rosie when she worked at the cafe, said that Rosie had high hopes that her mother and father might eventually settle down together, but that her Auntie Maggie was much less certain. Maggie believed that T.C. hovered around more out of pity than anything. Madame Zelda agreed and said her crystal ball didn't suggest that Cassie would end up with T.C., but she would find herself in a mansion 'out in the sticks somewhere'. Madame Zelda said she'd seen it as clear as day when she was crystal gazing for someone else entirely.

'Poor girl came to hear about her own love life and all I could tune into was Cassie's. It was bloody annoying, and in the end, I had to give up on the ball and do her tarot instead. I even had to throw in a free palm reading, to make up for the inconvenience.'

Freddy and Antony were also convinced that T.C.'s interest in Cassie was on the wane. 'You can tell, ducky, the eyes don't linger the way they used to. He beats a retreat as soon as the bevvy she's taken on board begins to show. He almost breaks his leg getting out of there. I've seen it, and so has Ant, haven't you?' Freddy turned to his friend for corroboration and got it.

'It's true, Liz dear,' Antony assured me languidly, 'there's none of the lingering looks that used to make him look like a lost puppy.'

'And the sparks *do* fly from the cove's heels if Cassie begins to look even the slightest bit the worse for wear. Ant and I think the stream of men gets to him too,' Freddy told me earnestly. 'Don't we, Ant?'

Antony didn't manage to speak before Freddy continued. 'It's true, sweetie. He couldn't complain when he was married to Pat. Bugger wouldn't have had a leg to stand on.' Freddy's

146

hand flew to his mouth and his eyes widened as he realized what he'd said. Pat had been crippled by creeping paralysis, or multiple sclerosis as I believe it was called. It meant that she spent much of her life in a wheelchair towards the end, and on crutches before that.

Sugar was convinced that he saw shy interest in T.C.'s eyes when they lit on me, but I have to say I hadn't noticed it myself and believe me, I was looking. Personally, I couldn't shake the feeling that somehow Cassie and T.C. were bound together and it would take more than me to unravel them. Even so, I couldn't quite extinguish the memory of the almost-kiss and the feelings it had kindled in me, however hard I might have tried to deny them.

As I ironed my blouse for work that evening, I wished and wished I'd brought the subject of Cassie up, so that I could put myself out of my misery by finding out if there was any hope for me. But I hadn't. Then another thought occurred to me. I hadn't felt a feeling as positive as hope since my Jenny had died. Now that I had found it again, perhaps I wasn't prepared to give it up.

15

Relations between Peace and Bandy were much more cordial once Peace was settled into her new routine and home. To begin with, Peace was not as dependent, having made some friends. Being out at school all day helped, too. She was diligent about her work at the cafe as well, and Maggie was very pleased to have taken her on.

'She's a good little worker, the customers like her, and what's more, she's sweet with Rosie,' Maggie informed me with a large smile. 'It's a case of "Peace says this" and "Peace does that" with our Rosie at the moment. She hero-worships her. She follows Peace around like a puppy, and Peace is very good, always taking time with her and treating her like someone of her own age. It's really sweet. It's as if Rosie's found herself a big sister.'

I noticed that I saw more of Rosie, too, now that she could come to Peace for help with her homework, especially the sums. And Rosie returned the favour by helping Peace with her written English, which sometimes seemed stilted. Had all been well, it would have been Jenny that shared the trials of homework. Although the thought brought a lump to my throat, it didn't feel as desperate as it once would have done. I was simply glad that Peace and Rosie had each found a friend, or an honorary sister.

Peace spent more time out and about once spring came and the evenings began to draw out a bit. She'd meet Bubbles after school and they'd repair to the milk bar for a good gossip and the general chit-chat so loved by adolescent girls and, come to think of it, girls of all ages. There is nothing like having a really good girl or woman friend, because we tell each other all the things we wouldn't dream of telling our parents or our husbands.

Occasionally, they'd go to the cinema. We

quickly came to an understanding that evenings out were fine as long as certain rules were observed, and they were that she was home by nine on a school night and ten on a Friday or Saturday, and that all homework must be completed to the satisfaction of her teachers. Or else. I don't think we ever discussed what the 'or else' would be, because the occasion never really arose.

I was mildly surprised the first time Peace missed her weekday curfew. It was only by a quarter of an hour the first time, so I let it go with only a mention. It was more serious the second time: half an hour. I discussed the problem with Maggie, the person I discussed all child-related topics with. I admired the way she'd brought up Rosie, so was happy to receive any tips and hints she might give me.

'Peace has started being late in on a week-night,' I confided to my friend. 'Just a couple of times, but still it's not like her.'

Maggie grinned knowingly. 'I think I might know what that's about,' she said. 'She's got a crush on someone. Rosie let it slip.'

'She never said a word to me.' I felt just a little put out. After all, we saw each other daily.

'Well, she wouldn't, would she?' Maggie laughed. 'That's kids for you, once they get past being round your knees that is. The bigger they get, the less you know. Welcome to the club. You're always the last to know anything – it goes with the job of bringing the little buggers up.'

'What else did Rosie tell you?' I asked.

'Not a lot.' Maggie took a sip of her hot tea and thought for a moment. 'Rosie says Peace thinks he's gorgeous, but that he hardly noticed she was there at first. Rosie thinks he's paying a bit more attention now though.'

'What makes her think that?' I couldn't help it, I had to know, even if it did make me a terrible snoop. I was, after all, responsible for the girl in a way, even if Bandy was her proper guardian. That's what I told myself anyway.

'Peace told Rosie that they had met up at the milk bar a few times and gone for walks and things.'

I felt the stirrings of anxiety at the back of my mind, and then shook myself. There was nothing I could do, especially as I wasn't supposed to know anything at all about it. Peace had only been late a couple of times and it wasn't as if she'd rolled in after midnight or anything like that. I decided to keep a discreet eye on her, just the same.

That Saturday night the usual crowd was in, plus a few theatrical types who came with Freddy and Antony and one or two old wrestling pals of Bobby Bristowe. Bobby, like T.C., had time off from watching the erring husband, because said husband and his wife were at their country seat for a few weeks.

'He's been as good as gold, anyway,' said Bobby. 'My Pansy reckons he's twigged that his good woman is on to him and he's keeping his head down for a bit. That's what Pans reckons.'

'I did see him with that little crowd at the casino, more than once,' T.C. added thoughtfully, 'and then there's another little mob at the Mayfair Club, but I've yet to see him single out any one of the females. He always takes a cab home by himself. I reckon if he doesn't do something soon, we'll get the order of the boot. I've told her more than once that she's wasting her money, but she seems to think it's worth it at the moment. I feel a fraud, though, as if I'm taking her money under false pretences.'

'Hold hard there, mate. We do the work, we put in the hours, it ain't our fault the bugger's faithful. 'Scuse my French.' Bobby's eyes darted around guiltily. His Pansy didn't like him swearing. When he saw she wasn't there, he relaxed a little.

'True, true.' T.C. looked vague. 'Just the same, I do feel a fraud. The lady said she'd call me if he makes a trip away from the jolly old family seat. So until then, we're free.' He didn't sound very happy about it, though. I think that T.C. had enjoyed being employed, even if he wasn't that keen on the job. He liked the sense of purpose that work gave to every day. I could understand that, because I liked it too.

The club suddenly filled up with customers, and I was run off my feet for some considerable time. Sugar was doing duty behind the bar and I was doing the waitressing. Bandy was nowhere to be seen, and neither, thank goodness, was Malcolm. That was another line of inquiry that had dried up almost as soon as T.C. had started to look into it.

When Sugar, T.C. and I thought about it, we could date the end of the thefts to the night Bandy and Sugar had rowed about it in the bar. Someone must have tipped Malcolm off that he'd been twigged, because they'd stopped dead and

151

to date, hadn't resumed. Sugar had insisted on paying T.C. for his efforts, saying he'd acted as a damned good deterrent and that he'd saved the bar a bloody sight more money than he'd cost.

I did notice at one point in the evening that T.C. had left Bobby's table and drifted over to join Cassie, Toothy, Sylvia and Neville, and my heart sank. Try as I might, I could only keep half an eye on them as I was so busy running between the tables taking orders and delivering them.

There was a point when I thought that if Cassie draped herself over T.C. any more, he'd be wearing her, but I couldn't get into a position to read his expression to see if he was enjoying the experience. It was only when I finally sat down for a rest and a drink, that I realized that T.C. had gone and so had Cassie.

As luck would have it, I caught Sylvia's eye. She smiled and mouthed, 'I told you so.' I looked away hurriedly and felt the colour drain from my face. All of a sudden, I thought I was going to faint, then that I might be sick.

'Here, drink this,' said Sugar, holding out a glass of water. 'Are you all right?' Concern creased his large face. Close up I noticed he was wearing mascara and just a hint of eye shadow, a discreet and tasteful silver grey.

I took the glass. My hand shook so violently that I sloshed half of it on the floor, narrowly missing my posh frock. After several sips, I began to feel better. 'I felt a bit faint, that's all. Probably not enough to eat or something.'

'Well, get off home now, sweetie. I can finish up here. Get yourself a nice sandwich before you turn in.'

I went upstairs and straight to bed. I tossed and turned, and fell into and out of a fitful sleep that was full of distressing dreams of T.C. and Cassie together. Eventually, my lower sheet wound up in a wrinkled lump that was making sleep more and more impossible. Fed up, I got up to remake my bed.

Before I returned to bed for another stab at some sleep, I nipped out to the kitchen for a glass of water. It was when I was in the hallway that I became aware that the flat felt very empty. I listened hard, and heard not a sound that wasn't the building settling or that hadn't come from the streets. I crept on tiptoe to the spare room and stuck my ear to the door: nothing. I eased the door open a crack and peered into the gloom. There was no reassuring mound under the white counterpane, no sound of the soft breathing and snuffling of a sleeper safely in the land of Nod.

I turned the light on. A pair of pretty, dark pink silk pyjamas were neatly folded on top of the pale, smooth bed cover. It didn't look as if Peace had been back since she'd left after breakfast. I walked into the room and looked around, hoping that she'd left me a note. But she hadn't. I know it was silly, but I looked in the wardrobe and under the bed.

I walked around the tiny flat, just to make sure she wasn't sitting quietly in the living room, reading, or on the toilet. But she wasn't. Still I refused to take it in. I looked again for a note. Peace knew to leave a note if she was going to miss a meal, or be late, or change her day's plans.

She always left a note. But she hadn't.

I think it was then that I began to scream. I couldn't bear it. Somehow, I had lost another child.

16

Sugar was the first to answer my screams. Dimly, I heard him pounding on the flat door. 'Lizzie, let me in. If you don't let me in, I'm kicking the door in. Stand back if you don't want a face full of flying wood.'

It brought me round. I opened the flat door just in time. Sugar flew in, shoulder first and came to a sudden halt just before he crashed through the living-room door, which was closed.

'Sweetie, what is it?' He looked around, wild-eyed, for possible assailants, rapists or just plain cat burglars. But he found none of them, just me looking ashen and forlorn in the doorway to Peace's bedroom.

I motioned towards the empty room behind me and tried to speak, but the words wouldn't come. So I stood aside so that he could see for himself.

'Where's Peace?' he asked.

'I don't know,' I whispered, then staggered a bit with the effort and had to sit down on the corner of her immaculate bed.

Sugar stared at the bed, then at me and then back to the bed again. His large hand raked his hair back in his familiar gesture and he looked puzzled, then decisive. 'Right. You get on the blower in the bar to the cafe. See if she's there. That's the last place we know she was supposed to be, it being Saturday. If she's not there – which she won't be, otherwise someone would have told you – find out what they know about her plans, if anything.

'Then call Cassie's place and get T.C. over here toot sweet. I don't care if he's on the nest. Tell him if he doesn't come right now, I'll be round there to drag him off her. I don't care, just get him here. We need him.

'I'll nip upstairs and break the news to Bandy.' Sugar ran up the stairs two at a time, leaving just a hint of Shalimar hovering on the air. I did as I was told and went down to the bar.

I dialled the cafe and waited, sitting at the bar staring at the rings, ancient and modern, left by damp glasses. I was in a daze. Was I responsible? Had I upset Peace in some way that I was unaware of? Where *was* she? Then I thought it was all my fault. How *could* I have lost another child? How could I have been so careless? Luckily Bert picked up his receiver, which stopped any more questions from arising to torture my already fevered brain.

'Bert Featherby here, and it'd better be bloody good at this time of night.'

'It's Lizzie Robbins, Bert. Have you seen Peace this evening? She's missing.'

He must have heard the fright in my voice, as his voice took on an edge. 'Christ! She was in as usual to do her shift. She had her tea, plaice, chips and peas. Then she left.'

'Was she ... you know ... all right? Did she seem

155

funny in any way? You know, secretive or anything?' I didn't really know what to ask.

'No, I don't think so. No more than usual, anyway. She's always a bit quiet, like. But I don't really get to chat much when the tea rush is on. Maggie'd be the one to notice anything peculiar. Hang on a tick; I'll get her.'

I sat and traced patterns in a damp patch on the bar as I waited, then scrubbed them away in a panic, when I realized I'd spelt out 'Jenny'. Tears welled up and I thought I was going to choke for a moment. I put the receiver down and poured myself a glass of water, took a sip, felt better and picked it up again to hear Maggie's voice saying, 'Hello, hello. Is there anybody there? Hello...'

'I'm sorry Maggie, I was getting some water,' I croaked, then took a sip and resumed. 'Did Bert tell you why I was calling?'

'Yes, he did. Peace did seem a bit jumpy, as it happens. Just picked at her tea, and that girl usually has a healthy appetite, even being so small. The other funny thing, she asked if she could have her next week's wages early, said there was a birthday present she wanted to buy. It seemed reasonable.' Maggie's voice died away.

I felt a lump forming in my throat, then I heard Maggie's voice again. 'I've just remembered. I saw Peace and Rosie in a huddle, just before Peace sat down for her tea. Rosie nipped out for a bit, maybe twenty minutes, half an hour, no more. P'raps that had something to do with it. Shall I ask her?'

I thought it'd be a good idea.

'I'll call you back,' she said. 'Are you at

Bandy's? I'll call back, I promise.' She hung up.

I got Cassie's number from the tattered note-book of telephone numbers Sugar kept under the bar and asked the operator to put me through.

I was just settling down to some seriously morbid and frightening thoughts when Cassie saved me by croaking, 'Yes?' into my ear.

'Cassie?'

'Yes. Who's that?'

'Lizzie from the bar. Is T.C. there?'

'What if he is? What's it to you?' Cassie sounded belligerent.

'Sugar says will he come. We have an emer-gency,' I explained.

'I've got my troubles over here, you know. Can't you sort it out without him?' Cassie's voice was sharp.

I heard the rumble of a man's voice in the background, a brief scuffle then, 'For Christ's sake, Cassie, give me the bloody phone.' There was another scuffle, then T.C.'s voice boomed in my ear. 'Hello, who is it, and what's the matter?'

I explained again. T.C. listened in silence, then he said, 'I see. I'll be right over. Tell Sugar that I'm on my way.' And the telephone went dead. I could think of nothing else to do but sit and wait. I suddenly felt as if all my bones had turned to jelly and that if I attempted to stand, I'd collapse in a heap.

So I decided to wait for the others to arrive, and tried to stem the flow of images of Peace dead in the gutter. Then the stories in the Sunday papers came to mind. They detailed the activities of white slavers who took innocent girls off the

157

street and sent them God knew where to be sold as sex slaves.

My thoughts were shattered by T.C., who burst through the door. 'Where is everyone? What's this I hear about Peace? What the hell's going on?'

I had just finished telling T.C., when Bandy arrived. Sugar was close on her heels and Malcolm was bringing up the rear.

'Where the fuck's my niece?' Bandy demanded, glowering at me as if I was deliberately hiding the girl from her.

I shook my head, unable to speak. I felt this awful sense of dread, which I recognized as exactly the same feeling I'd had when I took Jenny through the doors of Great Ormond Street Hospital for the very first time. It seemed to gnaw at my stomach, clutch at my heart and grab me by the throat all at the same time.

Bandy's eyes blazed and a dark red stain began to move up from her neck to her face, her lips twisted into something resembling a snarl and she made to leap at me, hands outstretched as if to finish the choking job that the dread had already started. T.C. stepped between us and faced Bandy down until she took an unsteady step backwards, her eyes still fixed on me.

Sugar took a firm grip of Bandy's elbow and steered her to a table. 'Sit!' he instructed in a voice that wasn't about to take 'No' for an answer. Bandy sat. He turned: 'You too, Malcolm. Let's all sit down, keep our tempers and our nerves and work things through in a logical fashion.'

Everyone sat, except T.C., who went to the cubbyhole next to the bar, filled the kettle and put it on to boil. 'Tea, I think. It won't fuddle brains or fuel tempers like gin.' Nobody said a word until T.C. was seated and everyone had a cup in front of them. Both Bandy and Malcolm opened their mouths once or twice, but closed them again at a look from Sugar. Finally, Sugar invited T.C. to take charge of the proceedings. He nodded and turned to me.

'Start at the beginning, Lizzie, and tell us in your own words what happened.'

I opened my mouth to explain, but Bandy barged in, 'She's let my niece wander off to God knows where, that's what happened,' she exploded.

I had never seen Sugar so angry. He was usually such a gentle soul.

'Bandy, will you, for once in your miserable bloody life, take responsibility for your own cock-ups? If you had been at work, Liz wouldn't have been covering for you at the club. If you had trusted your sodding boyfriend, you wouldn't have off-loaded Peace on to Lizzie in the first place and finally...'

Sugar took a deep breath, only to be interrupted by Malcolm. 'I don't think you should bring me into it, old chap. What do you mean, if she trusted me?'

Sugar ignored him. 'And finally, if your brains weren't so bloody gin- and sex-sodden, you wouldn't have accused Peace of stealing from you in the first place and she would be safely tucked up in bed right now! So, let T.C. get on with it, keep your bloody mouth shut until it's got something useful to say and for Christ's sake,

159

sling that stinking bastard out on his arse, so that we can get on with the job in hand!'

Bandy sat with her mouth open, the ugly red stain having drained away, leaving her face white and stricken. Malcolm's mouth opened and shut but no sound came. T.C. looked suitably impressed by Sugar's summing up, but I was bewildered. What did Sugar mean about Bandy accusing Peace of theft? I asked the question into a deafening silence.

As if Sugar in a temper wasn't enough of a shock, what came next should go into the annals of history. Bandy took a gulp of tea, several deep breaths, stiffened her spine and looked around her as if seeing clearly for the first time that night. But I noticed that she didn't answer the question.

'You're absolutely right, Sugar,' she said, as if no one had spoken since Sugar's outburst. Her voice shook slightly. 'Elizabeth, I apologize. No one can keep tabs on a sixteen-year-old girl twenty-four hours a day, especially not a Bunyan girl. We tend towards wilful.

'Malcolm, bugger off home, there's a good chap. I'll ring you when this mess is cleaned up.'

Malcolm began to bluster. 'Oh, I say old girl, are you sure? I could help, perhaps?'

Bandy smiled wanly. 'You're a distraction, Malcolm. Sugar's right. I haven't kept my eye on the ball, and it's time I did. My niece has run away and I am responsible. Not you – me. I'll telephone you. Now fuck off, there's a good fellow.' Bandy made a shooing motion with her hands, as if sweeping him out of the door.

Malcolm looked exactly like an oversized and

very hairy small child as he trailed towards the door of the club. I'm certain his lower lip was thrust out in a pout as he stopped in the doorway. 'Are you sure?'

Bandy smiled weakly at him, her voice surprisingly gentle. 'I'm sure, Malcolm. I can't function normally when you're around.' She grew firmer. 'Now fuck off and let us get on with it. I'll ring you in a day or two.'

'Well don't leave it too long, I might not be waiting if you do,' he said stiffly, and left.

Sugar, T.C. and I sighed with relief. Somehow, a lot of the ugly tension left the room with Malcolm, and we were able to concentrate on the real problem.

The telephone rang. Bandy's face lit up. 'Perhaps that's her,' she said, hope making her voice sing out above the jangling.

'It could be Maggie,' I said. 'She was going to call back to report what Rosie knows, if anything.'

'I'll get it, shall I?' T.C. said, not waiting for the answer but vaulting the bar and landing nimbly beside the telephone. 'Hello?' He paused. 'Hello, Maggie. T.C. here.' He glanced over at our table and shrugged apologetically; we'd all been holding our breath, willing it to be Peace at the end of the line. T.C listened carefully, interjecting the odd 'Hmm' and 'I see'. At last he hung up and walked thoughtfully back to the table.

'Maggie's sure that Rosie knows more than she's letting on but it's too early in the morning to grill her properly. She suggested I drop in for breakfast and question Rosie myself. Seems as good an idea as any. Does anyone have any idea who her friends are?' We all shook our heads. 'Are you sure? Did she ever mention anyone, even in passing? School friends, anyone?'

'Well, there's Beatrice and Angela, but I know they're away for the weekend,' I said.

Sugar sighed. 'She did mention the milk bar, meeting a friend in the milk bar, but I don't recall her saying who that was. Do you, Band?'

Bandy shook her head. 'All we ever do is argue. Chatting about her pals never comes up. I'm not very good at small talk, young gels, that kind of thing. I wasn't any good at it when I *was* a young gel, damn it, and I'm buggered if I've improved a single jot over time.'

She took a deep breath and finally answered the question. 'My pearls are missing from my dressing table and I accused Peace of stealing them yesterday morning. I don't know what got into me. I was in a foul mood and I lashed out. It was wrong of me. I didn't really believe it at the time.' Bandy looked at Sugar across the table, eyes soft. 'I've been a stinker, haven't I?'

'An absolute cow, Band,' Sugar assured her. 'But there's no reason you can't make it up to her when we get her back,' he added bracingly. He took her hand in his and gave it a little squeeze. 'She's not the first teenaged girl to get into a paddy and do a runner and she'll not be the last. We'll find her, never fear.'

17

If I hadn't been so devastated and frightened myself, I'd have found the sight both remarkable and
touching. I don't think I'd ever seen Bandy cry
before, but she was crying now. She simply
couldn't forgive herself for accusing Peace of theft.

'I was tired and I wasn't fully awake. She'd
nipped in to run an iron over her work clothes.
She said something about the electricity running
out downstairs and she couldn't find a shilling
for the meter.'

I immediately felt terrible. If I'd stocked up the
meter pig, none of this would have happened. I
kept a piggy bank by the gas and electricity
meters and stuffed it full of shillings on pay day,
so that we had light and warmth for the week.
But I hadn't had any change on Friday night, so
I'd left it until I got home from work on Saturday
lunchtime, after I'd been shopping in the market
and had changed a ten-bob note into ten shiny
shilling pieces at the post office.

'We'd been to see Flanders and Swann, you
see,' Bandy continued. 'I'd worn my pearls
because we were going on to the backstage bun-
fight afterwards, so I thought I'd tart myself up a
bit.' Poor Bandy sounded so desolate as she
related her miserable tale that my heart ached for
her. 'Michael had invited us yonks ago and we
were looking forward to it.'

I realized that she meant Michael Flanders. He and Donald Swann came to the club whenever they were performing locally. Lots of performers did, it was somewhere open after the theatres closed and often they were too wound up and excited to want to go straight home to bed.

'I had a hangover. Malcolm and I had had a set-to about some woman we'd bumped into in the bar at the intermission – she was far too bloody friendly in my view – and I was still disgruntled when Peace woke me up crashing about with the ironing board.' Bandy paused again and stared blindly at the floor. I saw Sugar give her shoulders a reassuring squeeze.

'Now, I know I left my pearls in the bathroom when I took my slap off ready for bed, along with my matching earrings. Anyway, once I'd been woken up I went to the bathroom to spend a penny and realized that the pearls and earrings had gone. I searched thoroughly, but they weren't there. That's when I lost my temper with Peace and somehow I managed to accuse her of stealing them.' Bandy's head dropped into her hands and her shoulders heaved.

T.C.'s voice was gentle. 'Then what happened?'

'She denied it, of course. We had words and then she had it away on her toes. Said she was going to be late for work, slammed the front door behind her and buggered off,' Bandy whispered into the silence.

T.C. nodded, patted Bandy's back gently but absentmindedly then squared his shoulders and took charge.

'Right, I'll question Rosie as soon as she's up and

taking notice in the morning. Meanwhile, I think we should report Peace missing. Lizzie, will you check her room again thoroughly and see if anything has gone? We need to know if Peace went willingly, in which case she would have packed, unless she was too upset, or whether she's been taken, in which case everything should be as she left it.'

I hurried back upstairs. It was a relief to be doing something. I checked Peace's wardrobe – surely not as full as before? I riffled through the hangers frantically. My hand trembled as I tried to remember some of her clothes. Her blue jersey dress had gone and the dark green, tweed skirt with the slanted pockets that she liked to wear with a neat, cream twin-set. That wasn't there either.

I wrenched open her drawers. Her underwear was missing, along with the cream twin-set and some other jumpers. Her suitcase was gone from under her bed and her toothbrush wasn't in the bathroom. Finally, after I'd checked the kitchen from top to bottom for the umpteenth time, I had to concede that there was no note from Peace. I slumped in a chair with my head in my hands. I had been so sure that there'd be a note somewhere. Usually Peace left her notes to me propped between the teapot and my favourite cup and saucer, because she knew that I was gasping for my first cuppa every morning and that I'd be at it again in the evenings as soon as I got in from work. I simply couldn't believe that the sweet girl I knew would be so unkind as to leave without a word, I had been so sure that her note had fallen to the floor and lodged itself under the cooker or somewhere, but it obviously hadn't. There was no note. I heaved a sigh and got to my feet, I had to report back to the others.

I reached the bottom of the stairs and was just about to push the club door open when I noticed something white on the street door mat. Someone had delivered a letter at some point and not one of us had noticed. I bent to pick it up and recognized Peace's handwriting on the envelope. My heart lurched as I tore it open and began to scan the contents.

Dear Aunt Liz,

I have gone away. I know that Aunt never really wanted me here and that I have been a very big trouble to her, so it is the best thing to do. Do not worry for me, I am going with someone who loves and wants me very much and who will take care of me.

Thank you very much for everything you have done for me. You have been so kind and I shall never forget you. I hope that fortune will smile on you and that you too will find happiness once again.

Please thank Mr Sugar as well, he too has been very kind to me. Please give Rosie my red padded silk jacket and thank Mr and Mrs Featherby for everything. I shall hold the memory of you all in my mind and in my heart for ever. Peace.

P.S. I hope Mr T.C. learns to love you very, very soon and then neither of you need to be so lonely any more.

I sat down heavily on a kitchen chair and stared

blankly at my yellow table top. Selfishly, all I could think of at first was that I would be sitting there alone again and how much I would miss her. I'm not sure how long I sat but when I heard footsteps on the stair, the note in my hand was streaked with tears and virtually unreadable. I stuffed it hastily in a drawer and looked up in time to see T.C. and Bandy framed in the doorway.

'She's packed her underwear, some clothes and her toothbrush,' I told them and heard a sob from Bandy. 'It looks like she meant to go.' I wondered how on earth I was going to tell them about Peace's note, without going through the mortification of letting T.C. or, indeed, anyone else, read it. In the end I decided to tell the truth. 'Peace left a note saying that she's gone with someone who loves her and that she trusts enough to care for her.'

'Can we read it?' T.C. asked, 'It might help us to track her down.'

I shook my head, 'I'm sorry, it's too personal, she didn't mean me to let anyone else read it.'

Bandy's voice was thin with tension, 'But I'm her guardian, I should read it – it's my right.'

I shook my head again. 'I'm sorry Bandy, but had Peace wished you to read it, she would have addressed it to you and she didn't.' Desperation was making me bolder than I had ever thought possible.

T.C. spoke before Bandy could get a word in. 'That's fine, Lizzie, but can you just tell us if there's anything relevant that may help us to find her?'

'Not really,' I said, 'just that's she's run off with

someone who loves her. She doesn't say who and she doesn't say where. The rest is mainly thanking everyone for their kindness and she's asked me to give Rosie her red, padded silk jacket – that's more or less it. Except for the personal bits and they're between Peace and myself,' I said firmly.

'Right! In that case, all we can do is wait for a chat with Rosie,' T.C. said decisively and we all trooped downstairs to wait with Sugar for morning to come.

18

T.C. and I were at the cafe door by eight, leaving Sugar and Bandy to hold the fort in case Peace came back, field telephone calls and speak to the police when they turned up – T.C. had rung his old chum Smiley Riley, desk sergeant at the nick, the night before. Maggie let us in.

'She ain't up yet, it being Sunday, but I'll give her a call now you're here. I'll get us a cuppa while we wait.' Maggie turned and yelled through the kitchen door, 'Bert, get a couple of breakfasts going, will you?' I muttered a half-hearted protest, it was supposed to be their day of rest, but Maggie would have none of it. 'A couple of extra breakfasts ain't nothing, he's cooking for us anyway,' she assured me firmly.

'What's your pleasure, darlin'?' Bert's voice called back very good naturedly for a man who had found himself working on his one day off a week.

'A couple of full doings for Rosie and T.C., tomatoes on toast for Lizzie here and some toast for me. Thanks, love.' Maggie carried on to the door beside the counter; it led to the stairs to the flat above the cafe. She pulled the door open, stuck her head into the dark stairwell and roared, 'Rosie! Rise and shine! Your dad's here.'

She turned and took her place behind the counter and began loading a tray with cutlery, sugar, milk, strainer, saucers and cups. This done, she went back to the stairs and shouted again, 'Rosie! Your dad's here. Do get a move on, there's a good girl.' She hefted the tray, carried it over to our table and unloaded its contents with practised ease. The table was laid in seconds and she returned to the counter, issued the still invisible Rosie with more instructions to heave her lazy little carcass to the table – and collected a large, steaming teapot while she was at it.

'Tea?' she enquired, pot raised ready to pour.

We nodded and said 'Please' in unison.

Maggie poured and then sat, ready to relieve us of all the details of Peace's disappearance, Bandy's reaction to it and our opinions as to the cause and the outcome. We told her all we knew as we waited.

Our breakfasts arrived a smidgin before Rosie galloped down the stairs and rushed into the room, and Maggie laughed. 'I swear you've got radar, missy. You always arrive with your grub. It's a gift.'

Rosie was quiet, the memory of her early

169

morning inquisition with Maggie obviously still upon her. She looked sheepish and she wouldn't catch T.C.'s eye, or mine. She definitely knew something.

'Morning, love,' T.C. said mildly, shovelling egg and toast into his mouth and chewing slowly. For once, I couldn't really fancy my tomatoes on toast and I had to force myself to take a bite.

'Morning, Dad,' replied Rosie, a shade too politely, and tucked into her breakfast, eyes downcast.

T.C. took a sip of tea and eyed his daughter's curls reflectively, then took another sip before he spoke. 'You know that Peace has run away from home, Rosie.' His voice was quiet, gentle, un-hurried. 'What we need to know is, do you have any idea where she went, or why? Did she go on her own? Can you answer any or all of those questions, Rosie?'

Rosie kept her eyes lowered, her fork stalled halfway to her mouth. She shook her head. The fork continued its journey. She began to chew her bacon as if it was sawdust.

T.C. waited. You could have heard a sparrow cough in Berkeley Square. Then he waited some more; we all did. Rosie began to fidget and stopped eating. Still T.C. waited. I noticed that both Maggie and I were holding our breath. Only T.C. seemed relaxed as he chewed, swallowed and sipped his tea. At last, when I felt I'd burst, he spoke again in the same quiet, unhurried tone.

'Look at me please, Rosie.' Reluctantly, as the expectant silence drew out, Rosie raised her head and looked across the table into a pair of eyes very similar to her own. 'I need you to tell us everything you know. We're very worried about Peace. We know she's upset, and that might make her do something silly.'

Rosie's voice was small, tearful. 'I promised,' she whispered.

'I know, dear, but there are times, and this is one of them, when it's all right to break a promise because it will be best in the long run.'

Rosie didn't answer right away; she looked at her Auntie Maggie instead. Maggie smiled ruefully. 'I'm sorry love, but he's right. Peace could get into serious trouble. We know she had a fight with Bandy and Bandy's very sorry, but she can't say so until we find Peace, now, can she?'

Bert made everyone jump by adding the weight of his opinion. We hadn't heard him come from the kitchen, as we'd been so wrapped up in Rosie. 'Tell him, Rosie. If your pal's in trouble, best we get to her quick.'

Rosie shook her head and wailed, 'But I don't know where she went.'

T.C. nodded. 'I see,' he said slowly. 'Is there any possibility that you might know who she went *with?*'

His daughter stiffened; he'd hit a mark. He pressed his advantage, still in a quiet, measured voice. 'So she has friends. Do you know who they are?'

Reluctantly, Rosie's eyes were drawn to her father's face. They stared at each other for a moment. 'She's friendly with Bubbles, Mrs Wong's daughter. They go to the milk bar together. I've seen them there.'

'I see. Do you know if they planned to meet there yesterday, after Peace had finished work?'

Again, Rosie seemed to hesitate, then said nothing.

'Is that a yes or a no?' T.C. probed.

'I don't know.' Rosie looked at her plate.

'I think you do,' T.C. told her. Then he struck, voice hard and sharp: 'Who did you take the message to?'

Before she could stop herself Rosie had gasped, 'How did you know?'

'You popped out somewhere after talking to Peace, then half an hour later, she walks out of here and nobody's seen her since. So, who did you take the message to?' T.C. insisted.

'Bubbles,' Rosie whispered.

'I didn't know you knew Bubbles,' Maggie said sharply.

'I don't, not really. But I've seen her.'

'What did you tell this Bubbles?' T.C. asked, dragging the interrogation back to the point.

'That Peace would meet her at the usual place.'

'Where's the usual place? The milk bar?' T.C. asked, still keeping his eyes firmly on his daughter.

'No, not after six. The coffee bar in Berwick Street.'

'The place that belongs to Luigi's cousin?'

Rosie nodded silently.

T.C.'s voice was gentle again. 'Was there anything else you told them, besides setting up the meeting?'

Rosie hesitated a shade too long.

'I see, there was. Best to spit it out now, Rosie, along with anything else you know,' T.C. told her.

It all came out in a rush. 'Peace gave me the key to your flat, Auntie Lizzie, to give to Bubbles so she could nip along there and collect Peace's suitcase. She'd packed it but she hadn't wanted to bring it here. In case there were questions.'

T.C. looked around him, deep in thought for a moment. 'Have you any idea what she was planning, or where she was planning to go? Was she going alone, or was Bubbles going with her?'

Rosie's clear eyes began to fill with tears as she shook her head. 'Honestly, I don't know. All I know is that Bubbles was to collect the suitcase and meet Peace at the coffee bar. That's it! That's all I know.'

Maggie grew restive and began to fidget. Something was bothering her and, after a moment's thought, she seemed to come to a decision.

'No it's not, Rosie. Didn't you tell me a week or two back that you thought Peace might be interested in some boy she'd met? Do you know who that is?'

'I told you in secret!' Outrage filled Rosie's voice.

'I thought we'd established that now is not the time for secrets,' Maggie snapped back. 'That's a luxury we can only afford when all our girls are safely tucked up in the bosom of their families, not when they're wandering about Gawd knows where.'

'She's right, Rosie, and you know it,' Bert informed her. 'Cough it up right now if you know anything, or you'll fall foul of me – and that ain't wise.'

Bert adored Rosie. As far as he was concerned, she could walk on water and he'd not be surprised, so it was unusual for him to come the heavy-handed patriarch. It certainly shook poor Rosie up; she went pale at Bert's sombre tone.

'I think it was one of Bubbles's brothers. But she never said. Just said he was handsome and clever. I can't think who else it *could* be; she doesn't know any boys her own age round here. What with school, work and homework, she hasn't had much time for meeting them. She hasn't been here long enough.'

T.C. stood up and walked around the table and gave Rosie a little hug. 'Don't feel too bad, sweetie-pie. I know you promised, but if Peace is in trouble, she'll thank you for it later.'

'And what if she's not in trouble?' Rosie cried. 'Will she thank me then? She'll just think I'm some baby who can't keep her mouth shut.' She sprang to her feet, rushed to the door and stormed up the stairs. We heard a door slam, then we heard it slam a second time.

Maggie, Bert and T.C. looked at each other in a stunned silence. Then Maggie tutted. 'I'm sorry, one and all, our Rosie's got a bit of a temper on her nowadays. I reckon it's her glands. She's coming up to that age.'

Bert chuckled. 'Well, maybe we asked for it. How would you like everyone having a pop at you before you'd had your first cup of tea? I know I wouldn't. Go to her, Maggie, and see what you can do.'

Maggie nodded. 'Rosie, Rosie love,' we heard her calling, as she disappeared up the stairs.

19

'So, what do we know?' T.C. asked, then answered himself. 'We know that Peace planned to leave home, possibly with a boy she'd met recently. We know that she left a note saying that she was leaving with someone who cared for her, but that's the only clue in it; the rest is personal stuff. We know that Bubbles Wong helped her, and there may be a connection with one of the girl's brothers. It's not a lot. Do you know where I can find the Wongs, Bert?'

'Yes. Well, sort of. I think they live above Chang's Chinese Emporium in Gerrard Street, the one with all the pots and chopsticks, fancy silk jackets and little black shoes in the window. It's on the left. If not, then they live next door, above one of those places that are boarded up but seem to be busy all the same. I had to drop her wages in once and an old biddy in the shop took 'em off me. But I know Mrs W. got the money, so there's a connection there somewhere.'

T.C. started towards the door. Bert stopped him on the threshold. 'Perhaps you'd better wait for Maggie. Mrs Wong knows her, and it might make things easier. You ain't seen no one close ranks till you've seen those Chinese folks do it.' T.C. nodded, came back in and sat down. Bert disappeared upstairs.

'I'd better go,' I told T.C., though I was deeply

reluctant to leave. I felt responsible for Peace because she'd gone missing from my home, and I just couldn't shake the feeling, however much my friends reassured me, that it was all my fault. If only I'd kept the meter pig topped up!

T.C. could see that it was a struggle to tear myself away and took pity on me. 'If you've got nothing else on, you could help me make sense of what I find out.'

I agreed immediately. Anything was better than sitting around waiting for news. I'd done enough of that to last a lifetime already. I hated feeling helpless.

'I could use some help to canvass the railway stations, cab ranks and the bus station as well,' he added.

'Won't the police do that?' I was puzzled; it seemed right up their street.

'It'll take them a while to get going, despite my good offices. They'll take the view that Peace has got a strop on and will come around in her own good time. That's what mostly happens in these cases. So they'll take the particulars, then give it twenty-four hours or so to see if she comes back.'

T.C. thought for a moment. 'And I'm not sure it's wise to tell them she may have left with a boy. If they think she's eloped, even as young as she is, she can still be married without parental consent across the border. The police will drag their feet and suggest Peace's guardians rush to Gretna Green to head 'em off at the altar. By the time the police take it seriously, the couple could be on their way back, man and wife.'

T.C. paused, thought some more and came to

176

some rapid decisions. 'It'll be best to cover some or all of the exits while the trail's still warm. And although the Wongs certainly seem to be involved, I'm not that certain we'll find out much from them. As Bert says, they close ranks and nothing penetrates if they don't want it to. We used to call it "The Great Wall of China" at the station. We came up against it whenever we had to question the Chinese about anything. I don't think we ever solved a single crime that involved them. Not that there were many; well, not that we heard about anyway.'

The moment we walked through the Emporium's doorway, it was as if we were in a foreign country. A tiny, wizened lady appeared from a doorway behind the counter and waited silently for us to approach. Her dark eyes were wary and watchful and her expression was utterly blank. Maggie and I waited by the entrance as T.C. took a few steps towards the counter. I took the opportunity to look around. Like the other shop I'd been in, this one was packed to the rafters. Every possible inch was taken up with something. Piled around the edges of the room, on the floor beneath some shelves, were large parcels wrapped in thick, white cotton cloth. Others were wrapped in hessian or heavy paper. There were also some wooden crates. Each was stamped with Chinese characters, in red, or black or gold. One or two had fierce-looking printed dragons wrapped around them as if for protection.

Shelves held china, tea bowls, teapots and a wide variety of mixing bowls, serving dishes, saucers and eating bowls. On others there were large jars and tins containing dried goods I couldn't even guess at, and there was one long shelf devoted entirely to what I thought were different kinds of tea. There were also some brown slabs, stamped with characters and designs that I couldn't identify. Piled in wooden boxes were lots and lots of knives and wicked-looking cleavers, some of them wrapped in brown paper.

Hanging from hooks in the ceiling were bundles of cooking pots, and brushes of various shapes and sizes, from twiggy besoms right down to small jobs that looked as if they were meant for brushing crumbs off tables or dandruff from mandarin collars. There seemed to be a brush for every possible occasion. Several bundles hanging from the ceiling were made up entirely of cloth shoes tied together in pairs, so that they hung like bunches of strange fruit. There were plain black ones and others that were embroidered with flowers or friendlier looking dragons than those on the parcels.

Another bundle was of plain, padded jackets of thick cotton, in a variety of sizes from tiny children's ones up to man-sized. The colours were dull, dusty blue, grey or black. Along one whole wall ran a garment rack filled to bursting with tops, tunics and trousers. One end sported plain, cotton garments for day-to-day wear, very similar to Mrs Wong's working clothes. At the other end of the rack there was an explosion of silk in jewel-like colours, turquoise blue, amber yellow, red, emerald green, sapphire blue, gold. These were the clothes for high days and holidays, those special occasions like wedding parties, betrothals and births.

Almost blinded by the sudden brilliance, I wandered over to a glass cabinet beneath the counter top, the better to listen in to the conversation between T.C. and the lady. The cabinet held smaller items, like combs and pins to keep long hair tidy – some fancy, some plain – and bundles of chopsticks, from plain wooden ones right through to splendid ones decorated with mother-of-pearl. The cabinet was a whole lot more fascinating than the conversation, which was distinctly one-sided.

'We are looking for Mrs Wong,' said T.C., only to be met by an unblinking silence. He tried a little louder. After all, she was elderly and she could be deaf. 'We are looking for Mrs Wong.' Still there was no response. It was unnerving, as if she couldn't see or hear us. I could tell that T.C. was getting a touch irritated and was doing his best not to show it. He tried for a third then a fourth time. He just had his mouth open for the fifth attempt when Maggie's voice made me jump.

'That's her!' she said urgently. 'Over there, just going into that shop.'

T.C. and I retreated to the door, the unwavering, dark gaze of the woman still directed at the space between us. 'Where?' T.C. asked.

'There.' Maggie pointed. 'In that shop. I swear it was Mrs Wong.'

We wrenched open the door. T.C. turned to the little old lady, smiled and thanked her, although what for, I really couldn't say. We ran across the road and piled into the grocery shop I'd visited once before. Sure enough, there was Mrs Wong

179

talking to another woman as they waited to be served.

The talk stopped dead the moment we were spotted. For a second, Mrs Wong stared at us as if she'd seen a hippo in her wardrobe, definitely recognizable but way, way out of its proper place. Then she murmured something to her companion and glided over to us as if she ran on castors. I'd noticed that before. Mrs Wong didn't appear to walk like the rest of us, as if she actually made contact with the ground. There seemed to be no friction at all. It was eerie.

We reassembled outside and Mrs Wong simply waited to see what we wanted, volunteering nothing except a smile and a small bow of polite greeting. Maggie took over. 'We're sorry to track you down in your own time, Mrs W., but we're looking for Peace. She's disappeared, you see, and we're worried.'

Mrs Wong looked from one to the other of us then asked quietly, 'And Miss Bandy?' The implication was clear: where was Peace's aunt, and why wasn't *she* worried?

'She's waiting by the telephone in case Peace rings her, and the police want to talk to her before they begin their search,' T.C. explained. 'She's asked me to start looking on her behalf. Have you seen Peace, Mrs Wong?'

'I saw her on Wednesday, at the cafe, before I left,' Mrs Wong replied.

'And you haven't seen her since?' Maggie pleaded.

Mrs Wong simply shook her head.

'What about your daughter; Bubbles, is it?'

T.C. asked.

Mrs Wong grew very still. 'My daughter?'

'Rosie took a message from Peace to your daughter just before she disappeared,' Maggie explained gently. 'We don't think Bubbles has done anything wrong at all, but we do know she was meeting Peace after Peace finished work.'

'I know nothing of this,' Mrs Wong replied.

'Do you think we could talk to your daughter, Mrs Wong? It might help us enormously,' T.C. asked.

Mrs Wong looked startled for a second, then shook her head vehemently. 'No, my daughter not here.'

'Has she gone away?' Maggie asked eagerly. 'She might have taken Peace, Mrs W. She might have taken Peace with her. We only want to know she's safe. You'd want to know your girl was safe if she went missing, wouldn't you?' Maggie's voice took on a pleading note, one mother to another. 'It's only natural to worry when they're out of your sight, isn't it?'

Before Mrs Wong could reply, a man appeared from the empty shop beside the Emporium on the other side of the road, and approached, smiling and bowing as he did so. He was well dressed in a dark suit, white shirt and silk tie. Speaking in beautifully precise Oxbridge English, he said, 'Perhaps I can be of assistance?' as if there were no perhaps about it. Then he spoke rapidly to Mrs Wong in Chinese, and she answered him briefly. He bowed towards us again, smiling rather sadly. 'Ah, I understand. Children are such a worry, especially the girls. Sadly, Mrs Wong's daughter is

181

not available to answer your questions at the present time.'

T.C. frowned slightly and asked, 'And you are...?'

Another smile, another small bow. 'I am so sorry. My name is Chang.'

'And you're absolutely sure that Miss Wong can't help us because... ?' T.C. inclined his head slightly, all polite interest.

'She is looking after a visiting relative and is away attending to her duties.' Mr Chang smiled and made another little bow.

'And when will she be back?' T.C. asked.

'That is very hard to say, but not soon,' Mr Chang replied.

T.C. sighed. 'Well, thank you for your help.'

Mr Chang bowed but Mrs Wong stood rooted to her spot. She hadn't moved or spoken since he had arrived on the scene. I had been watching her throughout the exchange between the two men. As ever, her expression was hard for me to read, but her eyes were different; I thought I could see fear in them.

20

Maggie and I were very despondent on the walk back to the cafe. It seemed to us that we'd wasted our time in Gerrard Street and we'd come away with nothing.

T.C., however, looked and sounded positively

182

chirpy. 'Don't worry, girls, it was only ever a very long shot. I didn't really think we'd get any help from that quarter. The Chinese folks don't bother us, and they like us to return the favour.'

'Still, I would have thought Mrs Wong...' Maggie didn't finish the thought, but I could tell that she was a little hurt.

'But that Mr Chang didn't give her a chance, did he?' I pointed out.

'What makes you say that?' Maggie asked me.

'She looked frightened to me. It was her eyes,' I explained. 'They went sort of dead and still the minute she heard Mr Chang's voice and they stayed like it. But they were bright and busy before. She was interested in why we were there and embarrassed at the same time, so she kept looking around to see who was watching. Then he spoke and the life went out of them.'

'Did you get your Brownie badge for "Sitting Up and Taking Notice" by any chance?' Maggie asked in an awed tone of voice.

I smiled. 'No, I wasn't allowed the Brownies. Wrong church.'

'Well, in the Scouts it was knots and map reading.' T.C. grew more serious. 'See, it wasn't a wasted journey after all. We've learned that Mrs Wong could be afraid of Mr Chang; that Mr Chang is an important member of the Chinese community hereabouts; and that they both say Bubbles is away. That means one of two things – that they're lying because they don't want us to talk to Bubbles for some reason that we can only guess at, or that she really is away. Either way, that doesn't mean that Peace is with her, any more than it means that she isn't. It simply means that we still don't know.'

'How do you know?' Maggie asked.

'How do I know what?' T.C. was looking puzzled.

'That Mr Chang's an important geezer,' Maggie answered a shade testily.

T.C. smiled. 'Oh, that's easy. The way he glided up, took over and, as Lizzie said, terrified the life out of Mrs Wong.'

'And the way he was dressed,' I added. 'I've noticed that powerful people usually dress well.'

'That's true,' Maggie agreed. 'It's all that money, I expect.'

'I really would like the chance to ask Bubbles a few questions, though. After all, she is Peace's friend, and girls like to talk, they like a confidante. So, if anyone knows who the chap Peace is involved with, Bubbles will.'

'Well, Rosie did hint that Peace was interested in someone not too long ago. I could probe a bit and see if she has any idea who,' Maggie suggested. 'I could also have another go at Mrs Wong. Things might be a bit different if we're in the cafe.'

'And I can go to her school tomorrow and find Beatrice and Angela. You never know, she may have talked to them,' I said.

We walked Maggie back to the cafe in silence. T.C. and I carried on to Bandy's place and found both Bandy and Sugar in the club talking to Bobby Bristowe. Bobby was really upset by their news.

'I like that kid. She'd often drop in for a chat while I was working *and* she'd help me with the

184

dusting. Tell us if there's anything we can do, won't you? Me and Pans – we'll help all we can. We like kids,' Bobby said awkwardly, clutching his duster. He was a shy man. Pansy usually did his talking for him.

'Thanks Bobby, we appreciate it,' Sugar said wearily. The strain was beginning to show on his dear face. Deep lines were etched between his eyebrows, as if they were clenched, like fists.

'Actually,' T.C. began, 'there is something you and Pansy can do. You can help me and Lizzie to ask at the stations, taxi ranks, stuff like that. Until the police extract their digits, they'll not get on her tracks straight away. They'll think it's probably just a spot of flouncing and that Peace will be back right as rain by teatime: it is usually the way of things. However, it won't do any harm to get going while the trail's still warm.' Rapidly T.C. assigned railway stations and nearby taxi ranks to us. 'I suggest you split up at each station and one of you take the station and the other the taxi rank.

'Bobby, how about taking Charing Cross? Again, if you go with Pansy, split up, you'll cover more ground much quicker. Lizzie and I'll take Euston, then on to Victoria and the bus station. Then there's Waterloo, King's Cross, Liverpool Street, Fenchurch Street, Paddington...' His voice trailed off. He thought for a moment, then pulled himself up straight. 'Yup. That's the way we'll do it. We'll start at the closer ones and fan out. It makes the best sense.

'There's no point in searching for a lead if it's already been found, so Bandy and Sugar – you stay here and we can telephone in from each station, report back and then, if one of us finds something, we can decide where to go from there. Is everyone clear?'

We all nodded and headed for the door, ready and eager to get going. I felt sorry for Bandy and Sugar, being the ones who had to sit and worry.

T.C. and I chatted easily as we sat on the tube, heading towards Euston. I felt so much better being able to *do* something that I was able to chat about something that had been niggling me for a while. 'I've been meaning to ask you, T.C., do you know what goes on in those places in Soho that look deserted? You know, the ones with the tatty curtains or the boards? There's always Chinese men going in and out, but no clue as to what goes on in there.'

'Some of them are kind of social clubs,' he said, 'where the men sit around, gossip, drink tea, play this game with loads of small ivory tiles and generally get together. Most of them have left their families behind in Hong Kong or somewhere, and the poor sods get lonely. So when they're free for a few hours, they want to relax with fellow countrymen. It's only natural, really. They often don't speak the lingo, either, which makes socializing outside of their own tight little groups a bit tricky.

'See, they work like stink – I mean, real sweatshop stuff – and grab a few hours a week with mates. The rest of the time, they must be sleeping. So they have these clubs. At least, on the surface they're clubs. They're also benevolent societies, sort of.' T.C. frowned, trying to find a way of explaining something he didn't fully understand himself.

'We had a talk once, from an inspector in the Hong Kong Police. He said that these clubs – Triads he called them – are partly social groupings, with the members mostly coming from the same area of China, and part secret society. They're all things to all men, 'specially when the men are working a long way from home. They arrange marriages, and finance and organize weddings and funerals, that kind of stuff. They sort out jobs, favours, travel plans, moneylending, places to live, health care, banking, gambling, prostitutes, drugs, revenge. You name it, your branch of the Triad'll arrange it – if it suits the men in charge, that is.

'But if they do a member a favour, it is for a price. And members *must* pay their dues, regularly and on time, even if there are no favours. Even some poor sod sweating away for eighteen hours a day in a laundry pays somebody for the privilege. They call this boss type a "gangmaster", and because he speaks English, he gets the jobs, negotiates the pay and takes a large cut. That's what the inspector said. The only thing is...'

T.C. paused. 'The only thing is, the members can't resign. It's not allowed and I *mean*, not allowed. To leave your Triad without permission, apparently, is asking to have your right to breathe rescinded on a permanent basis.'

'Is that a copper's way of saying they risk being killed?'

T.C. laughed and crinkled his face at me. I liked the way he did that. 'Our stop,' he said and stood up. He offered a hand to steady me as I rose and the train stopped rather abruptly.

No one at the ticket office in Euston remembered a small Chinese girl with a suitcase buying a ticket and no one at the barriers remembered letting anyone fitting her description pass on to a train. T.C. had no better luck with the cab rank. No one had picked her up or even seen her. We rendezvoused at the buffet and resumed our chat over a cup of tea and a rather tired British Railways Chelsea bun.

'So, have you ever been in one of these social clubs or dens of iniquity or whatever they are?' I asked. I was really interested.

'A few times, I suppose, a very few. When I was on the Force, we'd be informed of some sort of fracas at one of those places, but it'd mostly melt away before we'd arrive, and we'd find a couple of harmless old chaps having a peaceful game of mah-jong – the game with the tiles.'

His voice grew sombre. 'But there were stories. Gruesome ones. Once or twice officers found little bits of Chinamen strewn all over one of the gambling clubs and their spokesman would assure us that it was merely a little local difficulty that they'd sort out amongst themselves.

'They did, too. More bits of Chinamen would turn up somewhere else and then it would all go quiet again. We'd never find out what it was about, let alone who did it. Never a hint, never a whisper, nothing. Getting information really is like chatting up a brick wall, only you'd get more change out of the wall. No wonder the powers that be on the Force just tend to let them get on with it. Their view is, if the Chinese want to kill each other – fine, as long as it doesn't spill out on to the streets and involve us in any way.'

'What's your view?' I asked.

T.C. stared at the wall for a moment, choosing his words carefully. 'I believe that no human being should be allowed to kill another unless his or her life, or the lives of their loved ones, depends upon it. Simple as that. I don't care if they're Chinese, Maltese, Jewish, African, Indian or English, Welsh, Scottish or Irish, I think basic humanity should apply to every living soul. If Hitler didn't teach us that, then all those men, women and children died for nothing and that doesn't bear thinking about. It makes us animals. Worse; animals don't do murder, mass or otherwise, simply for the sake of it.'

I thought about his answer and realized that I agreed with him. 'What about the death penalty?'

'I don't see why another killing somehow magically evens the score. One more murder doesn't pay for the murder or murders that led to the execution in the first place. I mean, the victim's still dead, the family's still grieving. Hanging – just because it's official – doesn't make it right, in my book.'

T.C.'s voice grew passionate. 'There's been too many bad calls for hanging to be right. Look at that poor, simple boy, Bentley, he should never have been hanged. That was disgusting, that was. Then there's that Welsh bloke who was topped for killing his wife over in Notting Hill, and the main witness against him was Christie. It can be a wicked world, but two stranglers living in the

189

same house is hard to take.'

'I agree with you,' I told him. 'And what about Ruth Ellis? After all, she was a mother. How can it be right to deprive a child of his mother like that? I know she did wrong, killing her lover, but the poor woman was half-crazed with jealousy. They should never have hanged her. The French would have called it a crime of passion and put her in prison, that would have been the best thing to do. After all, she wasn't likely to make a habit of it, was she? Then that poor boy would still have his mother at least and some chance of seeing her.'

T.C. nodded. 'And what do you do when you find you've made a mistake? You can't dig 'em up and say, "Sorry mate, bit of a ricket on the trial front, seems some other bugger did it." And if you find someone else who you think *did* do it, what do you do then? Hang him as well and hope you got it right the second time? Personally, I think that sort of justice is best left up to God, if there is one, and we should bang 'em up in a nice jail somewhere.'

I felt pretty much the same and was ridiculously pleased at our meeting of minds on the subject.

'You know,' I said, 'I've been thinking. Do you think it'd be a good idea to check the buses? I don't mean just the Victoria bus station ones, but the local red buses. You see, the more I try to put myself in Peace's place, the more I can't see her getting on a train to leave town. She barely knows England at all, but she does know her way around London a bit now. She understands the tubes and the buses.'

I heard my voice trail away uncertainly. I didn't

want to try to teach my grandmother to suck eggs, as the saying goes, although anyone less like my granny than T.C. was hard to imagine. 'Besides, it's the only place in which she has friends,' I added, almost in a whisper.

T.C. grinned. 'You should join the Force. You've got a knack of knowing what makes people tick, you have. I think you're right. Once we've done the bus station, seeing we're already here, we'll nip down the local depot and ask a few questions in the canteen. The canteen's the place to find a load of conductors all at once. If we can have a word with some of them, we might find a trace. It won't do any harm to ask them to put the word out among their mates while they're at it.'

We had no luck at Victoria Bus Station either, so we headed back to Soho with a view to nipping in at the club first. If there was nothing doing there, we'd head on to the bus depot. And just for form's sake, I made up my mind to check Peace's room again before we left, just in case she'd slipped in while the coast was clear to have a nap or a snack, or to pack another bag. I didn't hold out much hope, but I'd feel an utter fool if we were trawling London while she was catching forty winks in her own bed.

It was only when I arrived home, once again checked Peace's room in vain and sat for a moment with a cup of tea, that the thought that had been nagging at the back of my mind finally surfaced. I had forgotten to ask T.C. if he thought that Mr Chang, the man Mrs Wong had been so afraid of, could be anything to do with the local arm of one of these Triads he'd been talking about. After all, T.C. had said that wherever there were Chinese folk, then their Triad was right there with them, organizing things.

It was obvious that Mr Chang was an important fellow. Perhaps his importance, and his obvious wealth, stemmed from his position within the Triad. Perhaps he was even the chap in charge?

21

T.C. and I had agreed to meet at the cafe for breakfast. I had to ask Freddy and Antony if they'd let me have time off to question Peace's friends at school. T.C. was planning to have another go at Rosie, but she'd already gone to school. Maggie was very apologetic.

'I called her and she scoffed her breakfast in double-quick time, then shot out of the door when my back was turned, the crafty little madam. I'll have to get her at dinnertime, sorry.'

'That's OK, Maggie,' T.C. said. 'I'll put in some more legwork and chivvy the police while I'm at it. She's been gone since Saturday teatime and they've had well over their twenty-four hours.'

We agreed to meet back at the cafe at about one, and I hurried over to St Anne's Court to beg Freddie for some time off.

'Of course you must help all you can. Ant'll be back from his mother's in Tunbridge Wells by lunchtime, and Monday mornings are always quiet: people are getting over their weekends.

Well, they are if they've had a good time. Mine was quiet, Ant being away. Still, it was nice to have five minutes to myself. It made a change.'

Then Freddy remembered the gravity of the situation and shooed me out of the door. 'Fly, Lizzie, fly and grill those girls for all you're worth. Find out what's happened to our poor little Peace. Don't trouble to come back after lunch if T.C. thinks you can be helpful. We'll manage between us, Ant and me.'

So I flew, to Peace's school. But Angela and Beatrice said that they knew nothing and, judging by their shocked reaction, I thought they were telling the truth. They knew that Peace liked a boy, but they didn't know which boy, as they'd never met him. According to Beatrice, Peace had been very cagey on the subject and they had found that really annoying.

'She said there was nothing to tell because he barely knew she was alive,' Angela told me.

'She promised to tell us if she made any progress with him, but she never did,' Beatrice told me earnestly. Angela nodded her agreement. 'She never even told us his name. She just said she'd met him at some kind of party and that she thought he was gorgeous, if a bit older than her.'

Maggie insisted that we had lunch and a hot drink while we listened to her news. She wouldn't utter a word on the subject until she'd plonked two plates of food and two steaming cups of tea in front of us. Both were welcome: it was cold outside.

'You can grill Rosie when she gets in for her dinner. She won't dare mess around with you, T.C.

'It's likely to become a power struggle if I tackle her, you see. She's just coming to that age where it's a point of honour to argue with me. Anyway, dinnertimes are busy and I probably won't get the chance to talk to her properly until tonight. So if you have a bash now, and get nowhere, Bert and I will have a go later.

'As to Mrs Wong: well, she wasn't very forth-coming neither. I reckon you're right, Lizzie, and that Mr Chang gives her the willies. She does still swear that Bubbles is away with this important visitor, and that Peace is not with them. And I believe her. What she doesn't know is whether Bubbles saw Peace before she left.'

'Do you know who this important visitor is?' asked T.C.

Maggie shook her head. 'You could try asking Mrs W. before the dinnertime rush starts. She's in the kitchen with Bert, bashing spuds.'

'I've got a better idea,' said T.C. slowly. 'Why don't you have a go, Lizzie? She won't find you as intimidating as a man and anyway, you'll be able to "read" her better than me.'

I was flattered. 'If you think it'll help, of course I'll try.'

We took a moment to discuss my strategy and it was Maggie who came up with the winning formula. 'I know everyone likes to say that the Chinese don't have no feelings just because they don't wear them on their sleeves, or indeed, on their kissers. But that's cobblers, of course. If I was you, I'd play on her maternal instincts; one mum to another kind of thing. I know for a fact that she was upset when your Jenny passed away. I don't

194

know if you noticed, but if Mrs W. served you when it first happened, you got larger portions than usual. She was subtle about it, but I saw her topping you up with extra more than once. Now that's not our Mrs W. She may be quiet, but she's got the instincts of a businesswoman that one, and she normally doesn't give nothing away.'

In the end, it happened quite naturally. I strolled into the kitchen, trying to look nonchalant. Bert greeted me cheerfully as he threw several calves' livers into a frying pan and some bacon under the grill. Liver and bacon was the special that day. I noticed the onion gravy keeping warm on the gas and some hot potatoes waiting to be mashed.

Mrs Wong kept her head down and carried on peeling yet more potatoes at the sink with deft, economical movements.

'What can I do you for, Liz?' Bert asked.

'Maggie sent me in here to get warm. I've been traipsing around Peace's school, then stations and cab ranks asking if anyone's seen her, and I'm frozen,' I explained.

'Right you are; thaw away. Put the chair beside the oven and you can toast your toes nicely there.'

I settled myself down while Mrs Wong peeled and Bert cooked in silence.

'Any luck on the Peace front?' Bert asked me eventually.

When it came to it, I didn't have to fake anything. I really was genuinely upset; I simply hadn't realized just how much. 'No, not a dickie bird. She's disappeared into thin air. And Bert,' I wailed, voice breaking because of the real lump in my throat, 'I feel terrible about it. She's dis-

195

appeared on my watch and I can't help the feeling that it's all my fault. Perhaps I should have talked to her more, listened to her, drawn her out a bit. I mean, we know nothing about her life, her friends, her feelings, nothing.'

Tears welled up and began to slip down my cheeks, to land, splish, splash, on my hands, which were clutched tightly in my lap. I could not rid myself of the feeling, however irrational, that if I had been a good enough mother, Jenny would still be alive, and if I had been a good enough friend, Peace would still be safely in our circle, instead of God knew where and with God knew whom.

Bert came over to me and handed me a clean tea towel to mop myself up with; I was really sobbing by then. He knelt down so that he was on my level and looked me earnestly in the eyes, while patting my hands with one of his.

'It ain't your fault, Liz, none of it. Seems to me that the poor girl's always been a stranger, wherever she's been, maybe even in Hong Kong. It was just bad timing that she turned up when Bandy was busy with Malcolm. She's always been like that, Bandy, sort of obsessional. Now if Peace'd been able to catch old Band between boyfriends, she might've been in with a chance. But she didn't, and that's not down to you, Liz.

'I'll tell you what. I'll work on our Rosie later. At the moment, she's a bit of an uncle's girl because she and Maggie are clashing over homework, keeping her room tidy and whether or not Maggie'll let her have this particular pair of shoes. They've got a bit of a heel and Maggie says she's too young and she's to stick to her Clarks. Rosie

196

says they're old-fashioned and that she looks stupid in the clumping great things.'

Bert rolled his eyes towards the ceiling, as if calling upon the Almighty to explain females to him. 'Me, I'm neutral, I just stick me hand in me pocket when we get to the till. What do I know about girls' shoes? I wear your basic bloke's shoe, in black or brown depending, and always have done. Maybe a drop of suede on a posh night out, but that's about it for me. Same with frocks; they either look all right, or they don't look all right – but don't ask me if one that looks all right is better than another one that looks all right, because I'm buggered if I'd know.'

He patted my hand, then groaned as he got to his feet. 'It ain't your fault, none of it. Uncle Bert says so, and he knows. Now I'd better get the liver and bacon on to plates. That bacon's just about to catch, I can smell it.'

I stared at the oven blindly, trying to think of a way of opening a conversation with Mrs Wong. I could hear her knife chopping and the splash and thud as the potatoes were tossed into their pot, then Bert's voice sang out, 'I'll just deliver this lot. Keep an eye on that bacon, Mrs W, and don't let the liver stick. I'll be back in a tick.'

It was a golden opportunity, and I seized it. 'Mrs Wong, do you know if Peace was *very* unhappy? I know she enjoyed visiting you and your family. It must have reminded her of a proper home,' I said wistfully, then suddenly realized I was choking up again. I was mortified. I was on a mission and this was my one chance to succeed. I swallowed hard, willing the tears to go back down and then bloody

197

well stay there, at least until I'd finished what I'd started. I felt a small hand on my shoulder and hardly dared to breathe.

'She always say you kind to her,' Mrs Wong said. 'She grateful for that. And Mr Sugar, he kind too, but Miss Bandy, she not kind. She wishes she had no niece. Same way, Peace own mother, she wishes she had no daughter. It is a hard thing.' For a moment, Mrs Wong and I stared at each other in complete understanding – it *was* a hard thing.

I cleared my throat. 'Do you know where she might have gone and who she's with? If she's safe, but doesn't want to be found ... well, I expect that will be all right. As long as we're satisfied she's safe and, if not happy, at least content where she is.'

Mrs Wong shook her head sadly, and turned away from me. I racked my brains to think of some way to keep the conversation going. 'In the note Peace left me she said that she was going to be with someone who really loves her. Do you know who that could be?' I asked as gently as I could. Again I thought I saw fear flit across her face. She shook her head and went to check the liver and bacon for Bert. I stood up and followed her, the better to see her when I asked my next question. 'Who is Mr Chang?'

Her eyes flew to my face, then swiftly back to the liver sizzling in the pan. She turned it over with a fish slice, to brown it a tad more.

'Mr Chang a very important man, very important,' she answered briefly, laying strips of crisp bacon on to plates, piling on creamy mashed potato beside it, then finally adding the liver and onion gravy. 'He married to a beautiful lady,

Madam Brilliant.'

'I see,' I said, not seeing much at all, beyond the bare facts. 'Madam Brilliant Chang. What a wonderful name. Us women are hardly ever told we're brilliant, or even just plain clever.'

For a moment, the briefest moment, Mrs Wong's expression lightened. 'Madam Brilliant is very clever, and most kind to my children,' she said enigmatically, then dried up as Bert returned to his kitchen.

22

I returned to the cafe to see T.C. and Rosie talking at our table. Maggie had retreated to her counter and the place had filled up with hungry customers, one of whom was Freddy. He signalled rather urgently for me to join him.

'I was talking to T.C. when I came in. When he saw Rosie arrive, he asked me to ask you to leave them to it for a minute or two, so grab a pew, do. He says you're proving to be a natural sleuth.' Freddy grinned at me, poured me some tea and we settled down to drink in companionable silence.

'When's Antony due back from his mum's?' I asked, more for something to say than anything.

'Any time now. I've told T.C. that I'll do a few cab ranks and stations after work and tomorrow if he likes, and I expect Ant'll help. There's a lot of ground to cover with just a few sets of feet to do it.

I mean, Peace is so *young*. For all we know she's been nabbed for the white slave trade. You read about it all the time in the papers. Did you see last week's *News of the World*? All those nice blond English girls winding up in foreign brothels, and even harems.' Freddy shuddered extravagantly. 'And those poor eunuchs! Now that *is* a fate worse than death.'

'But Peace isn't blond or English,' I pointed out. 'Do you think she'd still appeal to the white slavers?' This was something new to worry about.

Freddy shrugged. 'I don't know, really, girls not being my thing, as it were. I find it hard to imagine what those coves would consider valuable in the flesh line. I expect there's a market for Oriental girls as well as blondes. I mean, you could view them as exotic, and there's always a market for exotics. It doesn't matter whether you're talking fabric, fruit, furniture or females, some people crave the unusual, while others like to stick to the tried and tested.' His voice trailed away as the enormity of the situation dawned on us both.

Until that moment, it hadn't really sunk in that Peace's disappearance wasn't simply an unhappy girl's prank. The fact that we didn't even know who she had gone with or where she was suddenly seemed very dangerous. A lonely girl with a suitcase lost in a city would be easy prey.

I felt my flesh crawl as my imagination got to work. But as the beginnings of panic started to creep in, I made myself snap out of it. Working myself up into hysterics buttered no parsnips and found no lost girls. I stiffened my sagging spine, finished my tea and said, 'Excuse me, Freddy.'

I approached T.C. and Rosie just in time to hear him say, sharply, 'Loyalty is a very fine thing in its place, Rosie, but this is serious. If you know anything at all about a boy, a man, or anyone that Peace may have run away with, you must tell me.'

Rosie stared at her plate mutinously. 'I promised,' she said stubbornly. 'I promised not to breathe a word to a soul. And I haven't.'

'I've got to warn you, Rosie, you are starting to get on my top note.' T.C. thumped the table with the palm of his hand, making the china jump, not to mention the rest of us. He was normally such a calm man.

Rosie's eyes were still fixed on her plate, but I could see big, fat drops dripping down her cheeks and her bottom lip was trembling badly. 'I'm sorry,' she whispered, 'but I gave my solemn word when she made me her blood sister. We pricked our thumbs, swore an oath and everything!'

T.C. grew red in the face and had his mouth open to shout at his daughter when I cut in. 'We understand, Rosie, honestly we do. But you must try to understand too. We are afraid that if Peace is wandering about, all upset, with someone none of us know, she might come to terrible harm. Now, you wouldn't want that, would you? So, if you at least tell us who she's with, we needn't worry quite so much, need we? Do you see?'

Rosie finally looked up. She looked solemnly into my face, then back at her father, whose complexion had mercifully returned to normal, then she looked down and wiped her eyes on the sleeve of her cardigan. 'I don't know for sure. She could have gone away with her ... er ... friend, but

I really don't know. She honestly didn't say. She just asked me to give the message to Bubbles, so that's what I did.'

'Who is this friend?' asked T.C., more gently this time.

It made no difference. 'I can't tell you,' she said miserably. 'I promised.'

And this is what we had to make do with for the time being. I knelt down and gave Rosie a little kiss on the cheek and whispered, 'Thank you, sweetheart.' T.C. also kissed his daughter, giving her a friendly pat as he did so, and then we headed for the door. I was just about to step into the street when I realized I had forgotten to find out from Mrs Wong who was the important visitor that Bubbles was looking after.

I told T.C. to carry on and that I would catch him up, then nipped back into the cafe, winked at a very subdued Rosie as I passed, raised my eyebrows at Maggie for permission to enter the kitchen and, having got it, went in.

Bert was nowhere to be seen, but Mrs Wong was there. She was over by Bert's desk, which was wedged into a corner and held a telephone, a large and vicious-looking spike for sticking bills and invoices on, to keep them in one place, and a greasy address book filled with suppliers' names, addresses and telephone numbers.

Her back was towards the door, but there was no mistaking the fact that she was talking quietly into the telephone. I waited and listened, but it did me no good because I didn't understand a word of Cantonese.

Bert's voice behind me made us both jump.

'Forget something, Lizzie?' he asked.

Mrs Wong started, hastily replaced the receiver and turned towards the door guiltily – which told me she hadn't asked Bert's permission to use the telephone. And that simply was not done. No one used another's telephone without permission. It was very bad manners; everyone knew that. Luckily, I was blocking Bert's view, so he didn't see that Mrs Wong had strayed so far from polite behaviour and from his precious liver and bacon.

I smiled reassuringly at Mrs Wong. I wouldn't betray her, my smile said. 'I just wanted to ask Mrs Wong something, Bert. May I?'

'Don't ask me, petal, ask Mrs W, but let me past first, so I can get at me dinners.' I stepped aside and Bert returned to the stove.

'Mrs Wong, I've been wondering, who is this visitor that Bubbles is with?'

Mrs Wong stared at me blankly for several moments, no doubt wondering why on earth I wanted to know. It was a good question, because it was none of my business, but it was something that had been nagging quietly away at both T.C. and me all morning.

At last Mrs Wong decided to answer. 'He important man, very important. He come from Hong Kong for business with Mr Chang.'

'What is his name?' I asked, pushing my luck.

But Mrs Wong didn't answer. She seemed to be weighing things up in her mind, I could see it in her eyes, and a tell-tale flicker told me the moment when she decided against offering anything more.

23

It was early afternoon and the club was looking rather tired and dispirited in the weak sunlight that filtered through the grimy windows high up near the ceiling; it fitted everyone's mood perfectly.

As soon as we arrived, Sugar waved some money at T.C. 'Bandy and I thought we'd better lay in some readies to grease the odd palm, so I got a hundred quid out of the business account. You'd better take it and use what you need for expenses while you're at it.' He glanced at Bandy, to be sure she agreed.

Bandy simply nodded and lit yet another Passing Cloud. Judging by the ashtray, she'd got through half a packet in the few hours we'd been gone. It had been a long morning that had started early.

Sugar was gentle with her. 'You nip upstairs for a bath, Band, something to eat and if you can manage it, a bit of kip. We'll hold the fort between us and see to what needs seeing to.' He looked around for T.C.'s agreement and got it readily enough.

'Good idea, you look all in. Grab some sleep and then you'll be all the fresher to lend us a hand later,' T.C. assured her.

Bandy nodded wearily. It was eerie. She'd been unnaturally quiet and withdrawn ever since

Peace had disappeared. All her normal impatience and irascibility were gone. Her voice was husky. 'I've been thinking while I've been sitting here. I'd better alert the family. You never know, she may have tracked my sisters down.' She laughed a graveyard laugh. 'That'll put a nest of hornets amongst them.' She paused, and looked puzzled. 'Do hornets have nests?'

'I think so,' I answered warily.

Bandy sighed. 'I'd better get to it, I suppose,' she said as if she'd suggested ritually disembowelling herself before her nap.

'Why don't you have the bath, nosh and kip first, Band?' Sugar urged. 'A few more hours won't make a great deal of difference.'

I agreed. 'I'll come up with you and whip up an omelette or something while you bathe, how about that?' I was rewarded by a tired smile and a nod.

While Bandy ran her bath, I checked my flat. It had that unmistakable air of having been untouched since the door had closed behind me early that morning. It had taken me a long time to get used to that feeling when first I'd lived alone. Now I was going to have to get used to it all over again. A lump formed in my throat and I made an effort to pull myself together. I simply couldn't keep on bursting into tears. People were depending on me to do my bit.

Some of my stiff-necked resolve must have showed, because Bandy greeted me with, 'Good God, gel, has some blighter shoved a poker up your fundament?' as I walked through her door.

'No. I shoved it up myself,' I snapped – rather more sharply than I had intended. Normally I'd have considered that being sharp towards Bandy displayed definite suicidal tendencies.

'I beg your pardon?' said Bandy, genuinely puzzled.

'I keep blubbing, and it does no good,' I explained tersely.

Bandy nodded. 'Ah. I see. I understand it relieves tension; some people swear by it. Wouldn't know myself. Tension just gives me a blinder of a headache. Fancy a slug of strong coffee? It'll give you a spurt of the necessary for your afternoon's sleuthing.'

I accepted gratefully. I was flagging after my lunch, and could do with a jolt of energy.

I was surprised that Bandy knew what to do with the coffee pot and the gas ring. I had only ever seen Sugar making drinks or cooking. I don't think I'd ever seen Bandy nearer to the stove than the table. But she was surprisingly efficient. A few minutes later she announced 'café au lait' and placed two large, dark green coffee cups on the table, filled to the brim with strong, bitter coffee and creamy, warm milk. She lit a cigarette with a gold lighter and offered the packet to me. I shook my head. I'd never really liked the habit much. I'd tried it once, but it made me dizzy and sick, and that put me right off.

We sat down and I plucked up my courage. 'Which sister is it – you know, who is Peace's real mother?' I asked. The subject had been taboo over recent weeks and months, and it had been one of the reasons Peace and Bandy hadn't got along.

Bandy blew out a long stream of smoke and stared at the floor for so long, I thought she wasn't going to answer. 'Charity,' she said finally. 'Charity's Peace's mother. There are three of us, Faith, Hope – that's me – and Charity, the baby of the family. And my God, is she the bloody baby! Everyone's still cleaning up Charity's messes for her,' she said bitterly, then added, 'Not that I'd call Peace a mess, exactly; she's a nice enough kid. It's typical that although Charity had her, it's the rest of the family who look after her.'

'Where is Charity?'

'Buggered if I know. She married some Foreign Office johnny with a family seat somewhere in Gloucestershire.' Bandy coughed and I thought I smelt whisky. I sniffed my coffee suspiciously. I didn't want to be drunk on the job. Bandy laughed huskily. 'You don't think I'd waste the Almighty's blessed brew on you, do you? You're a comparative virgin, sweetie. I've seen you reeling after a sniff of the sweet sherry cork. You'll not cope with this stuff.'

I smiled in relief. She was right. I wasn't brought up to it, any more than smoking. I'd never really acquired the taste – though I had tried quite hard with booze when I was younger.

'And where's Faith?' I asked, taking a sip of coffee and enjoying it.

'Northants. She's married, too; a farmer. It's appropriate: she yaps like a bloody sheepdog. Always trying to get people back into line. She hates slackers, stragglers or renegades. Made my life a bloody misery when we were at school.' Bandy sounded sad rather than angry, which was unusual. Losing Peace was definitely having a strange effect on her. I would have expected all bossy action, barked orders and much dressing down of the troops if they didn't live up to her exacting expectations. Instead, Bandy seemed to have collapsed in on herself. She'd grown reflective and melancholy.

'Are your parents still alive?'

Bandy shuddered and her eyes were bleak. 'My father is. He lives in Shanghai nowadays, I believe, with my wicked stepmother. We used to live in Hong Kong when I was a gal. Father was in business. I expect he still is. He's not the sort to retire.'

I whispered, 'You don't like your family much, do you, Bandy?'

'No,' she said, 'I loathe them. My father's a glacial bastard and my sisters are... Well, they are who they are.' Her tone was so bitter, it would have made lemons pucker. 'Charity's as thick as pig shit and half as useful, and Faith could bore for England. That's when she takes a rest from ordering it about, that is. Great organizer, Faith, or so she'd have you believe.'

'Can I help in any way?' I asked tentatively. 'I could telephone to your family for you, if you like. After all, Peace was in my care when she flitted,' I said.

'Good of you,' Bandy said heavily, 'but the gal was my responsibility, not yours. I simply didn't make much of a fist of it, that's all. I'll do the calling. But I'll have a swift dunk in that bath first. It'll be getting cold by now. Next I'll have that omelette you promised me and a drop of shut-eye. Then I'll tackle the damned relatives.' She headed for the bathroom but stopped in the kitchen doorway.

'Thanks for everything, Liz,' she said awkwardly. 'The chat, the legwork, the omelette.' As she disappeared into the bathroom, I got busy with the eggs and an omelette pan. It was a distinctly odd feeling – feeling sorry for the usually terrifying Bandy. I had never expected that at all.

24

The club was more or less empty when I came back downstairs. Bandy was asleep in her flat, and Sugar was off asking questions at the local tube stations. The place looked forlorn, so T.C. and I decanted ourselves into my flat, leaving a note on the door so that the others would join us.

We toasted crumpets in front of the fire, not because we were hungry, but because it was a warm and cosy thing to do. Spring was really nippy that year, and there was an arctic wind in the streets outside. We stared quietly at the yellow and orange flames as they hissed and bubbled and sent off little jets of blue. T.C. turned the crumpet on his toasting fork, to brown the other side. I waited with a knife and some butter to spread as each crumpet arrived hot on the plate.

When we'd divided the crumpets between us, T.C. asked whether I knew where Peace kept her passport; it had a picture of Peace to show to anyone who might have seen her. I went to her room and returned with her passport, a recent photograph and her birth certificate all tucked safely in a crimson silk bag with a chrysanthemum embroidered on it.

'Well at least she's not in a position to go abroad,' I remarked as I handed it over. 'That's something to be grateful for.'

T.C. smiled. 'It depends on who she's with. It's not difficult to get a passport if you really, really want one. It depends on your connections. There's no shortage of dodgy paperwork left over from the war, and some of the men who produced it for King and Country are now producing it for all kinds of other people.

'The Chinese have their own lively trade in bent documents as well, doubtless. The Triads are very well organized, according to that inspector from Hong Kong, and maybe half the Chinese workforce over here are illegal.'

It took a moment for this to sink in. Suddenly I sat bolt upright as a thought occurred to me. 'We haven't tried her old school,' I said, awed by our stupidity. 'She had that friend, the one who left last term. We haven't checked her out either. We should get her address from the school, in case Peace decided to get in touch, or at least ask for help.'

T.C. slapped his forehead. 'Of course. What a bloody fool I am! Do you know the name of the school and where it is?'

I rapidly supplied what information I could, and T.C. charged downstairs to the club to use the telephone. I cleared the plates, washed them up and waited for his return.

He was gone for an age. When I could stand the

suspense no longer, I followed him down. It would be ironic if Peace had simply taken herself back to her hated school. I thought it doubtful, but it had to be checked. If she'd decided to contact her school chum, she still might have needed to get in touch with her school for the address. It was definitely worth a try.

I heard slightly raised voices before I'd reached the last step, and paused outside the door. It was open a crack but I could see no one through it, which meant that I couldn't be seen. One voice was T.C.'s and the other was a woman. I paused, telling myself that I didn't want to interrupt. 'Don't give me that nonsense, T.C. You left without a word, a by-your-leave, nothing. I'm not some tart you can use, then forget about, you know.'

T.C.'s laugh sounded just a touch bitter. 'Oh, I know that, Cassie love, I've never been able to forget about you for very long. Apart from anything else, Rosie's a constant reminder, bless her cotton socks.'

'The fact remains that you can't use me up and then toss me aside when you feel like it. I won't have it.' Cassie's voice was getting shriller and louder as she worked herself up.

This time, T.C.'s laugh was more sad than sour. 'Cassie, I didn't "use you up" as you so delicately put it. Neither did I throw you aside when I'd finished. The truth is, we never got started – you passed out cold more or less the moment your head hit the pillow. I'm not such a cad as to take advantage of an unconscious lady. I prefer the lady in question to be awake, consenting and taking notice. It's like dancing – far better with

211

both parties conscious.'

But Cassie was not to be mollified. 'Then why didn't you wait around? You know I like making love in the morning. It's when I'm at my best.'

'Because, Cassie my sweet, your morning is usually mid-afternoon by the time you've had something to help with the shakes, and I simply couldn't spare the time.' T.C. spoke briskly, but not unkindly.

Cassie's voice was sulky. 'Don't you love me any more, T.C.?'

T.C. sounded exasperated. 'I'll always love you, Cassie. You're the mother of my only child, after all. I'll always love you.' There were shuffling noises then, as if they'd moved closer together. My heart was in my mouth, but it had stopped beating.

I waited, knowing that I ought to make it clear that the pair had an audience. T.C. stepped into my line of vision, and then so did Cassie. They were standing close together, but not touching. T.C. reached out and stroked her hair briefly. 'I'll always love *you*, Cassie, but equally, I'll always hate your drinking. I can't cope with your drinking or the things that it makes you do.' He paused. 'And the things it stops you from doing. You're a gifted person, Cassie, but you're throwing your gifts away.'

'Oh, don't start on that again, T.C.! Boring old fuddy-duddies like you and my aunt are always on about it. So I enjoy a little drinky now and then. So what? There's nothing wrong with that. I rarely start before noon and I hardly ever drink alone. Isn't that what drunks are supposed to do:

nurse their bottle all by themselves? Do I look like one of those shambling wrecks you see in the parks, down the dark alleys?' Cassie's voice was getting shriller by the second. 'I'm well turned-out. I take pride in my appearance. It's a well-known fact that real dipsomaniacs do not!'

T.C. sighed deeply. 'Have it your own way, Cass. I'm not your keeper. Right now, I've got things to do and I can't waste time arguing the toss with you. I left before you woke up again because Sugar and Bandy sent for me. Peace is missing and they wanted my help to try to find her. So, if you don't mind, I'd better get back to it.'

'And if I *do* mind?' Cassie sounded belligerent.

'It'll be too bad,' answered T.C.

My heart started beating again, painfully and hard. I moved at last, plastered a smile on my face and stepped into the room.

'Hello, Cassie, T.C.,' I said, with false heartiness and just a touch too loud.

'Oh bloody hell!' Cassie muttered just loudly enough for me to hear. I ignored her.

'Did you speak to the school?' I asked T.C.

'Yes. They haven't seen her or heard from her. But they did tell me that her friend, Sally N'kozi, had gone home to Africa, due to some family crisis. Peace may have written, I suppose.'

'Who wrote what?' asked Sugar from the doorway. Freddy was with him. I looked at my watch. T.C. and I had been so busy, I hadn't realized that the working day was over.

'Thank Christ for that!' said Cassie with feeling. 'Get me a drink will you, Sugar? Make it a large one.'

T.C. shot Cassie a look of such sadness, tinged with something that looked remarkably like contempt. 'Have you found anything?' T.C. asked Sugar as he passed on his way to the bar to fill Cassie's order. Old habits died hard, obviously, even in a crisis.

Sugar poured a large shot of gin into a glass. 'Anyone else fancy a drink while I'm at it?'

'I'll have a teensy little whisky,' Freddy answered. 'I'm fair frozen. That wind cut through me like knives, duckies, knives! We trolled up and down Oxford Street and Regent Street, doing all the tubes, buses and rattling coves we could find.'

'Rattling coves?' I was mystified.

'Cabs, Liz. "Coves" as in friends, "rattling" as in, well, rattling along,' Freddy explained.

'Yes, but did you find anything out?' I demanded, a shade testily. I was thoroughly rattled myself, as it happened, by the scene I'd so recently witnessed and my unsettling reaction to it.

'Yes and no,' Freddy answered. 'Dennis, the bloke with the news-stand outside Piccadilly Circus, saw a little party of Chinese youngsters hanging about at a bus stop, three of them, two girls and a bloke. It was on Saturday night, when the hordes were coming in from the sticks for a night on the tiles.

'It was damp, dark and miserable and everyone was huddled up in their coats and scarves, but he noticed the youngsters because one of the girls seemed to be arguing with the bloke. The other girl was saying nothing and was so bundled up in her scarf, all that was showing was her eyes.'

214

T.C. looked thoughtful. 'Did he see if they got on a bus? If so, did he happen to notice which one?'

'That's the not so good part. There was a bit of a stampede at his stand and when he'd finished dealing with an awkward bugger with no change, the trio had gone. He didn't see where or how. They could've walked away, jumped on a bus, or they could have caught a rattler or they might have gone down the tube. He said he really couldn't say which,' Freddy answered sadly. 'Sorry.'

'You've done really well.' Freddy looked pleased and T.C. carried on, 'I know the stop you mean; it's by Dennis's pitch.' He thought for a moment. 'The number 15 goes from there, doesn't it?'

Freddy looked baffled, but I knew the stop. 'Yes,' I said.

'The bus to Limehouse,' said T.C. 'It's worth checking out. I'll ask around. Can I use the phone?'

'How about calling it a day and getting some food down us before the club opens?' Sugar suggested.

'Good idea,' Bandy answered for us all. 'How about convening round at the cafe and taking advantage of Maggie and Bert's good offices?'

We all agreed, except for Cassie, who was casually pouring herself another gin at the bar.

25

That night at the cafe, Freddy and Antony had given me leave to help T.C., Bandy and Sugar as and when T.C. thought it necessary.

'We're on top at the moment, ducky, so you take all the time you need,' Freddy told me earnestly. 'Bandy's even offered to pay some of your wages, but for the time being, we've said it'll be our contribution to the cause. We like the kid, don't we, Ant?'

'We do indeed, Freddy dear, so all the help we can give is freely given.'

Bandy had been duly grateful and so was I. I found that working with T.C. in the search for Peace was the only thing that stopped the misery and guilt from overwhelming me. I could not shake the feeling that I should have seen that Peace was troubled, and kept a better eye on her.

'But you couldn't know that Bandy was going to lose her marbles and accuse Peace of theft,' pointed out Sugar reasonably when I told him how I felt. 'If anyone's to blame, poor old Band has to carry that particular can. And I, for one, wouldn't fancy being in her shoes.' He paused and his face split into a gleeful grin. 'Well, just this once I wouldn't. Normally, of course, I'm your man...'

So, on Tuesday morning I was lying in bed and thinking things over. T.C. was due early and we

216

were going to follow the lead Freddy had got from Dennis the paper-seller. I was putting off getting up. Ever since Peace had disappeared, I had found the breakfast table unbearable. I had taken to gulping down a piece of toast and a cup of tea in bed, just so that the gaping hole across the table wouldn't stare accusingly at me.

I'd had my breakfast and was washed and dressed by the time T.C. arrived. As he walked through the flat door, I noticed that his hair was just beginning to grow out of its regulation police short, back and sides, and the natural spring had begun to assert itself once again.

As T.C. smiled at me, my heart lurched slightly. Just for a second, I had to fight the urge to trace some of the deeper lines on his face with my fingertips, to smooth the strain out of them with a little tenderness. I felt myself blush at the thought and made myself concentrate on something else.

Because I worked in a costumier's, I naturally concentrated on his clothes. As I tore my eyes from his face, I noted the fat Windsor knot in his wool tie, and that its tiny flecks of blue, mauve and grey were picked up in the colours of his Harris tweed jacket. I wondered, briefly, who had matched them: him or his late wife, Pat. Whoever it was had an eye for colour.

The jacket was old, but obviously well loved, with its brown leather patches at the elbow and at the cuffs. Beneath it, he wore a blue pullover and his trousers, with their sharp creases, were navy blue woollen worsted. His black brogues were old, much-mended but polished to a dazzling shine. Only policemen and ex-servicemen seemed

217

to get a shine like that on their shoes.

We stood for an age at the bus stop, and as we waited, T.C. began to confide in me. 'I'm worried about Cassie,' he said, apropos of nothing.

'Really?' I kept my head down, conscious that I was blushing with my guilty knowledge of his conversation with her the evening before.

'She drinks too much and lands herself in far too much hot water for my liking,' he said impatiently.

'What about for her liking?' I asked, playing the devil's advocate.

T.C.'s eyes crinkled again. 'Ah, there's the rub. She can see nothing wrong with it. And you're right of course; it's none of my business.'

'I said no such thing,' I retorted indignantly. Well I hadn't, not in so many words.

'You don't have to. I'm not her keeper.'

'No, you're not. But if you're fond of her...' I let it trail limply.

'I knew you'd understand. I *am* fond of her. I hate to see her do it to herself, or to Rosie. That poor child cringes sometimes, when Cassie's around. She's an embarrassment to the kid, even if she's only slightly the worse for wear. And of course, we were close once.'

It was like jabbing a sore tooth with my tongue, but I just couldn't help it. 'I thought you were close now,' I said, a little sharply. 'After all, you did go home with her the other night and I thought she'd surely disappear down your throat at one point in the evening, before you left. Sugar said he hoped she had her name tattooed on her feet, the way she was carrying on.' Which was an

218

absolute lie. I don't know what got into me.

'I don't know why I went. Loneliness, perhaps. There was a time when Cass was the most exciting woman I had ever known. Dear God, when she walked into a room...' T.C.'s eyes had that faraway look of a person gazing back upon happier times.

'But it's been a long time since that Cass has been with us. The one we've got now is sad; desperate and sad. I forgot, or I hoped, who knows? But I shouldn't have done. It's not fair. It's unfair to her and it's unfair to Rosie. Poor Rosie dreams of her mother and me ... well, let's just say she longs to be a bridesmaid.'

I tried to sound bracing. 'Well, it still might happen, you never know. If you love her...'

T.C. shook his head. 'No, that moment has long passed – if it was ever there in the first place. Cassie and I weren't made for a domestic life together. Well, she's not made for it anyway. She's a party girl and I'm a boring old slippers man. I like quiet evenings in, listening to the wireless, maybe half a pint at my local and roast beef on Sundays.'

I nodded in understanding. 'And she likes dancing at the Ritz, gambling in Mayfair, and gallons of gin and caviare daily.' I winced slightly at my bitchiness.

He laughed. 'That's about it,' he agreed.

I was saved from falling into further unkindness by the arrival of two number 15 buses. 'You take one and I'll take the other and we'll meet at the next stop,' T.C. suggested and I agreed.

My conductor, however, was unable to help. 'No, love. I didn't get no Chinks on Saturday night, not going towards Limehouse. I did get a

219

whole load going the other way mind, four blokes, but that was earlier, much earlier, around six maybe.'

I thanked him and hopped off the bus at the next stop. A few moments later T.C. arrived, but he'd gleaned even less information from his conductor than I had from mine. We waited for the next number 15 and I took my courage in both hands and continued the conversation we'd been having when the buses had arrived.

'So, you don't think you and Cassie can make a go of it, despite Rosie's fond hopes?' I tried for a light tone. Half of me was disgusted with myself. Here I was pumping T.C. for his feelings towards Cassie when I should be concentrating on finding Peace. But I couldn't help it. He had begun the conversation, after all. The opportunity to clarify things was there and I simply couldn't let it go.

T.C. shook his head sadly, then his face lit up. 'Ah, here comes the bus.' He stuck his arm out to make sure that it stopped for us.

'Yerse,' the conductor said, scratching his head slowly and dislodging his uniform cap slightly, so that it settled at a rakish angle. 'I do remember them. Two got on and one of the girls stayed behind. She was saying something to the geezer, didn't sound very friendly. The other girl looked a bit scared, I thought. But she seemed to be with the bloke willingly, so it was none of my business.'

'Where did they get off?'

'Limehouse, right down near the docks. Last I saw of 'em, he was leading the way and the girl was following, carrying the case.' The conductor sniffed disapprovingly. 'Didn't seem right – tiny little slip of a thing like her.'

T.C. fished the passport out of his pocket. 'Is this the girl?' he asked, holding the little book open at the right page. We held our breath.

'Yerse. I reckon it is,' the conductor confirmed. T.C. and I breathed freely again. At last, a sighting!

We jumped off the bus at the next stop and caught one heading back to base. I was so thrilled at what we'd learned at the depot, our first real lead, that I even forgot to finish off my conversation with T.C. about Cassie.

Freddy was filling Antony in on our detecting as I walked through the shop door that afternoon. 'I think I'll stick to the rag trade; it's easier on the feet and you get to keep warm. I've trolled bloody miles asking questions. Lily Law are on the case now, though, so with luck and all those lovely boys in blue, they'll get further than we did.

'Ah, here comes "Robbins of the Yard" now,' Freddy sang as I came into view. 'I've just been telling Ant what a whiz you've turned out to be on the detecting front. It's your eye for detail, I'm sure it is. T.C. says you have a gift for noticing things. What do you notice about me, Lizzie dear?' He fluttered his eyelashes.

I smiled, 'I notice that you're taking the mickey, for one thing, and judging by all that fluttering, you're parched and could do with a nice cup of tea for another.' I headed for the kettle.

'See! Right on the nail! Sherlock Holmes has nothing on her, Ant. It's like she was born to it.'

As we enjoyed our tea I told Freddy and

Antony about how Freddy's vital clue had led us to Limehouse. 'So at least we know roughly where she is, if not exactly. All we have to do now is work out how we find her. If a Chinese person wishes to disappear, Limehouse or Liverpool are the places to do it, according to T.C.'

Antony smiled lazily. 'Speaking of T.C. – what's this I hear about you having a bit of a "thing" for him?'

I blushed deeply and Freddy cried, 'Ooh, you pig, Ant! I told you in strictest confidence.' Freddy glared at his friend.

'And I told you nothing of the kind, Freddy!' I protested loudly. 'You shouldn't start rumours like that. Say it got back to T.C.? It isn't even true!' I wailed.

'If you say so, ducky, if you say so,' murmured Freddy as he examined his immaculate manicure once again. 'But you should see the way you look at him. I can't see as how it would hurt, anyway. You're both footloose and fancy free. Never be the one to stand in the way of true romance – or even a quick knee-trembler – that's what I always say.'

I blushed so deeply I thought my eyebrows would spontaneously combust. 'I'm still married to Sid, remember.' It was true, I was; and what's more, I had no idea where he was.

'But in name only, and I'd say that didn't count! Of course, I'm not the law,' Freddy conceded.

'No you're not – and the law takes a dim and expensive view of divorce,' I pointed out.

Antony nodded. 'It's true, they're difficult to get even if your other half's caught with his trousers down and *wearing* the co-respondent.

Trickier still if he's missing altogether. It's just a question of waiting out the time then.

'Anyway, I agree with Freddy. Why not wait as a pair and blow the marriage part? It's only a formality, after all. Us queer folk manage without it all the time.'

'Because I am not after T.C.,' I said firmly, between gritted teeth. 'And even if I was, he's still interested in Cassie and she is still interested in him. So there!' I almost stuck my tongue out; it felt so much like the sort of conversation I had in the playground when I was at school.

'Yes, but Cass isn't the settling down kind, whereas you are,' Freddy patiently went on, echoing my thoughts eerily as he so often seemed to do. 'And T.C. has "married man" stamped all the way through him, like a stick of Brighton rock.'

'Anyway,' said Antony, 'I don't see why you shouldn't look just as good as Cassie any day. You don't try very hard, that's the only problem. Look at your hair and those nails! Have you even heard of nail polish?' he asked severely.

'Yes, I've heard of it,' I snapped back. 'I simply have more important things to spend my meagre wages on.'

'Oh! *Touché*, Ant, *touché*,' Freddy giggled.

'What do you say we make the baggage our project, Freddy? We'll procure the necessary, where possible, and we'll create an overall look for her. Something coherent, vibrant, something altogether different from the Chapel Look she's got at the moment. Let's see what we can make of her.'

'I like it, Ant,' enthused Freddy.

'But I don't.' I was mortified. 'You make me

sound like a pathetic old bag of rags!'

'Not an old bag of rags, Lizzie dear, a young bag of rags. Own up,' Freddy asked gently, 'apart from that pink gown we made, have you changed your style or bought new clothes since your Jenny passed away?'

To my horror, I burst into tears.

Freddy's arm found its way around my shoulder and gave me a squeeze. Antony handed me my tea and a spotless hanky and smiled sympathetically.

'We may not win any subtlety competitions, but we mean well,' Antony assured me. 'We don't mean to upset you, but there's no other word for it: you *are* a teensy bit drab and it's time for a change.'

Freddy nodded eagerly. 'And we promise it won't cost a fortune. We'll get the girls and boys on to it.'

My stomach clenched. By 'girls and boys', Freddy meant the theatrical crowd. I tried not to imagine what they would make of me. Antony must have read my mind: 'He doesn't mean let them loose on you. He means to supply the where-withal; you know, make-up, hair, that sort of thing.'

'I've got my own hair, thank you,' I said with as much dignity as I could muster.

'He doesn't mean actual new hair, he means a riah shusher, a hairdresser, somebody to do something with that barnet of yours. Do you cut it yourself with a pair of nail scissors?' Freddy asked severely.

'No.' It was almost a lie; I didn't use *nail* scissors.

224

'Well, it certainly looks like it, ducky,' he replied, rather unkindly I thought.

'So what do you say, Elizabeth? Let us tart you up, so you are at least a contender for the affections of T.C., and in return, we'll get to turn you from duckling to swan. What do you say?' Antony's elegant frame leaned against the counter as he eyed me speculatively, as if I were a lump of clay just waiting to be moulded. 'And in return, we'll let you abandon the counter to help T.C. whenever he asks, how about that?' he added.

'I thought you were going to let me go anyway,' I said indignantly.

'We were, but I just cheated and changed the rules.' Antony smiled smugly.

'I bet you were an insufferable little boy,' I told him.

'I was, and what's more, I've grown up into an insufferable man as well,' he said without a trace of regret or remorse. 'Ask Freddy.'

'It's true, I can bear witness to that. Once he gets a notion in his noggin, it's the devil's own job to get it out. It's best to let him have his own way. It's simpler in the end.'

'I'll think about it,' I conceded, still in a bit of a huff. But they had a point. I *was* dowdy, even I could see that. I might have had a lively appreciation of colour and style, but I hadn't been brought up to see it in terms of me, somehow. I think I was a bit afraid of trying things out on myself. It had always been discouraged with the most withering scorn.

'Oh, I shouldn't, dear, you haven't the hips for it. You could rest a tea tray on that backside, I'd

225

wear something to cover it, if it was mine,' Mother would suggest. Or, 'Ooh no, not with your complexion. I don't know why you're so sallow; it doesn't run in my side of the family, you know.' It wore away the will to experiment as a young woman, and what with one thing and another, I'd never really got it back.

I sneaked a peek in the salon mirror when I thought no one was looking, but Freddy swept into view behind me and joined me in my contemplation.

'You've got good basic colouring, you know. What you call "rich mouse", I call ash blond. Do something to lift that colour a bit, that's what I suggest. Your bones are good. A bit of emphasis here and there would take your mind off the weakish chin. Pluck your eyebrows. They're too heavy for a little face like yours.

'Colours? Blues, pinks, reds, obviously, and coral would be good, but not grey, absolutely not! You look bloody awful in grey. I'd knock all those browns on the head as well. They've never suited. I've never known anyone who could find so many shades of bloody brown, and not one of them of any use to you. You just weren't made for it. You can't carry it. It washes you out, the same way grey does.'

'My mother always said they were my best colours!' I protested.

'Well, she was a lying bitch then, is all I can say. What I can't understand is why, when you look in a mirror, you can't see it? If it was anyone else, a customer say, you'd be on it quicker than a rat up a drainpipe.' I thought about it. I was good at

226

seeing what suited other people, it was true, but I couldn't seem to extend the knack to my own appearance. I thought I was as plain as ninepence, and nothing on this earth was going to do anything about that. I *did* have a big backside and my colouring *was* a little on the sallow side. My hair was straight and mousy; I couldn't see where the 'ash' came into it and certainly not the 'blond'. I wanted to see it, though, I wanted to see it very much indeed, but still couldn't make the leap and come out and say so. I didn't need to. Freddy was planning anyway.

'I think we should start with her day clothes and move on to evening wear when she's got somewhere to go – and someone to go with,' he said brutally, as if I wasn't there. He reached for a pad to make a list of my requirements.

'Yes, and her hair,' Freddy continued. 'The riah must be shushed forthwith and given some proper shaping. We'll need an expert to sort it out. Who do we know who gives estimates?'

I was stricken. 'And who do we know who will pay for it all, pray?' I asked, with more than a drop of acid.

'That's easy. You! You can pay on the instalment plan. We'll stop a modest sum weekly from your wages and, before you know it, it'll be paid for.' Antony had obviously been giving the plan some serious thought.

'With our connections in the schmutter business, we'll get the discount for trade.' So had Freddy, bless him. 'Oh come on, what do you say? Give that Cassie a run for her money, why don't you? Give it a whirl at least. It's not natural to hide yourself and your assets away, the way you do.'

Finally, I nodded. It had nothing to do with T.C., I told myself. I simply needed a change.

Freddy and Antony went into action immediately. 'I'm getting on to that nice buyer we know from Bourne and Hollingsworth, to see what he's got in cashmere,' said Freddy, grabbing the telephone.

My blood ran cold. 'C-c-cashmere?' I stammered. 'I can't afford cashmere!'

'Trade, ducky, trade. Never forget the magic word "trade",' Freddy reminded me from the telephone as he waited for the operator to come on the line. 'And you have no idea how pleasant it is to slip an arm around a cashmered waist and to rest a cheek on a cashmered shoulder. There is nothing like it in this world. Hello, operator?'

The wheels had been set in motion, and I knew, with a certain trepidation, that nothing on this earth was likely to stop them. I sighed with resignation. I might as well give in to it. It'd take up some of those many hours when there was nothing I could do about Peace but worry.

26

I went home after work, changed and presented myself at the club for a progress report. T.C. was still out asking questions in Limehouse, but was expected back any minute. I felt as if every second should be spent searching for Peace, but it seemed as if the police didn't agree with me.

Bandy was far from happy. 'She went missing on Saturday, and there's still not a word of her whereabouts from our famed constabulary. T.C. says it's because her departure was obviously voluntary. They won't be putting many men on the job because, in their wisdom, they've decided she's old enough to know her own mind and as there's no evidence of abduction, well, what's the hurry?'

Malcolm was hanging around looking helpless – and a bit gormless, it must be said. He really was a useless lump.

Sugar was behind the bar being philosophical. 'That is the thought to hang on to, Band. She went of her own free will. Meanwhile, T.C.'s on the job and he has got some results already. If he's right, she's only a few miles away.'

'That's something, at least, Bandy,' I said. 'Somewhere to look.'

'Yes, it's something all right,' Bobby Bristowe agreed, 'but it ain't a whole lot.'

'No,' said Pansy. 'How is he going to find out anything from the Chinese people in Limehouse when we can't find out anything from the Chinese in our own patch?'

'Can't we go mob-handed and demand to see the girl if she's there?' Malcolm asked. Only Sugar thought it was worth a reply.

'Won't work. They've only got to say "No" and what are we going to do? Bash doors down? Ransack homes and businesses? I don't think so. Have you seen what those lads can do when someone gets on their nerves?'

Malcolm shook his head.

'No, and you don't want to. Not if you're squeamish. Tell him, Band,' Sugar suggested.

'Dog meat. An angry Triad boss, or even a gang master if the occasion demands, can arrange to have people chopped up into dog meat without turning a hair, lifting a finger or even getting their hands dirty. A word or two is all it takes. I saw it in Hong Kong and frankly, I don't want to see it again. Normally, they don't interfere outside of their own set-ups, but if we went barging in where we don't belong, uninvited, then I expect they'd make an exception.'

I sat quietly, trying to imagine the scene, then rather wishing I hadn't. I had heard the same from T.C. who knew about the silent bloodbaths that could take place behind those anonymous blank shop fronts. Just as my imagination was recoiling from the scene, the early evening hush was shattered by someone making an incredibly noisy entrance from the street. A loud voice boomed, footsteps thudded and eventually a large woman – tall *and* wide – burst through the club doors in a flurry of mackintosh, galoshes and a large rain hat. She stood dripping in the doorway and surveyed the room. Finally, her eyes rested on Bandy and she began to unwind what looked like a mile and a half of violently green scarf from her neck and most of her head. At last she was free, and a ruddy face appeared.

'Hope?' she boomed at Bandy.

Bandy's face set in hard lines. 'Faith?' she asked. 'It's been a long time.'

'Yes, and it would have been longer if you hadn't

230

cocked up your end of the bargain! Typical of you, I must say. I told Father you'd balls it up and sure enough, you have.' Faith climbed out of her mackintosh, revealing a baggy tweed suit in a ginger colour that picked up the brick red of her face and made her look like a particularly sturdy carrot.

'Aren't you going to introduce us, Bandy?' Sugar asked in a suspiciously oily voice. Sugar was never oily. Sweet, yes; oily, never!

'If I must,' Bandy said ungraciously. 'Faith, this is my partner, Sugar Plum Flaherty. These people here are our friends, Bobby Bristowe, his wife Pansy, Elizabeth Robbins and Malcolm Lamb.' Bandy paused. 'This is my sister, Faith Sneddon.'

Faith eyed Sugar with distaste, even though his mascara was lightly applied – to his own eyelashes and not a yard of falsies, as was sometimes the case – and his nail polish was a clear, natural one. She raised half of her top lip in a small sneer and said, 'Is he the best you could do?' as if poor Sugar was not standing there, hearing intact. 'You've always been drawn to the odd ones. You were like that at school. If there was a misfit to be found, you found her.' She sighed deeply, her bristly ginger chest rising to the occasion. 'I see you haven't changed in that respect at least.'

I heard Pansy mutter, 'Gawd, she's a charmer', and Bobby grunt briefly in agreement.

Sugar's smile became oilier. 'We've heard a lot about you, Faith.'

Up until recently, we hadn't even known she existed.

'None of it good, I'll be bound,' barked Faith.

'On the contrary. Hope has always been most

231

fond in her reminiscences of you.' He paused just long enough. 'Distance must have lent enchantment to the view.'

He turned to Bandy in the astonished hush. 'Would you like to fill your sister in on the situation, Bandy, or shall we throw her out? I'm sure Bobby will oblige. I'd rather not risk my nails.'

Bandy smiled a large smile. 'We'll tell her the situation, Sugar, then we'll throw her out at the first sign of any more unpleasantness. Faith, these people are my friends. Show respect when you're on my property, or leave. The choice is yours.'

Faith Sneddon eyed us all as if we were something she'd found in her farmyard, but she was slightly more conciliatory than I'd expected. This was a woman used to barging and bludgeoning her way through life. 'No offence meant, I'm sure,' was all she said.

'But plenty taken,' snapped back Sugar, utterly unmollified. 'I'd hate to see you when you did mean it.'

'Well, cough it up, all of it, then I can get back to the farm.' Faith obviously realized that the sooner she was put in the picture, the sooner we'd be shot of her and the happier everyone would be.

Between us, we told her everything that had happened since Peace had disappeared. It didn't seem possible that it had been just a few days; it felt more like weeks. To give her her due, Faith didn't interrupt us once, although we interrupted one another quite often.

We'd just ground to a halt when T.C. appeared. Seconds later, Cassie followed him in, looking radiant, like the cat who had just got her cream, in

232

fact. My heart lurched and I tore my eyes away from them. I liked Cassie well enough, but at that moment, I couldn't bear to look at her. I sneaked another look at T.C. Was it my imagination, or did he look more hunted than hunter? Or perhaps he simply looked haunted. It was hard to say. Then I began to wonder what on earth I was doing, wishing misery on a friend. I turned my attention firmly back to the Carrot from Northamptonshire.

She'd focused on her sister. 'Have you informed Charity?'

Bandy shook her head. 'No idea where she is. Last I heard they were in Egypt, but that was a while back now. Those Foreign Office wallahs do move around so.'

'Good. It wouldn't do to alert her other half to the situation. He knows nothing about Charity's half-breed bastard. He must never know about her,' she added icily, making me shiver. She sounded as if she was talking about an unwanted puppy. 'It's a good match and Father is adamant: no contact with Charity. That's why he put you in charge of the brat and me in charge of the money side of things. I take it there's no possibility that she's gone to Charity? No chance that she found out who her real mother is?'

'I didn't tell Peace, if that's what you mean. She was curious, though, and we had more than one disagreement on the subject. It's possible, though, that she found out. Perhaps she simply worked it out, who knows? I certainly don't.'

'But it is a possibility?' T.C. asked, before the Carrot could get a word in.

'What's it to you?' Faith asked belligerently.

233

The woman was more like a damned bulldog than the sheepdog Bandy had described her as.

'I'm looking into Peace's disappearance,' T.C. answered mildly.

'Well, to me, it sounds as if my half-witted sister here somehow let the cat out of the bag, and that it is highly probable that the gal would try to hunt her mother down.'

'You make it sound like a bleeding fox hunt!' Bobby Bristowe burst out. Pansy stroked his arm to quieten him down. 'Yeah, well, what does she know about anything?' he muttered, staring down at the floor and allowing her to soothe him. 'Peace ain't an animal! At the Home, we all wanted to find our mums. It was only natural.'

'It's certainly another aspect to look into,' said T.C. 'Do you know where her mother is?'

'I do, young man, but I have no intention of telling you, or any of you. I'll contact Charity myself and I shall see if the child has turned up there,' Faith informed him firmly.

'Right you are. You will let us know the outcome? We'll call off the search if she's turned up safely at her mother's,' T.C. replied, equally firmly.

'Where are you staying?' Bandy asked her sister, none too graciously.

'Claridges. Father's usual suite. You can contact me there if there's any news. But I must get back home in the next day or two. I can't be wasting my time here.' Faith stood up and, as abruptly as she had arrived, she left, leaving us stunned in her, wake.

Sugar broke the tension. 'Well, I can see that charm runs in the family.' Bandy burst out

234

laughing, closely followed by the rest of us.

'Isn't anyone going to pour the drinks?' asked Cassie, unmoved by the merriment around her.

I sighed and took a quick glance at T.C. It really did seem as if the fact that Peace was still missing had made no impression at all on Cassie and that the next drink really was the only thing that she thought about. For the first time, I began to believe it was possible that T.C. could get over Cassie. After all, it must be very hard, and deeply hurtful, to play second fiddle to a bottle.

27

Faith returned to the club the next day and surprised us all by showing a little civility and a touch of humour.

'I've had a word with Charity, and the brat, thank God, has not turned up there. Charity's in a frightful flap in case she does. But then, I gather she's in a frightful flap about all manner of things. Seems her father-in-law has fallen off his perch and the old family tree lost the older limb, in the form of the brother, in the war. Copped it in France, so Henry's the heir.

'Terrible shock to his brand new Lordship if he suddenly acquires a Chinese stepdaughter as well. Bit of a facer for the locals too, gentry and yokels alike. Can you imagine?'

Bandy laughed for the first time that day. 'Yes, you can hardly slip a "slant-eyed maiden" into

English village life without it causing something of a stir. Especially if she's the by-blow of the lady of the manor. I almost wish I'd told Peace everything, now, and given her a map and the bus fare.'

For a moment, as they laughed together, you could tell that Faith and Bandy were sisters. Despite their obvious differences, there was the fondness of a long association there, a shared history.

In my opinion, people underestimate the importance of witnesses to their lives. My mother was friendly with a woman once, who let go of all her friends and family over the years, one after the other. Mother managed to last longer than most, but even she had to go eventually. No one was ever sure why this woman took so much umbrage, but she did. All she had left in the end was a husband she had married late in life. This man could drum up a stream of criticism about anyone who passed even briefly through their lives. I can still hear his awful drone as he poured out his scorn on the human race in general and everyone they'd ever met in particular. I often wondered how she felt when she got older and found that there was no one left to share her memories. It must have been utterly desolate for her.

Maggie, Bert, Freddy, Antony, Sugar, Bandy, Bobby, Pansy and all my other neighbours and acquaintances could remember Jenny and Sid. They had watched our lives painfully unravel and then had helped me to stitch mine back together again. And they were still helping me now that it was time to change the cut, pattern and fabric of it. And I, in my turn, was more than happy to offer my help whenever they needed it. After all, it was the people of Soho who had taught me the true meaning and value of friendship over the years.

Faith was taking her leave. 'There's not a lot to be done until someone unearths the gal,' she said tactlessly. Bandy and I shuddered. 'So, I'm off back to the farm. Keep me posted, Hope, and don't do what you always do and take your eye off the bloody ball. You've always been a slacker. Look at you, you're not even out of your pyjamas yet.'

'I'll have you know that they're not pyjamas,' Sugar intervened. 'They're a stylish little number I designed myself to suit her rather difficult frame. You could do with a little attention in that direction yourself, you know, speaking as a man. What do you think, Antony, Freddy? They're in the trade, so they know a thing or two about dressing ladies,' he explained.

My two employers circled Faith with their fingers to their lips, eyes narrowed, considering. 'The suit's too small, that's the trouble, that's why she looks lumpy. And the colour! What do you say, Liz?' Antony asked me.

Freddy eyed Faith kindly. 'Liz is our colour expert. Absolute whiz, can match anybody up.' He paused. 'Even you.'

'Heather mixture tweeds, with a base of soft colours like pink or, better, mauve. You can get good heather mixture tweeds to go with all kinds of colours. Anything that appears in the slub, really,' I answered.

Faith looked down at her ginger chest, then at the group around her. She turned a brighter red and stumped sturdily to the door. 'What's a slub when it's at home? And what do I care what a

gaggle of ghastly nancy boys think of me?' I
realized the poor woman was embarrassed. Her
voice grew sharp. 'Keep in touch, Hope, and
don't let that girl anywhere near your sister.
Father's explicit instructions.'

'I'll do my best, but it's tricky if I don't know
where she is. It's possible she's in Limehouse,
and we don't stand a snowflake's chance in hell
of getting in on the inside there. If the Chinese
want to hide her, then they will, and there's sweet
Fanny Adams we can do about it. We'll have to
wait for her to emerge. *If* it's her.'

There was a pregnant pause, then Bandy's
voice took on a guarded note. 'Either that, or
we'll have to ask for help from her uncle.'

This stopped Faith's retreat mid-stride. She
lowered her sensible brogue, with the little fans
of leather at the ends of the laces, very slowly and
looked hard at her sister. 'You wouldn't!' she said
firmly.

'What choice do I have, if we can't find her by
other means?' Bandy asked in a reasonable tone.

'Father would absolutely forbid it,' Faith urged
her sister, eyes still locked on her face. 'Absolutely and completely. Our association with that
family ended many years ago and it is far better
to keep it that way.' She took a deep breath.
'Better and *safer*.'

'I agree, but if she's disappeared into Limehouse it may be the only way to get her out.
Anyone but a Chinese would stick out like a sore
thumb. What do you suggest?'

'Find someone other than her uncle. Anyone,'
Faith suggested, voice strained.

'Nowadays, that's easier said than done,' Bandy told her. 'Much easier said than done. He's been in London for some time, you know. His connections are many and wide reaching.'

The sisters stared at each other, in silent communication, remembering God knew what from their shared past. Then, just as suddenly as she arrived, Faith turned back to the door and left us. We heard her loud footsteps echoing on the stairs and then all was quiet again.

The moment she was out of earshot, Bandy turned to Sugar with a worried look. 'She's right, you know. It wouldn't do to be caught up in anything that might be going on in the Chinese quarter.'

Sugar looked pensive for so long, I thought he wasn't going to speak at all, but finally he heaved a sigh. 'You could be right. I've been trying not to think too hard about that angle. But then I don't know who her uncle or even her father is. I thought you didn't know, seeing you were long gone by the time he got your little sister in the pudding club.'

The rest of us looked at one another in bewilderment. If we were looking for enlightenment, we were to be sadly disappointed.

'Yes, well, best not to discuss it now,' Bandy said briskly. 'Let's wait for our next meeting with T.C. We need to talk it over with him.' Bandy turned to me. 'By the way, what the hell is a "slub", anyway?'

For a moment she'd lost me, then I remembered I'd been talking about heather mixture tweeds. 'It's the lumpy bits in some kinds of woollen fabrics, gives it a more textured look, something like bouclé, only that's loops not lumps. It comes from the way they twist the yarn.' I explained.

Bandy didn't look any the wiser, 'It's another bloody language, the way you frock-makers speak. Sugar's just as bad; I don't know what he's talking about half the time.'

Then her face cleared. 'Ah, here comes some clientele!' she said with relief as a clatter of high heels and brogues came down the stairs to the club. 'Boozers. I understand *them*.'

28

That night I found myself submitting to the attentions of one of Freddy and Antony's friends who, according to Freddy, wielded his scissors 'like a true artiste. If anyone can do anything about that hair of yours, he can. Ronald is riah shusher to the stars. The only reason he is coming down from the heady heights to do yours is as a special favour to us.' That and the slap-up three-course meal provided by Antony and Freddy, who loved to cook.

We decided to put our worries about Peace aside for a few hours and make a night of it. I brought my 'wayward barnet' and a bottle of what I was assured was a good wine supplied by the French wine merchant in Old Compton Street. I wouldn't have known a good wine if I'd drowned in one, so I was glad of his help.

Freddy and Antony lived above the shop in St Anne's Court – a lane that only took foot traffic and still had its cobbles and gas lamps, although they'd been converted to electricity after the war – and their flat managed to combine cosiness with elegance, which isn't easy. Before I went there for the first time, I had been expecting the very latest in interior design, lots of bright plastics and up-to-the-minute fabrics, with blobs of primary colours. I was in for a shock.

The building was old, Georgian, with high ceilings that boasted beautiful mouldings, and Freddy and Antony had decided to go with it, rather than to try to impose the twentieth century on it.

'It'd be the act of a philistine to put plastic where plaster should be,' Antony explained.

'Take no notice, ducky, he's from Tunbridge Wells. He can't help it. What he means is, when we have a Georgian building here, it seemed best to us to do it in that style. It sort of lends itself to that more than all the nice pretty plastic.'

'And we've had a lovely time collecting the furniture and finding the fabrics and paints,' Antony added. 'We've wound up in some wonderful places. Do you remember that wallpaper printer in Hoxton, Freddy? Still used the old hand-block printing methods, so that the stately homes of old England can be refurbished. There's paint-makers, fabric-weavers, rug-makers, all beavering away in little workshops in the most peculiar places. We've been all over the place, haven't we, Freddy?'

'Yes, and we're always adding bits to it. We're haunting the auctions when we get the chance at the moment. We want a couple more dining chairs to make the set, and some china.'

The effort was worth it. The flat looked like a stately home in miniature, with its fine furniture and fittings. It could have been a set from an historical film, except that it looked and felt lived in.

The evening went with a swing. Ronald proved to be good company and, as Freddy said, 'a demon riah shusher'. He set to immediately he arrived. I had to sit through dinner with a head full of curlers, but nobody seemed to mind. It must have looked incongruous, pink plastic curlers in a Georgian Yellow dining room.

The talk flowed easily between the three men and I felt a bit like a spare part until I gave myself up to the delights of the food, the half-glass of wine I allowed myself and the freedom of being a spectator. As the wine bottle emptied and another took its place, I ceased to understand more than one word in ten of the conversation anyway. All three spoke fluent Polari. 'Trolling', 'Lily Law' and 'rattling cove' were about the only phrases I understood.

I drifted off into a daydream as I waited for the curlers and the setting lotion to do their promised magic. I was just replaying the time when T.C. had been in my kitchen and had been about to kiss me – except this time I didn't freeze, but melted into his arms instead – when I heard his name spoken. Jolted out of my daydream, I was back into the dining room and the assembled company.

'Sorry, what was that?' I asked. 'It's the wine; I was away with the fairies.'

'What, on three sips?' asked Freddy incredulously.

'I'm not used to it,' I answered a little defensively. 'What were you saying about T.C.?'

Freddy rolled his eyes. 'And you say you don't fancy him. It's love, I'm telling you, or a thumping great crush.'

'Don't tease the poor girl, Freddy,' Ronald scolded. He stood up, walked around the table and unrolled a curler to see if my hair was dry. It was, so we all repaired to the living room to see what he'd made of it when the curlers were removed and it had been brushed out. Ronald placed me in a chair beside a small table with the tools of his trade laid out neatly upon it. 'So, tell me all about this man. Is he handsome?' His fingers deftly whipped out the pins and the curlers.

I blushed deeply. 'There is no man,' I answered, voice barely above a whisper. My face was so hot, I thought I'd scorch the wallpaper.

'My dear, nobody goes that shade of crimson unless they have someone on their mind. Tell Uncle Ronald all about him and ignore these two awful old queens. They've been together so long, they've forgotten what it's like to yearn,' Ronald told me, briskly plying his brush and comb.

'If you don't tell him, we will,' Freddy threatened. Antony nodded lazily, smiling gently at his friend. 'She's got the hots for T.C. Do you know him?'

Ronald paused and gave it some thought. 'I don't think so. Tell me all.'

'Well, he's a handsome cove, but naff,' Freddy explained.

'He'd have to be naff,' Antony pointed out. 'There's no point in her setting her cap at one of us. She'd wouldn't get very far; she's got the wrong equipment.'

'I expect her equipment's just fine, as long as you like that kind of thing.' Freddy laughed. 'You describe him, Ant. I'll make the coffee.'

'He's taller than average and well put together, and he has a good face. Think Kenneth More crossed with a touch of Richard Green and a smidgin of Trevor Howard thrown in for good measure and you've more or less got him: except he's fair, with curly hair. Freddy's right; he *is* a good-looking cove, in a craggy sort of way.'

Antony's description of T.C. set me thinking about him again, but I was disturbed by an excited cry from Freddy, who had returned with a tray full of cups, milk, cream and sugar.

'Oh, ducky! What a job you've made. She's *gorgeous*, or she will be when we've got some slap on her. Lizzie, nip into the bathroom and have a blimp in the mirror. You won't believe the transformation.'

He was right. Ronald *was* a magician. My mousy hair gleamed with the blond rinse he'd put through it. It didn't turn me into a blonde, but it brought out highlights in my hair that I hadn't realized were there. As Freddy had said, it 'lifted' the colour and made it richer; there was no better way to describe it. And he'd cut my hair so well that it framed my face with feathery little curls and wispy bits that softened the edges. He'd added

244

height at the crown and the whole shape took your eye away from my weakest feature, my chin.

I gazed for a long time and decided, for the first time in my entire life, that I had quite a nice face. I had really pretty eyes, I thought; they were large and so dark a blue, they looked almost violet, like Elizabeth Taylor's. The men had been right about my eyebrows, though. They were too heavy for my face. I raced into the living room to ask if anyone had any eyebrow tweezers.

'No dear. It's not something I've ever felt the need for,' Antony answered. 'And as far as I know, neither has Freddy. How about you, Ronald?' Ronald shook his head sadly. I was just thinking it'd have to wait until I got home when Freddy had a brainwave. He pushed up the bottom half of the window, and stuck his head out.

'Ruby, have you or any of the other girls got any eyebrow tweezers that we could borrow by any chance?' he called to the little group of prostitutes standing under one of the street lamps, advertising their wares to the few men who hurried past.

We heard women consulting one another and finally Ruby replied, 'Yes, we have. What's it worth?'

'Don't you slappers ever give anything away for nothing?' Freddy called back. 'Or even loan it out for five minutes?'

'Nope,' came the answer.

'How about a nice hot drink and a rest of your poor plates while you drink it? You must be bloody frozen out there, and in this weather, business has got to be slow.'

'Don't you believe it, mate. When blokes get the

urge for a quick one, a little thing like the weather don't stop 'em. A shag's a shag, whatever the climate, and there's fellas who just have to have it, no matter what. And thank Gawd for that, or we'd starve come winter.' There was a brief pause. 'We've voted for the little rest and the hot drink. Sling your key down, there's a love.'

Freddy duly wrapped the front door key in a clean sock specially kept for the purpose – to muffle its landing – and threw the small parcel into the street. Moments later we heard heels clacking on the stairs and two frozen ladies of the night piled into the living room, bringing the heady smell of perfume with them.

'Good evening all,' Ruby grinned. 'The others decided to carry on working. This here is Brenda. Who needs the tweezers?'

'Me,' I answered.

'Ooh, your hair looks lovely. Who did it?' Ruby sounded really impressed.

'It was Ronald here, he did it,' I told her.

Ronald looked modestly at the carpet.

'Cor! Can you do mine some time?' she asked.

They swiftly made a date while I took the tweezers from Brenda and hurried back to the bathroom with them. Fifteen agonizing minutes later I returned to the living room with a slightly lighter step and tidy, slender eyebrows, although the skin around them still looked angry from the plucking. I gave Brenda her tweezers back.

'Ta,' she said in a tiny voice.

'Don't you worry, love, all that red will go back to normal soon. It's the shock,' Ruby assured me. 'You won't notice it tomorrow, and you look a lot better for it, so it's worth the suffering. Come on, Bren, time we was back at work. There's blokes getting away out there. I haven't earned me money yet, and the old man will go spare.

'Thanks for the tea, boys,' she sang out as she headed for the door, trailed by Brenda, who didn't look keen to leave the warmth and safety of the roaring fire. I couldn't say I blamed the poor girl. It was very cold for spring and it looked and smelt as if a fog was forming; the air had that distinctive smell of sulphur. I decided to leave before it really got set in and ruined my hair on the walk home. Ronald joined me. We departed in a flurry of thanks and goodwill and found ourselves on the street.

'Goodnight,' we called to the girls huddled under the street lamp and they called their farewells back. 'I'll walk you home,' said Ronald.

'Thank you for the hairdo,' I said shyly. Now that I was alone with him, I realized that I didn't know anything about Ronald or what he liked to talk about. I needn't have worried. He was content to gossip.

'Think nothing of it. It was good to see Freddy and Antony again. It's been a while. They can both cook, I'll give them that. They've been together for quite a stretch, now, haven't they?' He did not wait for an answer. 'I never thought old Antony would settle down. He liked to put it about a fair old bit in his younger days, I can tell you. I never thought he'd stick to just the one, but he has, for years now. Old Freddy must have talents we can only guess at.' He paused and looked at me for a second, then amended the statement. 'That *I* can only guess at.'

I raced up the stairs when I got home, to have another look at my hair. It still looked wonderful. Before I went to bed, I tried some make-up on. I was astonished at the effect. The combination of the hair, the eyebrows and a little make-up made me look quite pretty, even I could see that. I turned this way and that and sighed with satisfaction.

That night I dreamed about T.C. They were silly dreams, like films where the hero falls for the beautiful stranger who turns out to be the girl next door, all grown up. But I woke up happy, and when I looked in the mirror the next morning, I was overwhelmed all over again. Freddy was right: Ronald was a magician.

29

Maggie noticed my new hairdo immediately when she saw me the next morning. I'd also powdered my nose, added a little mascara and just a touch of pink lipstick.

'Lizzie, love, you look lovely. Off somewhere special, are you?' she asked, eyes wide and her dear face alive with smiles.

I tried for nonchalance, but failed because I was so thrilled with the new, improved me. 'No, I'm just off to work,' I answered, as I heard the door to the cafe open behind my back. For a second, my heart stopped. I was hoping it was T.C., like in my dream, but it wasn't. It was Freddy, closely followed by Antony.

'Doesn't she look a dish?' demanded Freddy.

'Isn't it a vast improvement?' seconded Antony.

'She looks lovely,' Maggie said comfortably.

'Well, let's hope old T.C. thinks so. It's time he got his mind off Cassie. That'll never come to anything; there's too much in the way. Whereas Lizzie here is just the job, in our opinion. And what's more,' Freddy finished triumphantly, 'she fancies him like mad.'

I turned to clout him for his cheek – just in time to see Rosie's stricken face in the doorway that led to the flat above. It was the merest impression, but it sunk in deeply in the moment between Freddy's outburst and Maggie's reply, which I didn't hear because I was rooted to the spot, looking towards the place where I'd seen the pale, unhappy little face. Nobody seemed to have noticed but me.

The conversation carried on around me as I willed my feet to move. At last I was able to shift them. 'Excuse me,' I said. 'May I go upstairs, Maggie? I'd like a little word with Rosie.' I walked towards the doorway at her nod. I had no idea what I was going to say to her, but I couldn't bear the memory of the look I'd caught on her face.

Rosie was in her room, sitting on her bed with her knees pulled up to her chest and her slender arms wrapped around them so she made a tight ball. She was staring blankly ahead of her.

'Rosie,' I croaked from the door. She made no sign that she'd heard me. I tried again, louder. 'Rosie.' Still nothing. I upped the volume again and accompanied it with a brisk rap on the door, then followed up by walking into the room and standing in her line of vision. At last she moved and spoke.

'Did you want something, Auntie Lizzie?' she asked politely.

'Yes, I'd like to talk to you.'

'What about?' She wasn't planning to make it easy for me, then.

I took the plunge. 'About your dad and me,' I answered, knowing that there was nothing much to talk about in the way of facts, but also that this left the more difficult subject of feelings and I had no idea where to begin.

'What about you and my dad?' she asked, voice hardening and eyes growing wary.

'That's just it. There *is* no me and your dad. Freddy was simply gossiping. There is absolutely nothing between me and your dad besides friendship. We are friends – at least, I like to think that we are, I can't speak for your dad.' I looked her in the eye so that she knew I meant what I said. It had always worked with Jenny, so I hoped that Rosie would know I wasn't lying to her.

Rosie looked at me for a long time, breaking my heart with her resemblance to her father and the sadness in her face. Then she smiled and I was aware for the first time that it lit up her face in just the way a smile lit up her father's. It was like the sun coming out. I felt tears start to well up, and pushed them down again. This wasn't about me and my feelings, it was about Rosie and hers. The trouble was, nobody had told her that.

'Do you love my dad?' she asked, never taking

250

her eyes off my face.

I was cautious, not because I wanted to lie to her, but because I simply didn't know. 'I certainly like him very much. Your dad is a very special person, good company, intelligent and a decent man. What's not to like?' I asked, trying to make a joke of it. But Rosie was no fool either, and would have none of it.

'Auntie Lizzie, I didn't ask if you liked him, I asked if you loved him. I know you like him and that he likes you. I can tell,' she told me, her face solemn.

There was to be no escape, I could see that. I made a snap decision to be as honest as I could be and hope for the best. I thought I probably owed her that. To be frank, I think children usually do better with the truth, as long as it's pitched at the right level. They can sense lies and prevarication in much the same way that dogs pick up fear. And it frightens them, whereas the simple truth often doesn't. At least, that's always what I had found with my Jenny, and I had had to tell her some terrible truths in my time. I had been amazed how that child had taken things in her stride. She had put me to shame.

I took a deep breath. 'I'm not sure, Rosie, and that's the honest truth.'

Rosie nodded. 'But you do fancy him, as Freddy the Frock says?'

Again I paused. It served me right for bringing the subject up, I supposed. 'Well, I certainly look forward to seeing him.' I struggled to find the words to describe how I felt. The trouble was, I wasn't used to talking about such things, and especially not to a child. And not being sure of myself made it even more difficult. 'And I enjoy his company very much,' I finished lamely.

Rosie was impatient. 'Yes, but does he make your heart thump, do you get butterflies in your belly, the way they say that you should?'

'Now where on earth did you hear all that?' I asked.

'Peace told me. Now, answer the question please, Auntie. He *is* my dad and I like to know who he's with in his spare time,' she said, sounding more like his mother. 'I worry about him,' she added, sounding more like herself.

I nodded slowly. Now that she came to mention it, I suppose that I did. 'But I've never heard violins, if that's any comfort to you,' I said, trying for a lighter note. 'I know you're hoping that your father and mother will marry now that Pat's gone, but honestly, Rosie, I don't think it's necessarily on the cards. They are very fond of one another, but there are some serious problems...' My voice trailed away as it dawned on me that I was heading into very tricky country.

Tears glistened on Rosie's lashes. 'I know. There's my mum's drinking for a start. He hates that and so do I. But I thought if she was happy, it might stop her,' she said.

The poor darling child, I thought, having to worry about such things. 'I don't think it's as simple as that,' I said carefully. I didn't want to squash her optimism, but on the other hand, false hope can be devastating. 'I was reading in a magazine that I found at the doctor's the other day, that there's some people who think drinking is an illness. Even doctors seem to think so nowadays.'

Her face lit up. 'Perhaps she'll get better then, like chicken-pox.'

I groaned inwardly. 'Perhaps she will. But as I understand it, the only real hope is giving up alcohol altogether, every drop, and I don't think your mother is willing to do that just yet.' I was still feeling my way very carefully.

'You see, there is no cure as such, or so they think, but there is control by total abstinence. Or so I understood from the article. There's an organization that helps people. It started in America, and apparently it's arrived here. Funnily enough, I saved the piece to show one or two people and your parents were among them. Your dad was very interested, but I'm sorry to say, Rosie, that your mother wasn't. Not at the moment, anyway.' I blushed at the memory of Cassie telling me in no uncertain terms to mind my own business.

The tears were streaming down Rosie's face, and I found myself sitting beside her on the bed, arm around her heaving shoulders as she leaned in against me. It was good to have a child in my arms again, even a temporarily unhappy one. I knew Rosie well and was confident that her normally sunny nature would re-emerge. Yes, it was a tragedy about her mother, but Rosie was dearly loved and I hoped and trusted that it would be enough to see her through. Eventually, the heaving shoulders slowed to stillness and the sobs to snivels, then hiccups and finally to one almighty sniff. She mopped herself up with one of Bert's large, masculine hankies, blew her nose and treated me to a watery smile.

253

'It's not that I don't like you, Auntie Lizzie,' she said in a small, still damp voice. 'It's just that I had hoped...'

I gave her a little squeeze. 'I know, sweetheart. I like you too, you know I do, and I wouldn't ever deliberately do anything to hurt you or without your permission, you know that.'

She nodded at me. 'I know you wouldn't. And honestly, if you do marry my dad, I won't mind, I promise.' She paused, then grinned a wicked grin. 'As long as I can be your bridesmaid.'

'It would definitely be a deal, if it ever came to that, but just because I have feelings for your dad, it doesn't mean that he has feelings for me. It does take two, you know. Even if he does like me too, there's no saying it'd come to anything. These things often simply fizzle out.

'Anyway, I'm still married to Jenny's dad, so marriage to anyone else is definitely not on the cards. You needn't worry about that right now this minute, nor order a bridesmaid's dress either. But I promise, if I ever do remarry, and you're still interested, then it would be an honour to have you as my bridesmaid. I can't imagine anyone I'd rather have.' I gave her another hug.

Rosie's expression grew serious again and she turned and looked me full in the face. 'And I can't imagine a better stepmother.' Her voice grew smaller and more solemn. 'And if I really think about it, Auntie Lizzie, I agree with Freddy the Frock. You would be better for my dad than Mum would be. You don't drink a lot and there's no other men. I think my mum likes men too much, and I know it hurts my dad. I've seen his face when she walks in with one.'

My heart ached for her, but I couldn't tell her it wasn't so, because it was. Rosie might have been young, but she was obviously far from stupid, and in certain ways perhaps a little too old for her years. She'd seen her mother's behaviour, and there was absolutely no point in looking for a comforting lie. So I kept quiet.

Rosie was the one who finally changed the subject. 'Has my dad found out where Peace is yet?'

I shook my head. 'There's been nothing new since we found out she'd taken the bus to Limehouse, and everyone is worried sick.'

I took a deep breath, knowing I was about to push my luck, but I decided that for Peace's sake I had to. 'If Peace told you all about the fluttering and heart racing that goes on when two people like one another, she must have been talking about the boy she went with. Rosie, I know you promised, but this is so serious. Peace could be in terrible danger and neither we, nor the police, can do a thing about it until we have a clue as to who she might be with.

'If you know who this boy or man is, you really must say. She'd understand, I'm sure she would. She may even be longing for you to spill the beans, if she's in trouble and can't help herself.' I could hear the pleading note in my voice and shut up. It was up to Rosie and all I could do was wait and hope.

'I promised,' she said stubbornly. 'She's my blood sister, the only one I've got, and I promised.'

'I know you did, sweetheart, but sometimes, when the danger could be awful, it's right to break such a promise. You are her blood sister, after all, and for all you or anyone else knows, she could need help desperately. Who better to help her than her own blood sister, eh?'

The pause seemed to go on for hours. All I could hear was her quiet breathing, the murmur of voices from the cafe and the loud ticking of the clock. I waited, and at last Rosie nodded to herself. She'd made a decision.

'It's Lucky. Lucky Wong, Mrs Wong's oldest son. Don't tell her I told you,' she pleaded, sounding her age at last.

My heart began to hammer so hard, I could hardly speak. I should have known! First Bubbles, now Lucky. 'I wonder why Mrs Wong didn't tell us? She must know what it is to worry about the young,' I said indignantly.

'She doesn't know,' Rosie said miserably. 'It's a big secret. Peace met Lucky in the long summer holidays, and liked him a lot. I don't think he even noticed her right away but he did in the end. Bubbles helped, I think, sort of made sure they bumped into each other and things.

'That's partly why Peace ran away from school. She hadn't really wanted to go back there at all, but when she found her friend, Sally, had gone, she said that was the last straw. So you see, she just had to get away and come back to Lucky and Bubbles. They were her only friends in the whole world – until she met me and got to know you, that is.'

I took a deep breath. 'Well I'm glad you told me, Rosie. You've been a wonderful help. I'll find your dad and tell him straight away, so that he can get started on that avenue of enquiry. Meanwhile, try not to worry. I won't breathe a word to Peace. If and when we find her.'

Just then Freddy's voice floated up the stairs. 'We're off to work, Lizzie Robbins, if you'd care to join us.'

Rosie started. 'Then it must be time I was getting off to school. I daren't be late or there'll be a black mark in the late book and if I get one more, they'll write to Auntie Maggie.'

I could quite see why that was not to be contemplated and helped her to pack her P.E. kit into her satchel. She gave me one last grin, a smacking great goodbye kiss and said, 'I feel better for telling you, Auntie Lizzie, and honestly, if you want my dad, I hope you get him.' She giggled and rushed for the stairs.

I went to the bathroom and splashed water on to my face, then remembered the mascara and had to clear up the mess. Tears and mascara did not mix, I'd forgotten that.

I stood for a moment, longing for Jenny, and then pulled myself together, replaced my mascara, put my best foot forward and set off to work.

30

As it turned out I didn't see T.C. during the course of the day as I had hoped, but the chances of seeing him later on were better, because it had become the practice for everyone involved with looking for Peace to meet up at the club in the quiet early evening. We would swap information, air new theories and bounce ideas around, in case we came up with any fresh suggestions.

T.C. was looking pale and tired when I arrived at the club. My heart sank when I saw Cassie sitting next to him at the bar, because I had been itching to pass on to him the news Rosie had given me about Lucky Wong. I was struck temporarily dumb by being so disconcerted to see him with Cassie once again. She was rapidly becoming his shadow and I, for one, was uneasy about it. I tried to be fair and told myself I would be worried about Cassie's renewed interest in T.C. whether I liked him or not. She just wasn't good for him: she wore him ragged, and she hurt him every time her drinking led her into the arms, and usually the beds, of other men.

I swallowed the lump in my throat. 'Rosie's told me who Peace may have gone away with.'

'Oh, for God's sake, don't any of you people ever think about anything other than that wretched girl?' Cassie said sharply. 'She's not the first to run away from home, you know. I did it, and so did Bandy here. It's not the end of the bloody world.'

'Yes, and look what became of you.' The words were out of my mouth before I knew what I was saying. I could have bitten my tongue off.

Cassie eyed me narrowly. 'And what, pray, did become of me? What are you suggesting?'

I turned scarlet. What could I say? I could hardly tell her the truth, that she'd become a dipsomaniac, a high-class tart and a rotten mother

258

with an illegitimate child that had to be cared for by others. Besides, I wasn't at all sure that my opinion of her wasn't rooted in bitterness: despite her appalling neglect, her child had lived, whereas mine had died, despite all my efforts to save her. The only times Jenny and I had ever been parted was when she was in hospital and they'd forced me to leave her at night.

I flinched from these awful thoughts. They didn't mean I wished Rosie dead in Jenny's place. But it didn't seem fair, either, that I should lose the centre of my universe, when Cassie barely even noticed that she had one – or if she did, she thought it was a bottle of booze and a man with a wallet.

What on earth had got into me? I stood tongue-tied as the thought wormed its way into my mind that I was jealous of Cassie. It was as simple as that. I was jealous of her lovely daughter and I was jealous of T.C.'s love for her and, worse, I was jealous that she was just so damned beautiful. She seemed to have it all and care little for any of it. I wanted to stamp my feet like a spoilt three-year-old, and scream 'IT'S NOT FAIR!'

At last, from a hundred miles away, I heard Bandy's husky voice. 'What she means, sweetie, is that you and I haven't made much of a fist of things. And she's not wrong, by her lights. We *are* a pair of gin-sodden baggages who tend to make a dreadful balls of our domestic arrangements, if you look on it in a certain way. The fact that you and I may prefer to see ourselves as a couple of independent gals who have chosen to live by our own rules *could* be seen, in some quarters, as an excuse for being a couple of soaks with messy love lives.' She laughed heartily.

'Well, I still don't like to be judged by some mousy little shop assistant and found wanting,' Cassie snapped back.

'You take that back right now.' T.C. stepped forward, his eyes flashing. 'Lizzie is not mousy, and neither is she standing in judgement over you, and you know it very well. Shop work is honest employment, and I really don't think you're in a position to sneer at it, do you?'

For a moment, everyone froze; Cassie looked from T.C. to me and back again, shock etched on her face. But her mouth remained stubbornly shut tight – there was going to be no apology.

T.C. shrugged and turned back to me. 'You've done something different with your hair.' He smiled. 'It suits you.'

I had my mouth open to thank him for the compliment, but Cassie butted in as if nothing untoward had happened, although her expression spoke volumes. 'So, are you coming or not?'

'Not.' T.C. shook his head. 'I don't really feel comfortable in that crowd. You go and have a good time. I want to hear what Rosie told Lizzie.'

'Please yourself. You've always been a crashing bore when it comes to having fun. Anywhere but in bed; there you excel,' said Cassie, flashing me a triumphant look and leaning forward to kiss T.C. 'I'll be off, then. Harry said he'd pick us up at seven-thirty, and I'm not even dressed yet. Are you sure you don't want to come with me? I know someone would lend you some evening clothes.'

'I'm sure, but I can't afford roulette.' Did he

sound a little weary, as if he was trying quite hard to get rid of her? I felt my heart lift hopefully and told it sternly to settle down again. I was almost certain it was wishful thinking. 'And don't you mean Neville's picking you up?'

Cassie sighed. 'I do wish you'd listen sometimes. Harry's the member. We can't get in without him.' Cassie smiled a secret and rather unkind smile. 'Anyway, Harry's showing an interest again. He telephoned and said he'd be in town and fancied a night on the tiles, and as he can afford it, I thought I'd join him.'

She paused for a heartbeat. 'It's not as if you can afford to stand a girl a cup of tea, let alone a night at the roulette table, so a touch of luxury is just about due – I've slummed it long enough.' And on that note, she swept out of the bar with barely a backward glance.

We all stared at the swinging door for a moment, then Bandy's cut-glass voice broke the spell. 'So, who is Peace's boyfriend?'

'It's Lucky Wong, Mrs Wong's eldest,' I told her. 'Rosie says Peace's been in love with him for some time, and it seems likely that she's gone with him to Limehouse.'

'I wonder why Mrs Wong didn't spit this little gem out at the start?' Bandy barked angrily.

'Perhaps she doesn't know,' suggested T.C. reasonably.

'Children rarely tell their mothers everything,' I reminded Bandy, 'especially when they get older. It's in their nature to be secretive; it's a bid for independence.' I didn't add that I thought Mrs Wong was very frightened as well.

'All right, oh voice of experience, have it your own way. But don't think I've forgotten or forgiven the slur you cast upon my moral rectitude. I may have bailed you out with the lovely Cassandra, but that doesn't mean the implication that I have somehow failed because I chose not to take the marriage and motherhood route, is not resented. For the most part I like my life, and don't you forget it, madam,' she said, trying hard not to laugh at me.

'I didn't mean...'

'I know that, you idiot. You were referring to Cassie falling prey to a randy policeman who promptly got her in the family way.' She chortled.

'I didn't mean...' I began again. I could see my face reddening in the bar's mirrors.

There was a cough behind me. I turned to T.C. 'If we could get back to Peace and this Lucky fellow. How did you get Rosie to speak? I almost, applied the thumbscrews and there was nothing doing, not a dickie bird, because she'd promised.'

'We had a little heart-to-heart, that's all,' I explained uneasily. Then I changed the subject quickly. 'So what do you think we should do now?'

'I don't know. I've been thinking about it ever since the first suggestion of a Limehouse connection. We can't go bursting in there, and we can't infiltrate. If we did the first, there could be a bloodbath, with Peace, and indeed us, providing all the blood. And we can't do the second, because we're not Chinese.

'If we inform the Force, they'll be duty bound to investigate; which would certainly get them nowhere, but would tip off Peace and her friend.

262

That's if he *is* a friend, and she's there voluntarily. And, of course, we don't know for certain that she's *in* Limehouse. We just suspect it. What we need is an insider.'

Bandy spoke up, obviously choosing her words with care. 'Sugar and I think we may have a way in to Limehouse,' she began cautiously. 'That's where he is now, trying to make contact with his friend.'

T.C. and I spoke at once. 'Who? How? Which friend?'

Bandy sighed deeply. 'You know I was brought up in Hong Kong?'

We nodded in unison.

'Well, of course we knew some Chinese people. My father was, and still is, heavily involved in the import and export business, mainly export, with several prominent Chinese businessmen. And we mixed socially with some of the more cosmopolitan types. Well, you know that. Peace was the product of one such social contact, obviously.

'So anyway, some of those contacts have found their way to Blighty. Quite a few years back now, I bumped into one of them, along with some of his family. And Sugar and one of these people formed what you might call a close bond. They've been having an affair for some time now, and that's where he slopes off to when he gets the chance.

'Naturally, it's top secret stuff. It's more than the lover's life's worth to be caught at it, so mum's the word. Not a whisper outside of the three of us and Sugar. Understood?'

Again we nodded. I was too dumbstruck to utter a word. Sugar had been having a secret and dangerous affair with a Chinese man for years and I couldn't utter a word to Freddy and Antony about it? It was almost more than flesh and blood could stand. I was so intrigued, I almost forgot all about my own problems.

'He's seeing if he can enlist some help inside the community, to see what's what. But it's tricky. Very tricky indeed. Delicacy is going to be required. That's if he's managed to make contact. Even if they arrange to meet, there's no guarantees. It often doesn't happen for one reason or another.'

'How do they make the initial contact, to arrange their meetings in the first place?' T.C. sounded as intrigued as I was. 'If it's all so difficult and dangerous?'

'An old spy trick from the war. They keep in touch via a number of dead letter drops. One's in the park, near the lake, so whoever leaves and retrieves the notes can look as if they're feeding the ducks. There's another in a suite my father keeps at Claridges. Father's business associates often use it when they're in town, and so do members of their families. Naturally, when there's someone important in town, the local Chinese jump to it to make sure he's comfortable and has all he could possibly need. Sugar's friend is often at Claridges as part of the welcoming committee.'

Bandy paused, took a deep drag of her Passing Cloud and a sip of her gin.

'Then again, in an emergency, I understand that Sugar is allowed to enlist the help of Mrs Wong to pass on a message. It's dangerous, though, and he's never had to do it until now. He's off seeing if it got through.'

A penny dropped. If Sugar's lover was Chinese it would explain why Freddy and Antony had never known who it was. It also explained how Sugar had always been able to get his hands on the silk for Bandy's outfits, rationing or no rationing. We'd all been as jealous as anything and had never known how he did it. Now I knew.

As if he had heard his cue, Sugar came through the door and looked around him. Seeing no one but us three, he grinned.

31

I went upstairs to my flat and made a light supper of sardines on toast and a cup of tea. It was all that my larder could provide. I had been so caught up in the search for Peace that shopping had been the least of my worries.

When I finally sat at my little yellow table, my mind was free to concentrate on the events of the day. Although we were no nearer to actually seeing Peace in the flesh, she felt closer now that we knew about her and Lucky Wong. It was also a strong possibility that Sugar's 'friend' could help us to make contact with Peace, or so Sugar and Bandy thought. We could at least find out if she was safe and happy, even if we didn't manage to persuade her to come back to us.

I was feeling considerably comforted by these thoughts and finally allowed my mind to wander on to the scene between Cassie, T.C. and me. I

265

played it over and over in my mind and each time the memory made my heart race. T.C. had stood up for me! He'd even noticed my new hairdo, *and* he hadn't gone off for a night on the tiles with Cassie. Even I, who had been so afraid – and so sure – that hope had died with my Jenny, was beginning to see a glimmer of it in my future. My heart fluttered at the thought.

I heard someone knocking at my front door. 'Hello, Auntie Lizzie,' said Rosie, as she came in and headed for my kitchen and the biscuit tin. 'I can't stop long because Auntie Maggie is on the warpath about homework – again!' Rosie rolled her eyes as she sat opposite my supper plate at the table.

'Sorry, I've caught you in the middle of your tea. I just came round to find out what my dad said about Peace and Lucky Wong.' Rosie looked worried. 'I wondered if it helped at all – if you'd found out where she's gone?'

I reassured Rosie that she had indeed been most helpful, and that her father understood the need to keep his secret informant secret. Once that was established, she settled down enough to enjoy a couple of custard cream biscuits, a glass of milk and a chat.

'So what's the homework that you're dodging?' I asked.

'Geography,' Rosie answered shortly, her mind on other things. 'Don't you think it's romantic, Peace and Lucky eloping the way they have?'

'I'm not sure that running away to Limehouse really counts as an elopement,' I answered cautiously. 'I thought you had to go to Gretna

Green for it to be called a proper elopement. Peace'll still need the consent of her guardian if she wants to marry in Limehouse.'

'Perhaps they're living in sin, then,' Rosie observed idly, as if she was a woman of the world.

'What do you know about living in sin?' I tried to sound shocked.

Rosie gave me what I can only describe as an old-fashioned look, just like the ones Great-Aunt Eleanor gave to anyone who whistled on a Sunday. 'Don't be silly, Auntie Lizzie. I'm not a baby – I *am* about to sit my eleven-plus, you know.'

I hesitated, believing as I did that it was Maggie and Bert's job to teach Rosie the facts of life, and not mine. 'I really hope not. I hope that Lucky is fond enough of Peace to respect and cherish her as she deserves. She is very young, after all,' I concluded firmly.

'My mum wasn't much older when she had me,' Rosie observed, and I realized that we had strayed on to very tricky ground indeed.

'That's true,' I said, as I tried to think of a change of subject.

'Well she wasn't,' Rosie insisted stubbornly. 'And Peace's dad wasn't exactly respecting Peace's mum either, was he?'

I could see that I was trapped. 'That's true, too,' I answered lamely. I could hardly deny it.

'Auntie Maggie says it takes two to make babies because they're too big a responsibility for one person. That's why people should be married first,' Rosie told me sternly. 'Auntie Maggie says that's the ideal way, but that sometimes people get carried away, being only human and a bit on the frail side. Auntie Maggie says all the saints are dead – that's why us living mortals get it wrong sometimes.'

I felt a wave of relief and gratitude. Thank God for Maggie. 'She's absolutely right,' I agreed robustly.

Rosie nodded solemnly. 'I know, Auntie Maggie is nearly always right.' She grinned. 'Auntie Maggie also says that sometimes, out of what some people might call sin, comes great treasure.' Her grin grew wider still. 'Like me!'

'That's true too!' I laughed. 'Treasure, like you and Peace.' I grew more serious. 'And on that note, young lady, I think it's time you went home and did your geography homework.'

Rosie left obediently, knowing that her Auntie Maggie would have her scalp if she didn't hand in her homework, complete and on time.

I realized quite suddenly, halfway through cleaning the bath after a longed-for soak, that I was utterly exhausted and wanted my bed badly. I was sound asleep half an hour later. Which is why it took me a while to respond to a quiet, but insistent tapping on my front door. I had no idea what time it was, but judging from the sounds drifting up the stairs, the club was still open for business. I lay for several minutes, groggily hoping the tapper would give up and go away. But it didn't stop, and in the end I put on my dressing gown and went to the door.

Caution made me put my foot against the door before I opened it a tiny crack and peered out into the gloom. I could see nothing but a human outline on my dark landing. Why hadn't my night visitor put the light on so I could see him properly?

'Who is it?' I asked. 'And what do you want?'

'My name is Lucky Wong. Peace sent me,' a shaky, young voice replied.

My first instinct was to fling open the door, but my second was to get a look at him first.

'Switch the light on, so I can see you. The switch is on your left,' I instructed, with more forcefulness than I felt.

He did as he was told. Under the bright glare of light stood a handsome, but obviously very frightened, young Chinese man. He was on the tall side for a Chinese, perhaps five foot seven or eight and so slender that I was afraid there was some risk that he'd snap in a high wind. His hair was glossy and black and his eyes were brown. He was dressed from head to foot in black, which made him look even thinner. There was something about his face, however, that left me in no doubt who his mother was. I wouldn't say he and Mrs Wong were like two peas from the same pod, but there was an unmistakable likeness that was elusive because it was more about his expression than his actual features.

'Please let me in,' he pleaded.

I stepped back and pulled the door open a little further. Lucky slipped inside. I turned off the landing light and indicated that he should go ahead of me into the living room. I invited him to sit, and he perched uncomfortably on the very edge of the chair, as if ready to take flight at any second. His entire body seemed to be trembling slightly. His eyes were darting everywhere and he couldn't keep his hands still, even though they were clasped together in his lap so tightly that his knuckles were as white as stripped bone. His hands were like his mother's too, with long, slender fingers that gave the impression that they were used to hard work, and plenty of it.

'Hadn't you better tell me why you're here?' I said, when the silence between us grew unbearable.

'Peace has been taken.' Lucky's voice shook. 'We'd just stepped out into the street, when these men took her. They walked up behind us, lifted her off her feet, pushed her into a big, black car and drove away.' His voice cracked and he had to wait a moment to get control of it again.

'There was nothing I could do! We didn't hear them coming. While two men carried Peace away, the third gave me a chop that made my legs give way, so that I was crawling on the ground like a beetle. My legs were dead, completely useless, numb. There was nothing I could do!' His voice and expression were so desolate that my heart hurt for him. 'Peace screamed that I should tell you. It was all she had time to say, before they gagged her.' Lucky paused again, swallowing hard to stem the tears that threatened to overflow from his glittering eyes. He looked so young, frail and frightened as he sat there, manfully fighting not to shame himself by crying.

I knelt beside him and patted his icy hands. I didn't know what to say, so I said nothing for a moment or two. 'I'll get help,' I assured him eventually. 'Just sit tight and I'll run downstairs.'

Bandy and Sugar left it to Bobby and Pansy Bristowe to get the last of the customers out of the club while they followed me upstairs to my flat. Lucky still sat tensely on the edge of his seat, his hands clasped as if in prayer. I made brief introductions but the terrified young man was barely able to look up, let alone stand. I noticed that he'd managed to control his tears while I was gone, so that he presented a more stoical face to Peace's aunt.

'Lucky, you tell Bandy and Sugar everything you know, while I make us all a cup of tea. You need something to calm you down and warm you up.' I tried to smile reassuringly, then stood in the doorway to listen to their conversation while I waited for the kettle to come to the boil.

'What's this about Peace being snatched?' Bandy demanded without preamble. 'Did you recognize the chaps who took her?'

Lucky was struck dumb. Peace's aunt was not a comforting presence at the best of times and she looked even more ferocious when confronted with the young man who had run off with her ward, and then apparently lost her. Bandy looked around her in exasperation and was gathering breath to launch another salvo of questions at Lucky when Sugar stepped in diplomatically.

'How about if I ask the questions and you answer as best you can; will that help?' Sugar asked gently, his voice soft and soothing, in a distinct contrast to Bandy's edgy, sharp tones.

Lucky nodded, his delicate features drawn and pale with fear.

'When was Peace taken, and where were you

when it happened?'

'Earlier this evening. We'd just stepped out...' Lucky ran through his tale again, explaining that they had had rooms with friends in Ida Street, off the East India Dock Road.

'Did you know the men? Did you recognize the car?' Sugar kept his voice low, unthreatening.

'I did know the men, by sight only. Also the car,' Lucky answered in a whisper, his eyes searching the corners of the room, as if he expected listeners to be hiding in the shadows cast by the lamp.

'What did you do next?' Bandy could contain herself no longer, and her sharp tone shattered the cosy atmosphere Sugar had created.

Lucky shrugged his slight shoulders helplessly. 'Once I could walk again, I hurried to...' Lucky hesitated, obviously searching for a word, and then said something in Cantonese, when he couldn't find the English for it.

Bandy translated in her husky, Passing Clouds voice. 'He means the Triad Social Club, where he knew he'd find people to tell him what the hell was going on.'

Lucky nodded. 'I hurried to the club where my friend has a little influence. He told me that there had been instructions for Peace to be shipped home on the next boat to Hong Kong.'

'Whose instructions?' Bandy barked.

'I do not know.' Lucky shook his head. 'But someone important. It must be. To arrange a kidnap and to keep everyone too afraid to speak his name.' He straightened up suddenly and looked Bandy in the eye for the first time. 'But I do know where she is being held.'

272

I joined the trio in my living room, bearing a tray of tea. All eyes were on Lucky.

'Well, spit it out, lad. Where the fuck's my niece?' Bandy demanded.

'In a warehouse near the docks,' Lucky answered promptly.

Sugar produced his diary and a tiny silver pencil. 'Write the address down here and draw a map if you can,' he instructed.

We all drank our tea and talked quietly about tactics, while Lucky did as he was told and drew a map. In the end, we decided to do nothing irrevocable until we'd had a chance to talk to Sugar's contact.

'We need to know what we're walking into, and my friend may know the lie of the land down there. Best to go in properly informed, if it's necessary for us to go in at all,' said Sugar. 'And we ought to get hold of T.C. and tell him what's happened. We need all the help we can get.'

32

It was arranged: I was to go with Sugar to meet his friend. He was going to pick me up at St Anne's Court after work. I was to ask Antony and Freddy to lend me a dress suitable for an evening meeting in the bar at Claridges. Once in the famous bar, I was to act as if we were a couple out in polite society. 'There's no need to lay it on with a trowel, sweetie,' Sugar assured me, 'it's just a little insurance. A couple attracts less attention than a lone male in places like the bar at Claridges.'

The dress didn't need much work, because the side seams and the bust darts had only been tacked. It didn't take Freddy long to let them out slightly and sew them up again with stitching that was stronger than tacking, so it didn't fall apart, but not so strong it would be difficult to undo and put back the way we had found it.

As Sugar said, if anyone objected, he'd simply pay for the bloody thing from the business account and I could wear it for the nights I worked at the bar. 'You need more than one evening outfit, apart from anything else. We can't have you covered in booze stains and reeking of fags. We run a high-class establishment, we do. You need one on and one at the cleaner's, at the very least.

'And as your employers, Bandy and I should provide it,' he added kindly.

Freddy bit down on a piece of blue thread. 'Now, nip into the changing room and try it on.'

I did as I was told. The dress made that lovely sighing, rustling noise that good quality silk taffeta makes. It whispers to you as it slides over your body like water. I luxuriated in the sensation for a moment and then got on with the business in hand, although I couldn't get the zipper done up at the back.

I was as surprised as Sugar as I stepped out into the lighted workroom and saw myself for the first time. The bluebell shade picked up the blue of my eyes and made them sparkle, and my normally rather dull skin responded with a glow. The long, narrow skirt made me look taller and the nipped-in waist and boned bodice showed off my figure, as did the low neckline. I'd had to take off my bra, which was a serviceable, sturdy white thing, and hope that the boned bodice would support what had suddenly become my obvious assets. It did. I looked really good, even to my critical eye. And I had a cleavage, something I'd always secretly wanted.

Sugar was less inhibited. He clapped his hands in delight and his dear face lit up like Leicester Square. 'Gordon Bennett! Talk about turning into a swan. You look lovely, Lizzie, really lovely. I shall be proud to have you on my arm. All you need now is your slap, some heels and a smaller handbag and we're off.'

We were back in my flat within ten minutes and Sugar was urging me on to greater speed with my make-up, while he sorted out some shoes he thought would do. 'Have you got a decent evening bag?' he asked. I shook my head. I didn't have any kind of evening bag, decent or otherwise. 'You'll have to borrow mine. I'll just go and get it. Meanwhile, do hurry up, time's short and we need to see T.C. for a final briefing before we go.'

He stopped at my door and turned. 'A bit more mascara wouldn't go amiss. You've got good eyes, let's get the full benefit. Don't bother with eye shadow, though. Your lids are too heavy, you'll look half asleep, like Victor Mature. I've never found that dozy look sexy myself. I prefer mine wide awake and taking notice, thank you very much.'

Twenty minutes later he was back waving a small silver clutch bag and wearing an immaculate black evening suit, complete with waistcoat, dickie and bow tie, beautifully tied. He really was a fine figure of a man. Tall, with long legs and a straight back. Although his face wasn't classically handsome, it had regular features and a rather square jaw. His hair was thick, brown and well cut, but kept a little longer than when I'd first met him; then he'd had the regular short back and sides most men wore. Sugar was not a Brylcreem man, preferring to sweep his hair back from his face with his hand whenever it flopped, which it did, often.

'Just shove a hanky, your powder compact and some lipstick in there. And your comb, don't forget your comb, it's windy out. Don't bother with money, you won't need it. I've got your coat.' He thrust it and the bag at me and shrugged into his own overcoat.

We clumped down the stairs to the club and walked in. Bobby and Pansy had joined Bandy and T.C. at the bar and they turned as one as we barged through the door.

'Bloody hell! Is that you, Elizabeth?' Bandy exclaimed, but I wasn't looking at her. I was looking at T.C., who was staring at me as if we'd never met before.

I hadn't had time to take a final look in a long mirror, so I turned and stared at myself in the big gilt ones that lined the club's walls. It didn't matter which one I looked in, the result was the same. I looked like a completely different person. It was all I could do not to faint at the sight; I'd never known I had it in me. Then my eye was caught by the reflection of my audience at the bar and they all looked as stunned as I felt. Obviously, none of us had known that I had it in me.

Pansy was the first to recover. 'Gawd, Lizzie love, you don't half look a picture. You look like a million dollars in that, doesn't she, Bobby?'

Bobby nodded. 'Two million!' he said firmly.

'I'd say so,' Bandy added.

Sugar simply beamed at me, like a proud mother hen. That's if hens can beam.

At last I was. able to turn away from the mirror and walk back towards the bar. T.C. stood up to help me into my coat. As he stood behind me he whispered, 'You look gorgeous, Lizzie, absolutely gorgeous. I wish I was coming with you.'

Claridges' bar was discreetly lit and sumptuous. The thick carpet, velvet curtains and luxurious upholstery made the atmosphere hushed but welcoming to those who could afford it. The rich mahogany bar gleamed as if Bobby had just given it an extra special buff up with his soft cloth, and the gilt fittings glowed in the lamplight. There were a good few people in, but it certainly wasn't packed, and I couldn't spot a single Chinaman among them. However, I could have sworn I glimpsed the Aga Khan or someone very like his newsreel image, almost hidden by the entourage that accounted for most of the customers.

'We're a bit early, the pre-dinner crowd isn't in yet,' Sugar explained as he steered me towards the far end of the bar and away from the group. There was a cluster of small tables half obscured from the room by a low decorative screen. I looked around and saw several other such areas around the edges: not exactly booths, but private places for a few tables, away from the main body of the room.

'What would you like?' Sugar asked after we'd claimed a table.

'Something non-alcoholic,' I answered. 'I want to keep my wits about me and take all this in. It's the first and probably the last time I'll be here.' I looked around me at the splendour I'd suddenly found myself in. Here I was, in a borrowed dress held together with some hasty stitching, one or two small safety pins, a lot of whalebone and a great deal of prayer, in one of the poshest hotels in the world. For a moment, I couldn't help feeling overwhelmed. What would my mother and the aunts say if they could see me now?

'Right you are, I'll get you a citron pressé. In fact, I think I'll join you. I'm going to need what wits I've got as well.' He smiled and turned towards the bar, then his expression froze. I followed his gaze. Two Chinese men had entered the room. I wondered which one was Sugar's lover. Both were handsome in their evening dress. When I looked harder, I realized that they could even be brothers. Recognition was niggling at the back of my mind, and I strained for a better look in the dim lighting. I heard Sugar's sharp intake of breath. Standing in the doorway behind the two men was one of the most beautiful women I have ever seen.

She was tall for a Chinese woman, slender and elegant in her straight, black evening dress. Her thick, glossy black hair was piled high to add some more inches, and peeping from the shiny coils were diamond pins that glittered in the lamplight. Her slender feet were encased in gold, stiletto-heeled shoes and she clutched a small gold bag. The woman looked slowly around the room, then moved forward to stand beside one of the men and murmured something to him.

The man glanced at our table, and nodded very slightly as he saw Sugar. It was then that I recognized him. It was Mr Chang. I felt an army of geese crawl right up my spine, pushing their famous bumps before them, until it felt as if my hair must be standing on end. I had just enough time to gather myself together when the beautiful woman drifted towards our table. She moved as if her feet made no contact with the thick pile of the carpet. Sugar did not move from his spot. He simply waited, wearing a complicated expression that I couldn't read.

'Mr Flaherty, such an unexpected pleasure,' said the beautiful woman in perfect English. Her voice was so soft it sounded like the sigh of a gentle breeze. Her eyes were fixed demurely on a spot at Sugar's feet and her slim hand was outstretched towards him. Sugar bowed slightly and took the proffered hand, with its immaculate long, scarlet nails. It was a hand that had never seen a sink full of washing up, dragged sudsy sheets over a washboard or hefted a duster; had I been a gambling type, I'd have put a week's wages on it and thought the money safe. Sugar lingered for a moment, the little hand clasped in his large one. He bowed his head over it, kissed it in a courtly manner and finally, a shade reluctantly it seemed to me, released it.

'Madam Chang,' he said. 'Always a pleasure.

May I introduce Elizabeth Robbins, a good friend of Bandy's and of mine.' He turned to me. 'Lizzie, may I introduce Madam Chang.'

I stood up and shook her hand. Madam Chang had a surprisingly firm grip. She smiled and inclined her head. 'A pleasure, Mrs Robbins.' I wondered how she'd known I was a Mrs rather than a Miss. I hadn't worn my wedding ring since I'd split up with Sid. With a start, I heard Madam Chang ask whether we would mind if she joined us for a moment or two, while her husband and his brother discussed some tedious business. So they *were* brothers.

'Certainly. Please sit.' Sugar pulled a seat out for her and she sank into it like a feather drifting to the ground. 'May I order you a drink?' I had never seen Sugar so formal or stiff, but then he was talking to the wife of a rich, powerful and – if rumour was right – very dangerous man. It didn't seem to matter which Chang brother was her husband, they were probably both dangerous. Of course Sugar would be on his very best behaviour – it stood to reason.

'A champagne cocktail would be very nice, thank you,' she said graciously, and he went to order the drinks at the bar.

I decided to make small talk while Sugar was away, but found it difficult to think of a thing to say. In the end, I plumped for something safe. 'Cold for the time of year, isn't it?' I said lamely.

Madam Chang smiled wider. 'Perhaps, but it *is* still only early spring,' she pointed out gently. She leaned forward suddenly. 'Quickly,' she said, although her expression of benign amusement didn't change. 'Come to the ladies' room with me and tell me what has Sugar in such a flap. I don't have much time. He can give me any extra details when he gets back from the bar.'

I followed Madam Chang towards the table where her two companions sat. She stopped briefly, said something rapid in Chinese, then turned to me. 'Mrs Robbins, may I introduce my husband, Mr Douglas Chang, and his brother, Mr Henry Chang.'

'How do you do,' I said politely. Neither man replied, although both nodded their heads briefly. I noticed, too, that neither of them had stood up at the approach of a brace of ladies. Perhaps it wasn't usual in China.

It was in that instant that all became clear to me. If Douglas Chang was Madam Chang's husband, then she must be Brilliant! Brilliant Chang, the woman who had taken on something of a fascination for me the moment I'd heard her name. I stood open-mouthed like an idiot, while she slipped the attendant a pound note to make herself scarce for a minute or two. There was no one else in the room, and Madam Chang asked the woman to try to keep it that way until we came out, promising another crisp note if she managed it. The woman slipped the first pound into a capacious pocket in her uniform and strode purposefully towards the exit.

I looked around me at the large room that glittered with mirrors and discreet lighting. It was the first time in my life that I had come across a Ladies that had a kind of salon attached. I was almost overwhelmed by the sheer luxury of it. There were elegant, upholstered chairs, a settee and a chaise-longue, in matching silk brocade, with a motif of sprigs of pink flowers on a *café-au-lait* background.

Mirrors lined one wall, and beneath the mirrors was a long dressing-table affair, with a series of mirrors and a chair at each. Each place was laid with a dressing table in coffee-coloured glass to match the chairs. Various bowls contained balls of white, fluffy cotton wool, soft, goose-down powder puffs and loose pink powder, so that you could simply dust a shiny nose. There were even perfume sprays made of cut glass, with silk-tasseled bulbs. I was dying to try them, to see if each held a different fragrance, but Brilliant's tone was so urgent that I concentrated on the business at hand.

'Right. Now we're alone, explain everything as quickly as you can. Time is very short.' Brilliant Chang was used to being obeyed, I could tell.

I explained as succinctly as I could. Her eyes narrowed as she listened, but she didn't interrupt. 'I see,' she said when I'd done. That was all she said for a while. I kept quiet too.

'You must tell Sugar that I will look into it and shall report back tomorrow,' she said quietly. 'I fear that this could be far more complicated than anyone thinks. It is a matter of great delicacy.'

'But Lucky seemed to think that time was very short and that Peace should be rescued urgently,' I explained, 'before she can be shipped out to Hong Kong on the next boat.'

'I understand, but I must urge you to wait,' insisted Brilliant. 'The situation is very difficult, very delicate. It involves powerful interests that you cannot understand. I must consult with my people, and you must not act before I report back to Sugar.'

Reluctantly, I agreed to convey the message to Sugar, Bandy and T.C. I wasn't entirely happy, though. I had seen how frightened Lucky had been.

Madam Chang smiled at me, her head to one side. 'Tell me, are you another of Sugar's lovers?'

I was shocked. 'Certainly not,' I spluttered.

Her laugh tinkled around the room. 'Don't be so shocked! Sugar is a beautiful lover.' Her grin widened. 'And he has the most enormous penis, like a donkey almost. You should try him. He will spoil you for any other man.'

She laughed louder at my wide-eyed expression. 'Truly, you should try him,' she urged. 'It'll be worth it, believe me.'

Was it possible? Could Brilliant Chang be Sugar's lover? I could hardly believe it. There must be some mistake. Everyone knew that Sugar preferred men – didn't they?

Although, the more I thought about it, the more I realized there had never been the slightest evidence pointing either way. No one had ever seen or even heard of him being entangled with anyone, except his mysterious lover, the one nobody had ever seen – except Bandy, and until now she'd kept very quiet about it. Brilliant Chang. Who'd have thought it?

'I don't think he'd co-operate,' I managed to say, caught between astonishment and merriment. 'I think you've spoilt him for anyone else. He seems to be a one-woman man.'

283

It was Brilliant's turn to be shocked. 'Really? Is that true?'

I nodded.

'How touching. How very touching,' she said as she glanced at her watch. 'We must go. We've stayed too long.'

Back at the bar, Douglas Chang looked up as his beautiful wife re-entered the room. He spoke to her sharply in Chinese as we approached the table and she stooped and whispered something into his ear. Goodness knows what it was, but his expression cleared and he laughed quietly, then gave me a strange look.

'I told my husband that Sugar is your demon lover with a huge member to keep you satisfied,' Brilliant tinkled as we joined Sugar. 'He was very interested.'

She stayed long enough to finish her cocktail and then abruptly stood. 'My husband and brother-in-law have finished their talk, I must rejoin them.' She bowed graciously to us both and said, 'It has been very pleasant. Thank you.'

The Chang brothers stood as one, and a few pleasantries were exchanged, judging by all the bowing and smiling. Then the trio left the bar. Sugar and I watched them go.

'So what happened?' Sugar asked the minute we were safely in the taxi heading back to the shop so that I could change out of my borrowed finery. 'On second thoughts, keep it zipped, even cabs have ears.' We rode the rest of the way in silence.

It wasn't until we were safely in the workroom at the shop and I was dressed in my own clothes, brewing a cup of tea while Sugar unpicked the frock and tacked it up again to its original dimensions, that he finally thought it was safe for us to talk about it.

I tackled him head on. *'Brilliant?'* I spluttered. 'Your lover is *Brilliant Chang?*' I was still having trouble fully grasping the idea.

'Yes,' said Sugar simply. 'Yes, Brilliant's my lover, but you mustn't tell anybody, not even the two reprobates you work for. Nobody knows, not even Mrs Wong.'

'Brilliant!' I said again, nonplussed. 'But I always thought your lover would be a *man.*'

'I never said I was that way inclined,' said Sugar with mock severity. 'Not that it would matter if I was; it's just that I never said.'

'But the dresses, the jewellery, the false eyelashes, the *wig?*' My voice rose to a squeal of disbelief.

'Just because I'm a transvestite,' said Sugar with some dignity, 'doesn't mean that I like to roger men. No, darling, I'm a hetero right down to my false tits.'

'Well, I never knew!'

'That's because you never asked,' Sugar answered, and I suppose there was no arguing with that.

When the frock was safely stowed on its hanger once again, Sugar and I strolled back to the club. I was too shaken to say much. It had been quite an evening for surprises. What I didn't know was that there was more to come.

33

The walk back to the club was the calm before the storm, and in those peaceful moments, I was able to tell Sugar everything that had taken place in the Ladies at Claridges. Except, that is, Brilliant's endorsement of Sugar's special asset and talent; I found that I was far too embarrassed to bring that up.

We had reached a companionable silence as we entered the alley and made for the door that led down to the club or up to the flats above it. We were on the threshold when it became obvious that there was an argument in progress down below. Sugar and I exchanged brief, questioning looks and then hurried down the stairs.

Lucky was standing in the centre of the room, apparently surrounded by hostile forces, all of whom seemed to be talking at once. He looked so frail standing there. It wasn't that Lucky was unnaturally small for a Chinese, because he wasn't, but he was very slender. His shoulders looked so narrow as he tried to stand up to the barrage of questions, opinions and recriminations that were raining down upon him.

Sugar took pity on him and bellowed at the top of his considerable voice, 'What in hell's name is going on here?'

Everyone turned to the doorway, and I jumped as a familiar voice behind me said, 'And I second that!' It was T.C., whose arrival had been masked by the hullabaloo that had greeted us.

Bandy, Malcolm, Bobby and Pansy Bristowe and several others stared back at us for a moment, then all began to speak at once. Sugar raised a large hand and yelled, 'Belt up, the lot of you!'

'Perhaps just one of you should begin?' T.C. suggested into the resulting hush. He smiled encouragingly at Lucky, who, although obviously terrified, was standing his ground.

'And you must be Lucky Wong?' Lucky nodded slightly and T.C. continued, 'Maybe you'd like to give us your side to begin with, then we'll hear from everyone in their turn. How about that?'

T.C. didn't wait for a reply, but ushered Lucky, Bandy, Sugar and me to a corner table. Impressively, even Bandy went quietly. Everyone else returned to their tables, except for Bobby and Malcolm, who were manning the bar. Although they tried to hide it, eyes kept straying to our out-of-the-way table and you could almost hear the creaking of a dozen sets of ears or more, as they strained to listen in.

Instinctively, I noticed, Lucky turned to T.C. 'A ship is due in from Hong Kong very soon. My friend says that they plan to take Peace to Liverpool. They are setting out before first light tomorrow morning, so that she is ready to go on board as soon as the ship arrives there.'

He looked around the table at the rest of us, his eyes pleading. 'We must rescue Peace straight away, before they can take her away. It will be too late if they get her on the ship. We'll never be able to get aboard. I'll never see Peace again!'

'And whose bloody fault is that, I'd like to know? If you'd left the gal where she belonged, none of this would have happened.' Fury and fear made Bandy's voice tremble slightly and her eyes flashed.

'Getting your dander up won't help, Band. Quieten down and let's think about this,' Sugar urged.

'What's there to think about?' I asked sharply, much to everyone's surprise, including mine. 'We've got to rescue her and it sounds to me as if the sooner the better. We haven't got time to debate the pros and cons of the situation. In a few hours, Peace will be gone, way beyond our reach.'

'But my friend said to wait,' Sugar reminded me. 'Because the situation was delicate and there were forces at work that were beyond our understanding.'

'Is your friend referring to who I think?' Bandy asked enigmatically, strain sounding clearly in her voice.

Sugar nodded grimly. 'I think so, yes.'

'Oh bloody hell!' Bandy spat, then turned her venom on poor Lucky. 'If you had left my niece where she belonged, then we wouldn't have the fucking Triad breathing down our necks! What the hell have you unleashed on us, you little bastard?'

Lucky's downcast eyes snapped upwards and he glared at Bandy, full in the face. I knew from Peace that to stare an elder full in the face was insulting behaviour for a Chinese, and there was no doubt that Bandy knew it too. The fine bones of Lucky's face made him look as if he'd been sculpted, and his blue-black hair shone in the lamplight as he held the look but said nothing.

T.C. took control of the situation once again, before more insults could be hurled about and time wasted. 'It would be useful to know exactly what we're walking into,' he said in a placating tone, 'before we attempt anything.'

'But Sugar's friend isn't due to report back to us until tomorrow, and that will be too late. I, for one, refuse point blank to stand by and let someone take another child away from me. I just won't have it!' My voice was shrill with tension. I turned to Lucky and said, with far more resolve than I felt, 'It's time we went. Show me where they're keeping her.'

I began to walk towards the door. T.C. grabbed my arm to restrain me. I shook him off. Fury bubbled up out of nowhere. I hardly recognized myself. 'We can't just stand around and let it happen, T.C.! Someone's got to do something, and I am going to try!'

T.C.'s voice was very quiet. 'You don't know what you're taking on.'

'But I can't just stand...' I began.

'I know, I know, you can't just stand by and let it happen. In that case, if I can't talk you out of it, I'll have to come as well. Any other volunteers?' T.C. looked around the club.

'Are you mad?' Bandy roared.

'I'll come,' Sugar said softly, 'although I think you're off your trolley. But I agree, we can't just let Peace be dragged off against her will. That's all there is to it. Bandy, I want you to stay here,' he said firmly.

'Balls to that,' Bandy replied, thrusting her chin

out defiantly. 'If Lizzie feels obliged to help that bloody niece of mine, then I am duty bound as well. I couldn't live with myself if I sat on my arse and waited.'

T.C. held up a hand to stop the argument. 'Actually,' he said, 'I think we should keep the number who go to an absolute minimum. We can't have hordes of us milling about in the dark. It isn't weight of numbers that's going to win this day; it's how sneaky we can be. And sneaky's easier with just a few of us.

'We'll take Lucky as our guide and interpreter, in case there's any negotiations. Lizzie's coming as a familiar and trusted face to look after Peace, who'll be very frightened. And anyway, it'd take a stronger man than I to stop her. Bobby, you should come for sheer muscle, and then there's me, for my previous experience in breaking and entering. That'll be enough, I think.'

After much heated discussion, Bandy and Sugar were eventually persuaded to stay put and to send help, in the form of the police, Brilliant Chang's friends, or both, if we didn't return from Limehouse by morning with Peace safely in tow. So in the end it was T.C., Lucky, Bobby Bristowe and me who formed the rescue party.

'Right you are,' said T.C. with false heartiness. 'Perhaps we should take one or two things that could come in useful. Sticky tape, rope, that kind of thing. Perhaps a few tools. Do you have anything that might make a useful jemmy, Bandy?'

We made a strange little group as we queued, each of us holding a lumpy bag, for the number

15 bus at Oxford Circus. After a brief debate, we had decided that it would be easier to plan some kind of strategy on the top deck of a bus, where we could go into a huddle, rather than crammed into a cab, with the cabbie listening in. Anyway, Bobby was a large man, and cabs were small.

As usual in a crisis, T.C. took command. 'I know it's probably dangerous, Lucky, but I think you may have to make the first approach when we get to the warehouse. You speak Chinese and it could help to lure one or more of Peace's captors to the door. It will certainly divert attention from the back of the building, where I think we should be able to gain entry. I had a look at your map, and it looks OK, but you'd better tell me what's there first, before we commit ourselves.'

T.C.'s careful questioning discovered that there was a lean-to with a flat roof that butted up against the high wall that separated the yard at the side of the warehouse from a cobbled lane. Lucky thought it would be possible to use a plank or ladder to bridge the gap between the lean-to and the warehouse's first-floor window-sills.

'I took another look round last night, late, after I left you,' Lucky told us. 'It is the best way into the building. There is a door at the back, but the yard is well lit and there are big, iron gates to get through first. The side windows are best.'

'Where are we going to get a plank or ladder?' I asked.

'We'll have to improvise when we see what awaits us,' T.C. said grimly. 'And hope that providence will provide.'

We continued our planning as the bus rattled along the city streets towards God knew what in the narrow, dark alleys of Limehouse.

34

The bus dropped us somewhere on Commercial Road.

Lucky immediately hurried down a side street that led to a maze of narrow, dark streets and alleyways. The whole area was a peculiar mixture of docks, warehouses, small shops and terraced houses. Some were old, sooty buildings, made to look even grimier when they were crammed up against brand new ones, replacements for some of those flattened during the Blitz. There were still gaping holes where the wreckage of bombed buildings had been cleared, but something new had yet to take their place. Then there were the actual bomb sites, virtually untouched since the night they were bombed – except by looters, children and time. In the East End, you were never far away from reminders of that awful war, a testament to the dreadful hammering the people took.

The street lighting was poor. In one way, this was a good thing, as it gave us the cover of deep shadow between the small pools of light, but it also meant we had to tread carefully and stop frequently to get our bearings. I picked up a broken piece of plaster from a bomb site and used it to mark a cross at awkward junctions where several alleys or roads met along our route. I thought it might help me get out of the tangle of streets again, should I find myself all alone and pursued by hostile Chinamen; the thought made me quake in my shoes the closer we got to the warehouse.

We arrived at last and took refuge in an inky black doorway to listen to T.C. whisper his instructions.

'A recce first, I think. Let's get a look at this lean-to and see what equipment we'll need to get in from there. I'll go with Lucky. You two stay here until we get back.'

Bobby and I just had time to agree before T.C. and Lucky stepped out of our refuge, faded into the gloom and disappeared into the black mouth of a narrow alleyway. I was very glad to have the reassuring bulk of Bobby standing beside me, because all the gung-ho bravado I'd felt at the club drained away when faced with the reality of the situation.

I had been so determined that no mere mortal was going to whisk Peace away from us that rage, fear and blind panic had buoyed me up. But the long bus journey, the confusing walk in the dark and the brooding presence of the warehouse all brought it home to me. I hadn't been reared to clamber over roofs and tackle kidnappers; my training had been for wearing my knees out in prayer and scrubbing the front doorstep to prove our godliness to our neighbours. I hadn't had any practice in the physical aspects of rescuing people; I hadn't even been allowed to skip and play leapfrog. And nice girls certainly did not *climb* anything more taxing than stairs and hills, or biff anything other than a cushion, a pillow or a rug, and then only for plumping or cleansing purposes.

A hysterical giggle caught in my throat as I tried to imagine what my mother and the aunts would make of me skulking about the docks in the dead of night with a huge all-in wrestler, a foreigner and an ex-copper. I rubbed my sweaty palms against the rough cloth of my coat and concentrated hard on not letting everyone down by collapsing into a gibbering wreck. After all, I'd got us all into this by insisting on trying to save Peace, and it wasn't the moment to change my mind.

I think Bobby must have sensed my thoughts, because he gave me a reassuring squeeze and whispered, 'Don't you worry, Lizzie. Them Chinks is only little geezers. I'm sure I can sling a few about if it comes to it. You just stick by me.'

I bit my tongue before I could point out that although there was truth in what Bobby said, the 'little geezers' he was talking about put the wind up such formidable types as T.C., Sugar and Bandy, all of whom were used to dealing with men intent on mayhem. Luckily, at that point, T.C. detached himself from the darkness, appeared in our doorway and gave me something other than fear to think about.

'Right you are,' he said softly, 'we've found the way in, and we've also found where they are in the building. They've got the lights on, and there are figures moving about. We've lifted a ladder and a couple of planks from a building site round the other side and I think it's all systems go. I've left Lucky guarding our ladder until we get back. Are you ready? Do you remember the plan?'

Bobby and I agreed that we were ready and the plan was lodged firmly in our minds.

'OK, then let's get going.' T.C. took my hand in the dark, and led me and Bobby to where Lucky waited by the ladder. The second we arrived, Lucky and Bobby made their way to the front of the building. Lucky was to kick up a fuss and, if possible, lure Peace's captors out to where Bobby, lurking in the shadows, would do his best to put them temporarily out of commission.

Once T.C. and I were alone in the alley, I was able to have a good look around. It was narrow, with a high wall on the warehouse side, topped with jagged broken glass set in concrete: it glittered evilly in the dim light from the single lamppost that guarded the exit. Either T.C. or Lucky had taken the precaution of throwing a thick piece of sacking over a section of the glass, so that we could get over it without cutting ourselves to ribbons.

'Won't be a tick,' T.C. whispered, then whisked the ladder down the alley and up against the offending lamppost. He was up the steps in a flash, there was a dull thud, a brief tinkle of glass and the light went out. For a moment I couldn't see a thing, but as my eyes adjusted, I saw that T.C. was back and busy propping the ladder against the wall ready for our ascent. He whispered in my ear, 'Wait for the ruckus kicked up by Lucky to start, then climb up after me. I'll guide you. We've already put the planks between the lean-to and the windowsills. All you've got to do is drop down a foot or two to the roof. It's fairly easy after that.'

The quiet night was shattered by loud banging

and shouting. Lucky had gone into action. Swiftly, T.C. shot up the ladder and straddled the wall where it was protected by the sacking. He leaned down to guide me up. Once I was at the top, he helped me over and between us we made sure I landed quietly. T.C. followed. The commotion at the front of the building grew louder.

Suddenly, a light came on. It streamed through the windows and lit us up for all the world to see. Instinctively I dropped to my knees then lay flat, pressing myself into the lean-to roof. I felt T.C. slither on his belly till he lay beside me. We hardly dared breathe.

It seemed that our windows lined a corridor that had three doors off it. The rooms looked like offices. Two men stood in the passageway. They were arguing about something, judging by the arm waving and the mouth movements. One of the doors was ajar; it must have been the room they'd come from when they switched on the corridor light. I thought I could see movement from the room behind the door, but couldn't be absolutely sure. I drew closer to T.C. and whispered very near to his ear, 'I think there's someone in that room behind them. I think I just saw some feet – a woman's feet.'

I felt T.C. nod once and whisper back, 'It could be where we saw the lights from the other side, when we did the recce.'

We waited silently for the men to stop quarrelling and *do* something. Still the shouting came from the front of the building, but now it sounded as if Lucky was banging a dustbin lid with a big stick, to add to the uproar. Eventually, one of the men began to walk along the corridor towards the front of the building, but the other returned to the room and closed the door behind him.

'Bugger!' T.C. breathed. 'They've left the bloody light on. Still, we can't help that. I'd better get a move on. You stay here: if I get in and that is Peace in there, I'll try to get her out to you safely. Be ready to guide her. At least it looks as if there's only one man in with her at the moment.'

T.C. crouched by the planks that bridged the gap between the lean-to and the windowsill; the whole thing was bathed in light. 'We just have to pray that no one comes along,' he muttered.

He turned to me, looked deep into my eyes, and said, 'I love you, Lizzie Robbins.' Then he kissed me, passionately, but all too briefly.

He stood up and stepped on to the planks, which bent alarmingly under his weight. Heart in my mouth, I looked down to assess the drop. It would not kill him, but it could break an ankle if he fell badly. I looked up again to find that he'd made it across the divide and was fiddling with a window.

Cursing under his breath, T.C. took a reel of parcel tape from his pocket and laid strips of it across a section of window, just like we did in the war to stop broken glass from flying about when bombs dropped nearby.

He removed his jacket, wrapped it around his elbow and jabbed it hard at the glass. It smashed, but the tape held so only a little of it fell, landing on the floor with a faint tinkle. Faint to me, that is. For all I knew, it could have sounded like a full milk crate falling down stairs from inside the building.

297

T.C. threw his jacket to me. I caught it while his hand snaked into the hole he'd made and unhooked the window latch. He levered the bottom window open as quietly as he could and slipped inside the moment the gap was wide enough to take him.

The hall light showed me every move he made clearly. I found myself babbling prayers to a God I was no longer sure I believed in. 'Please God, keep him safe. Make sure no one else is looking. Bring him safe back to me, please, please,' I begged.

'I didn't tell him that I love him as well,' I told the night, that merciless yellow light and, if He existed at all, an equally merciless God. I'd begged for Jenny, too, but He hadn't listened. 'Dear God,' I prayed again, 'please let Rosie and me have him back safe.' I was hoping that if God wouldn't let me keep him, He'd at least take pity on T.C.'s little girl. I was praying so hard, I'd had my eyes squeezed shut. When I opened them again, the hall light had gone out.

T.C. was now a shadowy figure, bent almost double with his eye to what I presumed was the keyhole of the door. I saw him stand up and heave his shoulder against the door, once, twice, three times in rapid succession. I heard a high-pitched scream just before the door crashed inward. In the well-lit room stood a Chinese man holding a wicked-looking knife. He was looming over Peace, who was seated beside a large desk.

Once again, the light went out. I heard thuds, muffled screams and crashes and then Peace shot backwards out of the door as if thrown, closely followed by T.C., who muscled her over to the open window then turned as a figure flew threw the air and landed on him. He went down.

Peace hesitated and I screamed at her, 'Peace, come here. I'm here. Come to me. Across the planks. NOW Peace, *NOW!*'

Peace did as she was told and I stood up and caught her hand as she reached me. 'Follow me,' I instructed and dragged her over the flat roof to the wall. I climbed up on to it, scrabbling against the flaking brickwork with my feet as I heaved myself up, then sat astride the sacking and leaned down to take Peace's hand and haul her up after me.

'There's a ladder here,' I told her, feeling for the top rung. 'Climb down into the alley and wait for me. I'm going back for T.C.' I was vaguely aware that the noise from Lucky and Bobby had grown louder, as if there was a free-for-all going on. But it was T.C. who was the main worry. He hadn't made it through the window. I crawled across the planks, which wobbled dangerously, grabbed for the safety of the sill and landed on it all right. I slid through the window, aware now of a grunting heap on the floor to my left. I stood over the heaving bodies and realized that T.C. was underneath and the man on top was systematic-ally banging his head on the floor.

I looked around frantically, grabbed a handy, if cumbersome fire bucket full of sand in both hands and brought it crashing down on the back of T.C.'s assailant. The head-banging stopped immediately as the Chinaman went limp. I flipped off the bucket, then put my foot under his torso and heaved him off T.C. 'Are you all right?' I asked.

I was answered with a fuddled moan. I knelt

299

down, got my arms under T.C.'s armpits and heaved as hard as I could, yelling as I did so, 'Get to your feet, get to your feet this minute!' I sounded shrill even to my own ears, and worse, I sounded just like my mother on the warpath.

I could hear distant feet thundering up stairs and along a corridor. Every fibre in my body was screaming at me to 'run, run like hell', but I couldn't get T.C. to move. He simply swayed where he stood, dazed and unaware of the imminent danger.

There was a second bucket and an axe where I'd found the first one. I prayed briefly that, as was usual, this bucket would hold water, not sand, and it did. I grabbed it and, without ceremony, threw the contents all over T.C. He spluttered, blinked several times then glared at me glassily. 'Wha...' he began. I didn't let him finish.

'Get out!' I hissed, and shoved him towards the open window. Instinct, and the memory of Bandy's graphic phrase 'dog meat', made me turn and grab the axe from the wall; one less axe between them made good sense to me.

I followed T.C. through the window and guided and shoved him, on his hands and knees, across the bendy planks. I was still standing on the windowsill with the axe in my hand when I heard men crash through a door at the end of the corridor. That galvanized me into action. I shot across those planks like a seasoned Big Top star, and stopped only to topple them into the yard, so they couldn't be used by our pursuers.

Let them make their own bloody bridge, I thought grimly as I pushed T.C. over to the ladder. I straddled the wall once more and hissed at Peace to take the axe that I handed down to her. I heaved and cajoled poor T.C. up on to the wall after me, then stepped on to the top rung of the ladder and told him to follow.

I guided his feet, one after the other, on to each rung by the simple expedient of hanging on to the ladder with one hand and grabbing his ankle with the other. Progress was painfully slow as I swapped hands and ankles for each rung, and once, he slipped and almost landed on my head, which would have brought us both down.

Eventually, though, we landed, breathless and damp, him with water and me with sweat, beside Peace, who had been holding the ladder down below in the alley. The darling girl had not deserted her post, and without her help we both would have come a cropper. She also had the sense to lay the ladder flat, once we were safely down, to confound anyone on our tail.

Not that it did us a whole lot of good. We were catching our breath when we heard an eerie scream, like a wild animal in pain. But Lime-house didn't really run to any night prowlers more exotic than the odd scrawny stray cat, mangy mongrel and rats, plenty of rats. None of which ever made a noise like that. It came again and I looked up just in time to see a man fly through the air and land lightly on the lean-to roof and look over the wall straight at us.

'Run!' I screamed. We did. Peace went in front and T.C. was in the middle, being dragged by Peace and pushed by me. Desperation lent strength to my efforts, air to my lungs and muscles to my calves, as we pounded along that alley and tumbled out, to be met by Bobby and Lucky.

'Lucky!' Peace cried and ran into his arms.

'No time for that!' yelled Bobby, sounding masterful. He'd worked out that T.C. was past it and I was exhausted, and had taken over as our general, thank God. 'Get going. I'll block the mouth of the alley.' It was then that I realized I still had the axe. I thrust it at him and marshalled my little party into a trot.

'Going somewhere, mateys?' roared Bobby as he swung the axe in a wide arc so that its head struck the wall and threw off sparks. The men in the alley stopped abruptly, crashing into each other as they did so. It gave us time to dive down the first of the many side streets and alleyways between us and a main road full of witnesses and safety.

We lost them in the end, although we could hear faint cries and clangs as the axe head hit masonry. We also lost Bobby. We waited in our pre-arranged rendezvous for some time, but he never showed up. Eventually, we started the long walk home.

'Cheer up, it may never happen!' yelled a meat porter as he lugged half a cow on his shoulder from a wholesaler's store to a waiting vehicle in Smithfield Market in the early hours of the morning. Porters were rushing this way and that, their bloody overalls garish in the harsh lights. It was another world, and it brought the memory of poor Bobby with his axe back into sharp relief.

'It already has,' I yelled back sadly. A thought suddenly occurred to me. 'Is there a cafe open around here?'

'Yes, love. Just round the corner, you can't miss it. Does a bloody good fry-up.' He grinned, hefted a dead sheep on his shoulders and sped off before I could thank him.

Nobody felt much like eating but I made them. My knees were wobbling, my teeth were chattering and my brains felt like cotton wool. Upset or not, my body was telling me that neither I, nor poor, soaking, shivering, fuddled T.C. could go another step until we'd topped up on food and had a hot drink to warm us up. Even though we had to choke down every mouthful, it did the trick, and both T.C. and I were better for it. T.C. stopped shivering, my teeth stopped chattering and my knees were restored to working order. Even our brains began to stir into life again, and I sent Lucky to find a cab.

Enough was enough: it was time to go home by the quickest possible means.

35

It was a subdued and dishevelled little group that trailed into the club in the early hours of the morning. Bandy, Pansy and Sugar had been sitting vigil and the relief on their faces at our arrival turned to consternation when they realized Bobby was not with us. We, in our turn, felt hope fade when we discovered that Bobby wasn't there, big grin on his face, waiting for us to appear. Nobody could enjoy Peace's homecoming with the thought that that dear, gentle giant might be lying injured or worse in an East End alley. Although Bandy and Sugar did try, and so did Peace.

Bandy was so relieved to see the girl that she didn't even shout, she just enfolded Peace in her arms and held her there for some time. Sugar was more demonstrative; he swung Peace off her feet and gave her a big, smacking kiss on each cheek between feasting his eyes on her. But Bobby's absence from the scene definitely put a dampener on the reunion for us all.

We had just decided to send the police to Limehouse to look for him, when there was a hammering at the street door. Sugar went to answer it while I tried hard not to imagine a gang of Chinese, armed to the teeth and intent on vengeance, on our very doorstep. We were simply too shattered to rise to the occasion. We were sitting ducks.

I looked at the group around the table. Peace looked crumpled in on herself as she leaned against Lucky, not looking at anyone and crying quietly. The poor girl must have been reeling with fear, exhaustion and guilt, feeling that her running away had led to all this trouble for people who cared for her: she was fond of Bobby and he of her. Lucky had his arm firmly around her shoulders. Although he, too, seemed stunned, the set of his jaw declared he was also determined never to let go of Peace again.

When my eyes rested on T.C., I realized what an awful state the man was in. He'd lost his jacket, left behind on the lean-to roof, his shirt was filthy and wet, and so were his trousers, while his face was deathly pale. Every now and then, his body would convulse in a bout of un-controlled shivering that made his teeth rattle like empty beer bottles in a shopping bag. It was time he found a change of clothes and a warm bed. I said as much to Bandy, who nodded and said she'd go and get Sugar's dressing gown.

'It's all right, Band, I'll get it,' sang out Sugar from the hall. 'Look what the cat's dragged in!' He flung out his arm like a conjuror's assistant, trilled 'Tra-la', and stepped aside as the mighty bulk of Bobby Bristowe filled the doorway.

Pansy was the first to react. She flew across the room, launched herself at her husband and was swung off the ground as she sobbed, 'I thought you was dead, darlin'. I thought you was dead.'

'Well, if I am, someone forgot to mention it to me,' Bobby laughed. 'Glad to see you lot got back safe,' he added, looking over Pansy's head at the rest of us.

It was some time before we could all stop smiling, laughing and chattering long enough for Bobby to tell us everything. Sugar returned with his dressing gown, a stunning creation in pink velvet, with several ostriches' worth of feathers around the collar and cuffs. Washed out as he was, T.C. looked so appalled when Sugar tossed it to him that the rest of us had virtual hysterics as we tried to persuade him to try it on at least. I'm sure the uncontrolled laughter was largely relief at seeing Bobby safe, sound and in one, large, happy piece.

In the end, with much tutting, Bandy went and got her dressing gown, a much more sensible creation in wool. T.C. was finally talked out of his wet clothes and into something warm and dry.

A fresh pot of coffee sat in the middle of the table and we all took reviving sips from our cups as we listened to Bobby's tale. We'd last seen him defending the exit of the alley we'd had to leave in such a hurry, and although he was able to hold our pursuers long enough for us to disappear into the labyrinth of streets and alleys, he'd had to give way eventually.

'I thought I was a goner, then I heard this Gawd-awful racket from behind me,' Bobby explained. 'I thought there were more of 'em come up on me rear flank. I didn't know which way to turn. Then I heard this Paddy shout out, "Hold on, big fella, we'll give you a hand." And about half a dozen bleeding great navvies waded in. Well, the Chinks – begging your pardon, Peace, Lucky, no offence meant – decided to leg it. I reckon it was the bloody great shovels what did it, all the Paddies had 'em and there's no getting near enough to grapple with a Paddy with a shovel,' Bobby concluded, giving Pansy a hug as he did so.

I looked across the table at Lucky and Peace, who were both relaxed enough, at last, to laugh and smile at Bobby's tale.

T.C. looked puzzled. 'It's good that the Irishmen turned up in the nick of time, Bobby, but where on earth did they pop up from?'

'They're in digs round there. When they heard Lucky kicking up at first, they decided it was purely a Chinese matter. Later they heard the fighting and decided anyone could join in, so they did. 'Cause of all that building going on, they stay in the area to save travelling. Gives 'em more lolly to send home to the family in Ireland that way.' Bobby beamed. 'Lucky for me, eh?'

Bandy took charge. 'Now you're all back safely, I think you need some shut-eye, the lot of you. We'll do all the celebrating and any more explaining later, how about that?'

It seemed like the best idea anyone had ever had. Peace took her old room at my place, while Lucky wound up upstairs, at Bandy's insistence. 'I want to keep a close eye on you, you young tyke,' was how she put it. You could hardly blame her. Anyway, it seemed best not to send him home to Mrs Wong until we knew the lie of the land and it was a more respectable hour. For all we knew, Peace's thwarted captors could be waiting for him to go home.

T.C. crawled into Sugar's bed, on the grounds that he needed comfort to soothe his bruises, and anyway, his own bed was too far away. Sugar slept on my living-room couch to provide protection, in the unlikely event it would be needed that night.

We all slept like the dead; it wasn't until a late breakfast that Peace and I had the chance to say 'Hello again' properly. Sugar had gone home and we had the kitchen to ourselves.

Peace could not look at me at first. 'I am so sorry, Aunt Liz, for all the trouble I have caused you. You have been good to me, and it was very wrong of me to bring so much trouble to you.'

I didn't know quite what to say, so I didn't say anything. I just caught her up in my arms and held her for a moment, and tried very hard not to cry. After a while, I let her go, handed her a hanky and went to find another for myself. We wiped our eyes, blew heartily and eventually I was able to say, 'The main thing is that you are back with us and in one piece – at least, I hope you are. They didn't hurt you, did they?'

Peace shook her head. 'No, I was frightened only. They did not beat me or molest me.'

I simply stared at her. I had run out of words. I was just so *glad* to have her back.

'Thank you for saving me from those men, Aunt Liz,' Peace said with great formality.

'Oh,' I waved my hand airily, 'it was T.C., Bobby and Lucky, really.'

Peace shook her head. 'No, Lucky told me – it was you who insisted that I had to be saved from those men. He said that you said you would go alone, but you would not stand by.'

'Well,' I told her, 'it wasn't quite like that. But yes, I did want to get you back.' I paused. 'I missed you.'

Peace nodded slowly, her eyes glistening with tears that overflowed again. She dabbed with my hanky. 'I missed you too.' She spoke so quietly, I almost didn't hear her.

Someone knocked at the door. I went to open it, with much more caution than usual, but it turned out to be Lucky, desperate to see Peace. I have to say, they made a very touching couple. It was not the Chinese – or indeed the English – way to show too much affection in public, but I could tell that the young pair were very much in love. It was the way their eyes constantly sought each other and their fingertips brushed lightly together at any tiny opportunity, like when they walked close together, or both reached for the sugar, or at any excuse at all, really. I knew the feeling all too well. Often, my own fingertips itched to smooth T.C.'s anxious brow or to pluck imaginary lint from his shoulders, but I was more reticent about it than they were.

'What now?' I asked the pair, who looked at me blankly. 'What I mean is, you're back, so what are you going to do now?'

Lucky answered me first. 'We wish to marry,' he said simply. 'That's why we ran away. We wish to marry and we did not think that Miss Bunyan, Peace's aunt, would allow it.'

'What made you think that? Did you ask her?'

Peace shook her head. 'I did not need to. Aunt Bandy does not like me very much.'

I thought about that for a moment or two. 'I'm sure that's not true, Peace. Bandy suffered badly while you were gone. I think she's fond of you, but doesn't know how to show it. Remember, she spent most of her childhood in schools a long way from her parents or in the care of nannies. I don't suppose she had much in the way of motherly affection herself, so doesn't know how to be motherly, but that doesn't mean she's not fond of you. You should have given her the chance to listen to you, before you ran away,' I chided as gently as I could.

'She told me that I had stolen her pearls.' Peace was like a fawn in the forest, as twitchy as anything and ready to run at the slightest sound, and I certainly didn't want to drive her away again.

'Yes,' I said sadly, 'she told us. She knows it was very wrong of her.' I changed tack. 'Do you have any idea who kidnapped you, or why?'

Peace and Lucky looked fearfully at one another, but said nothing for a second or two. Lucky answered for them both. 'We thought it might be a rival Triad but we don't know why. And it does not explain why members of our tong would be part of it, and why they wanted Peace.' Lucky looked down for a moment, almost as if he was ashamed. 'I am not important enough for it to be because of me, I think. I have no money to pay a ransom and they would know that. It must have been to do with Peace herself, but they gave no clue.'

Peace took up the story. 'It is true, they would answer no questions. They pretended they understood no English.' She smiled for the first time since she clapped eyes on Lucky that morning. 'And I pretended I had no Cantonese. So I heard them talking, but they said nothing about who wanted me to go back to Hong Kong.'

I brought the conversation back to the beginning. 'You cannot marry in this country without the permission of your guardian, unless you're prepared to wait until you are twenty-one.' What I didn't add, but felt keenly, was that they had better do something about this. They had been missing together for some time. Peace's reputation was going to suffer badly. People would wonder if Lucky had respected her; many wouldn't believe them even if he had. I was pretty sure the Chinese would take a very dim view, along with their English counterparts.

As Maggie would have said, glands had a lot to answer for, especially in the young and inexperienced. 'So, someone is going to have to approach Bandy if you want to be safely married before

Peace's twenty-first birthday.' Once again, Peace and Lucky exchanged stricken glances. It seemed to me that they would be happier to tackle the Triads, all of them, than take on Peace's aunt.

36

It was late afternoon. Peace and Lucky, accompanied by Sugar and Bobby, were in Gerrard Street, explaining themselves to Mrs Wong. Sugar and Bobby had gone along as both escorts and guards, to make sure they arrived safely and also that Peace was returned promptly to Bandy's jurisdiction.

Bandy, Peace and Lucky had had a long and private chat about things before they'd gone, which had left the young couple chastened and Bandy quiet and very thoughtful. And T.C. slept on in Sugar's bed, oblivious to the romantic and domestic dramas going on around him.

I was sharing a quiet coffee with Bandy in her kitchen upstairs, when his dishevelled figure finally appeared, yawning and wondering if there was any breakfast; then, once informed of the hour, tea.

Bandy looked so alarmed at the thought of having to tackle a frying pan that I laughed and offered to do the honours. The relief was plain on Bandy's face, and I set to while T.C. went to wash, shave and borrow a clean shirt from Sugar's flamboyant wardrobe.

'What do you think?' T.C. shouted through the doorway. 'The pink or the purple?'

I squinted at him through a cloud of Bandy's cigarette smoke. 'What about his cream linen?' I asked. 'That'll suit you better.' I tried hard not to look at the muscular lines of his body. My mum had taught me not to, and old habits die very hard, especially when a person is caught unawares.

T.C. looked bewildered. 'I'm sorry, I'm not really up on clothes. A shirt's a shirt to me, although I think pink might be going a little too far for my liking.'

Bandy had been watching me throughout this brief conversation and now she laughed her husky laugh. 'Liz dear, the cooking is making you hot and bothered. I'll keep an eye on the bacon while you show the poor, ignorant man what cream linen looks like.'

I joined T.C. in Sugar's bedroom, acutely aware that he was half naked. The moment we were through the door, he pushed it to and caught me in his arms. 'I've been aching to have you to myself since I walked into the kitchen,' he said softly, and kissed me. It was a long, long time before we came up for air.

So long, in fact, that Bandy's voice called out that it was time to turn the eggs over and she didn't want to break them. 'I always mangle the bloody things,' she explained loudly.

I broke free, laughing quietly to myself, found Sugar's cream linen shirt and handed it to T.C. 'For goodness sake, make yourself decent before either Randy Bandy or I jump on you,' I said, and ran out of the room before he could grab me

312

again. There was a time and a place for everything and right then, with Bandy grinning like a smug Cheshire cat in the kitchen, it was time for a very late breakfast, or perhaps a high, very high tea.

It was certainly a jolly meal and we saw Bandy at her most human. 'I want to thank you two,' she said gruffly, unable to quite meet anyone's eye; she looked at the gap between us. 'You've been bricks, the pair of you, fine chaps to have at one's wicket. If ever there's anything...' Her voice trailed off, but the message was understood. T.C. and I tried hard not to fidget with embarrassment, so as not to make Bandy feel any more awkward.

'Well, you know,' T.C. began, 'we're all friends, and friends help out in times of trouble. Well, good ones do.'

'And having Peace to stay was lovely and I missed her. Of course I'd want to get her back. I've already lost one child. I was blowed if I was going to lose another without an argument. So it was purely selfish, you see.' I blushed deeply. It was the truth: I *was* being selfish. 'I just couldn't face the pain of another loss, especially if I was never to find out what had happened to her, so I simply had to get Peace back.'

'None the less, I'll not forget it.' Bandy heaved herself to her feet. 'Time I got going. There's a welcome home party to organize for a start. I'll leave you two to it. When you've finished eating, just pull the door to when you leave. I'll be in the club if you want me.'

T.C. and I didn't rush. We ate up every crumb and cleaned up after ourselves, chatting and kissing as the mood took us, all sense of urgency and panic gone.

'You saved my life,' T.C. said eventually, nuzzling my neck while I tried to concentrate on a sink full of washing up. 'Clobbering the bloke who was smashing my head on the floor almost certainly saved my life.'

'You wouldn't have been in that position if I hadn't threatened to go on my own,' I pointed out. 'I had to do something. It would have been all my fault if you'd come a cropper.' I couldn't mention death and T.C. in the same sentence, I was superstitious about giving God or fate ideas.

I don't know who brought it up. I think it must have been him, because I would have been too shy. 'I've not been sleeping with her, you know,' he said.

'Sleeping with whom?' I asked as archly as I could manage through the happy haze of warm washing-up water, a full stomach and feeling safe at last.

'You know "whom" – Cassie. It's just that she's started seeing snakes again when she's been drinking heavily. She's afraid to be alone at night sometimes. I try to be a comfort to her.' He tried to catch my eye, but I wouldn't let him.

'Well, I've heard it called some things,' I said, keeping my eyes fixed firmly on the washing up. I felt the heat start in my neck and rise steadily until my face was burning brightly. I didn't know what had got into me, besides relief that is; I usually wouldn't be so rude. I stumbled on: 'But I've never heard it called a snake watch before.'

'Don't you believe me?' T.C. sounded a little hurt.

314

'How can I? The woman is gorgeous, you've loved her for years and years and now you're free, why shouldn't you rush back to her?' It seemed a reasonable question to me, but then I hadn't reckoned on his response. When I finally took a peek at him, I realized with horror that he was crying silently.

I didn't know what to say, so I dried my hands, sat down quietly and said nothing, trying hard to pretend that I hadn't noticed. I had never seen a man cry before, except Uncle Cyril at his friend's funeral, and that didn't count: they'd come through the trenches together. Uncle Cyril had been lumbered with looking after me for an afternoon, so he'd taken me along to his old comrade's 'do'. He hadn't troubled to mention it was to be a funeral. As my aunt said, he always knew how to show a girl a good time. T.C. spoke at last, his voice dreamy with memory.

'Cassie was such a live wire. Always so full of life.' He sighed, his eyes grew unbearably sad and I thought the tears must start again, but they stopped at his long lashes. 'And it was so different at home. Poor Pat. We knew what was in store there, and it wasn't a lot of fun. Obviously, it was far worse for her. She was the one losing the battle by a little bit every day. It was remorseless, and she was so brave...'

His voice drifted off and he was quiet for so long, I thought he'd finished, but he hadn't. 'It was Pat's idea, you know. "Take a mistress," she said. She'd been saying it for years, ever since that side of things, you know...'

He paused again, the memory painful. 'She

315

told me I was a young man, had natural urges, all that. I just laughed at her, told her not to be daft. She was my wife.' He stopped again, then whispered, 'She was my wife', as if that explained everything. And I suppose that it did.

'So what changed your mind?'

T.C. came back from the bleak place. 'Cassandra did. She was so gorgeous.' He laughed bitterly. 'You could say she swept me off my feet.'

'But is it completely over now?' I asked tentatively, just to make absolutely sure. Nobody could ever accuse me of being overburdened with confidence. Although T.C. had said he loved me, that had been on the lean-to roof when he was about to go into God knew what.

Part of me, the bit that had been likened to a mantelpiece, a plank and a cow by my husband Sid, had been nagging away at me ever since, telling me that people said all sorts of things in the heat of battle. The other part, the part that was thoroughly enjoying having her ear and neck nuzzled from time to time during the conversation, knew that his affair with Cassie was long dead, and was appalled that I needed to ask.

T.C. gave me a little squeeze and kissed my ear. 'Yes, it's over now, although we'll always have a history between us. And there's Rosie too, she'll be another connection. I hope you can cope with that?' It was his turn to feel insecure.

I said that I thought I could, and we stayed quiet for a while.

A little later, after we'd cleared Bandy's kitchen of washing up, we moved downstairs to my living

316

room where we enjoyed a cuddle on the settee and moved on to other topics. We exchanged a little of our histories, the way new couples do.

'Where were you born?' I asked him, hungry for every little detail. I tried to imagine him as a young boy, which was easy: a picture of a rather more masculine version of Rosie came to mind.

'On the borders of West Hampstead and Kilburn, at number twenty-three Garlinge Road,' he answered. 'And before you ask, my dad was a printer in Fleet Street and my mum was a housewife.'

'I see,' I said, trying to sound like Sherlock Holmes. 'Do you have any brothers and sisters?'

'I had an older brother, Peter, who bought it over France in 'forty-three. He flew Spitfires. And I have a younger sister Margaret, who married an Aussie and lives in Sydney. Mags and Jim have two kids, Terry and Theresa. So I'm a proud uncle twice over.' He beamed. 'How about you?'

'No, no one like that. Our lot didn't go in for having children for some reason. Of course, some of the aunts never married. It was the shortage of men when they were young, what with the Great War and the Spanish flu after it, there simply weren't enough men to go round.'

'So you were a one and only. Were you a lonely kid?'

I nodded. 'Yes, especially as I wasn't allowed to play with the other children in my street.' T.C. raised his eyebrows questioningly. 'They didn't belong to the right church, and anyway, they were "common", according to Mum. It never seemed to occur to her that we were common, too, seeing

317

as we lived there as well.'

T.C. nuzzled my neck and whispered, 'Well, you can play with me all you like' as he moved in to kiss me again, long and hard.

He coughed as we came up for air. 'Time I went home I think, before I start to take liberties.' He disentangled himself and stood up abruptly. 'Better not to rush things,' he said gruffly. 'We have all the time in the world to take things steadily.'

I was reluctant to let him go, but I was also aware that the last twenty-four hours, with all its highs, lows and downright frightening moments, had really taken their toll. I wasn't sure that there was a single muscle in my body that didn't hurt from all the exertion. I needed a long, hot bath before Peace's welcome home bash that night and I thought he probably did too. 'You'll be back for the party tonight?' I asked.

'Try and keep me away,' he laughed. 'But I've got to go home, clean up and get out of this bloody shirt. I can't get used to this open-neck thing.' T.C. flapped the floppy collar of Sugar's shirt. 'I'm definitely a tie man myself.'

37

The party that night was a small, intimate affair that managed to upset all the serious drinkers of the locality, because Bandy and Sugar decided to close the club to everyone except a select band of invited guests. It was safer that way. Bobby

Bristowe's wrestling pals were deputed to man the door and to keep out anyone out who wasn't on Bandy and Sugar's brief list.

I went to town on getting ready, with Peace's help. I wore my posh frock and full make-up, and my hair was set beautifully by my young friend. I was getting better at this dressing-up business. Peace looked lovely in a Chinese silk outfit in a shade of olive green that would have looked awful on me, but with Peace's colouring, looked stunning. And rather sophisticated too, which I expect was the effect she was after, seeing that she wanted to impress on everyone her readiness to enter into matrimony. The outfit had woven into the fabric a pattern of peonies that was so subtle it only showed up when the light struck it in a certain way.

Although she'd said very little on the subject, I gathered that the meeting with Mrs Wong had gone better than either she or Lucky had anticipated. Mrs Wong was probably simply relieved to have the couple home safely. She had refused to be drawn on the question of the hoped-for marriage of her son, beyond saying that she would consult an astrologer to cast their horoscopes to see if they were suited or not. I was fascinated. I hadn't known about the astrological aspects of a betrothal.

'We have deeply offended the Chinese custom already,' explained Peace. 'It is very wrong to elope. Marriages are arranged by a matchmaker and the two families. When they all agree, the astrologer is consulted. Sometimes, in traditional families, a couple do not even meet until the betrothal feast. I do not think I would like that,' she said earnestly, but then, she was very young and madly in love.

Personally, I could see some sense in such parental involvement. Experience was not to be sneezed at. If I hadn't ignored my family's opinion of Sid, I might have been saved a very unhappy marriage. But then there would have been no Jenny...

'Mrs Wong thought that Lucky may be forgiven for running away with me, because my parents are unknown and anyway, I am half "ghost" – that is what some Chinese people call foreigners.' Peace smiled at me in the mirror as she wound another roller in my hair. 'So I have no face to save as far as a lot of Chinese people are concerned.'

I thought that the same sentiments, more or less, would be held by a lot of English people. Luckily, few of them lived in Soho, stone-throwing not being that wise for people living in glass houses. Soho was made up of misfits and we all rubbed along together pretty well for the most part.

'How did Bandy take the news?' I asked. Peace had said very little about her private reunion with Bandy beyond the fact that she, too, had been nicer than Peace had dreamed she would be.

'She said that she personally had no objection to our marriage, but that she first had to consult with the Bunyan family and my Chinese family also.' Peace paused with a roller in her hand and a faraway look in her eye. 'She still will not tell me who my parents are. It is most annoying. But Aunt is very firm, she says she must consult with the families first, that she needs their permission to break such a long-held secret, even to me. Or, perhaps, especially to me,' she finished sadly.

We talked of other things for a while, and finally we were both ready to make our appearance downstairs where everyone had gathered to welcome Peace back into our midst and to reassure her that she was a valued member of our little clan. It was a message she badly needed to hear, or so Sugar, Bandy, T.C. and I thought. The poor girl had felt so unloved and so unwanted for most of her life, and we were determined to change that if we could. We walked in single file down the stairs, me in front. When I reached the club door, it was closed, but I could hear the murmur of voices on the other side of it.

I coughed – the signal to Sugar to throw open the doors – and stepped back, so that Peace would be first in. The doors flew open to reveal Bandy and Sugar grinning like two Cheshire cats, arms flung wide in welcome, and as one the entire company assembled behind them roared, 'Welcome home, Peace!' Then the throng gathered around the delighted, but utterly bewildered girl to welcome her more personally.

Rosie was first in: she simply launched herself at her friend, flung her arms around her and danced a little jig of pure delight and relief. 'You're back, we've missed you, *I've* missed you ever so much. Everyone's missed you,' she shouted.

'Hear, hear!' Bert echoed solemnly.

'Too true. Best little Saturday girl we ever had.' Maggie smiled.

'But she's the *only* Saturday girl we've ever had,' Rosie protested and everyone laughed, including an overwhelmed Peace.

Bobby and Pansy shyly presented the guest of honour with a posy of flowers they'd had made up by Cissie at the market. Freddy and Antony presented her with an IOU for the frock of her choice to be made at her convenience. The Campaninis had come bearing food for the party and piled it up on the tables for people to help themselves. T.C. simply gave her a speechless hug and then came over to join me. 'You look lovely, Lizzie,' he whispered in my ear, as he slipped his arm around my waist, thus announcing to the entire company that we were now a couple.

I thought I'd die of happiness right there and then, but stood up fairly well to the scrutiny and smiled proudly at people's knowing looks. But I blushed like mad under my make-up.

It was a good evening and towards the end of it, Lucky and Mrs Wong put in an appearance and were welcomed by one and all. Poor Mrs Wong, she looked so shy and lost, despite the fact that everyone knew her from the cafe and there wasn't a stranger in the room.

Malcolm wasn't there, I noticed. I wondered, briefly, if anyone had invited him before my attention was drawn elsewhere.

It was only when the party broke up, quite early as these things go, in deference to the exhausting and frightening time Peace, Lucky and their friends and families had endured, that we heard that Mrs Wong had passed on a message from Brilliant to Sugar in a quiet moment.

'My friend has asked to meet you tomorrow,' Sugar said as he, Peace, T.C. and I enjoyed a cup of cocoa and Bandy enjoyed another gin. The other guests had left and we were not far off making for our beds. Once again, we had guards to make sure we were safe. I wondered if we were being just a little over-protective, but bowed to Bandy and T.C.'s superior knowledge of Triads and their activities.

'It depends what they wanted Peace for in the first place,' T.C. explained as he kissed me good-night. 'They may stop at nothing to get her back, in which case the situation is extremely dangerous. But I'll be upstairs again, Sugar and Bobby are bedding down in your living room and there's the odd wrestler in a sleeping bag here and there in the building. It'll be hard to break in unchallenged. You should be all right.'

I was reassured, but couldn't help wondering why T.C. was so determined to sleep in Sugar's room. I didn't ask; I suspected it had something to do with protecting my reputation.

I felt a warm glow. I'd got myself a real smasher and a thoroughly decent man. Even Mother might have approved.

38

The next morning, much refreshed, I got up and had breakfast with Peace and set off in good time. I was to meet Brilliant Chang in the perfume department at Selfridges at ten, and wanted to nip into work to pick out an outfit from my brand new clothes, which I'd been told had arrived, thanks to Freddy and Antony and their lovely friend, the buyer.

Although I was on full alert for any unknown Chinese men loitering with intent, or worse, approaching me on the street, I was also amazingly happy and light of heart and step. Reason suggested if there were any lurking men, they'd pounce on Peace, not me, and Peace was surrounded by all-in wrestlers, Bandy, Sugar and T.C., so I thought she was about as safe as we could make her. Her long-term safety was more of a problem, and I had been carefully coached by Sugar, Bandy and T.C. to approach Brilliant on the subject.

'Brilliant's seriously connected in the Triad pecking order,' Sugar reminded us. 'She's the one to make the approaches to, and she'll deal with the powers that be for us. Never underestimate Brilliant.' Sugar smiled a faraway smile. 'If anyone can swing Peace's continued safety and future happiness, Brilliant can,' he said proudly.

I was also to bring up the subject of Peace being allowed to marry and how to go about arranging that to the satisfaction of the Chinese branch of her family. The couple already had Mrs Wong's provisional agreement, depending on their horoscopes and the prevailing attitude of the local Chinese community. Mrs Wong was desperate not to offend anyone, particularly the Changs.

As I walked through the shop door, Antony whipped a leather suitcase on to the counter and flung the lid open. 'Feast your eyes on this lot, my dear Elizabeth.'

It took Freddy, Antony and me a while to decide just what I should wear to my meeting with Brilliant. 'The dirty pink cashmere jumper then,' said Freddy, standing back, finger to lips and eyes half closed in contemplation, 'and the navy skirt. But it needs something to lift it. That neck's a bit severe. What do you think, Ant?'

'For a start, Freddy dear, I don't think you should call a perfectly respectable shade of dusky pink, "dirty". You'll put the lady off.' Antony smiled. 'But I think you're right about the neck. Are there any scarves in the case?'

We searched, but there wasn't one suitable and there also wasn't time to run one up from some silk from the stock. 'We haven't the time to hem the edges,' said Freddy. 'You can't go out with ragged edges.'

'I've got it!' Antony shouted from his workroom. He returned to the shop holding up a necklace made up of three strings of beautifully shimmering pearls. They looked almost real in the shop lights. We kept a small stock of costume jewellery – tiaras, earrings, necklaces and brooches – so that the customers could get an idea of what sort of thing went well with their dresses. Antony clasped the necklace around my neck, then he and Freddy stood back to admire the effect.

'Just the thing, Ant. Moves the whole outfit up from nice to classy. Classic and classy – you can't go wrong. All you need now is a touch of powder on your nose and a spot of lipstick to finish off. The black shoes and bag will do. So will the gloves.'

Antony held my coat out for me, and put

forward his opinion while he was at it. 'Your coat's a disgrace, but you can whip it off as you go through the door and carry it over your arm.'

'I wish you'd tell us who you're meeting. Must be important, to go to all this trouble. Future mother-in-law by any chance?' Freddy asked, brows raised to reveal eyes sparkling with curiosity.

It was so *hard* to keep Brilliant's existence a secret from my bosses, especially as they loved good gossip and I actually had some for a change, but I simply couldn't break my promise, so I smiled what I hoped was an enigmatic smile and buzzed off quickly before I got the third degree.

I arrived a little early and waited beside the Chanel range as instructed. I had thought Sugar might put in an appearance as well, but he was being careful. Too many 'accidental' meetings would look unnatural, should anybody be watching Brilliant.

She was a little late, and I spent my time trying some of the perfumes that I couldn't afford to buy. I was rather taken with Chanel No. 5, until I realized that a single bottle would cost several weeks' rent, and my chapel upbringing was appalled. It was at that moment that Brilliant arrived, all smiles and apologies for being late.

'I am so sorry. There has been a bit of a flap. A family member is causing difficulties – as usual,' she explained ruefully. 'It seems that most families have one such member, yes?'

I nodded. 'Yes, but I'm afraid that in my family, I'm the one.' I smiled shyly; Brilliant put me in the shade, even in my finery. Perhaps that was why she was called Brilliant. Maybe she put everyone in the shade, even her troublesome relatives.

'Do you come from a large family?' I asked politely. 'I was an only child myself, so if there was any disappointing to be done, I had to be the one to do it. Marrying Sid and leaving the Church were my greatest sins.'

We'd strolled into the ladies' clothes department. Brilliant idly flicked through some sensible, tweedy skirts. I couldn't imagine Brilliant in a sensible, tweedy skirt somehow. That afternoon she was dressed in an elegant, grey fitted suit, worn with black accessories; bag, leather gloves, stiletto-heeled shoes and the sweetest little hat perched on the back of her head. On top she wore a long swagger coat, in a black and white fleck. Her blouse was white linen, with a starched collar, lifted to frame her face. She wore her long hair gathered into a heavy knot at the nape of her neck, so that it didn't foul that dear little hat. A long crimson scarf of heavy silk damask, with self-coloured chrysanthemums woven into the fabric, added the final flourish. That splash of red lifted the whole outfit from smart to gorgeous.

'I have many many cousins, uncles, aunts, but there were only two of us born to my parents, myself and my little brother.' Brilliant laughed her funny tinkly laugh. 'Although he is not so little. My brother is fat, fat.' Brilliant spread her arms and puffed out her cheeks to show me just how fat. 'He lives in Hong Kong and has many fat children.'

I was so charmed by the image that floated across my mind, of a variety of balloon-shaped versions of Brilliant Chang, that I wasn't really very aware of my surroundings.

Luckily, Brilliant was not so slack. 'There, over by the raincoats,' she said under her breath. 'I know that face, it's one of my husband's chaps. Let's make our way to the Ladies where he may not follow. Suspicious husbands are such a bore.' She swept over to the bank of lifts and waited impatiently to be whisked off to the ladies' cloakroom and a few moments of privacy.

Once we were safely away from prying ears I quickly told Brilliant that we'd got Peace back and were very keen to keep her in Soho. I explained about Peace's wish to marry and our concerns about her safety from another kidnap attempt. It took a while to tell it all. Brilliant did not interrupt once, but listened attentively to every word.

'So, you see, we need to find out who kidnapped her and why, and we have to see if we can come to some arrangement so that it isn't attempted again,' I finished breathlessly, anxious in case I'd forgotten anything.

Brilliant was thoughtful for a while, then seemed to come to a decision. 'Remember the troublesome relative I told you about just now?' she asked, and I nodded silently. 'Well, it is my husband, Douglas. Henry is Douglas's elder brother and...' Brilliant paused for so long, I thought she wasn't going to finish her sentence. 'They have never really...' Again she paused and sighed deeply. 'My husband has always been so jealous of his brother. Well, today they had a terrible argument; what about, I do not know.'

I opened my mouth to speak but she held up her

hand imperiously and I closed it again. 'Your story could explain a lot about the flap he was causing this morning. I think I may understand now why he was so angry with the men who brought the news. It takes great tact to talk my husband out of his rage. I was afraid of what I might find when I got home. That is why I was late.'

'Do you think you can help us?' I asked. 'Do you think you can help Peace and Lucky with their plan to marry?'

Brilliant shrugged. 'I can only try. I will do my very best to help them.' She smiled ruefully. 'We are women, we know what it is to be in love, yes?'

'Oh yes,' I said, with more emphasis than I had intended.

Brilliant looked at me knowingly. 'Ah! I see. You are in love now – at this very moment!' She clapped and tinkled at me, 'You must tell me everything! Let us leave our sanctuary and have morning coffee in the restaurant and a nice fattening cake. Then you may tell me all about your lover.'

Her face lost its animation suddenly. 'We Chinese, we do not often marry for love; we marry for duty. To form alliances, to join families, it is all arranged. That is why I cannot promise that my brother-in-law will agree to Peace's marriage. Lucky is from a much lower class.'

I wasn't sure what Henry had to do with anything, but I ploughed on anyway. 'But Peace is half foreign, as well as illegitimate. That doesn't make her a very marriageable prospect either, does it?'

Brilliant's attention sharpened. 'That is true. All I can do is put it to the family.' Her smile came back. 'Time for coffee and cake and tales of your handsome lover. We've been in here far too long.'

Over coffee and a most delicious chocolate confection, I answered some of Brilliant's questions.

'Tell me, is he handsome?'

'I think so,' I answered shyly.

'What is his name? Does he work? What does he do?' The questions came thick and fast, and before long Brilliant knew almost everything, including T.C.'s involvement in rescuing Peace from the warehouse.

'Is he a good lover?' Brilliant asked finally.

I blushed deeper than my jumper and admitted that I didn't know.

She was aghast. 'You do not know! Well, you must find out straight away. There is no point in taking a bad lover to your bed more than once.' Brilliant paused a fraction, then said, 'Unless you are married to him, then it is your duty, of course.'

I shuddered as the thought of Sid crossed my mind. I resolved there and then to consult Sharky Finn at my earliest convenience. It was time I tracked Sid down and began the long, drawn-out, tedious and often humiliating business of divorce.

39

I was working an extra shift in the club that night, as Bandy was too weary to cope: although not too weary to sit in her corner, drinking steadily with Malcolm. I liked to keep busy myself, as the strain was telling on me too. True, Peace was back, but she was still in danger and under heavy guard and everyone was feeling it.

Sugar was out on an errand somewhere. He was due back to give me a hand, thank goodness, because the place was already pretty full and I was run off my feet. Sylvia was in with Toothy, and Cassie soon joined them with Harry in tow. Some of Bobby Bristowe's pals were taking a break from guard duty, while Bobby and Pansy did the honours upstairs and sat with Peace. Last I'd seen, they'd been playing cards. There was also a whole mob in from the BBC.

My heart fluttered as I noticed T.C. stroll into the club around nine, just after Cassie and Harry had taken their seats with their friends. I had poured some drinks ready to deliver to their table, so I simply smiled 'Hello' at T.C. and indicated that he should wait for my return at the bar. As I neared the table Cassie raised red-rimmed eyes and caught sight of me approaching, then she saw T.C. at the bar and her expression hardened. Her eyes returned to me. 'Why the fuck are you wearing my pearls?' she demanded.

My hand flew to my throat. 'Am I?' I asked, wide-eyed with horror.

'Yes you bloody well are,' Cassie replied, her lovely face purple with booze and rage.

'Hold hard there, Cassie,' T.C. said firmly. He'd come up behind me and had heard everything. 'Don't go accusing anyone before you're in full possession of all the facts. What's more, look who you're accusing. Lizzie isn't capable of theft.' He sounded very angry and it was enough to give

Cassie a moment's pause.

Bandy got up from her bar stool and weighed in as well. 'Lizzie's our good friend, and you know that. So shut up, Cassandra, and let me handle this.' Bandy looked at the pearls at my throat. 'So where did you get them, Liz? May I have a closer look?'

I took the necklace off and handed it to Bandy with shaking fingers as I explained about the shop, the costume jewellery and Antony's lending the pearls to me. 'I thought they came from our usual stock.'

I felt T.C.'s comforting arm around my waist and tried not to look at Cassie's thunderous expression.

'I must have left them there last time I had a fitting. Antony had no right to lend out my necklace. The bloody nerve!' Cassie spat.

Harry looked startled and managed a strangled, 'I say...' before Bandy butted in.

'The thing is, Cassandra, these pearls are mine. I can tell by the clasp. It's made out of my initials in diamonds, you see.' Bandy held out the clasp for us all to see. Sure enough the letters were H.B. – for Hope Bunyan. 'Your initials are not H.B., are they? So the question is, what are *you* doing with *my* pearls?'

T.C.'s arm tightened around my waist as we waited for some kind of explanation. Then Cassie rounded on Harry, who was blinking madly behind his spectacles. 'Where did you get them?' she demanded. 'You gave me the damned things! Where did you get them?'

Harry cringed slightly, but spoke up manfully.

332

'I bought them for you from a chap in a pub. You were there! Don't you remember? I paid him twenty-five pounds, as I recall.'

Cassie began to shake her head uncertainly, then said, 'Come to think of it, I do have a dim recollection. Wasn't it at The French House?'

'Could you give us a description of the bloke, by any chance?' T.C. asked Harry hopefully.

'I can do better than that, I can point him out. That's the chap over there.' Harry indicated Malcolm, who was creeping quietly towards the door, only to find it barred by Sugar who was just coming in.

'Grab him!' T.C. shouted with such authority that Sugar did as he was told without question or understanding. He caught Malcolm by the collar and marched him over to our little group, grinning with pleasure.

Harry nodded firmly. 'That's the fellow. He said you had fallen upon hard times,' he told Bandy, his eyes enormous behind his glasses, 'but wanted to keep it hush hush. He said you were letting a little jewellery go on the quiet, through him. Said you didn't want your business creditors getting wind. I thought I was doing my bit, as it were, in helping to keep the old watering hole afloat.'

Sugar shook Malcolm slightly, as if he were a rat. 'When in fact,' he said, 'you were buying stolen goods.' He shook Malcolm a little harder. 'What do you want me to do with this, Band?'

The look that Bandy shot Malcolm would have pickled vinegar. 'I'll deal with him. Leave him to me. I've had a lifetime of dealing with vermin.'

'With pleasure. Where do you want him?

333

Upstairs?' Sugar enquired politely, while getting a firmer grip on his prize.

I almost began to feel sorry for Malcolm. He seemed too paralysed with fear, embarrassment, or possibly both, to move, struggle or protest. Of course, he was completely surrounded by hostile forces. Some of them, namely Bobby's pals, were very beefy forces indeed, so resistance would have been not only useless but probably damaging to his health.

Bandy nodded and followed Sugar and Malcolm towards the door. It wasn't until they'd gone that I realized I'd been holding my breath.

T.C. was the first to speak. 'How about a drink?' he asked, and so I returned to the bar and gave him his beer, aware all the time that Cassie's fiery eyes were following us malevolently.

Sugar returned to the club and grinned. 'We should hear the merry tinkle of breaking crockery any second now,' he said. There was a tremendous crash, right on cue, followed by several smaller ones in rapid succession.

'There goes another tea service.' Sugar sighed and rolled his eyes towards heaven. There was a thunder of big feet on the stairs, then another almighty crash, followed by an ominous skittering sound, as something heavy hit the landing, then scattered its broken parts around and about. 'That'll be his typewriter,' Sugar told us knowledgeably. 'I heard his previous one go the same way. She had to buy him a new one. Still, I don't suppose she'll trouble this time.'

Another pair of feet thundered down the stairs and a fine old set-to began in the hallway, close by the club doors, so that we could hear every single word. Although, as T.C. remarked later, the good people of Slough had probably heard it all quite clearly too.

'Stealing from me is one thing, you loathsome pool of ordure.' There was a thud, and Sugar mouthed that Bandy had just delivered a left jab. 'But letting Peace take the blame is beyond the bloody pale, even for a slack-jawed, craven prick like you.' Another thud.

'Right hook!' Sugar grinned with glee.

'How do you know?' I asked.

'She always leads with her left and follows up with a right,' Sugar explained.

'Does she often beat men up?' T.C. asked.

'No, not often. Only when they piss her off.' Sugar smiled. 'And then it's only her boyfriends. She's never whacked me, and very few of the customers.'

'I'm not sure that that makes it all right, though,' I said doubtfully. I mean, I didn't think it was all right for men to beat their women up, so it seemed to me, in the interests of fairness, it shouldn't be all right for women to beat up their men, surely?

'She's right, you know, Sugar,' T.C. said. 'It's not really on. We ought to intervene.'

'Be my guest, mate. Personally, I'm taking the view that the man stole from her, then let a sixteen-year-old girl take the blame, so if Bandy didn't whack him, I would. If you think Lily Law can do better, make a citizen's arrest and do it the legal way. But will the punishment really fit the crime? Will the judge take into account that Peace was out there, up to her neck in God

335

knows what, because that prick wouldn't own up to being a light-fingered bastard?'

T.C. shook his head. 'I shouldn't think it'd be taken into account, no.'

'Then I say let her beat the shit out of him, because if she doesn't, I'd probably have to do it,' Sugar observed. 'The man did wrong. He betrayed her and Peace. He deserves a whack.'

'But to err is human, to forgive divine,' I found myself saying, to my utter astonishment. I sounded like my mother – not that she'd ever forgiven anyone in her life. My mother could have won medals in grudge-holding.

'Well, Bandy is erring,' Sugar shrugged, 'and she *is* human. But nobody ever suggested she was divine.'

Further sounds of Bandy being human followed. 'Now you can fuck off, you slimy low-life! Don't ever come near me, my club or my friends again. Better still, bollock-brain, get out of Soho, otherwise I'll turn the Chinese on to you and they won't leave enough of you for your own bloody mother to recognize.' She drew breath. 'That's if you weren't hatched like all the other fucking snakes in the grass.'

For the first time, Malcolm's voice managed to penetrate the furious tirade, the hail of blows and flying pieces of china. 'I can explain,' he began.

'HOW?' The word rang out like a thunderclap. 'You stole my pearls, got drunk and sold them in a public house. Then you allowed a frightened, unhappy child to take the blame. How can you possibly explain such treachery?'

'We'd parted,' Malcolm said, as if that

explained everything. 'You remember? You'd thrown me out and I thought we were all over.'

Obviously, Bandy didn't think any more of that excuse than I did, because we heard another crash and then, 'Oh for God's sake, get out of my sight and never soil my eyeballs again, you repulsive little man.'

The street door slammed with a resounding thud and a flushed Bandy appeared in the doorway to the club. She wiped her hands down her thighs as if to clean them off, grinned at the assembled company and said casually, 'Well, that's got shot of that bastard. Anyone feel like a drink?'

The club took on a party atmosphere after that and it was getting late by the time Sugar told me to go home to bed. I took him up on it gratefully. T.C. escorted me to my door. 'Tonight has been fun. Thanks, Lizzie.' He moved a pace or two towards me and stared at my face for so long, I felt sure he could have painted a portrait from memory.

I stared back, hardly daring to breathe. What was he thinking? I couldn't tell. Finally, our eyes met and he moved another pace forward, put his arms around me and kissed me so softly on the mouth, it felt like the beat of a moth's wing, nothing more.

It ended all too soon, and I was too dumb to speak and too paralysed to move. T.C. smiled at me, touched my cheek gently, and whispered 'Goodnight, Lizzie, sleep well and sweet dreams.' Then he disappeared into the night, taking my heart with him.

40

'No!' Freddy breathed the next day, as I told him all about the previous evening and the way it had ended. 'Did you hear that, Ant?'

'Yes Freddy, I did, because I am standing less than three feet away and I am blessed with average hearing.' Antony gave Freddy a little smile, to show that the sarcasm held no real sting.

'I could swear you sleep in the knife drawer sometimes, Ant. There's nothing wrong with a little romance, even if it is second-hand.'

Freddy turned back to me. 'So what happened then?'

'He went home,' I said. To me, that was self-evident, but not to Freddy, apparently.

'*He went home!*' Freddy positively screeched in mock horror. 'He went home?' he repeated, not sure he had heard right. 'You didn't jump on his bones while the jumping was good?' He turned to Antony in exasperation. 'Did you hear that, Ant?'

He continued without waiting for a reply, especially a sarcastic one. 'She had him at the end of her lips and she let him *go home!*' Freddy threw his hands in the air. 'What *are* we going to do with you?'

I was contrite. 'What else was I supposed to do?' The moment the question escaped me, I realized I'd asked the one man who was likely to tell me in graphic detail.

'Grab the bugger gently by the goolies, haul him off to your bed and roger him rigid while the rogering was good. What the hell did you think you were *supposed* to do with him?' Freddy asked with heavy patience. 'Learn bleeding square dancing?'

'Now who's being sarcastic?' Antony enquired mildly. 'What he is trying to say, Liz, in his rather crude way, is that T.C. is a man of honour. Had he slept with you, he would have felt obliged to take responsibility for you. It's his pattern. Look at Pat, look at Cassandra.'

I thought about it for some moments. It was a way of looking at things that simply hadn't occurred to me. It felt wrong to me, but when I examined the idea closer I realized that this was how a man was supposed to behave, if he was honourable.

'I wouldn't want to trick him into anything,' I offered lamely. 'I don't want him to feel responsible for me.' I paused for a moment, struck by an extraordinary revelation. 'I am quite capable of taking responsibility for myself, thank you very much.'

'All right ducky, keep your hair on,' said Freddy. 'I didn't mean any offence, but I thought that's what respectable women were supposed to want. And they don't come much more respectable than you, now do they?

'What I mean is, I thought that if a man got his end away before matrimony, with a respectable girl and not a professional, then he had to marry her. And if, for some reason, he couldn't do that, then at the very least he had to provide for her and any joint spring-offs. Now, I know there's a million toe-rags out there who don't play the game, but T.C. ain't one of them, now is he? Look at his record.'

It was true that T.C. had looked after Pat until she'd died, and that he continued to try to look after Cassie, even though she often defeated him. He could have denied paternity of Rosie, and everyone, including her mother, would have believed him, but he hadn't. And I knew for a fact that, when he was working, he'd paid towards her upkeep, even though Maggie and Bert had tried to convince him he needn't.

He'd also often paid Cassie's fines when she'd appeared in court on Drunk and Disorderly charges, and worse. Maggie had told me that too. He'd turn up at the cafe to hand over the money for someone else to pay, so that his employers – the Police Force – wouldn't find out about his involvement and sack him.

Antony was right. T.C. really did do his best to be an honourable man, a thoroughly decent cove. It was only his humanity that sometimes let him down. But then, that's what made him interesting. If he'd been too honourable, he'd have been as dull as ditchwater.

Our humanity lets us all down at times, let's face it. I'd married Sid in a burst of all too human fallibility. I had wanted so badly to get away from home and to live a little, that I would have done almost anything. But marrying the first man who asked me had seemed the only way. Respectable girls didn't leave home unless they married.

The war had changed all that for lots of girls, but

not for me. My mum made sure of that. Defiance hadn't occurred to me. Being an idiot, I hadn't thought much beyond the magic ceremony that would spirit me away from the drab four walls of home and the cheerless piety of Mother and the aunts. Marriage itself had come as a bit of a shock, and motherhood as an even bigger one.

I loved being a mum once I got used to it. I can't say the same for marriage, but then, Sid wasn't really husband material. He'd tried, but responsibility didn't suit him. He was a free spirit chained to domesticity and it stifled him. In the end, he'd broken free, and I wasn't sorry, not really.

Freddy's voice finally penetrated. 'Are you in there, Lizzie?' His tone was edged with concern. 'You was gone then. Miles away and it didn't look no picnic neither, or if it was, you was supping on ashes.'

'I was thinking about marriage and responsibility. I was thinking that I didn't think much of it really. I mean, if a grown woman decides she wants to sleep with a man, why should either of them be chained for the rest of their lives to an institution that doesn't suit them? It didn't suit Sid, and look what a disaster that was.

'I wouldn't want to feel that I'd tricked T.C. – or any other man – into that kind of set-up again. If I'm honest, I didn't marry Sid because I particularly wanted to be married to him. What I wanted was a passport out of home and chapel.' I swallowed painfully. 'And if I'm brutally honest, I used the poor man to get it. Now that kind of thing never does,' I said with certainty. 'It causes bitterness and resentment and everyone feels cheated.'

'Do you know something?' Antony drawled. 'You are one formidable female. If you don't want all that, what do you want?'

'I'm not sure. I just know that I don't want that. A partnership should be just that, where you care for each other. The way that you two do, and Maggie and Bert. Perhaps it helps to work together,' I mused. 'But when the man earns all the money, that kind of equality goes straight out of the window.

'Somehow, even though you're skivvying and caring for the children, it's never enough to make up for the fact that he earns it and doles it out. He holds the whip hand, he has the power. I hated it,' I said vehemently, shocked at how strongly I felt. I hadn't realized that I'd held any views at all, let alone such unorthodox ones. My mother must have spun in her grave like a Catherine wheel, spitting and hissing furiously, to hear such blasphemy fall from my lips.

'Well, good luck to you, ducky, we hope you get it.' Freddy thought for a moment. 'Especially as we're your employers, and it means we won't have to break in anyone new.'

He paused, eyed the door and hissed, 'Hands on your wotsits, girls. Here comes the opposition, with her rich bod in tow. She must be here to collect her frock.'

The shop bell tinkled and Cassie breezed in on a wave of expensive perfume and cold air. All talk of T.C. ceased immediately. Even Freddy knew better than to tease, and he was normally incorrigible.

'Good afternoon, slaves,' Cassie sang airily, then stopped, brows creased. 'But you're not slaving.

Does that mean my latest creation is ready?'

The shop bell tinkled again and Sugar entered, smiling widely.

'Can I borrow Lizzie? She's wanted for a meeting.' His smile widened still further. 'We're off to tea at the Ritz,' he explained enigmatically.

'The Ritz, no less?' Freddy was impressed. 'What do you think, Ant, shall we let her go?'

Cassie butted in: 'Say "no", then I can go in her stead. It's been a while since I've had tea at the Ritz.'

'Sorry, Cassie, you won't do. It's got to be Lizzie, she's been invited specially.' I thought I detected just a note of satisfaction in Sugar's voice.

Antony finally got his consent in edgeways. 'I think we should let her go, Freddy dear, then she can report back. Try to steal a menu while you're at it, I do so love a good menu.'

Sugar told me all as I trotted beside him trying to keep up with his long strides. 'Brilliant swung it. She called the club. We can stand the troops down. There won't be any further kidnap attempts on Peace. She's safe. And you and her are going to meet the Changs for tea at the Ritz at four o'clock today.'

'Why me? Not that I'm complaining, I've never had tea at the Ritz,' I assured him hastily. 'But why me?'

'Bandy insisted, said that Peace'd feel more at ease with you there,' Sugar told me. 'It's to be Peace, Bandy and you, that's all I know. Bandy took the call.'

'So why have you got me out of work before lunch?' I asked, mystified. Even I couldn't take

343

more than four hours to get ready for tea.

Sugar's smile looked as if it would split his face in two. 'When I saw Cassie going into the shop, I thought you might like to get out. And anyway, T.C.'s at the cafe looking lost without you. You could have lunch together.' Sugar gave a little wave. 'See you around half three, tarted up and ready to go.'

41

T.C.'s face lit up like a lighthouse as I walked through the cafe door. There was absolutely no mistaking that he was delighted to see me and I almost floated over to his table. The conversation with Freddy and Antony was fresh in my mind and as I looked at T.C. rising to greet me, my insides felt like jelly.

'This is a wonderful surprise,' T.C. told me. 'Wonderful. I was feeling lonely for you.' He held a chair out for me and his fingers brushed my neck lightly as he helped me off with my coat.

We found it very difficult to hide our feelings during our lunch. I can't even remember what I had, except that it tasted like sawdust because my mouth was so dry. Our eyes seemed to be locked, and we were barely aware of our surroundings. Every time our knees touched under the table, a shock like a surge from Battersea Power Station ran through me. I found, as I lifted my cup to my lips, that I was trembling and I had to hold it with both hands. When T.C. went to the counter to pay Bert, who happened to be standing by the till, Maggie slipped over to me, her hands full of a tray of dirty crocks from the other tables.

'Why don't you two find a room? You can barely keep your hands off each other. I'll have you know, we run a decent establishment here.' She laughed and clattered away with her brimming tray.

I was blushing furiously as T.C. returned to the table. 'Are you on your way back to work?' he asked.

'No, I'm off to the Ritz for tea. There's been a summons,' I said briefly, aware that there were sets of prying ears on several of the customers. 'So I'm going home to choose an outfit. Would you care to come home with me to help me choose?'

T.C. looked into my eyes. 'I'd love to,' he said simply.

I explained about tea with the Changs as we walked briskly around the corner, through the alley and up the stairs. The relief to find the flat empty rushed over me like a wave as we went through the door. Peace was out. I felt weak in the knees and very shy and I didn't quite know what to do next. I could offer him a cup of tea, but we had just had one. I offered one anyway, my voice suddenly so husky it was barely audible.

'No thanks,' he said, 'but I'll take a kiss.' He pushed me gently back against the flat door and moved towards me. The kiss was long and passionate and neither of us could speak for a moment when it ended. I slipped round him, turned and took his hands in mine. I began to walk backwards as I tugged him towards my bedroom.

'Come with me.' I whispered, 'I want you...'

'I'd love to,' he said, 'I'd really love to.' He let go of one of my hands, dropped the latch on the front door so that we could not be disturbed, then lifted me in his arms and carried me to my bed.

We woke with a start to hear someone pounding on the door. 'Aunt Liz, are you in there? We are just about to leave, are you ready? I cannot get my key to work.'

T.C. and I were still entangled in each other, the sheets and drowsiness and it took a second for our situation to sink in. My hand flew to my mouth and for a moment I had to fight the urge to break into guilty giggles. T.C. gave me a little shove.

'Up, up, you hussy. You're due for tea at the Ritz.' He smiled lazily at me and stroked me gently with one hand as he pushed me out of bed with the other. 'Me, I'm staying here to gloat over my astounding good fortune. Now kiss me quick and then get dressed; you, madam, are in a hurry.'

I did as I was told, put on my dressing gown reluctantly, and crept to the front door – making sure my bedroom door was closed first – and let Peace in. 'But you're not dressed, Aunt Liz,' Peace said accusingly. 'Mr Sugar said you left work hours ago, to have lunch then to get ready.'

'I won't be a minute,' I told her, unable to quite look her in the face. 'I must have fallen asleep. I'll just have a swift wash and I'll get dressed. How about waiting for me downstairs?' I practically shoved her out of the door again. 'You can tell Bandy and Sugar that I won't be long.'

I broke the land speed record getting ready.

T.C. lay idly in bed laughing gently at me as I fumbled with mascara brushes and lipstick.

'You look gorgeous. It's all I can do not to drag you back into bed with me again,' he teased. 'Come here and I'll kiss you goodbye on the cheek, so's not to smear your lipstick. Do you want me to wait for you here, or would you rather I left, so that you can pretend for a while longer that you are a respectable woman?'

I wanted him to wait for me, just as he was, but then there was Peace to consider.

'I'll get up once you're gone, and I'll wait for you downstairs in the club. Then, if you want to take advantage of me again when you get home, you can, and with pleasure.' I finally, reluctantly, tore myself away and skipped down the stairs to meet my friends. My heart was as light as my step as I hugged my secret to myself. I had a lover. I had a lover!

And I was so *pleased* with myself that, for once, I didn't stop to think about what Mother would have thought.

42

Sugar gave me a knowing look as I rushed into the club but Bandy and Peace failed to notice how flustered I was, thank goodness. They were too eager to get going. We took a taxi to the Ritz, partly to arrive in style and partly because we were running a little late, thanks to me.

The moment we entered the room behind the man in pinstriped trousers whose job it was to lead the customers to their table, we spotted not only Brilliant, but her husband Douglas and his brother Henry. All three stood and bowed slightly as Bandy, Peace and I approached their table. Very formal greetings were exchanged, and we were all careful not to look anyone directly in the face for more than fleeting moments. I knew from Peace that this would be considered very rude indeed.

Brilliant was the first to speak after we sat down. 'Francis,' she addressed the man in pinstripes, 'please send the waiter immediately. We should like to order and, when we have our food, we wish to be left undisturbed.'

'Certainly, Madam Chang,' Francis answered, then glided away, signalling *en route* to a waiter with a snap of his fingers and an imperious gesture. The waiter arrived swiftly and handed out large menus to each of us, then withdrew to wait at a discreet distance while we made up our minds. I wondered how on earth I was going to slip the big menu into my small handbag for Antony. Our order was given and we settled down to some small talk while we waited.

'How is Hong Kong?' Bandy asked Henry after a while.

Henry smiled for the first time. 'It is beautiful, crowded and busy. It has changed very much since you left, I think. It is even busier than ever, and there has been much building.'

I couldn't think of a thing to say, so I left it to the Changs and Bandy to maintain the conversation. No one was addressing me anyway. Peace and I sat quietly, listened hard and watched from under our lashes.

It was a magnificent room with large chandeliers that sparkled way above us. Heavy, rich, gold brocade curtains were draped at the lofty windows and a thick, gold and red Regency-striped wallpaper hung on the walls. The floor was carpeted in exactly the same red as the stripe in the wallpaper. I found myself thinking that it must be murder to get the crumbs up at the close of business each day. The tables were dressed in thick, crisp, white linen, white porcelain china with a thin, gold stripe at the rim and the words 'The Ritz' emblazoned on it. The heavy silver cutlery and silver tea service were engraved with the same legend. I was dying to examine the pieces to see if they were EPNS or real silver, but I didn't dare.

Waiters appeared silently on the thick carpet and loaded the table with plates filled with tiny, triangular, cucumber sandwiches, the crusts neatly cut off, as well as some equally dainty plain bread and butter. These were followed by a plate of scones, a large bowl of clotted cream, another of strawberry jam and a three-tiered cake stand. Each tier held a selection of cream cakes that looked mouth-watering. Finally, the waiters brought a rich, dark Dundee cake, and it sat looking sturdy and worthy beside those light, frothy, cream confections. The waiters withdrew as silently as they had come and we were left to our own devices.

Brilliant smiled radiantly at the assembled company and began to pour the tea elegantly and expertly for each of us in turn, first her brother-in-law and then her husband, thus showing their position in the pecking order at the table. Bandy came next, then Brilliant somehow managed to serve Peace and me simultaneously before pouring the last cup for herself. Once the cups were handed around, we were offered sandwiches in the same order. Finally, we were free to begin talking.

Bandy kicked off with a question in Chinese that I couldn't understand, naturally, but it obviously startled Peace.

'What did she say?' I whispered under my breath.

But Peace was too busy listening to Henry Chang's answer to speak, so Brilliant translated for me. 'She asked if she could reveal to Peace the name of her father.' Brilliant listened to Henry's reply with a small smile on her face and her head slightly inclined. 'My brother-in-law says that she may.'

Bandy answered briefly and turned to Peace. 'Stand up, child,' she ordered, and Peace obeyed immediately. 'Henry Chang, may I introduce you to your daughter, Peace,' Bandy began, 'the gal who has been causing so much trouble lately.' Bandy turned to Peace. 'Mr Henry Chang is your esteemed father, Peace. Douglas Chang is your first uncle and Brilliant Chang, your aunt.'

If I was expecting everyone to fall into one another's arms, I was to be sadly disappointed. The polite acknowledgments of the introductions were as stiff as the introductions themselves, with everyone bowing but saying nothing much. It took me a while to realize that the really tricky business of the day was not going to be broached until we had eaten, so the small talk continued to flow back and forth between the sandwiches and cakes.

Henry addressed Peace directly. 'You are good at your studies, I understand, particularly figure work. That is very good.'

'Thank you,' Peace whispered, hardly daring to look up and certainly not at her father.

Apart from that, the talk covered the weather, the food, the tea and a host of names that meant something to the Changs and Bandy, but nothing at all to Peace or me. None the less, it was interesting to hear about the lives of these unknown people who had married, given birth and died. It seemed that a great deal had happened since Bandy had left Hong Kong for the last time.

'And you?' Brilliant's husband, Douglas, enquired politely. 'You have no children?' He knew perfectly well that Bandy was unmarried and childless, but it seemed to be a necessary part of the conversation for someone to ask the question, all the same.

Bandy shook her head. 'Alas, no.'

'And your honoured sisters?' Douglas pressed, and I realized that he had been fishing for that information all along.

'No, no other children. Only Peace. Peace is the only child in our family – so far.'

Douglas's face hardened. 'Then it was most careless of you to lose her,' he observed.

Everyone at the table stiffened, but Bandy was equal to the situation.

'We didn't lose her,' Bandy answered. 'She was taken.'

'You had a responsibility and you failed to meet

it,' Douglas replied evenly.

'Only because your family shirked it in the first place,' Bandy pointed out, leaving her formal manners behind, but remaining in tight control of herself. I noticed she didn't swear when taking tea at the Ritz.

I sneaked a look at the others at the round table. Brilliant's eyes moved between the speakers as she listened intently to their conversation and Henry stared thoughtfully at the top of Peace's bowed head.

I patted Peace's hands, which were clenched tightly in her lap beneath the table. She hadn't eaten a bite of her sandwich.

Henry finally took charge of the conversation by addressing Peace directly, cutting across his brother's bickering with Bandy. 'I understand that you wish to marry, and that we know the young man in question.'

He waited for a reply from Peace but she was too afraid to look up, speak or even to nod.

I spoke up for her, and took one of her icy hands in mine. 'Yes, that's right, Mr Chang. Lucky's a nice boy–' I was cut off abruptly by Douglas.

'That is quite right, Mrs Robbins. Lucky Wong is a boy. The question is, can he do a man's job and be a husband?' Douglas Chang stared right into my face, so I knew he was being intention-ally rude. 'His family is not worthy to be joined with the Changs. They are peasants.' He spat the last word and glared at me.

I don't know if it was because I was buoyed up by the secret knowledge of how I'd spent my afternoon, or because I was so much in love myself that my heart ached for Peace, but I felt her desperation transmitted through her icy hand as clearly as if it was the Home Service. I suddenly found myself standing up to the head of the London branch of a secret and very dangerous society. 'That may be true, Mr Chang, but I understand that the fact that your brother sired Peace out of wedlock, *and* with a foreign woman, makes Peace a very poor marriage prospect indeed, regardless of her association with the Chang family.' I paused and took a rather ragged breath. 'Therefore, it would seem to me that the Changs should be grateful to the Wongs. It shows great generosity of spirit and it also shows that they are genuinely fond of Peace.'

A flash of anger sped across Douglas Chang's face. He was about to speak when his brother smoothly interrupted him.

'What's done is done, and there is truth on both sides.' He paused and looked at Peace. 'But Peace is my daughter, and I have neglected my duty to her for far too long. Mrs Robbins is right about that, Douglas.'

His brother tried to protest, but Henry would have none of it. He pulled rank. 'I am head of this family, and I will speak.' He turned his attention to Peace and his back to his brother. 'I may only offer my sincerest apologies, daughter.'

I felt Peace's hand clench at the word 'daughter', but apart from that, she remained still and silent as she listened to Henry Chang.

'There were many reasons at the time, and the family thought it best that we try to forget what was considered a very shameful episode in the life of their number one son.' Henry smiled ruefully, and I noticed that Peace was looking at him hard from beneath her lashes. 'But now that I am head of the family – your grandfather died only last year – I feel that, with your permission, Peace, I should like to get to know you better and to acknowledge you as my daughter and an honoured member of our clan.'

Douglas sat rigid with disapproval throughout this speech, but said nothing until his brother had finished. Then he exploded, although in a polite, controlled sort of way. 'I still say that to own her will seriously undermine our strength, brother, unless she makes a good marriage that will strengthen, rather than weaken, our position,' he argued, as if Peace wasn't sitting there, listening to every word.

Henry Chang looked directly at his brother. 'I have no ambitions for my daughter,' he said firmly, 'beyond getting to know her at last, and helping her where I am able.'

He turned his head to address us. 'My brother, however, is childless. Unless that situation changes, Cousin Philip Chang will become head of our clan when we brothers join our ancestors.' Henry smiled sadly. 'Not that any of you know about our cousin, but it is best, I believe, to keep him where he belongs, in charge of a distant province and well out of the way of anything...' Henry hesitated, then added, with great solemnity '...sensitive or important. My brother does not agree with me.'

Even though Henry Chang appeared to be putting his cards on the table, I could tell that there was still plenty of the pack being hidden. We were not being told even the half of it.

I looked at Peace, but her face showed nothing, even as her nails dug into my palm beneath the tablecloth. Bandy's expression was easy to read. She was waiting for the Chang brothers to get to the point – as was I. It seemed to me that, in their manoeuvring, the two men had almost forgotten Peace and her wish to marry and settle down.

I flashed a look at Bandy, who caught my eye, nodded very slightly and cleared her throat. 'The family history is no doubt fascinating, to those who care about such things. Personally, I'd also like to banish my lot to an obscure province and leave them to fester there for ever. But it doesn't answer the two main questions. Who kidnapped Peace? And what about this damned wedding?'

At last, I thought, someone to put bald questions. Henry smiled quietly at Bandy's straightforward approach, but Douglas frowned deeply. His look said it all: how dare this foreign woman with the bad manners and large nose question us?

'There will be no wedding,' Douglas told us. 'A Chang may not marry a Wong, and that is final.'

Henry's voice was soft, but there was no mistaking the edge to it. 'I will decide who my daughter may marry, little brother,' was all he said, but Douglas's mouth snapped shut. His eyes, though, signalled pure hatred for the quiet man sitting opposite. I looked to see how Brilliant was taking the fact that her husband was being put firmly in his place. I caught a look exchanged between her and Henry which told me that Brilliant was well aware of the power play

355

going on and had already picked her winner.

Henry Chang surprised me, and everyone else, by showing an important card in his hand. 'And your view, sister-in-law?'

Brilliant bowed her head slightly in acknowledgement. 'I think a marriage arranged with Cousin Philip's first son could well ensure a Chang has a place in the next generation to lead our tong, as my esteemed husband believes.' Brilliant's face grew more serious. 'But also, I think that it would be a terrible mistake to give Philip any promise of future power. He is, in my opinion, untrustworthy.'

Brilliant stopped for a moment, and chose her next words with obvious care. 'I also believe that our neglect of Peace means that we have no right to dictate what her future is to be. Whether Peace marries Lucky Wong, or marries Cousin Philip's heir, as my husband wishes, or chooses to remain a single lady, should, I believe, be her decision. If she chooses to take advice from her family – either side – then that will be a very good thing, as older heads carry more wisdom.'

Henry Chang considered Brilliant's answer for quite a while. 'And Miss Bunyan, your family's position is...?'

'As her guardian in England, I say let the gal get on with it,' Bandy replied shortly.

'And you, my daughter. Tell me your hopes and dreams.' I noted that he had ignored Douglas altogether, and I also noticed that Douglas was well aware of it.

'I would like to marry Lucky Wong, Father,' Peace whispered. 'And when we are married, we would like to open a restaurant here in Soho.'

Peace suddenly found her courage. Her voice grew stronger and more certain for the first time that afternoon. 'I should also like the Wongs to be a part of the business. That is what Lucky and I hope to work towards, the proper family life that I have been denied.'

She took a deep breath, looked up at last and addressed her father's chest region, being too polite to look him in the eye. 'I should like to know who my mother is. And I should like your assurance that I will not be taken away and married off to my second cousin Philip's first son.'

I was so proud of Peace. Most people would have been utterly intimidated by the situation, but not Peace. Her desperation to stay in Soho with Lucky had given her a strength I'm sure she didn't know she had.

Henry considered his daughter without expression or comment for a while, then he turned to Bandy. 'Do you think it is realistic? Can Peace apply herself to hard work?'

'Yes, to both questions,' Bandy answered shortly. 'If she puts her mind to it, that is. Your child is a determined and intelligent young woman, traits that I believe she has inherited from both lines of her illustrious ancestors.'

Once again Henry Chang nodded thoughtfully. He came to a decision. 'You have earned the right to know who your parents are, daughter. I think Miss Bunyan will agree.' He did not trouble to confirm his statement with Bandy herself, who shrugged philosophically. 'Your mother is Miss Bunyan's younger sister, Charity. She, I believe, is now married to a diplomat. Whether your mother wishes to acknowledge you is something you will have to ascertain from Miss Bunyan. I cannot influence their decision.

'As to the marriage,' Henry continued solemnly, 'my brother is right. The Wongs are not worthy to join with the Changs. Such a connection would normally bring no honour to our family.'

Peace opened her mouth to protest, but her father held up his hand for silence, and got it. 'However, in this instance I am inclined to agr–' Henry got no further.

'You cannot allow this, brother!' Douglas shouted, all pretence at good manners, as well as caution, gone. 'You cannot bring more shame upon us! You live in Hong Kong. The shame will not meet you every day, but I live here. It is my face that will be lost.'

'Your authority should withstand any loss of face,' Henry said firmly. 'The performance of your duties to the tong and your family need not be in conflict if you stamp your authority firmly enough. But brother, be told. *I* will decide what happens to my daughter, both as her father and the head of the tong. *You* will abide by my decision, both as my younger brother and as my subordinate within the tong. You will understand this.'

I looked at the two brothers as they confronted one another across the table. Then I looked at Brilliant, who was listening intently.

Bandy, eyes gleaming, flashed a wicked grin at me and whispered gleefully, 'Here's a fight I get to watch for a change, because I didn't start it, and I'm not in the thick of it.'

'This is a celebration of a father reunited with his daughter, Douglas, so I shall show mercy and overlook your bad manners. Just this once, as an act of thanksgiving.' Henry's eyes bored into his brother's, until Douglas was finally forced to drop his. 'There will be no alliance with Cousin Philip through a marriage with my daughter. Not ever.'

'You are wrong, Henry,' Douglas hissed. 'I worked long and hard to get Cousin Philip's agreement to this match and I will not let you throw the opportunity away when we are so close to a satisfactory conclusion. Your bastard should be on her way to China and her wedding by now. It was all arranged. My men had her ready to ship.' Douglas made her sound like a cargo of coal.

I heard Brilliant's sharp intake of breath but I kept my eyes on Henry to see how he would take the news that Douglas had betrayed him and kidnapped his only child.

But Henry's expression gave nothing away. 'Yes, your men have been most helpful in explaining everything to me. Indeed, they took little persuading. Sadly, brother, you do not seem to inspire much loyalty among your people. Personally, I have found that a carrot is worth two sticks, but then, you've always rather enjoyed using the stick, haven't you?' Henry turned to Peace. 'I will see to it personally that you will never be taken away again.'

He clapped his hands together smartly, and two Chinese men appeared from nowhere, gliding across the room to stand each side of Douglas, where they waited silently for instructions.

'You may take him now,' Henry told them,

without troubling to glance at either the men or Douglas.

I shot a look at Brilliant, who seemed neither surprised nor worried; she was in Henry's confidence, obviously. Bandy, Peace and I held our breath as we waited to see what happened next. Several emotions flitted rapidly across Douglas's handsome face – fear, defiance – and then his eyes darted around the room as he looked for an escape route. Seeing none, he suddenly capitulated and stood up. Perhaps he hoped to escape once he was out of the opulent confines of the Ritz. The two unsmiling men closed in, took an arm each, bowed to Henry and marched Douglas away.

Henry had kept all his attention on his daughter, as if nothing had happened to interrupt his train of thought.

'You may marry, daughter. Consult the astrologers about the day that is most propitious, after your own horoscopes are cast, of course. And, as to the restaurant–' Henry pulled his lower lip thoughtfully – 'it is a sound business proposition. More and more Chinese will be coming here to escape the political situation at home and they will need to eat. I will back you in this venture if you guarantee that you will deal with the money. With your aptitude for figures, the work should suit you.'

He smiled. 'And you should also guarantee that your old father has a bed on his visits to London. I have a feeling that Mr Bunyan will not wish to lend me his suite at Claridges again, after news of your wedding and Douglas's disgrace reaches his ears.'

There was a stunned silence that lasted and lasted. Then, as the news sank in, Peace gave a squeal of unbridled delight, and launched herself at her father. She wrapped her arms around his neck as he sat rigid with surprise, then she kissed him on both cheeks. Great, big, heartfelt kisses. 'Thank you Father, thank you Father,' she cried, over and over again.

After the initial shock at such an un-Chinese public display wore off, Henry's expression became smug as he soaked up the attention.

'I blame the foreign side of the family for such unseemly displays,' he said to us, but he looked a very happy man, none the less.

43

Life settled down.

Peace was allowed to leave school and went to work alongside Maggie and Bert to learn about the restaurant trade in Soho and how to cook English dishes. As she solemnly explained to Bandy and me when she put her case for leaving school before her aunt, 'It is good to offer as wide a variety as possible. I am learning to cook Chinese food from my future mother-in-law and from Bubbles. In this way, we can cook for whoever walks through our doors. Lucky shares my lessons as it is my intention that we should all be able to deal with every aspect of the business.'

She giggled prettily. I was delighted to notice

that love, not only from Lucky's family, but from her own father and, indeed, the rest of her 'chosen' family in Soho, had turned Peace into a good giggler. 'Bubbles and I may have babies later on and when we are giving birth, someone has to cook and count the money and shop and do all of those things. This I learned from Aunt Maggie and Uncle Bert. They can cover each other's jobs, should the need occur. In this way, you do not lose trade.'

I looked with awe upon the slip of a girl who had become something like a daughter to me. She really was a clever one, but then life had taught her how to look after herself. Bandy agreed to let her leave school and to pursue her studies at the cafe and in Mrs Wong's kitchen.

As the wedding plans progressed, Peace continued to stay in my flat, while life upstairs, without Malcolm, returned to its old, much quieter, routine. Relations between Bandy and Peace improved tremendously as Bandy took an active interest in her niece's wedding plans. There was to be a church ceremony to please the English authorities and a traditional Chinese wedding to please everyone else. I was looking forward to it. I'd never been to a Chinese wedding or even seen one, and neither had T.C. Bandy took charge of the English preparations with all the zeal of a bride's mother, and Brilliant undertook the organization of the Chinese side of things. Mrs Wong also offered her help, and it was gratefully accepted.

Not long after tea at the Ritz, I was summoned to Brilliant's flat, which was in the little bit of

Wardour Street that was marooned on the Leicester Square side of Shaftesbury Avenue. As I stood outside the discreet entrance, I looked up to see a large, egg-shaped clock jutting out over the pavement where I stood. It bore the legend 'Perruquier' in curly script at the top, and 'Costumier' at the bottom. It seemed as if Soho had had shops like Freddy the Frock's for a long, long time, because the dates for the original owner began in the eighteenth century. The clock was witness to an old, proud tradition of costume-making, of which I had become a part, and it made me feel as if I truly belonged; that the narrow streets of sooty bricks and the razzle-dazzle neon lights of the theatres and cinemas, their ornately decorated frontages calling to mind giant wedding cakes, were my real home. I belonged. I pressed my finger to the bell.

Brilliant herself answered my ring, smiling widely. 'Come in, come in,' she urged and skipped up the stairs ahead of me. 'Douglas is now in Hong Kong, so we have the place to ourselves.'

She led me into an enormous room that had at least three distinct seating areas in it: one by the row of windows, and one at each end. I realized that several flats had been knocked into one. The furnishings were sumptuous, with lots of heavy silk and red and gold lacquer furniture and boxes. But I didn't have time to get a good look around, because Brilliant engaged the whole of my attention almost immediately we sat down.

'So,' she breathed, eyes dancing with merriment, 'you have taken T.C. as your lover at last. You must tell me everything. Is he passionate? Is he big? Is he inexhaustible? Most importantly, does he satisfy you?'

The woman was incorrigible, but infectious. I laughed like a teenager and answered, 'Yes, I'm not telling you, I'm not telling you again and yes. And how did you know?' I knew for a fact that she hadn't seen Sugar since my afternoon with T.C., so how *did* she know?

Brilliant gave her tinkly laugh and clapped her hands together in delight. 'I knew it! I knew it! I knew it the moment you walked into the Ritz. You had little clouds under your feet and you glowed like a perfect pink peony on a dew-kissed morning. Only one thing makes a woman look like that at four o'clock in the afternoon and that is beautiful lovemaking at two.' She cocked her head and eyed me narrowly. 'But what is this? The glow is fading. You have not been loved since. Why is this?'

How *did* she do that? I was to learn over the years that, to Brilliant Chang, I was as transparent as a recently washed window, whereas I never knew what she was thinking or doing from one moment to the next, unless she chose to tell me. I explained that I had Peace staying with me until the wedding and T.C. and I didn't want to set a poor example. After all, we weren't married.

Brilliant was appalled. 'You have your lovely man at last and yet you don't? That is ridiculous. There is his home: isn't his wife safely with her ancestors?'

'Yes, she is, and I think that's it really ... that neither of us feels right about ... you know, doing it, in her home.' It sounded a bit lame as I said it, but it was the way we felt. Surprisingly, Brilliant understood.

'That is simple. Use hotels. Use hotels until Peace is married. Hotels are fun, they make you feel racy, sexy and very, very naughty. It is very exciting.' It was an idea that, I have to admit, had not occurred to me. You don't think to stay in hotels when you live in a place.

'Sugar and I use them all the time. Sometimes for an hour only and sometimes for a whole night. Now Douglas is in Hong Kong, we plan a week in Nice, at the Negresco.'

We drank fragrant jasmine tea and gossiped and shared confidences like old school friends. I believe it was that Saturday afternoon that cemented our friendship once and for all, and we made a point to meet often after that.

'About Douglas trying to arrange this marriage with Cousin Philip's boy,' I began, and felt my friend stiffen slightly. 'It's like royalty, isn't it? They arranged marriages for dynastic reasons. You know, alliances and so on. Is it usual in China?' I felt her relax again.

'Oh yes. My own marriage was to cement a relationship between two rival families. It works very well sometimes.'

I took a big gamble and asked, 'Did it work for you and Douglas?'

'It worked well for our families, but personally, not so well. Douglas and I, we did not truly like one another, but it was our duty,' Brilliant explained. Then she laughed. 'That is why I took a beautiful lover.'

'Do you think Douglas knew?' I asked, noticing

as I did so that Brilliant and I were talking as if Douglas had 'gone before', as the aunts would have said, which in a way I suppose he had.

'What, that I did not like him? Of course! He did not like me much either. But there was tolerance. There had to be. But did he know about Sugar? I do not believe so, because if he did, I think...' Brilliant hesitated, 'I think we would not be having this conversation.' She smiled. 'And now, it is time to talk about weddings.'

The rest of the afternoon disappeared in a blizzard of menus for the obligatory feasts, as she explained what had been chosen. 'Henry knows that feasting goes a long way with a Chinese. He knows that this is a controversial marriage, so the feasting must be the most wonderful the community has ever known. He knows that full bellies can smother tongues that wag with disapproval,' Brilliant explained. 'And he knows that handing out contracts for all that is needful for feasts, weddings, ritual gifts and, indeed, the small matter of creating a restaurant, to the local businessmen and paying them well for their labours, will ensure that memories are lost also. Peace and Lucky will be all right in Soho. You need have no further worries about that, Elizabeth.'

We had a bottle of champagne back at the club to celebrate not only that Peace's safety was guaranteed, but also that Sugar was a lot safer, too. Poor Sugar. He must have loved his Brilliant very much to risk dying for her for all those years. It occurred to me that night, for the first time, that she must have loved him too, to risk so much.

They may have been safer with Douglas Chang back in Hong Kong, but their affair still had to remain a secret to everyone except a small inner circle. Brilliant was charged with maintaining the Changs' authority in London and that would have been difficult, if not impossible, if rivals had realized that Sugar was the great Brilliant Chang's Achilles' heel.

And she was great. Under her leadership, the local Chinese businesses prospered and grew. Unlike her husband, who had always used fear as his weapon, Brilliant used her charm, her powers of persuasion and sheer guile in the main, to achieve even better results.

As Bandy pointed out, 'Douglas was never the brains of their outfit, Brilliant was. And now, without him, she's got rid of her main liability, because he was always wilful, that one, no discipline to speak of, even as a boy. I remember my father talking about him, because it's so unusual for a Chinese. For them, duty to the family and the Triad is almost everything. Balls that up or rebel against them and you're in deep trouble, as Douglas has proved all too well. Henry won't forget, little brother or no little brother. He won't forget and Douglas knows it. He'll have to spend a lifetime watching his back – that's if he's not dead already.'

'Just as well the bugger's well away from Brilliant, then,' Sugar observed.

Bandy looked at him with something approaching tenderness, I thought. 'Yes, it's just as well,' she said sadly. 'It is just as well.'

44

The wedding was approaching fast and there was lots to do. One day, Bandy handed Peace a large number of crisp five pound notes and told her she must go shopping for her dowry.

'Under normal circs,' Bandy explained, 'it'd be the bride's family who supplies household stuff like crockery, bedding, pots and pans, that kind of thing.' Bandy smiled ruefully. 'But, as you may remember, a lot of our china got caught up in the Malcolm wars and I don't think Sugar would be happy to see his kitchen stuff disappearing either, so you'd better buy it all.'

Peace and I went shopping with a will. We had a lovely time haunting the department stores in Oxford Street and the Chinese emporia in Soho and Limehouse. We turned these shopping sprees into outings, and took lunch or tea out while we were at it. I learned a lot about Chinese food and Peace learned a lot about department stores and pretty soon we had a modest mountain of household items in the corner of my small living room. Finally, there was the chamber-pot. Brilliant was adamant about the chamber-pot.

Peace and I were bewildered. What was the point of a chamber-pot in a time and a country that was amply supplied with flushing WCs?

'It must be filled with fruit, sweets and strings of money when it is presented, with the rest of

Peace's dowry, to the groom's family,' Brilliant informed us when she joined us on one of our jaunts as our chief adviser. 'It's symbolic. Of what, I am not sure, but it's important. Every bride must have her chamber-pot.'

After much discussion and laughter, we settled on a trip to Bermondsey Antiques Market at the crack of dawn one morning. If she had to have a chamber-pot, we decided we'd go the whole hog and get a splendid Victorian one, complete with fruit or rosebud decoration. In the end, Peace found a set that included a large washing bowl, a jug and a matching chamber-pot and was enormously pleased with herself for getting three items in one go and at a bargain price.

She'd haggled with the good-natured stall holder like a pro and got him down by a whole pound. The decoration was a rich mix of cherubs, fruit and full-blown roses, all of which were auspicious, said Brilliant, if you took the cherubs to be plump, healthy babies, that is.

'I'm going shopping with Lucky tomorrow,' T.C. told me after work one Friday as we lay snuggled up in Manzi's Hotel, which had rapidly become our favourite of all the local hotels. It was small, friendly and had a homely atmosphere, which suited us fine.

Brilliant had been right about sneaking off to a hotel being exciting. It felt deliciously wicked, especially when I allowed myself to think about what my mother would have had to say on the matter. Thoughts of mother and the aunts at such moments just seemed to increase my ardour somehow, much to T.C.'s surprised delight.

'When I was young and fancy free, the lads used to say it was some of the convent girls who had the loosest knicker elastic,' T.C. told me, 'but I'm beginning to think you lapsed chapel types could take the title.' He laughed as he moved in closer. 'Where was I?' he asked with a mock leer.

'Going shopping with Lucky,' I answered promptly.

'We've got to buy the bridal bed. It's Lucky's job to see to that, so while we were at it, I thought I'd buy a new bed for when I move into the flat. What do you think?'

'Can you afford it? I know I can't at the moment, I'm still paying for all my new clothes and then there's Peace's wedding and every-thing,' I answered doubtfully. A new bed would be nice. The old one had a nasty dip in the middle, which was all right when I was alone, but a nuisance when I wasn't.

'My posh lady client coughed up when I made my report on her wandering old man.' T.C. lay back on the pillows, his arm firmly around me. 'She was generous. Seems she was itching to divorce him and proof was all she needed.'

It had been an extraordinary thing, but solving the case of Bandy's missing pearls had also solved the case of the posh lady's roving husband.

'I knew I'd seen her old man before, the minute I looked at that photo, but I simply couldn't place him. I'd just seen him the once at the club, then only briefly,' T.C. explained.

But once Peace had gone missing, he'd left the watching the roving husband to Bobby and

Pansy, and they'd never seen him before, so they didn't twig either. As luck would have it, their various paths simply hadn't crossed at the club until the night of the pearls. It shook everyone rigid that Cassie's Harry was the same bloke they'd been following, not least of all Harry.

I smiled contentedly as I remembered once again that it was during that time that T.C. and I had changed from being friends, to being more than friends, and finally to being lovers. I had a lot to thank Peace for, in a funny way.

Quickly I touched wood, to ward off the possibility that she, or my happiness, could disappear again. Hanging around with Chinese persons was making me as superstitious as they were. They seemed to see portents and omens everywhere. Either that, or feeling joy once again had made me desperately afraid of losing it.

'Buy the bed,' I said, 'it'll bring us good luck.'

45

The wedding day finally dawned in September, soon after Peace's seventeenth birthday. The bride was up with the sun. There was such a lot to do before her groom arrived to carry her back to his home.

'Shall I run your bath?' I sang out happily. Peace's joy at her coming wedding was infectious and my own excitement had been growing with hers until I thought we both might burst with it.

I had learned so much about Chinese customs over the past months and I found it endlessly fascinating. Superficially, some of their wedding customs seemed to be remarkably similar to ours, but with the Chinese, there's always a wealth of symbolism invested in each act. For example, most brides like a nice bath before they dress in their wedding finery, but a Chinese bride-to-be must add a kind of grapefruit essence to hers, to purify her ritually.

While Peace wallowed in her steamy bath, I prepared our final breakfast together in the kitchen. A lump formed in my throat the size of one of those damned grapefruit. I was going to miss her, even if she was just moving around a few corners.

'Just think, tonight you and Uncle T.C. can be together at last, just like Lucky and me. I am so happy for you.' Peace paused. 'Do you mind very much that you may not marry Uncle?'

'I do mind, rather. I was brought up to be respectable, but I'd mind being kept apart from him more. I have never been so happy, except when Jenny was a tiny baby.'

'It is very sad,' Peace said, but I wasn't sure to what she was referring: my inability to marry T.C. until I'd found and divorced Sid, or the loss of my beloved Jenny. Possibly she was talking about both.

I stood in the kitchen for a long moment, caught up in a vision of Jenny's wedding, had she lived to have one. She'd always so loved to play at being a bride, with her granny's old net curtains draped cunningly around her hair and from her little shoulders to form a bridal veil and a long train. I often acted as train bearer, mother of the bride, and bridesmaid all at once. Teddy, Bunny-face and her doll, Joyce, were the guests gathered at the table laid with her pink plastic tea set, ready and waiting for the wedding breakfast of rock cake and Marmite sandwiches or whatever I had in the larder. It had been a favourite game for rainy days, when playing out with Rosie hadn't been an option.

It was the hot tears streaming down my face, dripping off my chin and landing on the back of my hand, that brought me round. I heaved my shoulders back, stiffened my spine and drank a glass of water slowly, in an effort to pull myself together. I *would not* ruin Peace's day by bringing my sorrows to it – even if it killed me. Peace's wedding day was a time for joy and not for wallowing in self-pity. I could almost hear my mother's voice telling me so. I made a supreme effort to sing out my reply as cheerily as I could.

'Never mind about me, sweetheart. Just think, this time tomorrow, you'll have spent your first night as Mrs Lucky Wong. Now there's something to be happy about.'

I could smell the grapefruit from her bath as I laid out the pretty, red silk underwear I had had made for her to wear under her beautiful bridal outfit. My mother would have had a purple fit at the thought of scarlet undies, the colour of harlots. Only an irredeemable slut would wear red knickers with black lace and tiny, black ribbon bows. But I happened to know that to the Chinese, red was the colour of joy, and there really couldn't be enough of it at a Chinese wedding. So red undies it was, and a red bridal outfit to boot, right down to her shoes.

T.C. and I had agreed that he would move in as Peace moved out, and in my heart, it felt like a kind of marriage to me, even if chapel, God and my mother would not have agreed. So while I was at it, I had a set of daring undies made for myself, only mine were black with red trimmings. They made me feel deliciously like what Mother would have called 'a slut', and no doubt that added to the illicit thrill they gave me every time I took them out of their tissue paper to gaze at them. I planned to wear them for T.C.'s first official night in residence.

Peace and I had had many a cosy evening talking about our men, our hopes and our dreams and she had said that if I was to stand at her side when she stood before the Wong family altar, at the actual moment of the marriage, then I too would be married – in Chinese eyes at least, in a way. I'm not sure that her argument held water, but I was deeply touched that she should want to share her day with T.C. and me.

Once she'd completed her preparations we sat down to wait for the bridegroom to come to claim his bride. Bandy, Sugar, Bobby, Pansy, Freddy, Antony, Maggie, Bert, the Campaninis and Madame Zelda convened in the club and we all waited together. There was definitely no mistaking Lucky's arrival, because it was accompanied by the hisses, crackles and loud bangs of fireworks being set off by his gorgeously dressed attendants. Chinese bridegrooms certainly know how to make an entrance.

'Remind me, that if ever I decide to get married, to do it Chinese style,' Sugar murmured in my ear as we stood watching the spectacle. 'Any old excuse to slip into a little silk number.'

We drew a fine old crowd on the way to Lucky's home where the ceremony was to take place. After the months of ritual betrothal, the feasts, the gifts, the dowry, the bed-buying and installation, the marriage itself was an understated, brief affair in front of the Wongs' family altar. Here, the happy couple paid homage to Heaven, then to Earth, to the family ancestors and to Tsao-Chün, the Kitchen God and, having done this, the couple bowed to each other and that was more or less it for the formalities.

To make sure that the couple were also married in the eyes of British law, a second marriage ceremony was set for a little later that afternoon. Peace, Rosie, Bandy, Brilliant, Bubbles and I disappeared back to my flat and, once again, wedding preparations began.

Freddy and Antony had gone to town on Peace's wedding dress. It was absolutely gorgeous with its antique lace, seed pearls and yards and yards of train for Rosie and Bubbles to carry. Sugar and I spent many happy and secret hours embroidering discreet dragons and phoenixes, as well as Peace's and Lucky's names in self-coloured silk all over the bodice and skirt. Rosie and Bubbles had also been dressed by my employers, in a reddish pink, to bring in the joy theme once again. All the dresses were ankle length.

I was to be maid of honour, and wore a silk

375

two-piece in blue, with my secret black undies beneath and little hat perched at the back of my head. As our procession entered the dark doorway of the beautiful Wren church, the organ began to play the triumphant wedding march. The bride and her maids looked so stunning standing there. Rosie's blond curls contrasted beautifully with Bubbles's glossy black hair and Peace looked enchanting. Each of them had a bouquet of pink roses and baby's breath clutched in their white-gloved hands.

I looked up the aisle and there was T.C. standing proudly beside the groom, ready to do the honours as best man. Everyone was there. The Chinese contingent had turned out in force, as eager to enjoy an English wedding as we had been to enjoy the Chinese one. I could see the Campanini clan, grinning widely. Madame Zelda sat with Maggie and Bert, whose chests were swelled with pride, along with T.C.'s, to see Rosie looking so pretty and attending to her bridesmaid duties so well.

Freddy and Antony sat towards the front with Sugar and Bandy, so that they could enjoy the effect their clothes had on the assembled company, to the full. The gasps of admiration were clearly audible as the bride's party entered the church and my employers smiled modestly at one and all.

At last the Vicar's words rang out, 'We are gathered here in the sight of God to join this couple in holy matrimony...' and yet again, my mascara was seriously threatened. I looked at Bandy and to my utter astonishment, saw that she was weeping like a baby beneath her large red hat. Photos were duly taken, the confetti thrown and the guests were getting ready to attend the feast laid on by the Wongs, when someone shouted that the bride hadn't yet thrown her bouquet. Peace looked bewildered, so I hastily explained the tradition that whoever caught it was going to be the next bride.

'It's a sort of good luck thing,' I told her. 'All you have to do is turn your back on the crowd and throw it over your head, so that you can't aim deliberately, and the single women and girls try to catch it.'

Peace nodded and did just that. I stood well away. I was not, technically, a single woman, and thus in no position to be the next bride, and didn't want to rob a proper qualifier of her chance. I needn't have worried. The bouquet flew high up into the air, described a beautiful arc and then landed solidly in T.C.'s hands. He'd been standing to the side, talking to Sugar at the time, so it was a sheer fluke. Everyone roared with laughter and Sugar clapped him on the back. 'Never mind, mate, I'll lend you a frock,' he reassured a totally nonplussed T.C.

I did have one very bad moment. It was as Peace and Lucky posed outside the church, with their bridesmaids, for photographs. Whether it was the sun slanting low over the church and lighting the scene with that mellow, misty light of autumn, or whether it was an overwrought imagination, brought on by all the excitement and not enough food, but I swear I saw Jenny. She was dressed in a bridesmaid's dress, her posy clutched in her white-gloved hands. She was standing a little to one side, away from the main group, in the shade cast by a London plane tree, and although I couldn't see her clearly, I knew it was her. I was sure of it. I was so certain that I took a step forward, my hand reached out and I called her name softly, 'Jenny?' I felt someone take my arm. I turned to shake them off. It was the worried face of T.C. that brought me back to the earth and business at hand. I turned back towards the plane tree, but the figure had gone. I shook myself. It must have been Rosie or Bubbles that I had seen. It was silly of me. It was also high time I had something to eat. I'd had nothing since breakfast.

At last, the banquet began. The Wongs had really gone to town to welcome Peace into their family. I lost count of the courses, but there were at least twenty-five. Thank goodness I had been warned by Brilliant that to leave food was very bad manners indeed, an insult to one's host. The trick was to take tiny portions of each course, perhaps only a mouthful or two, so that one reached the finishing course in good order.

Men and women ate separately, even the newlyweds, and it was some hours before I found T.C. by my side once again. 'It's been a wonderful day,' he said softly close by my ear, 'but long. Let's go home.'

'Yes,' I answered, 'let's.'

Author's Note

One of the great things about being the author of a book is that you get to play God in a small way. A Brilliant Chang really did exist in the Chinese community in London, but he was a man, a cocaine pedlar to the flapper generation, who flourished in the 1920s. However, I loved his name, so I pinched it, performed a magical sex-change on him (no nasty scalpels were needed, a few taps on the keyboard and it was done) and then moved her to the 1950s.

I've also taken a few liberties with just how big the Chinese community was in fifties Soho. Although I distinctly remember a Chinese presence in the streets of my childhood, I've exaggerated actual numbers. Historically speaking, the real influx began a little later, in the 1960s, when many people fled Communist China. Then, as now, Chinese workers were organized by gang masters who acted as middle-men between the workers and the employers. However, the tragedy at Morecambe Bay in 2004 has made the whole question of the exploitation of immigrant workers, legal or otherwise, much more obvious now than it was then.

Back when I was a girl, we could never have imagined the changes that have taken place in polite, and not so polite, society. I went to a delightful wedding recently where the happy couple's children sat on their parents' knees during the taking of the vows, and the rest of us all smiled indulgently at the delightful picture. This would rarely have happened in 1950s England, if at all. Illegitimacy was deeply shameful then and almost the worst thing that could happen to a young woman was to be pregnant without benefit of matrimony at least nine months before giving birth.

Living in sin was also deeply frowned upon. It happened, probably fairly often because divorces were so difficult to get, but few would have owned up to it outside of red light districts and my beloved Soho. In those days, a divorced person, however high born, would not have been allowed into the Royal Enclosure at Ascot, or indeed anywhere near royal circles. Nowadays, they'd have to sling out half the royal family if those rules still applied.

Although mixed-race marriages were still rare, the Second World War made a big difference. People who would normally never have left their village, suburb or the few streets around their part of town, were moved all over the world and were introduced to a huge range of new people, places and experiences, so things changed radically. Up until then, the odd colonial might turn up with an exotic wife, but an English woman certainly couldn't have married a Chinese, Indian or African husband and brought him home, and expected to get away with it. Life would have been very hard indeed for such couples. Thank goodness times have changed.

Finally, some thank-yous. Firstly, to the Chinese Cultural website I consulted about traditional Chinese weddings. It gave me loads and loads of information, most of which I had to leave out in the end, sadly, because when I crammed it in, the last chapter looked like a lecture on wedding customs, which wasn't the point at all. So I had to content myself with tiny snippets from a rich and fascinating subject.

Thank you so much to the team at Transworld, namely Linda Evans, Judith Welsh and Beth Humphries, for their sterling efforts to get this one on to the shelves.

Lastly, I'd like to thank Selina Walker for being a truly wonderful editor and for bringing this one home during a very tough time. What a star!

Pip Granger

The publishers hope that this book has given you enjoyable reading. Large Print Books are especially designed to be as easy to see and hold as possible. If you wish a complete list of our books please ask at your local library or write directly to:

Magna Large Print Books
Magna House, Long Preston,
Skipton, North Yorkshire.
BD23 4ND

This Large Print Book for the partially sighted, who cannot read normal print, is published under the auspices of

THE ULVERSCROFT FOUNDATION